2

J. L. Cross

Copyright Page

This is a work of fiction, and the views expressed herein are the sole responsibility and imagination of the author. Likewise, certain characters and incidents are the product of the author's imagination, and any resemblance to actual persons living or dead, or actual events, is entirely coincidental.

Bonds of Betrayal (*Crown of Deceit* Series, Book 1)

Published by: *Cross Roads Publishing House, LLC*

©*2022* J. L. Cross

All rights reserved. No part of this publication may be scanned, uploaded, reproduced, distributed, or stored in a retrieval system and transmitted in any form or by any means- electronic, mechanical, photocopying, recording, or otherwise- whatsoever without prior written permission from the author and publisher, except in the case of brief quotations embodied in critical articles and reviews and certain other non-commercial uses permitted by copyright laws. Thank you for supporting the author's rights.

Hardcover: 979-8-88796-327-8

Paperback: 979-8-88796-327-3

E-Book: 979-8-88796-328-0

Cover Design by: *Amy Rose*

Chapter Headings by: *Etheric Designs*

Interior Art Designs by: *Brothers in Arts*

Formatting by: *J. L. Cross*

Table of Contents

Copyright Page 3

Forward 6

Intro: 9

2 Kastell 52

3 Gideon 67

4 Ethal 76

5 Kastell 95

6 Yurdell 127

7 Kastell 135

8 Yurdell 199

9 Kastell 208

10 Yurdell 232

11 Gideon 238

12 Kendra 250

13 Kastell 264

14 Yurdell 294

15 Gideon 304

J. L. Cross

16 Kendra	338
17 Kastell	353
18 Kastell	392
19 Kastell	409
20 Gideon	418
21 Kastell	436
22 Kendra	451
23 Kastell	463
24 Ethal	484
25 Kastell	492
26 Kastell	509
27 Kastell	518
About The Author	535

Forward

In writing I've found solace. Those roots didn't grow from shade and inconsistency. I have my family to thank for all the encouragement and support they have provided to me over the years, especially the last two years that helped to shape this novel and its series.

There was no better feeling than pressing the publish button and waiting for the downpouring of negative reviews, it is our just as authors and artists, because everyone can't be pleased. Though I prepared for the naysayers, I was built on a sturdy foundation of support and encouragement that wouldn't be easily shaken.

There's a world I have created within these pages, one that I've grown found of as if it were a part of my very soul. I share in the hopes that others can connect and admire the characters and their home the way I have.

This is dedicated to those people that stood in my corner; the ones that had unshakable belief that I would accomplish my dreams.

J.L. Cross

J. L. Cross

8

J. L. Cross

Intro:

Blood.

    Violence.

        Hate.

            Tyranny.

I was an outcast that fled the mainland for a slim cut of peace-and-quiet left in the world. Scurrying back to that awful place with my tail between my legs was not an option. I sailed across the great sea for a new life, from Tarem to the Kingdom of Aylhm. My people came seeking a new beginning away from their old hardships.

Freedom.

This was supposed to be our great awakening; our great new beginning, but just as it was with Tarem, Aylhm had its own flaws and injustices.

There wasn't much left of the day. The sun crept through the sky stained with dark heavy clouds. There was plenty of daylight left to finish tilling in the fields. Hard work gave great bounty, and we were in desperate need of a decent fall harvest.

With the final hours of the day dawning on us I could barely see through the sweat pouring from my brow as I steadied myself. I stared up into the brooding darkness, pleading, I only wanted one day of rest. The untilled fields around me stared back, mocking my desire.

J. L. Cross

The rumbling sound of wooden wagon wheels and the heavy thuds of a horse's hooves into the malleable ground brought my attention back from the sky. I wiped at the sweat on my brow and groaned. Visitors, unwelcome visitors from the city.

Pulled by two horses and surrounded by a convoy of armed Ayles dressed in their polished leather and shining steel armor, a wagon rumbled and *jangled* over every lump in the road. The telling sign the wagon was filled in the back with coins and goods. None of which we had to offer.

The King's tax party. The day we dreaded for weeks came at last. We had nothing to give. Nothing but our lives and the little harvest we had to get us through until the fall harvest. The King knew we came here with nothing more than our own hands.

King Vor gave us land, tools, and the material to build. It was his first grand gesture that the Kingdom moved on from the feuds our people had from the very first of our voyagers. Now that he made himself appear gracious and benevolent, he intended to tax us until we were pulling our teeth to get by, or worse, selling off our loved ones. All generosity was eventually met with debt.

I took my garden fork and stabbed it into the ground of the dirt road that led to the center of our village. I would stop them here. I would put my foot down to this. Now, while I had the chance to use my words as weapons and not the beast within. *Things are still civil. Everything will be fine. Breathe…*

My wife brushed a hand over my arm, sensing the tension roiling through me. "Be cautious, Alcux. That's the boy Prince with them. I hear he's..." she lost the words. She tilted her head as she thought, her red hair, tightly braided, fell over her shoulder. "*Difficult.*" She said finally. "You know young boys, wanting to be men." Her eyes glinted at me. I had made many mistakes through my own arrogance as a young man. She stood to my left, ready to support me in the confrontation we both knew was coming.

As the small convoy came closer, I wasn't surprised to see the young prince force himself in the front. This was the destiny of this kingdom. The King's spoiled heir that wanted nothing but to take and take from his citizens.

I held my chin high as I raised my voice over the sound of the wagon. "Turn around Vlad. My people will not be paying tax."

The boy pulled his horse to a stop and slid from the saddle in a single motion. The men behind him looked anxious and fearful. They weren't ready to conform to the new prince either. It seemed that no one was fond of him, but all of the men with him were filled with enough angst that they wouldn't deny a single order given.

Vlad was tall and lean like his mother's family, a long line of royal blood flowed through him, and it showed. His skin was like ash and bone, a color of death and all things dying and unpleasant. His short white hair accentuated the gray in his skin, making him look less pale. He was a walking reminder of the Kings before Vor, the Varius dynasty lasted generations and generations. After being disrupted, the royal genes were coming back stronger than ever. The only indication that he was indeed his father's son was the banner colors he paraded and the leathers he was adorned with.

J. L. Cross

"You don't have a choice, *King* Alcux. There is a debt to be paid." A threat laced with honey. "For the supple land." Vlad gestured to our hard tilled fields with his thin ugly fingers. "For the tools." A raise of a white eyebrow as he noted the tool, I blocked his path with. "For the peace in which your family enjoys. The ability to lay your head down at night without fear." His voice was smooth and confident as he ticked off all the commodities of life that put us in their debt. "There's a price for all good things."

He can't win this battle. I shook my head, silencing the thought. "There is nothing for them to give. If the King finds fault, he will come here himself."

Vlad's eyes were a piercing deep icy blue that I'd never seen before. Those were the eyes that belong to generations of royal men. His mother's eyes. Those were the eyes of tyrants long since dead in these lands. King Vor's new reign made it possible for the Arvors to venture back to this side of the sea. Now, looking into the eyes of the next King, I knew Vor's kindness would only last as long as breath remained in his lungs.

"Your debts will be paid." Vlad bit out, catching me from my dazed thoughts, the new worries and fears festering in my mind, breeding a life full of doubt and anxiety in my chest… Every word was a solid warning.

I turned my back on him. The Arvor inside me howled in protest. *How dare you turn your back on an enemy!* If only this once I showed him my most vulnerable side, maybe he would feel triumphant and retreat back to the hole he crawled out of.

J. L. Cross

"Get off our land you delinquent bastard." My wife brushed a worried hand against my shoulder as I passed her, her words a cold and vile insult to the prince. By nature, she was a gentle and kind woman, but she was not a woman to accept any defeat. So much for caution. I chuckled, her hand falling away from me. Determined to make my way back into the field to pull the rotting plants from the ground in the last streaks of light.

Every following second pulled on my mind, anchoring it in place as the seconds felt like decade and the wind felt like thin blades of ice through my veins. Every fear in the very depth of my mind took shape. I felt the delicate glass walls I lived in shatter into a thousand pieces. Everything I built came to an inescapable end in a single breath that shuttered out of my lungs in a near scream that was etched in despair and agony long before it left my lips. I had turned around to coax her back to me, only to see blood splattering out onto my face. The scent of it made my stomach lurch and the Arvor halted in his pacing tracks through my mind. Every inch of armored scales rippled with hysteria. For a heartbeat the beast stalled, unmoving and with every sharp flash of steel brandished he retreated. Denial. I couldn't draw him out no matter how much I needed him now. *Anguish.*

The sound of guards dismounting, and shouting didn't register in my ears. I didn't hear Vlad's vehmenet insults as he stood clenching a blade doused in the blood of my wife. I didn't hear the screams erupt around me. Everything was quiet. Everything was still. An eternity could have passed.

14

Her body was draped heavily over my arms. Lifeless. I fumbled with the weight of her limbs as I clenched her into my chest. I collapsed in my struggle to balance her weight. My shirt, arms, and face were smeared in the hot dark red of her wasted life. She smiled at me only moments before. Vlad did this. Vlad slit her throat from behind as she turned away the victor, every word hitting its mark. He rammed the blade into her ribs without hesitation. A taxation party sent from the city turned into a slaughter...

Within a single breath I was defeated. I had wanted to part with them under civil circumstances. Here were the repercussions of my actions, a poor attempt to brush off something and *someone* I shouldn't have. I should have stood my ground. *You did this! You made her a target! You should have stood your ground.* My thoughts raced, finding every way I could have prevented the slaughter around me. *Why did I ever turn my back on him?* Everything I created with our new freedom burned to the ground around me. I could have given him something, anything, instead he took everything.

I carried my wife's body with me across the incinerated village towards the remains of our home. I cradled her close, tears leaked from my eyes; sounds of pain thundered out of me without any conscious control. My wife had a beautiful soul, how could this have happened to her? I trembled as I realized her brown eyes would never shine with life again. They vacantly stared up at me; hollowed endless depths of death. I kept her close to me as I watched the roof collapse inward. A shrill scream pierced the air. This time they were my son's. I howled, knowing that I'd have to rummage through the rubble to find

J. L. Cross

him, but I couldn't bear the thought of letting her go. Holding her close in one arm I pulled and dug with my fingers and nails to dislodge a few fallen rafters. I managed to see through the rubble only for a second before smoke clogged my vision. I heard him sputter and cough when everything was silenced by the last *whoosh* of the building's structure falling in on itself.

I raked my hand through my hair as I sobbed. I hauled my wife's body against my chest and sank my head onto hers, wishing that there would be the faint rhythm of her heart against her ribs, but there was nothing. I was filled with an emptiness I'd never wish on my worst enemies. My heir, my wife, my life stole out from under me.

I wasn't the only one that suffered.

Our homes set ablaze with torches thrown onto the low bearing thatched roofs. Brave villagers attempted to put out the flames and patted down their neighbors that were writhing in pain from the flames that ate their bodies; most of them were slaine and thrown into the destruction with the ones they desperately tried to save. Some made failed attempts to salvage bits of their lives. Others were either run down and butchered, or by some grace of our Mother goddess made it to the Western forest to escape the Aylish tax party.

The home I worked so tirelessly to create burned. Everything I cared about surrounded me in ash. Vlad strode through the destruction unscathed with a blade covered in blood. He held the blade upright and leaned his nose in, breathing in the scent of her. The little warmth of the life she had chilled by its steel.

J. L. Cross

"I don't concede to beggars and wanderers. My father will not concede to a vagabond and his trifling followers. I've only righted the wrong done here to my father. You were taking advantage of his limitless kindness and generosity, playing him a fool. Now, you are the vagrant you were born to be. Homeless and *alone*." Vlad smiled as he drawled out the former, his sharp white teeth pointed. "I don't win my battles with words, Alcux. I win them in my actions. Your Queen may have bested my temper, but I have won the battle she started."

Other Ayles began to close in on us. He pierced the ground with his blade and lowered himself. He leaned in, the smile only deepening. "I'll give you a moment to decide what happens next. You can run and I will spare your life. You will remember this moment for the rest of your life as the last thread of generosity my father will ever show an Arvor. Or, you can stand your ground, shift into the animal you are, and we can fight to the death here and now."

I looked into the faces of the men around me, none showing an ounce of fear. They wouldn't back down. They wouldn't concede the ground they've won here. Even to a lowly King with the strength and speed of an Arvor, I wouldn't win against so many. My heart… My mind…*ached.*

"Choose." Vlad hissed. His eyes flashed with the last of his patience. Calculating the final seconds that I'd have to decide.

I whispered in my wife's matted hair. "I'm sorry, I didn't save you, and I couldn't save our boy. Forgive me." A sob retched through my body as I loosened my grip on her. "Forgive me."

I decided to preserve my life instead of fighting like every fiber of my being wanted to. What was once here was lost. There was nothing left here to fight for. I ran to the forest, the laughter and taunts of the Ayles behind me woke the beast. He started to stroll through my mind in anger. He ached, he hurt. Every strand of our mind reached out for every possible way to kill Vlad.

I needed to let him out. I tore my clothing off as I shifted into the Arvor. I caged the Arvor inside for so long. He hadn't surfaced to fight, but to *run*. I cried an awful howl in anguish towards the sky as all four of my legs dug into the earth and propelled me to safety. With every step I looked over my shoulder time and again. I left my cherished wife and son behind, a decision that would torment me the rest of my life. She wouldn't have wanted me to throw my life away to preserve nothing more than her remains.

Screams of the innocent faded behind me as they pleaded for mercy and were quickly denied. My son was somewhere in the rubble, I'd be back for my family, to give them peace. Smoke rose, the taste of scorched flesh tainted my mouth and nose. Peace burned in the rubble that day.

It was a new era of war.

J. L. Cross

1 Kastell

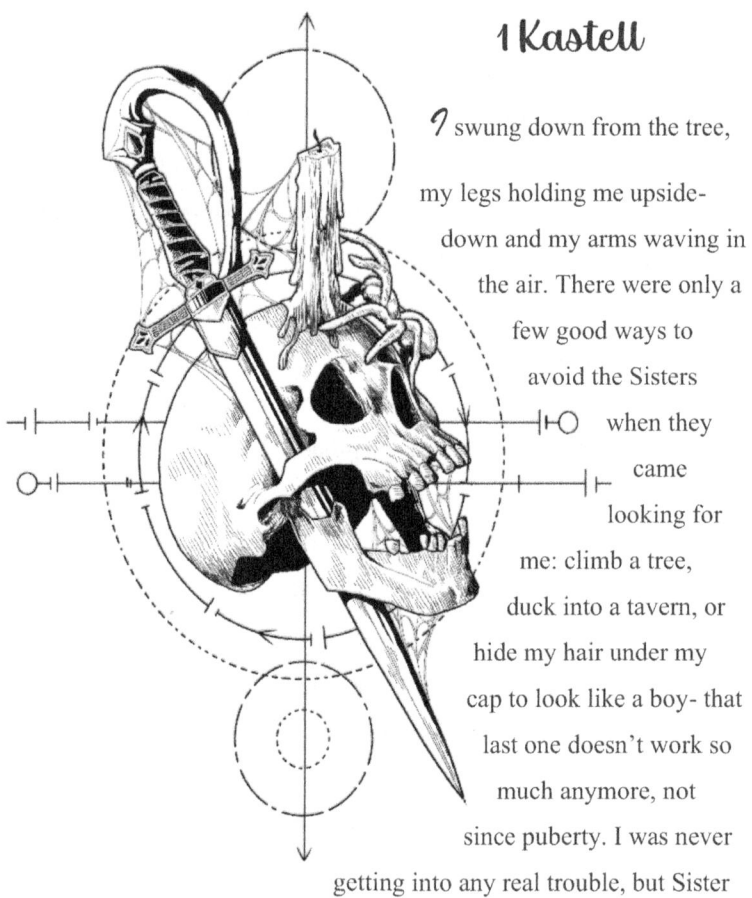

I swung down from the tree, my legs holding me upside-down and my arms waving in the air. There were only a few good ways to avoid the Sisters when they came looking for me: climb a tree, duck into a tavern, or hide my hair under my cap to look like a boy- that last one doesn't work so much anymore, not since puberty. I was never getting into any real trouble, but Sister Kendra always had to take the items I'd won gambling with others, mostly older men with the coins and riches to risk. Usually, senseless fake jewelry or bits of gold they panned. The older I got the more I won in coins and the harder it got to hide.

Today I wasn't in the mood to be surrounded by anyone, but recently those I came to know best, my own age, started to move away from the village. They were going off to make their own homesteads.

Many of the young girls were married off before seventeen. I fantasized all the time about having that kind of life; Someone to love, a husband, maybe a soulmate. Sometimes I just wanted a place that was truly my home. Kendra did her best, but the Sanctuary of Goddess followers was not really my home. I didn't belong there no matter how welcoming they tried to be. No matter how many years I spent with them, I never acquired a true sense of belonging.

I dropped to the ground and got my bearings, readjusting my trousers and my cap. The cap was small and simple, it helped to hide my ears, another clear reminder that I didn't belong here. This was a Witch's village.

I'm the daughter of the King. King Vor Kest to be precise. There were Kings all over, but my father was the King of the greatest Kingdom, Aylhm. He built his castle in the heart of it and a glorious city sprouted around it, Civith. I wanted to go back there, but the truth was hard to accept, it was dangerous there. My own mother was taken from me by an assassin and my brother had burned and slaughtered a village of innocent Arvors. After his banishment he became my next greatest threat. I had known my brother wasn't quite right… but I never took into consideration that he would come for me after my father's decision to cast him out.

A childhood of growing up in the Sanctuary wasn't what I had imagined. I missed my life in the castle, but here I was loved. It would be hard, but I knew it would come sooner than I wanted it to. Like everyone else, my time was coming, and I felt it pressing down on me, an invisible weight on my too slim shoulders.

J. L. Cross

I watched as the tavern bustled and people came and went. I sat at my favorite table and snacked on a loaf of bread for comfort. I didn't have any friends here. Leaving wouldn't be all that hard, nor bad for anyone. I could convince Kendra to come with me. I wasn't sure how I would be able to make it without her. She was the mother I needed when my own was taken so suddenly from me.

I snapped out of my daze and left for the Sanctuary. My playing cards and dice went untouched. A first for me. It wasn't a long walk, but enough for the rich mead's effects to wear thin. Partially the crisp air that was rolling in with the night was to blame.

Kendra waited at the gate for me. "Did you have a good evening?" A grim set line to her red lips. She didn't approve of my frequent escapades but learned to accept them. I rolled my eyes. Kendra liked to keep a short leash on me. It meant the lack of privacy, or the space to think clearly.

Living with a community of witches meant that there were no secrets. The Reflector was always nearby. She wasn't much different from the other women, except that she could see into my thoughts. The woman could touch them if she pleased. It was like an unwanted scrape against the consciousness. Sometimes it even felt vile, a complete intrusion of privacy. I made it clear I didn't want to be around the woman. After seven years in the community, I still didn't know her true name or her face. She kept herself hidden.

"It was just a beautiful night. I couldn't help myself." I said after clearing my thoughts. I looked through the gate to see the woman standing off to the side, cloaked and hooded per usual.

J. L. Cross

"Mother Reflector." I said in greeting. Her head dipped in a short recognition before she hurried away.

Kendra stiffened at the woman's persistence to probe my mind. "Don't mind her. Mother Reflector is only curious. She senses the conflict in your thoughts." Kendra waved it off with a flick of her fingers. "Tell me about the mead I can smell on you from here." She said and swung the gate open with the wind in a single motion of her wrist.

I smiled and passed through. Another flick of her wrist and it closed behind us. She rubbed her wrist and groaned. I didn't notice it much before, but she was aging. She gained weight that I never cared to recognize before, and lines on her face, around her eyes from smiling and across her brow from every word lashing she had to give me over the years. Kendra couldn't keep chasing me forever. It was time for me to make my way home.

"Kendra, you're getting older."

"Tell me something I don't already know." She snapped back. "The Mother can surely be cruel to us." She crossed her arms over her thick chest as she cursed the goddess she served. "Why are you pointing it out now?"

"Well, I'm getting older, too." I took the cap from my head and let my ears free. I pushed a strand of my white hair behind my left ear. She was piercing me with those sharp green eyes, daring me to go on. "I'm nearly twenty-one. All the other girls in the village have gone. The boys have married and I'm all alone. I shouldn't have to be here. I belong somewhere else now. Don't you think you've done the job you set out to do?"

She shook her head. "It wasn't a job for me, Kastell. I took you in because I loved you before I set eyes on you. The Mother brought you to me. I couldn't turn you away, nor could I have turned away your father. He needed me to take you and give you a good home, one free from the threats and violence. I loved every moment of it."

"It's time for me to leave." The words were clipped and short. I never wanted to drag out the unbearable. "I don't mean to be harsh. Only honest." I bit my lip, trying not to meet her eyes. I knew she wouldn't be happy, there was nothing that would make this any easier. "I've never felt this pull before, not until now. I've told you before that I don't believe in the Mother the way you and the other sisters do, but if there's anything I can say to make you believe that this isn't just what I *want* to do, but what I *need* to do- I'd tell you it's that if I ever heard the Mother's voice tell me what I need to do, then it was an hour ago when I was looking at the villagers. All of the other children grew up and moved on. That's when I heard her tell me it was time for me to leave, too."

When I finally had the courage to look up at her I was stunned to see the pride and joy that filled her eyes and dark face. The woman that raised me was ready for me to go as well. We were both ready.

"I'll let the sisters know to prepare us rations and horses." Kendra smiled; her eyes filled with tears that I knew she would never let me see fall. She wouldn't show me that weakness. She would save those moments for herself.

I held a finger up to stop her before she turned away from me. "I have one condition for this arrangement."

Kendra nodded. "Anything, Dear."

"You can't write to my father. He can't know that I'm coming. I'm twenty-one years and he has yet to send a convoy to claim me. He's not ready for this; he'd do anything to keep me away and safe. He must not know I'm coming."

Kendra rolled her eyes. "Have you ever thought that maybe he was waiting for you to decide to come home?"

"He wouldn't leave that kind of decision for me to make." I blurted. "He likes to exercise control. That's just what Kings do."

"Only over the people he needs to control. Would he really make a decision like that for you?" She said and turned on her heel to head to the barn. She would be sure our things were ready for departure first thing the next morning. Kendra was excited for me, not the reaction I was prepared to face.

Heavy dew formed on the grass in the valley. Fog drifted through the air as the sun came over the horizon. Rays pierced the sky throwing shades of blue, purple, and pink across the expanse in a colorful display. Birds sang in the depths of the thick forest behind me; flowers opened to the welcoming brightness of the sun. The further I traveled the more these beautiful sights and sounds were lost to the sounds of civilization. On the next hill a small stone watchtower rested as it was slowly taken back by nature. The walls were covered in patches of moss and vines that grew slowly under the vice of time. Daisies poked from small holes left in the walls. Those little pieces of beauty found a place even in the smallest cracks. Eventually the Mother would have her way and claim the entire building back to the ground and have it turned to dust.

    I rocked uneasily in my saddle. I wasn't ready for the next leg of our journey. My legs were chaffed, my back ached from the long ride. I wasn't so unfamiliar with horses or riding, but I wasn't accustomed to long journeys. I couldn't take my mind off of the fact that it would be very soon that I'd face one of my own kind. A tall eared snobbish guard or worse, a noble. Living with witches and magic folk that despised my kind made me a bit more distasteful to them myself. A small voice in my head echoed the guilt I should have just for being an Ayl as well.

    Ayles didn't travel into the forest or past the valley; I was one of the few Ayles that went so far from home, it's been a long time since interacting with my own kind. How hard would it be for me to find my place in their world? Seven years was a long time away from my own people. I looked and acted like a witch, apart from my oddly tall and pale ears that stood erect above my head. I wasn't around my own people in years, just the thought of interacting with them made my stomach turn. What if I wasn't what they expected?

    At the watch tower the view would be clear all the way to the gates of Civith, the city of Ayles. The city in which my father's throne sat, the same throne my ancestors possessed. Long ago that castle was once my home. When I would arrive at the city, the beautiful sounds of the forest would be a reminder of better days gone by.

    This was my home. Civith was ruled by the Kest dynasty, the name of my father, and before him, the Varius dynasty, the name of my mother. My father, King Vor, fought to the death against my mother's suitors, winning the right to the throne in blood and glory, as was custom for the suitors of all Varius' daughters. It was a custom upheld by many dynasties even before the Varius name. Was that what I had to look forward to? I was well past the age to marry.

    Only a man like my father with a deep desire for power could come out so victorious against so many enemies. I wouldn't call that a compliment, but it was my father's strength. He often told me as a little girl that it was his love for my mother that made him victorious, but I knew now that love didn't keep someone alive. Skills, practice, and diligence kept someone alive. Not to mention fear of death. A King was often challenged throughout their reign. It was average, normal to say the least. There was always someone that wanted the throne, and a King that refused a challenger was often seen as weak. My father was a skilled warrior long before he fought for his title as King. He was even a warrior in the Varius army, and not at all by choice. All our young men served when they wished to become a citizen of the Kingdom. My father hailed from a village that had very independent roots in the East. After taking the throne my father ruled for five years, unchallenged and undefeated. It wasn't until later those challengers came calling.

J. L. Cross

Ayles loved bloodshed, war, and death. We fought over everything and for everything. There wasn't anything I didn't think we wouldn't kill over. A shameful realization about my people. It was something I was often reminded about during the magic folks' community outreach. The last day of every month Kendra would take me to the homes of victims of the war, from both ends. We left them food, dried goods, and sometimes all they needed was a shoulder to cry on. Those people were the ones I was returning to the city for.

It wasn't long after the death of my mother that the Varius name was washed out of the castle and the Kest name was flying on every banner. I was next in line for the throne, but not by choice. Out of three siblings I'm the youngest. My older sister, Taria, was the only other child of our fathers endowed with the Kest name. Taria outright refused the life of royalty after our mother's death. She went to live with the Fae in the north. I haven't seen her since. Although I knew in my heart, she was safe and living in peace, the Fae were master magicians of time, unrivaled by any other species. Or so it's been told.

Vlad Varius was banished by my father for committing various crimes. He gambled, he tormented children, tortured slaves without cause, stole from the royal vault, and in some cases he murdered. Before his banishing, Vlad brutally murdered a whore in the throes of passion. My father tried to cover the mistakes of my brother, but every so often a new body would surface and eventually there was no way for him to cover up Vlad's horrendous actions. My father couldn't take the innocent bodies piling around my unstable brother. Instead of executing him for his crimes, *as he should have*, he was banished from the kingdom. King Vor had one great weakness- his children. My father loved all his children unconditionally. What father could take the life of his only son?

After his banishing, Vlad went under our mother's name, Varius. It suited him. Our father may have been a cold killer for power, but he wasn't a merciless murderer; those traits were directly from the Varius gene pool. My mother murdered her servant, claiming that the poor woman was plotting to kill her, and then killed herself when she couldn't cope with taking a life. She told my father she was hearing voices in her head. In the end those voices must have been screaming at her. Thankfully, I was spared from the craziness in my family. At least, that's what I thought.

A sour taste lingered in my mouth. My face was sweating. How could I be sweating? I couldn't take my mind away from what *could* happen during my arrival. Would my father recognize me? Would he try to send me back to the sanctuary with Kendra? *No.* She said that it was possible that he was waiting for me. I was sent to the sanctuary when the war with the Rebels had begun; to protect me as his only heir. Ending the Kest dynasty would be as easy as ending my life. Hiding me in the sanctuary was genius of him then, but now I'm a stranger to my own kind. The benefit: I could go about unnoticed. Would I see any familiar faces? Maybe even the faces I knew from my childhood would be gone, moved on to better things far away from the war.

I peeked out from under my hood to get a good look around. We had traveled for hours. It was the most tedious part of the journey.

Clusters of farms stood out against a background of meadows that went uncut and untended beyond them. We passed several farmers tending their fields or livestock. Each paid attention to themselves, not daring a glance up as we passed. They tilled and dug at the parched ground until it came loose and somewhat malleable. One boy chased after a stray sheep in a field of thick tall grass.

The forest disappeared behind us. It would only be a memory for me to reach out to when the city was overbearing. The closer to Civith, the uglier our surroundings became. A pattern of dirt roads and people that cared about nothing other than what they worked at. The village near the sanctuary was entirely different. You couldn't walk ten steps without being called a greeting from a friendly passerby.

Everything leading up to the city seemed more depressing. Some Ayles looked so skinny and depraved. Some even looked sick. At the heart of the city the King's mighty steel and stone castle stretched towards the sky. From the watch tower I would get my first good look at it after years of being so far from home.

This last leg of the journey was far more dangerous than the rest. Rumors of rebels, thieves, and trolls plagued the lands around the city. I wasn't sure if it were a lie to keep the Ayles closer to where they laid their roots, or if there was ever some fact to it. I never saw a giant or troll a day in my life, but I knew that they had a whole island to themselves in the East. Maybe that was nothing more than a fairy tale as well.

I couldn't wait to see Civith. The dangers around me worried me less than what it would be like to be home again. rebels are constantly wandering the lands around Civith. rebels weren't the only ones to fear, Ayles would be increasingly more dangerous the more starved they became. I had food, water, a horse, and clothing. Everything in my bags could potentially make me a target. What I had could last some poor Ayles a week.

 I started to sweat nervously. I wiped my palms on my robes and rubbed my pale arms. What if it was nothing like I imagined? What if it went to waste? I pushed the hood off my head and shed my outer robe. I was burning up with anxiety. It's been years since I had a conversation with another Ayl. What would that be like? They were different from the witches I'd spent so much time with.

 Not too far ahead of us there were a few Aylish soldiers guiding their horses down the path quitely. I loosened my hair and covered my ears before passing them, a force of habit. They had a stiff and rigid demeanor. Neither of them paid me any mind, but both of them stared pointedly at Kendra as we passed. She didn't seem to mind their candid rudeness.

 "Kastell, what's on your mind?" My elder companion brought her horse up beside mine. Her short curly black hair bounced on her shoulders, perfectly framed around her round face. My mare snapped in irritation when the stallion nudged her neck. Kendra pulled away slightly to separate the two.

 "You know she doesn't like his company. He's so high strung. It came as a shock to me when you chose him as your mount in the first place." I remarked after scratching my mare behind the ears.

Kendra chuckled. Her voice acquired a sharp rasp over the years as age took her ever so slowly. "He'll make my journey quicker when I return to the sanctuary without you." She took a long pause. I could feel her piercing green eyes on the back of my neck, but I couldn't look her in the eyes just yet. Not after she confirmed what I feared most. She was leaving me soon. I'd be in a new place and all alone, surrounded by people and places I should know and remember, but I would still be a stranger in the midst of it all.

"You know," she grumbled, "all the sisters will miss you dearly. I will miss you most of all. You were just a girl when your father brought you to me, and now I am sending you home as a woman. I'm honored to have raised you." I heard the swell of tears in her voice. Kendra wasn't comfortable with the silence between us. It was tense and hard for us, usually there was so much to say.

I still couldn't bear to look at her. "I'll miss you as well. You didn't just raise me, you were a mother to me, something I never truly had." I remembered my mother, I knew her and spent time with her that I would treasure, but even my mother had limitations as the queen. Kendra had an untapped vault of time for me. She really was my mother.

We just reached the base of the watch tower as the darkest parts of the sky on the horizon turned to blue. I stopped in front of the well and dismounted and quickly fetched the water for the horses as Kendra dismounted more methodically, her aching body making things more difficult for her. We sat on a few stumps that were being used as chairs around a burned-out fire while our horses rested. It was odd to see the post abandoned and quiet.

"I won't be going further with you." Kendra grumbled after a moment while looking at her feet. She seemed to look over my shoulder and then dip her gaze.

"*No*. You will not be. For your own good." A guard stepped out from inside the tower. He walked with a strut of arrogance. I had to glance over my shoulder to see him. He was a large man. He could easily lift me with a single hand and toss me aside, but I still rose to my feet to challenge him. The first Ayl I'd seen in years and I wanted to force his casually hate-filled attitude down his throat.

He smiled when he caught sight of my ears tucked into my hair. A mark of privilege in these lands. I was better than Kendra, I was worth more than she was. That's all he saw- value and prestige. I saw the way he surveyed my muscles and the position I stood in. He was pinpointing and marking every ounce of weakness I had, or my strengths. I stood nose to nose with him, a snarl coming from somewhere deep inside of me.

The guard gave me a smug smile, he'd won only with the power of words, eliciting a panic and rage inside of me to defend what I thought was mine to protect. He scoffed and stepped back. Winning the challenge was enough for him, he didn't have to be the last one standing his ground. *One for one*, my mind marked.

Kendra took my hand in her fragile ones and pulled me back towards her. "Witches are not allowed within the limits of the city, we've talked about this many times before. You know better. Witches often used magic years ago to hurt and punish the Ayles. In some cases, it was used to control them without their consent." Kendra smiled up at me, her ebony skin was glowing, flawless in the sun. "Your journey will end with only yourself to celebrate the victory of return."

"I wanted to show you my home." I was disappointed. Originally, I was under the impression she would be taking the whole journey with me, but I should have known better. We had talked about this many times. The guard watched us with dark eyes as if we would try to commit a crime against him here in the daylight and he needed to be extra cautious. There was something dark hiding in the depths of those eyes, something I couldn't trust.

Kendra laughed, patting my hands. "I've seen enough of the city from here. My home is beyond the forest. I don't care for the city anyways." She stood up and hugged me tightly.

"I love you." I whispered into her hair as my tears soaked into her shoulder. I tightened my grip, afraid to leave the small woman to travel home alone.

Kendra pulled away and held me at arm's length. She then wiped the tears off my flushed cheeks with the cuff of her wool shirt. "That's enough of those. Write to me, visit me, but promise me one thing," she paused until I nodded, gripping her wrists as her hands held my face. "Don't let Vor send you back to these woods. You make your own decisions from now on. Do not bend to his will."

I nodded and hugged her one last time. "I'll write." I confirmed. I wasn't so sure I would have the nerve to challenge my father's will though. That could only be known with time. I would miss the feeling of Kendra's warmth against me when I was sad or just in need of comfort. I would miss her cooking and her knitting, even her singing. Most of all I would miss having a mother.

"I expect no less." She kissed my cheek. "I love you, and don't you forget it."

She mounted her horse. I couldn't believe that this was it, this was the moment that made us sit in silence through a whole morning worth of riding. We had nothing more to say as we traveled closer and closer to this inevitable goodbye. I chose this for the both of us. I had made my decision, but she followed me blindly through it. She let me forge my own path and started me on it. What better mother could I ask for?

I watched her ride away without even a glance behind her. Kendra taught me right from wrong, taught me to be a lady, how to use a knife and sword, and how to use my first bow. Watching her ride away from me was like watching my heart split in two. She was right, I needed to go home. I made this decision for a reason; I was done hiding in the sanctuary, far from my destiny, but a part of me would always be in the forest with her.

I turned to the guard who looked me up and down, observing me more than ogling me. "What are you staring at?" I barked as I crossed my arms, sitting back down at the fire. My mare had to rest and drink before going on. He leaned against the crumbling door frame of the watchtower. There were flecks of old blood on his grieves. His leather armor looked too thin to protect him from much.

"You're dressed like a peasant." He mocked. Each step he took closer to me had my defenses rising again. He reached out and flicked my fair white ponytail once he was within an arm's reach. My hair wasn't nearly as fine as his. Mine was rough and dry. I combed my fingers through its length just to brush away his touch.

"What Ayl binds her hair in such a sloppy manner?" He chuckled and went to sit near the fire on the stump across from me.

I timidly watched and monitored his movements as he poked the ashes around so he could start a fresh pot of tea. "Is there something I can do for you, *peasant*?" He asked rudely. Yet his eyes still darted from under his guarded expression, looking me over like a threat. *Like prey.*

"Actually, yes. I'm not sure how to ask this..." I crossed my arms and turned slightly away from him in embarrassment.

"Out with it." He said, his expression softening a bit.

"Well, I haven't lived among Ayles for a few- many years. Mostly-"

"Sit." He demanded before I could finish my thought. "Just ask before I get bored." More a threat than a warning. Those eyes held something dangerous that beckoned for me to run away.

I took the cup of tea he offered from his last pot. Was he actually being kind to me after so casually threatening me? "How should an Ayl wear her hair?"

He covered his mouth as he chuckled at me, trying desperately to hide his amusement. "How do you not know such things?" His phrasing was proper, but still a bit informal. His tone was rich, his words enunciated. Every word passing his teeth and lips was clear and distinct. Witches mumbled and whispered frequently.

"I-I…" I stuttered, and then calmed my breathing before I attempted to answer again. He was making me uncomfortable, just by bearing under his scrutiny. "I was raised by Kendra, the witch." I gestured to where she had ridden off. "My father sent me away after my mother died. I don't know much about Aylish culture anymore. Only the small things that Kendra taught me and that from my mother's lessons as a young girl, but back then I never really did my own hair."

"What *did* Kendra teach you?" He killed the flames under his pot and leaned back to relax, kicking his leg out to make himself more comfortable. He was tall and handsome, if you liked a war-torn animal. Everything about him defined his prowess in combat. His boots were tight and worn in with his trousers tucked into the tops. A tattoo on his left arm was hidden under the sleeves of a thin stained white shirt that was cleaned so many times it was fraying at the cuffs. He wore a lightweight leather vest over his shirt, an awful attempt at armor. Yet, he was here, alive, a face covered in scars.

My thoughts raced from the sight of him to everything I was taught by Kendra to make me a proper lady. Her rules chanted inside my head: *Let men speak first, never attempt to touch anyone of the opposite gender. Women are meant to be engaged, not* to *engage. Be the Queen first, a Wife second. Always remain upright, shoulders square, and chin up. Always look the one you're speaking to in the eye. All questions can mostly be answered with* yes, *or* no. *Don't seek* attention from strangers and always keep your robes washed and clean, as well as your body. Ayles pride themselves in hygiene and presentation.

"Well, I think she taught me the basics and for the most part she told me to avoid strangers. Above all other rules, do not associate with Arvors. That was her last rule." I answered after I realized he was staring at me intently while I over analyzed everything Kendra taught me.

He sat up and listened when I spoke, not what I had expected from him, and not a witch's trait. Sometimes they would fidget or look away while talking, not the Ayles. His hair was down in a long braid behind his back and the sides of his head shaved with a tattoo that swirled around the back of his head and down his neck. His hair wasn't constrained with foreign objects like hair bands, which is what I used. I didn't know many types of braids, just the one plain one that never held well.

He cut through my racing thoughts. "You know, the basics are all you need. Proper mannerisms can get you a long way. Yet, you're already breaking one of the rules." He said as he gently elbowed my arm. "You're not avoiding strangers."

My skin trembled as if a spider just walked across my arm. I held my arms close to my body and across my chest. The minute Kendra turned her back I broke her rules. What kind of Queen would I be if I couldn't follow at least some rules?

"You're right, I think it's time for me to go." I quickly stood and went to my horse.

"Just a moment!" He shouted as I briskly untethered my horse from the post.

I turned to him as I gripped the reins tighter. "No, I think that was enough. I think this is where we part ways." I said angrily.

He bowed then, something Kendra hadn't taught me. "I apologize. That was rude of me. Will you allow me the honor of fixing your hair? An act of kindness," he paused, "for my behavior."

I thought for a moment and then agreed. He stood and pulled my long hair from its constraint and quickly braided my hair elaborately and allowed it to fall down my back. I could tell how he didn't allow his hands to idle on the nape of my neck and the way he was quick that he was now aware of my innocence, maybe more so than I wished.

"There. You don't speak like a peasant, so you shouldn't wear your hair like one. I suggest a new tunic or robes as well. Something to bring out your eyes." He then did a short bow, a sly smile on his lips.

I mounted my horse and turned her toward the city.

"Can I have your name?" The soldier looked up at me from where he stood. His arms crossed over his chest.

I shrugged. "Maybe, I haven't decided if I like you enough to be familiar."

He chuckled. "Kyier. When you see me again you can call me Ky."

"I don't think you'll be seeing me again, Ky." A small smile crept onto my lips. He was an intimidating man, a warrior, but there was something there that wasn't before, something friendly in his eyes and in his face. That darkness in his eyes receded if only slightly.

He turned and walked away. "Maybe not."

I got my first real look at the city of Civith. The blue and white banners were flying, more of a dangle. They weren't well taken care of and many were even torn, hanging by a thread from their old wooden posts. The colors were faded. The white turned gray, riddled with holes. How could it look so low and so disparaging? The walls wept from the clinging mist and fog surrounded the castle. It was still majestic in its place. It was beautiful in its own sad way. Yet, it stood tall, menacing in the shadows of the mountains just beyond the River to the North.

The city was falling apart. Some buildings barely stood the test of time. The village outside the sanctuary had better walls and sturdier Inns than what I could see. Roofs were caved in, and some were dark and black from smoke and tar used to manufacture a semblance of a repair, but it was like kissing a broken arm. The damage still lurked beneath it. The Varius dynasty had taken such good care of their people. I was embarrassed to be called a Kestro. Couldn't my father have done better by them? Without my mother the poor were all but forgotten.

Guards waved civilians near the gates to approach and checked the farmer's trading carts of goods. They looked for rebels and witches trying to sneak their way into the city, or children trying to sneak their way out. I used to be one of those mischievous children.

Excitement coursed through me. I wanted to be in the crowd, surrounded by the people, carts, and ecstatic children. The smell of fresh baked breads and pies; foods that made my mouth melt and water. I wanted to feel the fine linens embroidered with intricate designs and clothing of all types. I would be in the mix of the great disgust the city truly was- body odor, scrap, and Aylish waste tossed from windows into allies. I couldn't wait for all of it. I kicked my horse into a steady trot. If I was quick enough, I wouldn't miss the traders setting up their stands and displaying the best they had to offer.

The sound and sights of the trading bazaar opening for the day would make me feel like a child all over again. I once stood just inside the gates gripping Taria's hand, bouncing with excitement that first time I watched them open their stalls and wave their wares. My mother wanted me to see how food came to our table, and how we relied on our people to provide for us. My mother was the epitome of a remarkable Queen. If I could be even half of what she was- I could be proud. She was a proper soft-spoken woman, but stern on her children. I followed on her heels as she waded into the crowd of farmers flooding into the mouth of the city to greet them and thank them for their services. Some of them even rushed to her. They gifted her with loaves of bread, sewing materials, perfumes, and even a chicken. It was all the farmers had to offer. She took the flailing animal with as much gratitude as she received everything prior.

Riding towards those looming gates made my heart ache. The last time I was so close to them I was in a carriage barreling out of the city towards a new life. My entire existence was flipped on its head. The lavish clothing, jewelry, and delicacies were stripped away. I learned to fit in with the average.

I remembered seeing her body, my mother's, laid out on the marble floor of the throne room. I was rushed past it and thrown into a carriage. I would never forget the blood and the vacant stare of her eyes. Vlad was beside my father in his night garments, barely awake. When we ran through the throne room his eyes locked on her lifeless corpse and he was frozen in that moment. That was the last I saw of my tyrant brother. Two years later I received a letter from my father. I was the new heir, Vlad was banished, and the security of my life was of the utmost importance. Nothing more, nothing less.

No one knows I'm here. Panic surged in my gut threatening to make me vomit. Kendra wouldn't have sent word to my father of my return, would she? No. She would honor my request. We both worried he would turn me away, especially with the war only escalating throughout the years. Yet, she seemed sure that there was a greater chance he would accept me. His reaction was unpredictable.

How would I even get into the castle? *I'm a stranger here.* Would I have to request an audience with my own father? The thought made me chuckle. I was a stranger here. No one would know my face.

The thought comforted me. With no one to recognize me, the safer I would be. *What is there to fear?*

My mare startled as we neared a mass of people clamoring at the mouth of the city. Yet, the crowd was smaller than those I remembered from my childhood. It was early morning and the gates creaked open as the entrance was widened, sparking bittersweet nostalgia. As the mouth to the city swung open it began swallowing up all of the traders waiting for a breadth to get in rather than filing one after one through the half-closed doors. They were more frantic in their hurry than I remembered. These people were afraid to be outside the city walls. Even though most of these same people lived outside the walls, they clamored in angst to get in. Did any of them feel safe in their own beds or on their own lands? Was this the fear they lived in to preserve all they had left?

Guards stopped carts and hooded figures, double checking and ensuring that no outsider would gain access. Some of us slipped by unnoticed as the guards were overwhelmed with a pair of ragged teenage boys with short, braided hair that ran cart to cart picking out apples and oranges as they bolted through. The guards shouted and sent the youngest of their flock to chase after the two rascals that were clearly going to get away.

I dismounted and moved in front of my mare to control and calm her. I gripped her reins under her chin and let her press her head into my shoulder for comfort. Neither of us were so accustomed to the chaos. She willfully followed me through the crowd after I used my robe to cover her face. A blind trustful horse would follow you into the sea. I moved her onward to the gate but attempted not to brush up on any of the sickly-looking farmers with carts filled with rotting crops. Surprisingly, I wasn't stopped from making my way past the guards. Of course, I wasn't trying to hide from them either.

The market buzzed with children and elderly who shouted about the wares their stands sold. A town crier heckled at gatherers about threats from the rebels just beyond the walls of the city. I stood by to listen, drawn in by his alluring voice.

"Have you heard! Have you heard!" The man was reaching and trying to bring others to him. "Rebels are everywhere! Threatening the city, night and day. If you listen close enough, you can even hear the beasts barking in the night, fighting over the remains of their food. Their leader is creeping closer and closer to our beloved city as the days pass. Yet, the *mighty* King's men have yet to bring his head through those gates. What has the King done for us? We have encroaching famine, we have illnesses, and we have death. The King hides away in his castle and soaks Aylhm in the blood of our kin, leading them to uncertainty. Not to mention, witches -"

I couldn't help the furrow in my brow or the anger that snagged in my chest and boiled through my very bones, tingled on my skin. *What a lazy coward*! He stood on a pedestal and shouted lies. My father would never march anyone into battle unless he knew he could win. He was an intelligent and strategic man. One man couldn't bring illnesses down on his people. Though, he could do better with providing repairs for their homes and city. My father wouldn't hide.

"Excuse me." I shouted from the back of the crowd. I was irritated by his absurd claims. Everyone turned their eyes on me. He still rambled about the danger of witches and how my father conspired with them to undermine Aylish superiority. As I made my way forward, I had to shove past a woman that scoffed over her shoulder at me.

"Excuse me!" I yelled, and this time the crier stopped and acknowledged me with a scowl.

"Is there something I can do for you, little miss?" He asked. He stepped down off his wooden crate used to make him appear larger and more alluring. Really, he was a thin, malnourished, and gaunt man that hardly matched me in height. A runt. Suffering without food would make a man say anything for half a coin.

"Yes. You're spouting lies. Rebels aren't *just* outside the city." He tried to interrupt me, but we were standing face to face now. I narrowed my eyes. He halted and gestured for me to go on with a roll of his hand.

"No. There isn't much out there at all. Sure, you could say rebels are a threat, but they're not camped in the valley, or even in the forest. I grew up with witches." Someone let out a shocked gasp beside me. "They're far from the conspiring type. If the King is hiding away in his castle, then he's not making an effort to conspire with anyone. I guarantee they're less of a threat than the rebels are. Isn't it horrible what you're doing, filling the citizens with fear? So much fear that no one travels past the farms in the valley? Are you heckling at them for just a single coin? Do you enjoy making them fear their duty as soldiers and farmers, or do you just take some sick satisfaction in watching the mothers, wives, sisters, and daughters of those men weep with a fear that you've planted in them?"

"Who are you, traveler?" He spat, angry that I dared challenge his word. His breath was wretched and cascaded down on my face. I couldn't turn away. I wouldn't give him that satisfaction. I wouldn't back down to such a small and ugly man. It wasn't just his gaunt and sunk face that disturbed me, but the thing inside of him that made him say these things. Was it really my father that so easily bred these feelings into his people?

"Oh, I'm just as you say, a traveler." I said with a snarky smirk. "I only wish you would be more honest. Do the rebels really threaten the city so much?"

He laughed then. "The traveler doesn't yet know. Hundreds of Ayles were killed on the battlefield just north of the city only a few short weeks ago. She doesn't know how the leader of the rebels looks like the Devil and bathes in the blood of those that he's killed to turn his fur coat red." He whispered into my face, trying to fill me with the same fear that they held so close.

I shrugged. "There is a possibility that I'm wrong, but I was out there and there wasn't even a murmur from the Rebel Arvors. Battles have been fought all across Aylhm. I doubt one battle is enough to scare us. The Ayles have fought giants in Gorgon and forced the Soilts into the North. Is this the battle that you'll let sink us into despair? I think you may be exaggerating the circumstances, filling them with an unprecedented fear. *Heckling for crumbs.*" I teased.

He laughed, "Stay long enough, dear traveler, and see the carnage for yourself. Most here have lost their loved ones to the Rebel King… And soon many more might die when he brings the fight to the city walls, *or within them.*"

The crier took his stand on the box. If you looked at him for too long, you could imagine his brittle legs snapping under him like dead twigs. He was a weak little man with nothing better to do, and not much else to contribute to society. *A waste of good air,* I thought.

"Don't forget winter is soon approaching! The King will give rations in the coming weeks! Don't forget to claim your rations!" I tried to tone the heckler out, but his cracked voice was etched into my mind, an annoying repetition of scratching rocks against granit. I shook my head. His voice was like fine sand in my ears. I wished I could fold them or dull their sensitivity. I didn't want to hear him as I crossed the bazaar with my mare in tow. Yet, his voice sought me out. *Illness and Death. The King hides. We're abandoned. The next fight will topple the city into the dirt.*

A moment passed before something he said registered in me. *Famine over the winter?* Civith never saw famine in its history. Civith never needed strict rationing so early before the winter either. In recent years there was a plentiful harvest. Were the Arvors intercepting our harvest wagons as well? Maybe the Mother was choosing a side in the war.

Father could be anticipating a plague, something more devastating than the war. There was only one plague to pass through long before when our people first settled on the land. It was spread rapidly first by what was left of mankind, then to the witches and warlocks who were more resilient to such things, and then it came for our people. The first plague killed many Ayles, another reason for the divide in the races to deepen.

I guided my mare on to the iron castle gates. The city was small with only two divisions of residential homes. Most didn't want to live so close to the royals or in easily controlled districts. These homes were caving in, and some were in dire need of repair. It looked worse close up. The poor and unfortunate lived within the walls of the city, leaching off the King for support. I never minded it though, these people were elderly, or orphans, or even deformed and couldn't farm, mine, or wield swords in the army. This was supposed to be their haven, but the heckler made it sound like the city wouldn't remain safe.

I took in the sight of the wall around the castle. It was fortified and even had recent repairs that were noticeable. You would think my father was more worried about preserving his own life rather than that of his people. Maybe he should focus on finding an end to the war instead. If he put as much time into diplomacy as he did his own walls there could have been a breakthrough by now.

Soldiers were posted everywhere on the higher walls, there was only one lonely soldier waiting in front of the gate, studying it. He was dressed in royal blues and whites. The colors of my father's house. Only his most important men and slaves dressed in our family colors. These were clean and crips with golden embroidery, meant for only the most respected of their positions. He was a commander; his sword and bow were sheathed on his back and the hilt of the sword glistened in the rays of the sun. His golden blonde hair was combed perfectly down his shoulders without even the slightest knot or split end. He was tall and broad, a masculine masterpiece. His jacket was tight across the breadth of his shoulders.

The commander rolled his shoulders and stood up more straight from what he was looking at. His neck cracked as he straightened and moved his head side to side to loosen tense muscles. "Open the gate."

The gate swung open, he stepped over its heavily watched threshold. I attempted to follow, but a bolt from a bow stabbed the ground just in front of my feet. I almost faltered, I clutched my mare's reins to hold myself upright. The attempt on my life rattled me, *of course they won't let me in*. My breath caught in my chest and my heart raced, realizing that the only reason the bolt missed was because the anchor was shaking and beside himself. *Lucky me*. I wanted to hurl it back in the direction it came, but I knew better, rage wouldn't get me where I needed to be. I needed to be home. I need to be on the other side of this flimsy gate. I could rage-out another time after I assumed my role as heir. Maybe then I would shove the bolt down the trembling soldier's throat. I could hurl the bolt up the wall and nick his precious little stubby Ayl ears if I wanted, but for now, I would mind myself. I swallowed my pride. I rolled my eyes at my own stupidity.

"How dare you intrude into the castle, peasant!" He spat after gathering his nerves off the wooden floorboards of his little tower. The guard had a very false sense of security in his elevated haven. His lip curled in disgust as he looked down on me from the wall. *Peasant, again? Really?*

"I request an audience with King Vor!" I shouted back with as much gumption as I could muster. No matter my disposition to violence and self-defense, I was still unnerved. This place was foreign to me, but it was still my home. I had to be careful I didn't let the fear he instilled in me with his missed bolt sound in my voice. I was soft spoken, but I projected my voice in my defense.

The man waved me away. "He will not accommodate such a-."

"Enough." The order was even and just loud enough for me and the soldier to hear. The soldier scoffed and turned away from me. The commander stood in the shadow of the now closed gate. He watched me as I fidgeted with the reins in my hand. "What is your business with the King?" His eyes moved over my body. He stepped from the shadows; his face puzzled. *"Wait,"* His voice was soft. "I know you. Your face, it's very familiar to me."

I knew him. I knew this man from years ago. A slave owned by my father. We grew up together. Time made him into a man and the face of the teenage boy I knew back then was all but gone.

Inara. He was a close friend of my brother, Vlad. Does this mean that my father had long since passed and the Kingdom was mistakenly passed to my brother? How could this have happened?! Is this why I was kept hidden away from the city for so long at the Sanctuary? Was my father only trying to protect me by hiding me there?

I huffed and rubbed the back of my neck. "We've never met." It wasn't so far from the truth. Inara could be an entirely different man than the dark anus of a boy that I so clearly remembered. "Tell the *King* that I carry precious cargo for him." I flicked my hair over my shoulder and gave him more sass than he could probably handle from a woman.

He doesn't recognize me. I'm only familiar. I let out a long breath as I assured myself. As Inara had gotten closer to me, his scent was warm, enticing, and masculine. The aroma of vanilla and wine. *Not the anus you remember.*

I hated him when we were growing up. I still hated him, I was sure of it, but he looked and smelled so much different now. *Why does he smell so good?* Not the smell of a boy, but a man. I ignored that sweet enticing smell. This was the boy that harassed and chased me to appease the ill mind of my older brother. Inara didn't look like that boy anymore. I didn't want to know him. I didn't want to know if he changed.

Inara shook his head as if to disregard the possibility that I was familiar. "No, she's long since gone." He said to himself. I refused to meet his eyes, I could only tempt recognition so much from a menacing bully of my childhood so much before he knew me and became that same horror all over again. Commander Inara added to Kendra's list of things to avoid.

Loud women

Rebels

Arvors

Thieves

Gamblers

Strangers

And now... *The Commander*

Inara bullied me many times alongside my brother. It's a wonder he didn't place who I was. He disregarded the notion so easily.

Do I look that different? Back then I was a plump little girl they chased. He was a year older than me, sixteen, when he tried to grab me by the arm and unintentionally ripped the sleeve of my dress, forcing me to hold it up to my chin securely as I cried and ran from him. I was hardly flat chested then. Vlad was amused, but Inara blushed red at the incident. I never thought he was as horrible as Vlad, but I never took him to be innocent. Of course, Vlad only cared about torturing and killing his victims. Bullying me was only a hobby he entertained when he truly got bored.

Just as I was beginning to turn, the Commander turned on his heel to face me again. He had taken a moment to gather his thoughts, then met my eyes. Sure enough, his were gorgeous, brown with golden flecks throughout. "I will request an audience with the King personally. Do not stray far from the city."

I took the reins of my mare tightly in my hand. My knuckles were turning pale at the intensity. Was I mad at him for not recognizing me, or was I mad at myself for wishing he had? I wanted nothing more than to have this ordeal dealt with. Though, I was afraid that my own brother would be behind those gates. Was there even a chance and somehow, I wouldn't know? *Nonsense!*

2 Kastell

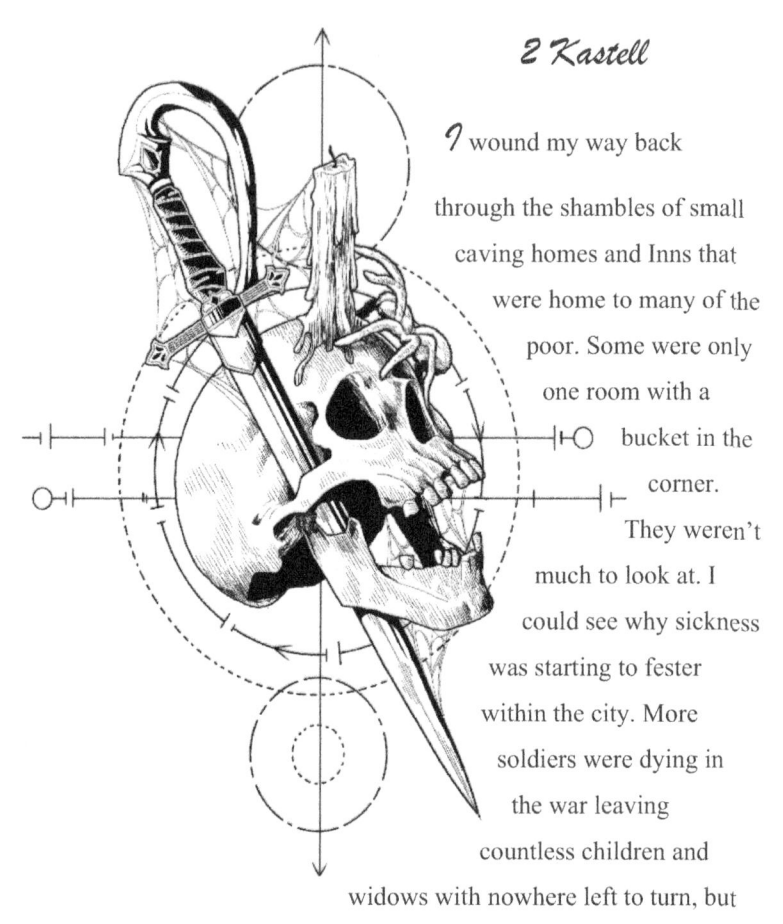

I wound my way back through the shambles of small caving homes and Inns that were home to many of the poor. Some were only one room with a bucket in the corner. They weren't much to look at. I could see why sickness was starting to fester within the city. More soldiers were dying in the war leaving countless children and widows with nowhere left to turn, but they came here seeking aid, and this was what they were offered. Rats scoured the allies for leftover scraps of bread and rotting vegetables.

Relief filled me as I broke through the end of the housing district and back into the market square. The smell here wasn't as rancid as in the housing district and the smell of oils and perfumes from the vendors mingled with the foods from the tavern. They washed out the smell of waste. I stopped in front of the city stable and used what little coin I had to stall my horse.

"She'll be well seen after." The dirty barn boy assured me. I hesitated before leaving, unaware of where I would go for the night.

I nodded. "I'll come back soon for her. If you groom her, I'll give you more coins." The barn boy smiled and hurried back through the rows of freshly swept stalls.

I left then to cross the market to the nearest inn, the only plausible place for me, but some of the doors were crooked and barely hung to their hinges. I could tell more than half of the rooms were vacant. It was a shame how worn and beat down the city became in only a few years. My mother would have never let things get so bad. I was shocked that the Royal Collective would let it go to waste so easily as well. They should have cared more about these things. The people depended on them.

As the sun started to set, children played in the open market with a ball and the city tavern overflowed with men and women alike. *The Dripp.* The sign hung by two thick metal rings and swayed with the passing of a breeze.

A woman sat perched in a young soldier's lap with no more than a sheer blouse to cover herself. Some women would do anything for a few coins, even humiliate themselves. This was normal for Civith.

I remembered my father in my ear as a child, *"don't ever disgrace my name, Kastell."* Now I didn't have any coins to eat and none to sleep.

    I would sleep with my mare, I finally decided. If I placed bets on the dice game in hopes of making a few spare coins I could easily find myself in debt or in a brawl, probably both. I wasn't confident enough in myself for either after traveling for so long. I would never humiliate myself that way.

    Things were different at the Sanctuary. As I got older, I snuck out more and more. I wanted to go into town and socialize. I stayed away from most men, but the women could never gamble or play as well as me; the men that did gamble against me were desperate and horrible at it- an easy win on my part. It was embarrassing for men that lost a handful to me, but I always slipped those coins into a purse under my floorboards. Kendra found them once, so I started donating them to the beggars on my way back to conceal my escapades. This time I was the beggar. I was only in a brawl or two growing up with other children, but eventually my late-night adventures ended, the allure dying.

    I stood from a distance, staring into the glowing lights of the tavern. The smell engulfed me. I wanted to taste the home cooked stew and bread on my tongue. My mouth was watering in anticipation, but it would not be satisfied. The overflowed mugs of wheat and barley beer called to me, but I would stay thirsty.

    A hooded man approached me from the tavern slowly, turning a coin with his fingers to catch my eye. His robe was dark, black, no embroideries and no insignias. He wasn't from around here. The stranger staggered once from the ale he already drank, but he straightened himself and proceeded much more gracefully.

"I am not selling anything here." I said sternly. I wasn't in the mood for another confrontation with a man. I had my fill for the day. I wanted to stand here and smell the wafting scents of the tavern in despair and hunger- without being bothered.

He chuckled, a deep rich sound. "I'm not paying for a service, my lady, I'm donating to your cause," he said. He pushed back his hood revealing a strong handsome face with short red hair and a trimmed beard.

"*You're a human.*" I accused him after noticing his short, rounded ears.

He smiled suspiciously. "Not quite, but good try. For two coins you can try your luck again, but it isn't very important, is it?"

"Men, warlocks, witches, and rebels are forbidden in the city." I recited what Kendra said to me thousands of times.

"Yet, *Hybrids* are not. The law was a little too specific, it has loopholes." He flipped the coin to me. "Fill your stomach. No one deserves to be hungry." He put up his hood and continued to pass me on his way to the stables. "Even a prejudice like yourself."

I sighed. Was that what I was? Suddenly I was ashamed of myself. I checked the coin in my hand. It seemed bright and clean. It would indeed fill my stomach, but it wouldn't buy me a bed. A haystack in the loft of the stable would do, I suppose. It would be cold, but not unbearable. It was good enough for me a moment ago, so it would be good enough now. One coin never changed the fate of a peasant.

I made my way into the tavern and sat in the only open space at the bar. Everyone seemed to be in decent spirits. It was a lively atmosphere with chatter filling every corner. It was impossible not to enjoy myself.

I slapped the coin on the bar; a cook instantly put down a hot meal. It was as if he knew I was trying to taste his food from across the market with my nose in the air like an Arvor in heat.

The food was delicious. The soup was as rich and flavorful as those aromas had convinced me it would be. The bread was fresh and scored on the bottom from a stone oven hidden somewhere behind the building. I could smell the next loaf roasting as I stuffed my face with the fluffy white piece that was haphazardly cut and shoved beside my bowl of soup, leaving me full and happy.

It was wonderful, surrounded by strangers, oddly exhilarating. This was no different than all the times I spent in the taverns at the witch village. I never had that feeling in the Sanctuary, nor had I ever felt so wired before from the mead.

There were only a few times I felt so ecstatic, the first time I shot my bow was at the top of that list. Kendra taught me to master the art of a bow and then that of throwing knives. She often said, *"No woman should ever be defenseless."* Even in my state of content, I was surrounded by strangers, and I was still the heir. Protecting myself was always her first concern. She would have never sent me scuttling back if I wasn't ready to do just that on a whim.

J. L. Cross

I staggered through the tavern door and back into the fresh night air. I filled my lungs and exhaled deeply. I crossed the market square to the stable. The doors were sealed. Candles were burning in some windows throughout the housing district. Soldiers and teens were just making their way home or to the barracks closer to the castle.

The stable was small and the back had a ladder leading into the loft. It was harder than I expected to crawl into the loft with mead rattling my brain around. With the barn doors sealed and locked I took it into my own hands to make an entry. At least I would be safe for the night, somewhat warm, and secure. There wasn't much more I could ask for. *A warm bath*, I could use a warm bath. I chuckled at the thought as I leaned back into a few haystacks, pulling my limbs in. I stared out the loft window into the night sky and tried to count the stars.

Thud.

Thunk.

Someone kicked me awake the next morning. My eyes had trouble adjusting to the intense light of the morning sun. It was barely over the horizon. I raised my hand to block the rays. The shadow of a tall man stood over me. I pulled my feet back from him and bolted upright. An irritated barn boy stood behind him, a permanent scowl on his face. *Trespasser.* A silent accusation. Was it too soon to tell him I didn't have the coins to pay him for grooming either?

The shadowy figure kneeled, revealing his face. *Inara, again.* That same smell of vanilla surrounded me. *What a rich smell.* Although, the sweet scent of wine was gone. Sober men weren't as easy to deal with, not as fun either.

"Good morning," he offered me his hand and brought me to my feet. His hand was surprisingly smooth for a warrior of his caliber. "The King will see you." He tossed a coin purse to the barn boy, changing his demeanor to one of outright pleasure and jumped down from the loft gracefully. "Now." A command.

I quickly fumbled my way from the loft. I had to move my legs twice as fast to keep up with his every step. For every one step he took, I took three. At a remarkable five foot, three inches, I looked like a doll compared to most Ayles who were naturally taller. Instead, I was short and thin; although I was curvy in the places it counted. That was the blessing of my mother's genes.

After entering the main gates to the castle, I was flooded with memories. I once played in the front lawn, rode my horses, and on many occasions, I had been chased by both Vlad and Inara. I wondered if maybe he recognized me now and chose to ignore it. Maybe he didn't want me to know that he knew. Did he know that I remembered him the moment I saw his face in the light? Did he even suspect me? Maybe he didn't want to remember me. Would those memories be plagued with a sense of guilt after all these years?

J. L. Cross

Beautiful small trees lined the path to the castle. They were in full bloom, deep pink and red leaves with small white flowers. They were delicate, if I stared for too long, they would fall. I reached up to snag one, but I was too short and had to hurry to catch up. I focused on my surroundings, each flower and every shrub. I tried to ignore his rigid jaw. His teeth were grinding against one another, a muscle twitched in his cheek. *He knew.*

"Keep up." He turned around to encourage me after he caught me gawking at the scenery. His pace slowed to walk beside me as if he didn't want to appear rude, but we were past that.

Everything had grown over, it reached out towards the path as if to snag our feet. Bushes, trees, and plants went untrimmed and in a state of disorder. Even the trees went wild and reached out into the path to push us together, forcing us to walk closely.

Walking in the main door was haunting. Memories of my mother were everywhere. I could hear her voice echoing through my memories and down the halls, calling my name. If I closed my eyes long enough, I could see it clean and pristine as it was before. Her hand dragging down a table cluttered with vases and flower clippings she took from the garden.

When I opened my eyes the reality was disappointing, she wasn't there waiting for me. Cobwebs gathered in corners and across the ceiling. Dust clung to every surface. The same disorder on the outside was reflected on the inside.

"Why is everything so unkempt? What happened here?" I asked as we stopped in the main room.

J. L. Cross

"There is no time to clean when most everyone is fighting a war or preparing for famine." Inara replied. I looked at him, seeing what I said register in his eye. I was here before. I noticed the change. I could see the dread and gloom in the dirty floors.

His jaw tightened again, and he moved his eyes away from me. "I'll get your father."

I sucked in my breath. He did know. How could I have been so foolish to think he didn't? "Wait!" I called after him. He turned to face me, his eyes narrowing. "Did you know this whole time but let me sleep in a barn away from my home... *in the cold*?"

He reached out and brushed a strand of my hair from my face. "It didn't occur to me until I saw you asleep this morning. You looked so much more... *woman*. Last I saw you- you were a little lamb." He wore a crooked grin. "Do you blame me? You're not the child I so vividly remember. Not at all. Why didn't you just tell me who you were?"

"You were so mean to me. Always chasing me with Vlad. What if it was him that was here now?" He tried to reach for my face again, this time to tuck the strand of hair behind my ear, but I slapped his attempt away. "Don't touch me. Don't try to flatter me. You couldn't stand up to my brother back then, you won't stand up to my father now if he tries to send me back to the Sanctuary."

He looked frustrated. "I never stood up against your brother because I was *his* slave. How could I? He was vicious to everyone, including someone as innocent as you. Vlad was alway jealous. He knew he would never be good enough to be heir. It was only a matter of time."

"You're a coward." I spat through clenched teeth.

He rubbed his jaw in anger. "If it weren't for me, there would be more bodies piled around this castle!" He was towering over me, trying to frighten me. I didn't back down. I held my chin high, staring into his angry brown eyes. I wanted him to plead for forgiveness before I gave it to him.

"If it weren't for me..." He seemed beside himself about what he was about to say. I cocked an eyebrow, daring him to finish his thought. He stammered, searching my face. "You would have been his first victim." His words were soft, a whisper only for me to hear.

He turned and stormed off. "Bastard!" I yelled after him. Why would he suddenly want to portray himself as my hero? What did it matter to him what I thought after all these years? He always antagonized me alongside my brother. I didn't want to forgive him for that, but when I saw those eyes boring into my own, it was hard to recall that he was once that boy. *You're an idiot.* On many occasions Vlad would hit me and shove me around. One time he chased me through the garden with a new sword. How could I forget those things? Inara never tried to protect me then.

I crossed my arms over my chest and took a gander around. A painting of my mother hung on the wall near the entrance. It was coated with so much filth that you could barely make out her face through it. I ran the back of my arm over the canvas to clear the grime away. Her smile was radiant. I remembered that much, and the artist had caught that delicate part of her. I wished I could be held by her again. In this very moment that was the welcome I needed.

"Kastell!"

That was none other than my father's voice. His voice echoed power, anger, and authority. I could feel it in the room, it vibrated through me. The anger in his tone made me freeze in the place I stood. He would try to send me back.

"Why would you ever consider returning during the turmoil of a war? You were safe with Kendra."

"I- I-" I stuttered. How could I stutter at this moment? How could I look so weak and feeble? This wasn't going to help me win my argument.

My father hadn't changed much, other than the few lines in his face that either came from stress or aging. His hair wasn't nearly as long as it was when I was sent away. It was customary for Commanders and warriors to cut their hair to their shoulders, so the braids weren't too long during battle. His hair still hung below his shoulder blades. Something as trivial as hair getting in the line of view could cost a man his life on the battlefield. Grunts usually cut their hair no longer than the bottoms of their ears, an aesthetic label to their service.

I steadied myself. I was ready for this. "As the heir, I will not spend my adult life rotting in a sanctuary of celibate women," I said. "I don't know the strife, fears, and struggles of my own people. I was called a peasant more than once. I need to be here, by your side, learning my duties as heir. Will you deny the people of your city a worthy leader if you pass?"

He crossed his arms with a smile taking him. "You have always been stubborn like your mother. Even in the face of death she shrugged." He wrapped me in his arms just then, surprising me. It felt so good to be home. My eyes watered. He smelled like warm apples, a smell I'd forgotten.

"Don't send me away." I begged in his ear, sniffling away the urge to cry. I didn't mean to sound so pitiful, or to beg, but I had nowhere I felt I would belong. This was where I was supposed to be.

He pushed me away to arm's length. "I can't make you leave. You're your own master now." My father smiled slightly. "You've become incredibly beautiful." He let me go. "I want you to know something very important. I need you to pay attention to me now."

"I'm listening."

"Your life will alway be in danger here. You are the only heir to this throne. You are *their* greatest threat."

"Who?" I asked, slightly puzzled.

"The Rebel King." Inara spoke. "And Vlad, of course. We don't know what the proxy king looks like, but we know he was also a victim of Vlad before his banishment. He would do anything to see the end of your father's line. He's been looking for a new lead for a long time now. Your brother, however, lives. With breath in his lungs, he remains your greatest threat, and your father's. The proxy King has been acting on behalf of the Arvor King for years now, it's hard to know if there really is any other King."

My confusion grew. Vlad was banished after I left for the sanctuary. I didn't fully comprehend the reasoning or even his crimes. "What could he have possibly done?"

"Your brother started this war. Every day the Arvors make it harder and harder for me to consider diplomacy." My father crossed his arms.

Inara let out a dark chuckle. "I spent night after night cleaning the messes your vile brother left behind. It was my duty to protect his life, and his image. We were young warriors, fresh out of training. We escorted a small party of Aylish tax collectors to the Arvor settlement. We were supposed to be delivering rations and collecting the tax. They were paying for their shares of wheat and barley. Back then our relations with the Arvors were… *civil*, at best."

My father interjects, "they didn't exactly come here with a warm attitude. They came here and asked for land. I gave them all I had, the burial grounds of their ancestors. They were the first Arvors to come here in decades since the last of them died." My father was a great diplomat and a strategic man. To think the war was worsening made me think it was more to do with the Arvors and less to do with my father, but I knew he was stubborn. I knew he had buried hate in his heart.

"What did he do?" I asked, slightly ill prepared for whatever Inara or my father would tell me.

"He murdered everyone he could in the village. Your brother couldn't control his lust for blood and death. He looked down on them like they were animals." Inara moved closer to us. Shifting his weight and leaning himself against the corridor wall. "The Arvors were left with a sour taste in their mouths. A rumor came of an Alpha Arvor that hailed from Tarem. He feared that Vlad would return to finish off his victims or worse. So, the Arvors banded together with other rebels, sleeping in caves and the depths of the forest. They're fighting to end the line of King Vor. I assume they rest most of the blame on your father for allowing such a boy to be armed to the teeth with weapons and soldiers that day. We hoped that the banishment of Vlad and my promotion to commander would show them that we weren't monsters, but that was foolish logic. There was already a deep rift between Arvors and Aylish in the first place, things that would never be easily forgotten. The only asset we have going for us is that they hate Vlad as much as we do."

"We hope that it remains so." My father chimed in. "Enough with the history lesson." He rubbed my arm. "I'll get you caught up, in time. Until I'm sure that I won't have to worry, Inara will not leave your side."

"*What*?" The both of us gasped in horror.

"Lord, you must be mistaken. The war-"

"Enough." My father settled. "You're not children chasing each other in the yard anymore. Kastell needs to be protected. I don't want her to be left alone. Not for a single moment. I trust you will defend her with your life?"

"Yes, King Vor, *with my life*." He repeated, dipping his head in obedience.

My father left us. His footsteps thundered down the hall, leaving us staring across the room at each other.

What a warm welcome home…

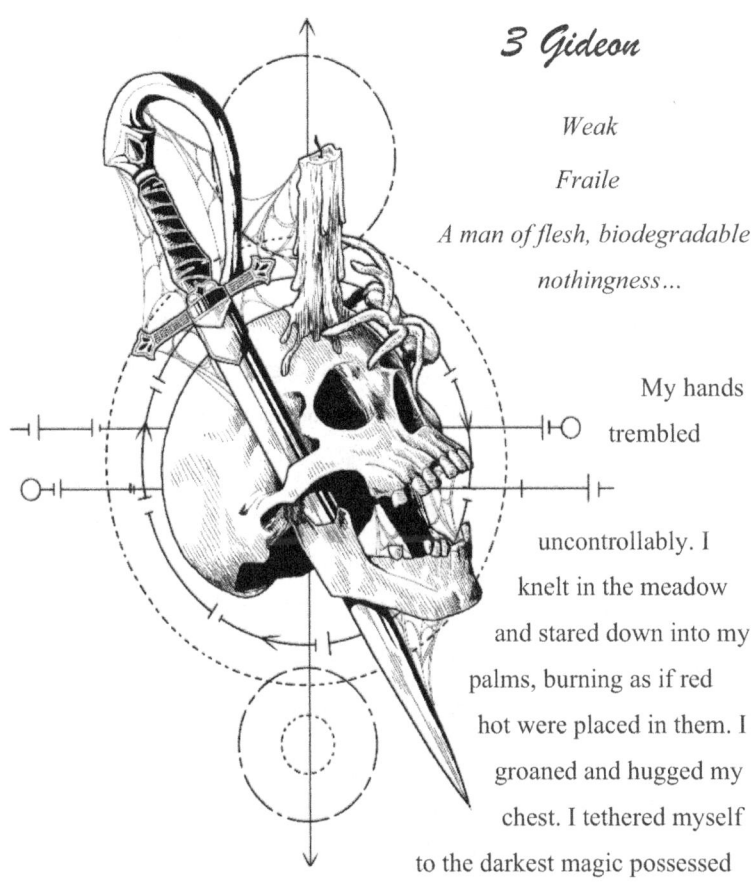

3 Gideon

Weak

Fraile

A man of flesh, biodegradable nothingness...

My hands trembled uncontrollably. I knelt in the meadow and stared down into my palms, burning as if red hot were placed in them. I groaned and hugged my chest. I tethered myself to the darkest magic possessed by the Earth, Claret Magic. I could feel it rattle through me as it tried to escape through every pore. When I looked up from the grassy meadow floor a warlock stared down at me. His face covered in scars, his mouth bleeding. His teeth dyed a deep red as his lips curved into a menacing smile.

"I'm here to warn you, Gideon, Claret Magic is consuming."
The man faded in and out, his voice steady in my mind. He grabbed

onto my core, the stem of all my thoughts, and curled his fingers around my brain. *"Sacrifice to appease its demands."*

Claret magic was volatile. Every man to wield it lived a short life. The cost of great power would be my life. There was no sacrifice that would saite the desire it had. I felt it pull on my soul and eat at my energy until it was too hard to look up from the dirt.

"Was obtaining power satisfying? Is this the way you wanted to end?" His voice was in my ear, yet the image of him hovered not far from me. He was inside of me, he was in the magic, he was everywhere. He lived in the magic. He cocked his head to the side, taking in the sight of me writhing in pain. The man enjoyed this.

The man knelt in front of me and offered his hand. I shook my head to clear the mirage away or to loosen his grip. I wanted to fight back against him and win. I wanted control.

"GO AWAY!" I screamed in desperation. My resolve melted away.

I pressed my searing hands against my head and pulled at my hair. I crawled back to put space between us, but he moved with me. I took in a shuddering breath and focused on the rushing sound of air as my lungs filled.

In..

Out..

In..

Out..

My ears rang until the pitch was an unforgiving wail. I clenched my eyes closed and I rocked myself back and forth to gain an ounce of comfort.

"Sacrifice to the Darkness!" The man demanded; his eyes turned a piercing swallowing black. I opened my eyes to find myself surrounded by faded images of warlocks and witches that were once consumed by Claret Magic before me. They had sacrificed for power and now they lived in the vacancy of my mind where I'd stored up that same greed for power.

"Sacrifice..." They moaned in unison. Each one was scared, missing patches of hair, pale skin, malnourished, and looked faint. They didn't belong here. *"Sacrifice..."* They groaned again.

I held myself. I cried into the Earth beneath me. Would the Mother ever forgive me? I dug my hands into soft soil and let myself fall sideways as my body began to spasm. Every muscle clenched and released in unison. My mind froze in its realization of suffering and my eyes rolled back into my head. There was no way out now. I needed to commit to my decision. I needed to stop trying to run away from this. I wanted this… Didn't I?

Was this really my end? I knew this would happen; I knew the cost. The Magic needed to have life and energy to feed from, and my life force was limited. I couldn't sustain it forever. Eventually it would ask for more than I could give. As my mind rattled and became foggy, confused and disoriented I knew this was the time. I had nothing more to give it that would satisfy its hunger.

J. L Cross

I breathed in the smell of cut grass. I laid there contemplating the power that consumed me. My spirit could escape back into the Earth. Or I could die fighting. I pulled myself up on buckling legs and stood on ill balanced feet. I took one step, and the force of the magic pulled me down onto one knee. I slammed my fist into the ground. I needed to harness the anger that was growing in me.

"*AAARG!*"

How could the day be so peaceful, but I was slowly taken with agony. Birds sang and the sun pierced through the trees. The whistle of the birds echoed through my mind with the brushing sound of the leaves rustling in the wind.

I pulled my jacket tighter around my shoulders. My body shivered impulsively. My boots were heavy, so I threw them off and did my best to stand again. I used what little magic I had left to make my body light. The Earth pulled me to it, trying to eat me up and press me into the dirt, but I stood. A dark red smog drifted out from between my gritted teeth. I clenched down and drew in a deep breath; it retreated down my throat, it seared every inch as it went. It wanted to be free, but it was mine.

The counterfeit crowd around me closed in. This was in my head. They reached out to me. I was afraid to let their hands touch me. I pressed my hands to my head to shut them out at first, but they were already in my head. They didn't plan to leave. They inched closer and closer.

It was time for me to stop trying to evade them. This was going to happen even if I didn't want it to anymore; but wasn't this what I came here for? I invited them closer. I let my hands fall open at my sides. I didn't retreat or resist when they demanded my sacrifice. They were here to collect. My pain would be my sacrifice. Each of them laid a hand on me, as our skin came into contact, they disappeared in a burst of red mist. It seeped in through my skin. Each one marred my body with a deep painful burn. With each touch they departed, a symbol seared into the canvas of my chest unique to them. They looked like wax seals, an emblem of who they once were. This was their way to live on, to empower me.

The numbers dwindled; my body shook with the pain I was too numb to feel. There was only one left to face. His clenched toothed smile dyed the color of barn wood with blood running down his chin. He hovered close, just as he did before.

"Take my pain and acquire immense power."

He held out his arm for me to grasp. This last one would be of my own choosing. I lurched forward and grabbed his arm before I had a moment more to hesitate. His skin was dry and flaky; if I shook him, would he fall apart into a pile of ash? He felt delicate and disposable. Yet, I touched him. They weren't a foolish trick of magic, they were real- their faces and their agony. They were in my mind, seared into my body, and they were here to collect.

He absorbed into my skin and his memories permeated me. They brought me to the ground. Witches were burned, Ayles chased them from the battlefield. The history of the first war. I knew these stories. There were images of him, forming a shape of a man from wet clay and earth. The last effort to defeat the Ayles, who invaded from far unknown places. He was the first Warlock to ever harness Claret Magic. He used his life to create new beings, beings that possessed untold powers against the Ayles. He harnessed a power that only came from depleting life from another being.

I was him. I walked the halls of his mind and toured his final memory. I saw through his eyes. The memories were strong, they could have been my own. The clay man he built began to breathe and gasped for air and from it came the first of his creations, the Soilt, built to harness every weakness the Ayles had. It turned the tides of the war.

Those memories ceased and my mind cleared, the dense fog that held my mind lifted. They were a short compendium of his life as it was lived with blood magic. I had felt his life and energy as it dissolved, every cell separated into a thin mist and seeped into the body of clay. That's where his memories came to a swift end. I knew some of this history, but not much of it. Some of these stories were lost through the centuries.

Pain that laid waste to my body slowly eased from my aching bones. I started to feel strength come back into my muscles. I could barely move. I held my hand in front of me and whispered an incantation under my breath. A small spell I learned from listening to other warlocks versed in fire magic. It wasn't a spell I was able to do. I anticipated failure when a burst of flames ignited before the words completely left my mouth.

Fire magic, a magic I never had access to before. Warlocks were known to specialize in specific magic classes. I mastered compulsion, but nothing physical ever came simply. Only a rare few warlocks mastered more than one class, some dabbled in others, but they would never know the full potential of more than one. Too much magic for one man would be imprudent and reckless. The Mother was conservative that way. It was hard enough to muster the energy for one, but two? *What about all of them?* The thought bristled through me, a wire brush against my nerves- painful, but something stirred under my skin. Power awakened at the thought.

    I grinned and let the flame die. Bright drops of blood landed on my chest. I wiped at my mouth and nose; blood leaked from my orifices. A sacrifice to wield such great magic. Not one spell could be cast without a sacrifice of blood, or life.

    I knelt in the dirt and prepared myself for the worst. No Warlock has ever attempted what I would. No warlock would obtain such power and then sacrifice his life moments after. I prepared myself for this. I knew what I had to do, and if I was right, I would become an unstoppable force to be reckoned with. Claret Magic has always required payment, but what if I already made the ultimate payment? I studied and researched every possible outcome. The worst was that I'd die, and the magic would go on looking for a new victim. Or I would overcome the power and control it. I would be its master for years to come. I came this far, no one would miss me if I failed.

    The spell I would use was more of a ritual, a dead practice after the Soilts were created. I watched that powerful warlock use it through his own eyes, in his own memory. I would use it again, just as he had... but I would rebirth myself. I knew the spell. I recited it over and over again in my mind, a willing sacrifice to the Earth. It was possible that this same spell would save me from my impending death. I could be a name history would never forget.

I withdrew a vial pendant from my pocket and used a stone to cut into my wrist until blood ran from the wound and turned to a drip. I held my shaking arm over the vial. As the blood collected at the bottom of the vial I chanted, letting my spirit shackle itself to the vial. I corked the vial and tossed it away from me to the edge of the meadow. As it traveled in the air, I felt the pull of my spirit as it tried to leave me. I had only minutes to stop my heart before the bond between my spirit and the vial broke. I needed to die to release my spirit. This would be my ultimate sacrifice, my entire life force. If I were right, then the Magic was already attached to my spirit and would remain so until my rebirth, locked away in a tiny vial hidden beneath the brush of the meadow.

I dug my hands into the earth and quickly made a small and shallow grave, I rolled into the cool dark depths of the hole. I fisted my hand, commanding the Earth to respond. Mud and moist dirt covered me up to my neck. I started to chant again, instigating death to come for me. Elder warlocks often sacrificed themselves to the Mother this way, beckoning the Earth to give their families and people a rewarding harvest for the following year. Their lives sacrificed to the Mother and to their loved ones.

My breath caught in my lungs. I stared up at the bright sky, I naturally struggled to take in air, but I was denied. The light at the end of the tunnel wasn't a light to walk towards like I wanted; it was the light of life fading from my vision as I was pulled to the depths of its endless void. If I wasn't mistaken, this was a horrible way to die.

    My spirit released from my body as the light faded. I was carried to the pendant, filled with the essence of the Claret Magic. If all my research proved to be right... My life would be the ultimate sacrifice, a source for the Claret Magic to constantly feed from once I was freed. The wait could be long, but the immense power coursing through my spirit would be well worth the wait, no matter how restless it became.

4 Ethal

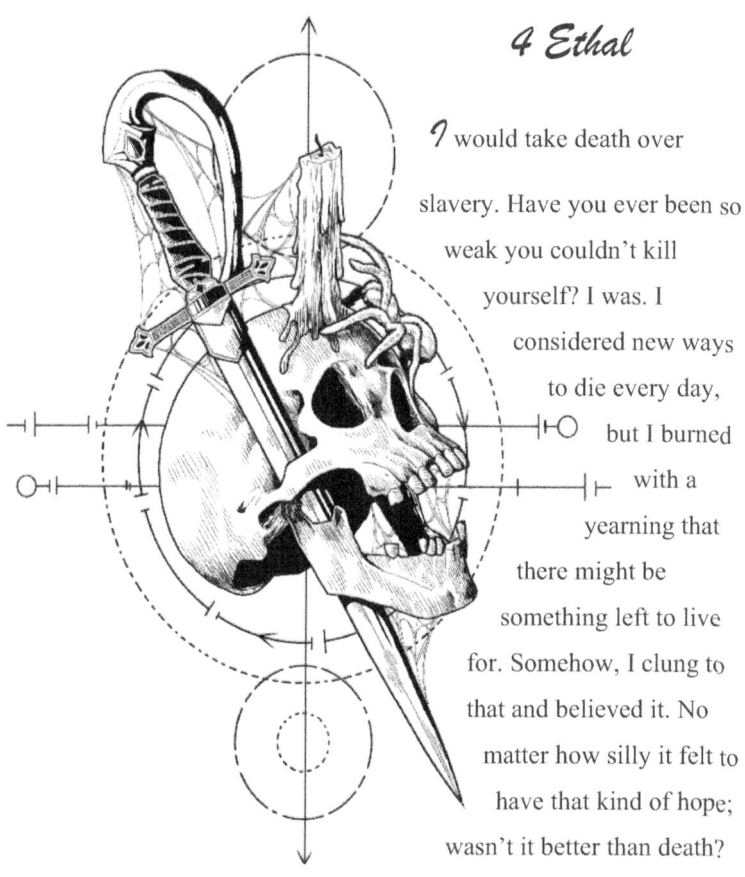

I would take death over slavery. Have you ever been so weak you couldn't kill yourself? I was. I considered new ways to die every day, but I burned with a yearning that there might be something left to live for. Somehow, I clung to that and believed it. No matter how silly it felt to have that kind of hope; wasn't it better than death?

The buckets in my arms were heavy and burdensome. I missed a few meals and lost a lot of sleep, rendering me weaker than usual. Rain poured down as I took the bucket of sow guts and dumped it on the edge of the forest. The pig's blood ran through the foliage and branched out through a puddle like veins. Arvors would be along to finish what I left. At least they would have a satisfying meal.

I looked into the puddle of blood and grimaced at my reflection. My eyes and cheeks were sunken, and my skin was pale and flakey. The bones in my shoulders were poking through and all the fat on my body had vanished. My hands trembled as I pulled up my sack dress and saw my hips and ribs close to the same, defined under tight dry skin. I needed to eat. If I was neglected much longer, I would be the next meal left for the Arvors.

"*Ethal*!" I was called by my master to return to the farm. "*Ethal*!"

I rushed back, leaving one bucket outside the barn doors. My master had the pig strung upside down so the blood could drain. I placed my remaining bucket under the head to gather the dripping blood.

"Bring the horse in." Dawson grunted and limped out of the barn without looking me in the eye. My master's weren't the worst, but they sure weren't the nicest in Aylhm. He was injured a few years before by a bull he raised. After the accident, he transitioned into agricultural pursuits. The farming industry became remarkably profitable for him. Everyone knew he sent half of his harvest to Arvors across Aylhm, but he wouldn't unveil that same information to the Ayles when they arrived to collect tax. He insisted that the crop was poisoned by bad weather or too much rain. I thought about turning him in. I wanted to watch him get strung up by his ankles, an example to the others, but I caught him putting his coins away under the barn floorboards in a messy sack and I pitied him. Dawson saved every spare coin to eventually leave his dreadful wife. He wanted his freedom as bad as I needed mine, but he was hesitant to grab onto it, staying here one day after the next.

J. L. Cross

I was a mage, born without a natural keen for magic, not even a specific class. I learned the craft with sweat and tears, but the only ones willing to teach me were the Soilts. A rather unfortunate circumstance. I was mixed up in the compulsion of my Soilt Master for so long that when he was beheaded by a renowned Hunter, Vivian, our bond broke and tore me in half. The hunteress took me to the nearest witch village and sold me off as a familiar, *a Soilt lover*. Disgusting really, being that she was a Soilt herself, paid to be the death-dealer to her own kind. I lived as a slave for three years. Each day that passed pushed me closer and closer to an untimely death.

Ayles were threatened by a colony of Soilts in the North. King Vor sent his paid huntress, Vivian, into the colony and had them slaughtered. It wasn't long after that there was news that emerged, Vlad Varius established himself there. The truth was that many Soilts lived. I wondered if the King ever questioned/ 1u; Vivian's allegiance to him when rumors surfaced of the colony growing again.

My humanity was all that was left intact. Vivian was a ruthless killer and huntress. Tales of her great feats were told across the Kingdom. Even witches and Arvors talked about her.

I would live the rest of my life carrying Dawson and his wife's, Tilda's, waste to be dumped, fetching their horses, and doing anything they demanded of me.

What a life to live. I pulled at the metal collar around my neck as I tried to scratch the skin that chafed beneath it. All I wanted was a moment of relief, but it was a shackle endowed with a powerful spell to inhibit my own magic, the little of which I retained from my dead Soilt master. The colar rendered me an average slave. The collar shocked my fingertips, they were already scarred from the collar. I attempted once to pry it from my neck and instead I withstood the tips of my finger burning until they were balls of puss and burnt muscle.

    The rain poured down and soaked my dress. It was more of a sack that barely covered my boney figure. As I walked out into the field for the gelding, I picked wildflowers that were closed to weather the storm. I ate the heads off each of them. I had to forage as best as I could; meals didn't come often.

    I stopped in the middle of the pin, my feet sinking into the mud. My toes were numb and ached to walk and bend. My eyes met the young gelding's, convincing him that I was a friend. The gelding came to me when I held out my hand for him. I gripped his harness and started to lead him back to the barn. He was a large work horse, brown and sturdy. I leaned against his frame for support when I needed it. I was tired and wanted to rest. The day was finally coming to an end.

    The barn doors were heavy for my frail body, but I got them to shut behind us. The storm roared on the other side. Lightning made the cracks in the door flash, and thunder rattled the walls. The gelding fidgeted; the storm made him restless. I filled his trough with rich grains, taking some for myself. It wasn't an appetizing meal, but it would tide me over.

    I used a brush to sweep away the heavy water from his thick coat. He was just starting to shed for the spring. I hushed him when he got antsy from the thunder. The humming sound of my voice calmed me down as well. I would be made to sleep with the animals again, per usual. I tossed the brush aside and made myself comfortable in the corner, leaning into a pile of hay.

Life didn't give me many comforts, but as I stared through a hole in the roof into the dark sky I realized that I made it another day. Electricity flared through the clouds cascading blues and purples across the expanse. The world around me was small, no matter how vast it truly was beyond the chains of a slave. The weight of what was beyond this life settled onto my shoulder, threatening to crush me under it. The stars hid behind clouds of gray, but occasionally, there would be the shimmer of one to see. The storm reflected all the anger I wished I could scream about that built up inside of me, but I didn't have the energy for that anymore. I only had enough energy to suffer. Rage was buried somewhere deep inside of me, begging to be let out.

Things were taken from me that could never be returned. The ache and absence between my legs was a steady reminder of what they took from me. Here I lay for the hundredth time, the same position and the same corroded rust colored knife hovering over my womanhood. The same chants echoing in my ears. The tongue that speaks them forked like a snake this time and I can nearly feel it flickering out over my skin in a long rope of words hissed into one.

"You're Property, nothing more." A reminder I haven't needed.

J. L. Cross

The ache of my wrists visited me in the darkness, pulling me back to the steep descending desolate remains of my reality, plummeting over the edge of my world. It's not the table I was spread open on anymore. There's nothing more after that aside from the pain that could have killed me. It's her voice that I hear in the echo of my nightmares time and again that draws me back from the descent. The truth of her words were a vice around my neck. Her hands were cold as she strangled me in the corner that I was allowed to sleep and piss in. She seethed and spewed from her mouth all the rage she clung to violently. Each word biting my skin, another scar left by her truths.

This was her release. She'd take and take from me as long as she eventually got what she desired. My blood never gave it to her. My raw genitalia she carved from me and ate as she sacrificed to her all-powerful god... never gave it to her. My use was coming to an end.

No bed. No warmth. The shiver in my bones, the reminder that this is a simple stage my mind has rendered for me to visit over and over again. A cruel punishment to suffer with no way to awake.

Punished for beauty.

Punished for the life I took.

Punished for the curses I threw, the ones that stuck.

Punished for the son that was stolen and outgrew his need for me.

Punished for my absence.

"You will have nothing." My master's voice again sensing all of my disdain for myself, all of the hate I've gathered into my core. The aged venom that rolls off of her tongue paralyzes me to the very core.

I'll try to sleep again at that moment as if I could block out the nightmare, but I know it won't come. I closed my eyes during the pain, but I still saw the light of the world spinning around me as I did.

The universe teeters back and forth on a dais of uncertainty. It inevitably pushes me towards the dark pit that's somehow rearranged itself to fit in this small corner but appeared so large. It'll engulf me again. Part of me doesn't seem to care. The panic inside of me wished for it. If only my life would end and the panic, the fear, the agony would drift away into that darkness to abandon me permanently.

I have more to live for. I have a life to regain.

This is the same reminder I hear every time the nightmare comes again to haunt me.

The searing pain of the brand that marked my neck sending the desire to die into every nerve ending as it left its lasting impression. Every muscle in my body bunched and strained against the bindings that held me in place, a taut ache over the skin of my ankles and wrists.

It's the jerking into an upright position and the flail of my limbs to swat away the brief remembrance of the pain that I wake to. I'd fought so hard to wake every time, but I'm not allowed to have the mercy of a reprieve from the punishments given to me. They only fade when the brand touches the back of my neck.

J. L. Cross

The sun broke through the barn. I awoke to see my master as he opened the barn doors to let the gelding out for the day. "Get up." He demanded shortly. Dawson was not the cruelest of my masters. I preferred his short bitter tones versus the rage of his wife. Tilda would beat me for the most minor mistakes. I was no longer allowed in the kitchen to cook when she realized how awful I was at it. The less time I spent in the main house, the less I dealt with her.

"Ethal," Her voice croaked from behind me. I turned to see her holding a sack. She threw it at me. "Go to the meadow and bring me mushrooms. Don't be long." Mushrooms she would mix with a cup of my blood and chant to the Mother for fertility. After everything the woman had taken from me, she still did this one ritual in hopes that she would eventually gain favor from the Mother. She was barren, and the Mother would have her stay that way.

Tilda was surprisingly in a pleasant mood. If it could be called pleasant at all. Maybe I would thank Dawson later. She was most often happiest after being pleased by her husband. Tilda remained barren. Her worst fear was Dawson would lay with me to have a child. But, to no shock, Dawson hated children and was often rude to them as they passed by the farm. He yelled for them to keep their tiny hands off the gelding.

I quickly moved past her thick short body. Thankfully the storm moved on, leaving the morning sky crisp and clear with a slight chill. A low fog hung in the air as the sun crested the horizon, casting beautiful colors across the sky.

J. L. Cross

The dirt road was muddy. Every step crammed thick balls of mud between my toes as I trudged on. The meadow wasn't far from the village, and I turned down the path leading to the clearing when I found it. Trees were beginning to bloom and were often being disturbed by teenagers. This time it looked untouched. The first time I found it years ago, bones were still protruding from an old dirt grave. I covered the poor remains and placed a boulder at its head to mark the unnamed body. It was a beautiful place to have a grave, but it was awful that he was buried alone so far from the formal burial ground.

I sat on the boulder to rest. I was entirely out of breath, each rise and fall of my chest rapid and short as I tried to regain myself. I didn't realize how worn my body really became. I sat back and inhaled the fresh scent of the grass as my breathing slowed. Dirt, moss, and crisp morning air. I shivered; a blissful smile crept over my face. The action was foreign. The sensation was odd and misplaced as the corners of my mouth twisted. I would rather be cold than anywhere near Tilda. I jumped at every opportunity to leave.

The trees around the meadow were full of leaves that protected from straying eyes. I went to lay in the grass next to the grave, the only peaceful company I kept these days. Just before I laid down I caught the glimmer of something shiny at the edge of the clearing.

The shimmer continued as the morning sun hit it. I went to the spot, covered by a bush and fallen tree limbs. I moved the debris out of the way and uncovered the object. On a thin chain a small vial with black symbols dangled. It was filled with a red liquid. The liquid seemed to have its own pulse, the surface of it vibrated.

"That would be mine." A voice cooed behind me. His voice was clear, an echo in my mind and thoughts. I felt it travel down my spine and leave a tingle in my belly. The vibrations of his voice caressed parts of me that I thought were long gone. *My magic.* He was calling to my magic. A second shiver, but this was of pleasure and excitement. I dropped the vial back to the ground and gripped my chest as my heart raced. I looked all around me and there was no one. I needed to see the face behind the voice.

"Who's there?" I was answered by silence, the rustling of leaves under the trees and a careful breeze.

I studied the vial for a moment without touching it. I knew these symbols; they were ancient warlock spells. This was a tethered object. I couldn't leave it there. I picked it up. Tethering spells were frowned upon now.

The voice came again, this time a hoarse plea. "Don't throw me down again, please." He begged. Sorrow dripped from his every word, luring me in. His voice was coming and going. Far and then close again, a whisper in my ear.

He was a pulsing mirage only a few feet away from me. He could only be heard and seen if I held the vial. I flipped the vial in my hands and looked over the symbols closely. Dark magic like this was dead for decades now.

I locked my eyes on the warlock covered in the same dark symbols, etched on his chest. He was nearly naked, only wearing a loose fitted pair of trousers that hugged his hips. His hair was a thick brown and a beard covered a strong wide chin and jaw. His eyes were a blazing red with hues of brown dancing in them.

I was drawn to him much like I was the Soilts. It was their magic that did that to me. I could tell his magic was far stronger than any magic I ever witnessed before. The two magics felt so similar, this was the magic that created the Soilts. A dark potent magic that poisoned minds. I felt it try to soak into my mind, but it was trapped in a dormant place. *Death?* Something about the magic was irresistible. I wished I could see it and touch it. It begged me for release and clung to me like tar. I wanted it... I needed it... I loved it.

I backed away from him, conceding a step as my chest ached for that power. I missed the way this power felt. I could feel the warmth and presence of my Soilt master's in it. Calling me. Only a handful of warlocks trifled with Claret Magic. I only ever heard horrible stories about it. It fathered the Soilts, but even their magic wasn't as deadly as this. The glowing red eyes were a telling sign that someone submitted to the power it had over them. Although, this man wasn't displaying the typical signs of weakness from the intense power coursing through him. Then again, I could tell it was trapped, harnessed somewhere other than with the living.

"Ethal, don't leave me here." A touch of despair in his voice. Every few seconds he twitched his head to the side, his eyes closed as if he were listening to it. His head tilted down to the side as if he heard someone in his ear. "I can't stay here another moment." He pleaded.

"Your memories are strong." He said with a grimace. "I can't see them, but they tell me things."

"No, no, I can't take you. Tilda can't ever know." I said frantically at his proposition to take him. I looked around for somewhere safe to hide the vial. With closer inspection I could tell it was full of blood. I looked down at it and groaned. It would only be my luck to encounter a spirit tether. These spells were done out of desperation to retain life before an inevitable death. How could I leave him here? He sounded as poor and lonely as I did. I could alleviate his pain. I could also give him an eternal rest and pour the blood out over what I now expected to be his grave.

I looked down at my feet, his eyes piercing and intimidating. "Why would you do this to yourself? Eternal suffering?" I questioned as I held up the vial. "Why would you tether your soul to something so fragile and disposable? Why would you want to remain here?"

He chuckled and moved to stand over the body. "I had nowhere else to go. You don't have to worry about your masters finding me." He said as he came to me. "No one but you can see me. It seems as if my spirit has claimed a master of its own."

"What should I do? How can I see you?"

He pointed at the vial. "Until you release me, my spirit is bound to this. It should break once I'm free. Very volatile magic. Now that I think about it, my head could have exploded doing this one. It was worth the risk." He drifted to stand beside me, looking down at the vial. "My theory was that I could perform the clay man spell." He stopped for a moment to think. "It's more of a curse, really. Look at the

Soilts, they don't ever catch a break. Anyways, I had a working theory that if I performed the spell, I could harness the darkest form of magic without fail. My life was the eternal sacrifice Claret Magic demanded. Now, I am equal to it in mortality." He wagged his finger, a deep chuckle coming from him. "There was only one thing I didn't consider…" He glanced over his shoulder at me. "I can't interact with the living world. I can't possibly do the spell myself."

I laughed at him. "You're joking, right?" I sat back on the boulder "This has been attempted multiple times before. Even the Soilts tried to recreate the spell, it was futile. Every Warlock that has tried becoming immortal through a spirit tether and a death chant has remained dead. Not to mention- when the object of the tether was broken or drained, they dissipated into nothing." I hung the vial around my neck from a string I pulled from my dress. "Your efforts are futile like everyone else's, and you will never have a physical form. The clay-man spell has never been duplicated in history. The warlock would have to harness Claret Magic for it to work, but with that comes death and no one has ever taken Claret Magic with them in death." I stuttered over my words. This man had done it, he had taken Blood Magic to the grave with him and trapped it.

"That being said," I went on, "any warlock that has attempted to replicate that spell has been killed by the magic. It's as if the magic itself refuses to repeat history. Soilts are essentially a plague on the living." I narrowed my eyes on him. I wanted to know how he did it.

He nodded. "No one has tried it with Blood Magic equally trapped in the eternal tether with them. This makes me much different."

I scoffed at him. "Even worse!" I gasped. "If it does work, however you want me to do it, I'll be resurrecting the most powerful immortal being in the world."

He came to stand in front of me. "My name is Gideon Urmon." He crouched in front of me to be level with me, his red eyes pierced me. "Tell me, Mayvel, a hungry slave with no family name. Do you wish to remain a slave?"

I shook my head. All I ever dreamed of was freedom. How could he even ask me something like that? I grew up being bullied and teased for not having any skill in magic and then I found myself in the hands of Soilts. I did whatever they would ask for a taste of their magic. I was a slave to them, addicted to the way it felt when their magic passed into me Now, as a real slave with nothing to my name and no one to love me, I wanted nothing more than freedom.

"Then you understand the Claret Magic. It wants nothing more than to be free again. This is why I know that my theory will prove itself. I studied this for a very long time before I attempted it." He paused and rubbed his chin. "See it this way, young mage. If I fail, then you will have the last laugh and the name *Gideon Urmon* can be laughed about at the table of your peers for a very long time."

I chucked the vial into the dirt in spite of him. I had been manipulated before. He knew this, he knew he could coax me into it. I'd be fooling myself if I said he couldn't. He was a mind-thief, a vial man to do this to me by listening to my thoughts and memories. Touching the vial inevitably connected me with him. Gideon knew my history with the Soilt and how I was so easily tormented back then.

What if he was right? If I did this, could I see my own freedom? Gideon would be the most powerful being in Aylhm, maybe even Tarem. He wouldn't let his rescuer return to enslavement, would he? He could even have the power to end the war or incite a new one.

"I will try to free you." I spoke into the emptiness, knowing he listened. "As long as I am a free woman afterwards, not a slave, not even to you."

I picked up the vial and he appeared again from a cloud of red mist. "I have faith in you, Mayvel. I would grant your freedom with my first breath."

I grunted as I knelt in the dirt that covered his grave, my brittle knees scrapping on the earth. "I can't do magic. I can barely do magic without my shackles."

"Take a drop of my blood from the vial onto your hands and pull off your collar. The Claret magic will live on your skin long enough to grant you strength."

I did as he said. I hesitated before I took the shackle in my hands. What if it didn't work? What did I have to fear? I was already nothing. I grabbed and pulled, the shackle shattered into a million pieces, falling around me in metal shavings.

Holding up my hands I snapped my fingers and the branches in the trees began to bend and sway. Taking a stick into my hands I rubbed it and pressed my lips to it. When I opened my hands, the stick turned into an insect that mimicked the light tree bark. I released it, watching it fly off my fingertips.

J. L. Cross

"I doubted you. I have no doubts now. What should I do?" I had no doubts that Gideon would succeed.

He gestured to his grave. "Use this soil and clay and mold the earth into the shape of a man."

This was the same magic the first warlock of Claret Magic used. He created Soilts with his life and blood. Claret Magic literally gave those creatures life. Witches thought that they could control the Soilts, but all they did was create a force of nature with abnormal powers. They were the weapon used to bring the first war with the Ayles to a standstill. Soilts had since created their own lives separate from the Witches and were despised by all species as a plague of Evil. I never thought they were so bad. They didn't ask for their creation. Of course, they never quite used their powers for good either.

"This won't work." My doubts swelled back to me. "That Warlock gave his entire life to create the beings that he did. This is absurd logic. If it doesn't work, you could be gone forever."

"I have sacrificed my life. I'm already gone. I sacrificed decades to wallowing in this meadow as a spirit, watching life change. I was here when the Arvors tore through looking for food, raiding the village. I was here when witches burned at the stake in Aylhm, just for being witches. I have grieved here for my people, for every soul lost to this horrendous war. If I die, I will die in the attempt to be the most powerful man to walk beside the Ayles, and in the ranks of the Arvors, and in the farms of the warlocks. I will live to visit the sanctuaries and be a part of the peace this land needs."

As he spoke, I started to form the likes of a man from the clay. His determination fueled my movements. My hands covered in dirt, the white of my skin gone. "Promise not to leave me when I do this." I felt tears welling in my eyes. After this I couldn't possibly return to the way my life was.

"I will *never* leave you behind." He whispered in my ear. As the form was finished, every curve of the figure was seeping water from the wet soil.

What was the worst that could happen? He would reign terror on everyone, or he would be the peacemaker in Arvor's clothing. Claret Magic was never used in a pure fashion. "I know what to do from here. I've studied the stories before."

He smiled, his teeth were white and straight. "I'm lucky to have been dealt a Soilt Familiar as my keeper." My chest tightened. I didn't want to live the rest of my life known as a familiar. I didn't want it to follow me.

I dropped a single drop of blood on the chest of the figure andran my hands over it as I chanted. I placed the vial and the necklace around my neck for safe keeping. His image started to mist away and seep into the soil. Either he was dead, or the magic would work. Only time would tell.

Hours and hours passed, and night came. Nothing changed about the figure. I slammed my fist into the soil. I would have been the first mage to stand beside him if it would have succeeded. I shrugged when the anger seemed to be gone. With his blood I would be powerful enough to do anything I pleased. This was a gift that I wouldn't waste.

I wouldn't let his life go to waste, nor would I ever laugh at his attempts. These were the sacrifices our kindred needed to understand magic and its capabilities. The greatest witches and warlocks usually died in horrible ways, but they constantly paved the way for our people.

With the vial snug between my breasts and hidden under my sack dress, I made my way to my master's home. The chimney still choked out plumes of smoke, lanterns lit the windows. It was a small cabin made of wood and stone. For the two of them it was too large, a barren wife made for a lonely life. I took the vial between my fingers and gently dispensed a dorp on my fingers. With a snap of my fingers the cabin was engulfed in flames. I held my hand up, projecting a barricade to trap them in their death.

The sound of pounding on the door made the frame rattle. Dawson coughed on the smoke and attempted to break free. Tilda screamed as I watched her catch fire through the window. She tried to get through, but there was no way out. Their skin became increasingly charred, their hair and clothing fried off. The flames stretched over the cabin and reached into the deep night sky.

The power started to die in me. I grew weaker by the second. Yet, I was satisfied. The rage I buried deep inside of me tore to the surface and had its vengeance. Looking at my hands they were burned and shaking as if I had held the flames with my own hands. I tried to walk away from the devastation I left. My insides grew tight, constricted by the dark power I used. My nose dripped blood. I wiped it from my face and tried to continue.

J. L Cross

Witches and Warlocks from the village started casting buckets of water onto the raging fire as I limped away. In the chaos I was just a woman, not the assailant, not a slave. I sat at the base of a large tree and sunk into the crevices of the trunk. I had nowhere to turn. After a short rest I would go to a sanctuary and seek refuge. The elder witches didn't care for pure magic or acquired. As long as I stayed in the village I would be recognized as a slave and no better. I needed to move on, a new beginning.

My chest ached as I tried to breathe. The constricting feeling was loosened, but the discomfort remained. The power of dark magic was everything legends said it was. It made me feel untouchable, a dangerous and an addicting feeling. I clutched the small vial of Gideon's blood against my chest, my most precious gift.

5 Kastell

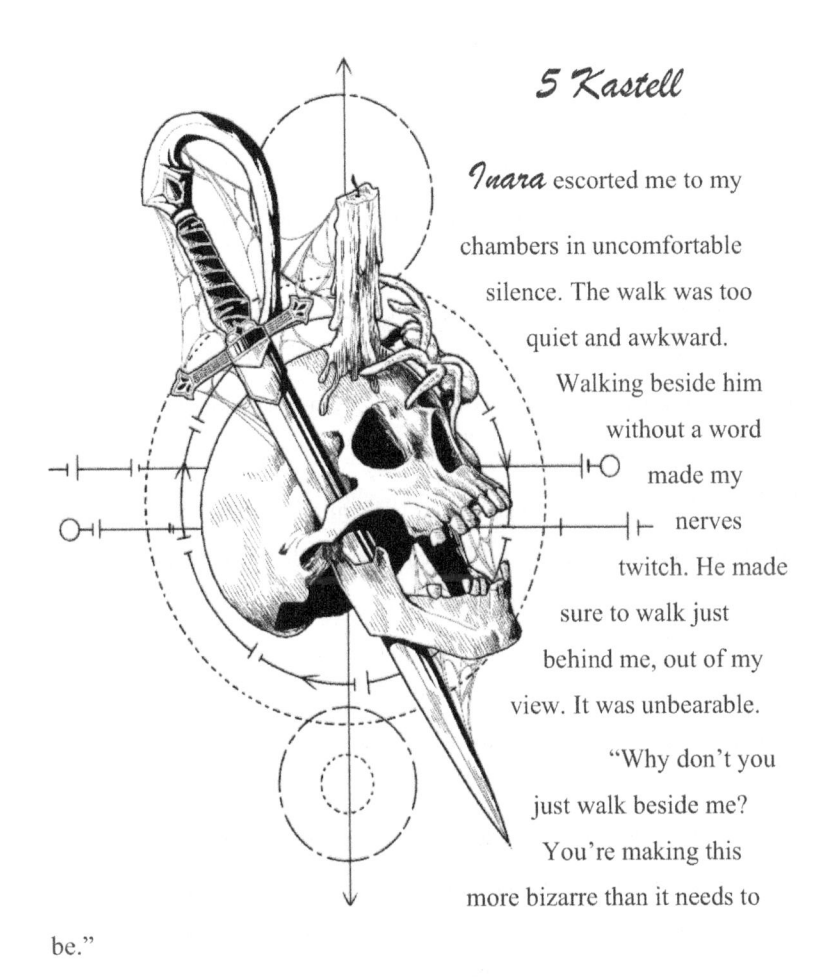

Inara escorted me to my chambers in uncomfortable silence. The walk was too quiet and awkward. Walking beside him without a word made my nerves twitch. He made sure to walk just behind me, out of my view. It was unbearable.

"Why don't you just walk beside me? You're making this more bizarre than it needs to be."

"It's not custom for anyone to walk directly beside someone of royal stature," he said. He continued to follow behind me. He cleared his throat. "So, what are your plans? Do you have any intentions?"

I laughed. "I've barely come home. Of course, I don't have any intentions. I just wanted to be home. I've learned to defend myself so I could feel safe about coming home. It's an insult to our people if I ascend to the throne from the shadows. How am I supposed to protect them if I don't even know why we're at war? I shouldn't have been hiding for so long. I wouldn't be prepared to be queen."

"You would rely heavily on me, as your first commander, if you would ascend. A woman shouldn't be concerned with the strategies of war or the gruesome acts of killing." Another man that looks down on women. I wouldn't have expected that from him.

"Commander Inara," I scoffed.

"Just Inara." He interrupted. "We might as well become a little more familiar with each other. It seems like we'll be spending a lot of unwanted time together." He despised his new duty. I turned quickly and shoved him with the palm of my hand. He was solid. It wasn't the response I intended, but my head spun with injustice. Was I really the problem, couldn't he see that he was? Was he only trying to antagonize me?

"*Commander* Inara, I would rather not be *too* familiar. The last time we were familiar with each other you were calling me a rat and shoving me through the halls." I reminded him of a time from when we were children. "My first act as Queen would be to rid the royal court of all the toxic men oppressing women; yourself included. I am fully capable of handling my own."

"You wouldn't last a moment without a guard as Queen." He gave a half smile as if his intention all along was to irritate me. "Ayles will be in an uproar if you ascend without a husband." He studied me for a moment, "do you enjoy reminding me of how awful I was?"

My teeth clenched together, trying to hold back the tide of rising anger he was stirring in me. "It's degrading that you think I'm helpless. I'm very capable."

He chuckled. "I don't think you're helpless, but I would rather treat you like you're helpless than watch you lose your life. If your father would pass- I only hope that you would know you could turn to me for your needs. I would never embarrass you, but I would never let you be ill informed either. This transition back into the royal court will be difficult. I want you to know, I am here if you need me."

I felt like a useless infant when he spoke, but was it possible he had good intentions? One thing he had said was repeating over and over in my mind. "Do you think my father will marry me off?"

He shrugged like it didn't matter. "He hasn't mentioned it yet, but it could be possible." He squared his shoulders and continued down the hall. He looked bothered. "The good news is that your father will match you well. There are a lot of worthy men in the Collective. You're the light of your father's life, he's asked about you many times throughout the years. I was constantly running letters between Kendra and him. He missed you very much." He glanced over his shoulder, a smug grin on his face. "And poor Vivian, she was tasked with countless hours watching over you from afar. What tedious work for a renowned huntress." Vivian was my father's paid hand. An assassin of sorts, but as long as she was paid well, she would do nearly anything he'd ask of her.

I remembered Kendra often reading me his letters, but even in his latest letters he never mentioned war or famine. Although his letters were a welcome comfort over the years, he left me in the dark with things that really mattered.

Inara stopped in front of a large wooden door. The metal hinges rusted. When he pushed the door open it creaked and cracked as if it hadn't been opened since the day I left.

"This is it." I remarked, stepping around him to push the heavy door open further. "Hasn't it been cleaned in the last six years?"

"No." Inara chuckled. "A lot has been forgotten since you left. "I'll send someone to have it cleaned. For now, there's a guest room just down the hall."

The guest room was smaller than the rest of the rooms in the castle, but it was comfortable for a night. The room was well lit by a single lantern on an old white vanity. The paint chipped on the aged wood causing small crackling lines up the legs and across the surface. The bed against the far wall was dressed in plain gray sheets and a beautiful white canopy of curtains. There was a matching tall wardrobe, empty. I left with nothing and returned to the same.

Inara saw my eyes traveling around the room and then resting on the empty wardrobe. "Your saddle bags were fetched earlier. They'll be brought to you."

"Thank you." All I owned was in there, and even though I didn't bring much, it would be nice to have my own things.

Inara stepped out of the room. "I'll be just down the hall if you need anything."

He hesitated on his way out. "There's a feast for your return in the dining hall. You might want to wear a dress." He teased my messy trousers and crinkled shirt. Most Aylish women wore dresses every day, but at the sanctuary I wasn't required to wear them at all. They weren't comfortable either. I found men's bottoms and a simple blouse to be efficient in combat training and other activities, like gardening. Women here were often treated like fragile glass figures. I didn't want that for myself.

Inara closed the door behind him as he left. I listened for his retreating footsteps down the hall before I poked my head out. A servant stood across the hall with a bucket in her hands and a frantic look on her face. How long did she wait for?

"Are ya ready for your bath, my lady?" She hurried into the guest room, her bucket sloshed sprinkles of steaming water on the ground. It was oversized for her, and she waddled to carry it in, a towel slung over her arms and my saddle bags that were resting around her shoulders only made the short journey for her harder.

"I didn't mean ta make ya wait." Her eyes looked scared, and I could tell she was worried about being punished. Maybe she was just timid?

"Oh, I wasn't waiting. I didn't know you were coming." I said as I followed her into the room.

The servant poured the water into a tall wooden basin and threw my saddle bag on the floor. "Get yourself undressed." She urged. This servant was older than I expected, a seasoned handmaid. She was most likely hand selected by my father.

J. L. Cross

"I'll fetch you a dress while you get in the bath." She said, breaking through my thoughts. She made her way out of the room quietly.

While she was gone, I stripped from my dirty clothing and sank into the basin. I laid back and let the warm water cover my face and let it soak into my long hair. When I came up through the surface the cool air stung. The servant had infused the water with lavender and eucalyptus. It was cleansing and refreshing on my body.

I relaxed into the warmth, letting it ease away my building worries. This was only the beginning of this new life. Every day would be filled with more dresses and formal gatherings than I would ever be used to. Seeing my father again after so long was relieving. I was expecting more anger, or for him to demand my return to the Sanctuary, but he conceded so quickly. I barely knew him. He wasn't the same man he was when I was a child. My mother's death confused and hurt him, leaving him changed. I would have to get to know him again. Would I measure up to all that he was expecting?

I inclined my head towards the door when I heard foot falls coming down the hallway. The sound stopped just outside my door, the floor creaking under the weight, and then they continued their way. Inara? Was he so dedicated that he would pass by my room and listen through the door? My heart raced at the thought that he was standing only feet away. I was vulnerable once; I didn't want to feel that way again. there was a stirring of fear in my belly, like I'd be hunted by him. He chased me once; why wouldn't he do it again?

J. L. Cross

He hates you. My mind whispered to me. He didn't want to spend his time following me around. He didn't want this kind of duty while his men were riding out into battle and to their posts, constantly in a state of danger while he remained in the safest place in Aylhm, by my side. I didn't want him here either. It made my insides twist knowing that he was so close. He would rather be fighting to the death for our people. I'd prefer if he were out there doing just that. For a moment I felt like we both needed this circumstance. His duty would make him face his guilt and forever be ashamed of it when he had to look me in the eye, but then again, I didn't want him close enough to look in the eye.

I rougly scrubbed my body and hair to scratch away the feeling left inside me by Inara. This was the most luxurious bath I had since the Sanctuary. Scrubbing my skin raw ruined it. Everything there was simple, even the baths. I didn't have infused bathing water there, nor did I have a servant to infuse it for me if I did.

"My lady," The servant came bumbling into the room with an olive green and white gown in her hands just as I rinsed the suds from my hair.

"Out, out!" She demanded as she got closer to the basin. "You'll get wrinkles if you don't get out. Ya've done scrubber yer skin to a cherry."

I stood and she handed me the towel. When I was done drying, she helped me dress and do my hair. She was quick and precise. "Can you teach me how to do my own hair?"

She laughed. "I can, but ya have the luxury of a servant doing it for ya every morn." That was something I didn't want to consider yet. There wouldn't be many times I'd be alone at all.

"You're right." I relaxed and enjoyed the treatment as she pulled a comb through my hair and braided beautifully in an elegant display. It was the same as having Kendra braid my hair, but the outcome was so much more extravagant. Not to mention the servant was quick and a bit rougher to get my hair where she wanted it, leaving my ears exposed and on display. They felt naked the way they protruded from my head and uncovered for the first time in years.

"What's your name?" I asked as I admired her working hands as she kept building to the design, creating pinned flowers from the twirled pieces of hair.

"Della, my lady." She answered. She wiped her hands on her apron and stepped away. She offered me her hand so I could easily get to my feet. I had to wear a thick petticoat to make the dress full. I wasn't going to enjoy dressing like this at all. This wasn't me. The hem of the dress had elaborate embroidery, leaves and pink flowers to stand out against the olive green. The flowers matching the ones she pinned throughout my hair.

Della escorted me from my room to the entrance to the dining hall, down the hall and back down into the main entry way of the castle and just outside the dining hall. We didn't pass through the archway. The dining hall filled with members of the court ever so slowly. The room was vast with a large and long table in the center and hand carved chairs at each place setting. There were a few settings that remained empty. The length of the table was decorated with flowers and the best dining china in the Castle. There was a small boy standing just inside the hall with a large drum strapped to his body and a mallet dangling from his hand. A traditional war drums.

The members of the court dressed in fine clothing and each according to their house colors. My dress, even though it was flowing and made of the best fabrics, was not bright in color and was not my father's colors. The olive green was the color of the Varius house, a symbol meant to honor my mother and her death with my return. I never enjoyed the flashy colors, or the lavish parties.

The fabric was soft and delicate against my skin. It was such a graceful sensation. It glided around me like air. I didn't mind being pretty. I didn't mind dressing up, but I hated knowing that everyone would be looking at me. Years have passed since I had this much attention. How did my father organize a last-minute gathering in my honor in the first place? The room was decorated in the same yellows, greens, and whites that adorned my gown. It also appeared to be the only room in the castle my father cared to have properly cleaned.

"I'll fetch you a drink." Della hurried off into the crowd to get a drink from a servant that was pouring. I stood back by the entrance, waiting. My father was never on time to these kinds of events; even when I was a child my mother had to hurry him along. I wasn't surprised I waited alone. With every moment that passed I gained a little more attention. I was being noticed by Collective members that kept peering into the entrance way at me. I felt like an animal in a cage. A part of me wanted to turn and go to my room. I wasn't really sure if I was ready for this life again, but I brought myself here. I had to be ready for it.

It was custom for guests and the royal family to be announced, but I wouldn't be announced before my father. Men were always announced before women, and the King before his guests. Unfortunately for the rest of us, the host always decided to show reasonably late. My father hadn't changed as much as I thought. He was still the same man, even if his face looked colder and more rigid than before. Mourning changed a person.

A soft warm stroke against the back of my arm made me startle and glance behind me. "Stunning," Inara whispered close to my ear. "Absolutely magnificent." Laced with mockery and menace, as should have been expected. "I'm glad to see the little boy has become a woman. Once plump and ugly is now plump…" he stuttered over the words, "but far less ugly."

I turned my face away as a flush of anger crept into my cheeks, the heat making me dizzy. He didn't appear to be the malicious boy he was when we were children but looks were deceiving.

"I won't entertain your pitiful insults. It would be best if you kept your distance. I can't focus with incompetent enemies in my ear like that." I shot.

He shrugged. "Be more resilient. I wasn't aware I could get a rise out of you so easily." A short chuckle and his warm breath touched my ear making me shiver. "Would you care to save a dance this evening? We can insult each other a bit more."

"Not with the likes of you." I saw the faint smile in his eyes at my retort. He enjoyed the mean banter.

I squared my shoulders when I spotted my father in the corridor. His steps were slow and even. He walked with an elegant sense of power and dignity, every inch of him demanded attention. He dressed in his best suit of ceremonial armor. It was a lightweight gold chainmail snugly fit over a silver shirt with rather puffy sleeves. His trousers were royal blue to match his banner colors. My father was also equipped with his ceremonial sword.

"Your Highness," Inara bowed and dipped his head in respect. He sounded and acted like a whole different man around my father. Not the way he was when he so casually talked down to me.

"Good evening, Commander Inara." My father pulled me into a quick embrace. "It's like a dream when I see you. It's like I'm staring at your mother." He took a deep breath and released me. "You will never know how lucky I am to have you home."

I touched his arm, hoping to comfort him. I knew he didn't agree with my return, not while the war was still raging between the Ayles and Arvors. "You didn't plan this, but despite your attempt to protect me from harm, my place is here with you."

He nodded. "It only feels right." He turned his attention to Inara and gestured towards the ball room. "Shall we?"

Inara moved into the ballroom and as he entered the young boy started beating his drum to draw the attention of the crowd. Inara silenced him after a short second. "I present the King," He paused.

These gatherings were not common in times of war. "Vor Kest, first of his blood, prevailing ruler and Vanquisher."

I turned to my father before he stepped out. "*Vanquisher?* You're joking?"

"I've killed a lot of foes on the battlefield. I didn't pick the name, the Collective did." Without further hesitation he stepped into the dining hall. The men bowed and women performed a steady curtsy. I rolled my eyes. These were the traditions I despised. You can be a King without so much subjugation.

After the formality was over and initial greetings were had, my father raised his voice. "It's abnormal for me to make any address prior to the feast, but it's also out of the ordinary for me to host such a celebration in a time of war," he cleared his throat. "Today is a special day for all of Aylhm." He reached his arm out to me. I took his hand and let his steadiness calm my shaking hand. He ushered me into the room beside him. "My daughter has returned!" The hall erupted with clapping, alongside the equivalent sounds of gasping and murmuring. My father held up a hand to quiet them. "*Sole heir to the throne.*" He let the words fall into the silence that filled the room, daring them to murmur against him. We both knew how the Collective handled Varius daughters, but I knew my father wouldn't let men fight to the death the way he did for my mother. "Undeniable Queen, the next sovereign ruler of Aylhm." He finished.

I carried on through the evening with my father. He introduced many of the territory overseers as well as District managers, none of which I would remember with the pace of the evening. Each he knew by name and knew even the most minor details about their families and health. I could tell my father still held the same passion for his people and the Kingdom as he did long ago. When I was a child, I thought my father chose the life and luxury of the Collective before his family, but it was obvious that the people needed a true leader like him. The Varius dynasty had been cruel to the Kingdom, leaving peace ties broken and destroyed. Although, through the decades my father repaired those relationships, others like the magic folk and Arvors were a long way off from peace.

I was drained and out of breath trying to keep up with all the conversations and Collective members. I would never be able to remember their names. I couldn't understand how my father made it look so flawless and simple. I would strive to be even just a fraction as great as him one day. The people of the Kingdom deserved that much. I wasn't sure I'd even hold a light to what he was for them.

Finally, my father walked me to the edge of the room where Della filled my glass and fanned me. I tried to take a deep breath. Every man offered lavish compliments, even in the faces of their wives, and some of the wives offered just the same. They all strung up flattery in my face. If I was ever going to know these people, it wouldn't be from within these walls. We only had just a moment alone before the feast was bound to begin. I touched my father's arm in a plea to get him to slow down and not run me off into another introduction.

"Please, no more." I begged. I wasn't sure I could handle any more attention than I was pressed with.

He laughed. "You must be overwhelmed." He held my hand and squeezed. "This will become second nature to you. You've always been a commanding presence like your mother. I see no less than a worthy Queen inside of you."

I nodded and tried not to brush his compliment off as pure flattery. "Why are they being so kind? They don't know me, but they're so desperate to seek my favor. I'm not sure I can handle being called beautiful again in one day."

My father chuckled and rubbed my back, easing some of the stress. "They're meeting their future Queen. They know they'll need you on their side."

"It's fake." I said dryly.

"All is fair. Fake or honest, these people will need you on their side or they'll lose all they have." His hand fell away from me. "It takes a while to get used to, but it's always the same. They'll always be this fictitious. Some of it is plain mockery, don't let it bother you. They just want to please you. Everyone will want to be on the Queen's good side."

He took a swig from his glass and handed it back to Della. "With that said, there is one very important introduction that must be made." He tilted his chin towards a man standing near the exit. "I would much rather feed him to the dogs, but he's made his place here."

This man clearly never stayed a minute longer than needed. He stood confidently, but unlike any other Ayl I saw in my life, his brown hair was voluntarily cropped and brushed over one side. His tall thick ears were emboldened by the hair style, not as elegant as ordinary

Ayles. His tall slender shoulders were back and his head high. He was brazen and imprudent, but thin, fragile even. He didn't wear an overcoat, instead just an unevenly buttoned shirt, which was only buttoned half the way up his chest, exposing his strong physique. He was taller than me, but shorter than average.

"Who is he?" I asked, impatient to know. Apart from every man present, this one would not be easily forgotten.

My father grunted at my interest. "He's a wanted man. Desired by many."

I chuckled lightly, "I'm not sure that I care. He doesn't have an escort with him tonight." Anyone with a claim would never leave a desirable man to entertain himself at a gathering. "I won't compete with other women. If a confrontation arises I will concede my interest. A man that doesn't know that I'm the superior match has more heartfelt feelings for another. They'll deserve each other. I will run no contests over men in my life."

"Very well." My father remarked. "His name is Yurdell. He commands the market district and farming districts, of which there are multiple. Yurdell is the most powerful man in this room aside from you and me based on the challenges he has won to secure his titles and lands. Should I reiterate how much land he owns. Frankly, he owns almost more land on the continent than I do. Yurdell is a greedy bastard and doesn't know when to quit. He is by far our dynasty's largest threat that lives within the city walls. What's more, Yurdell is not of pure blood. In the case of our demise, a washed out Soilt lineage would acquire the throne, assuming the Collective doesn't want Vlad on the seat of power. Yurdell's impurity is disgusting; a science experiment."

The disgust was written on my father's face, but he quickly hid his dismay when Yurdell began to approach, a young slave boy following him with a jug of liqure, limping and struggling to keep up. He passed his empty drinking goblet to the dirty boy dressed in tattered rags.

He extended a short bow, "Let me introduce myself, I am Yurdell Revaine, District governor of the Farmlands and the Market." His voice was soft and soothing but filled with pride. He bent low in an elaborate second bow and kissed the back of my hand. "It's an honor." He looked up from under his eyelashes, devilishly handsome. His skin was remarkably pale and flawless. He clearly stood out from everyone in the room. He was different from the other Ayles and it made him even more enticing to look at.

My father didn't attempt to hide his evident disgust. This man of the Collective held power and an overwhelming interest for the throne; this was the man I needed to root out the secrets of the Collective. What would it take to make him show a little more interest? What would it take for him to propose courtship? Inara would be infuriated when he learned I picked a halfbreed of all beings to court. *A very handsome halfbreed*, I admitted to myself. It would be the festering hate for Yurdell's species that infuriated Inara. His anger would be oddly satisfying.

"It's my pleasure." I batt my eyes and cast down my gaze, attempting to look flustered and shy. This man desired the presence I brought into a room. He stared at me and watched my movements.

I would need a strategic approach. Yurdell was educated and a man of finery. He was a man that clearly desired being the authority and control in the room.

"It's intriguing to meet the man behind our farming and food distribution, despite the recent gossip of famine." I said after a moment. I would need to engage his mind. I needed more than a flattering smile and a pretty dress to make this man look twice.

A half smile came to his face. "Are you sure you want to insult my capabilities on your first day home?" His eyes narrowed but softened again after a glare from my father. "*My lady.*"

"I have been back for such a short time." I fanned my face and turned my gaze away from his, glancing back to him, appearing as innocent as I could. His dark eyes sparkled for a moment. "Of course, I meant no offense. Maybe you could tell me more about the obstacles we're facing."

He dipped his head in agreement. "Famine is still only a rumor, *a fear.* Those flames are fanned by the war and the encroaching forces of the Rebels. Has this fear gone so far as to reach you wherever you've been resting your head all these years?"

"The food touches many mouths, even the ones in hiding." I said, making a motion to brush my fingers over my lips. His gaze followed.

He nodded. "You're right. How could I be so foolish? Of course, you know these things. Food and market profits are the foundation of our society. Without the principle of the coin, we would be nothing but everyday commoners. Do you have an interest in these things?"

I gave him a nonchalant nod, agreement, but barely. The most I knew about markets and values was how much coin I could win in a hand of dice. That wasn't the market he was interested in talking about. "Not quite, but I'm sure you could give me an earful of knowledge about it. Sit beside me during the feast." A man of his position would be offended at a woman assuming higher authority. Challenging a man's pride was an easy way to get attention.

He smiled and when he did, I could see fangs hiding in the front of his mouth, a dangerous display of dominance in the Soilt community. "It seems you're confused, my lady," he paused and offered me his hand, "your father will head one end of the table, but I represent the other members of the Collective, as their executive dignitary. I will sit at the opposite head of the table. It would be an honor to have you seated at *my* side."

Just as any predator would, he snapped at the bait. With his level of ambition, it wouldn't be long before he proposed a courtship offer. It was only my luck to set my sights on the Executive Dignitary by mistake. He was held in high regard or feared just the same. There was only one executive dignitary at a time, determined by land ownership and riches. Though, any Executive Dignitary could be challenged in a duel for his title. By the look of him, Yurdell had fought in a few, if not many duels.

My father relinquished my arm with a sigh of discontent. He wasn't supportive of the choice I made, but he reigned in the anger I could see in the twitching muscle of his jaw. I moved with Yurdell across the room. His footfalls were fluid and soft. The man hardly swayed with every step he took, like a shadow gliding across the ground.

Yurdell wasn't fazed with my presence on his arm, or from the stares from the other members as we walked by.

"Don't mind them." He said in a hushed tone. "Most of us were expecting the banished bastard to return. They're pleasantly surprised. However, you might have a hard time with suitors in your near future. There are whispers that the Collective will need to ensure a good King ascends. I'm foreseeing the annoyance of match making."

I swallowed the bile that rose in my throat at the thought of contemplating marriage so soon. I only just decided to come home, I never considered that marriage may have come with that.

"Not to worry." Yurdell said as he pulled a chair out from the table. The other guests were making their way to their places as well. "You seem like a brilliant woman, capable of making her own decisions. I personally can't wait until you shove their suggestions down their throats or up their ass where they belong."

I sat as he held out the chair. Yurdell could see my strength buried inside of me, even though the formalities. Would the other members of the Collective see that as well?

The meal was multiple courses and I found that I couldn't stomach such delicacies. I ate the plain grains and fowl, but there were far too many sweets offered for my taste.

"You so casually mentioned there is famine on the horizon, yet you leave food untouched." Yurdell commented.

I shrugged. "The food at the sanctuary was always plain, I never had so many delicacies. The strawberries are delicious, my favorite in fact, but there's way too much for me."

He took a remaining piece of fruit from my dish and popped it into his mouth. "What would you do as a benevolent ruler to uplift the threat of famine from your people?" A question to slyly challenge my intelligence and knowledge. Was he trying to gauge how strategic my own mind functioned compared to his own?

A loaded question. He liked to get straight to the point. "I'd defend my sustenance transport heavily. On my trip from the Sanctuary, it's clear to see that the harvests could be plentiful. Why are we expecting such a famine in the first place?" I posed. "There's a slim possibility that our harvest is being routed elsewhere in exchange for something." A challenge of integrity and honor for him. We both knew that Soilts only held one of those two things in high regard. He controlled transports. I saw the flash in his eyes of recognition. I was blatantly throwing insults at his capabilities as a man of responsibility.

I pressed on, "or Arvors are simply intercepting our goods to feed themselves, their population has increased by 30 percent in the last decade. They now outnumber the villages of witches and warlocks combined. Though, there aren't many of their kind left either." These were the things Kendra educated me on. The witches feared the Ayles, but everyone feared an unchecked population growth of predators. Maybe there were more of them than we've seen.

"Their species does seem to be growing at an unprecedented rate." I reaffirmed, meeting his eyes. He was intrigued and leaning towards me, his hand holding his head, the insult forgotten. A sharp and broad chin resting on his palm, interest flaring in his eyes.

"Although, we should consider all facets of information before we immediately speculate that heinous crimes are responsible for an impending famine."

The table became unusually quiet. I was being watched. My cheeks started to burn with embarrassment. My father held his hand up, gesturing to me as if he wanted to put me atop a pedestal. *Pride.*

"My very blood, gone for a decade and returns with more sense than any dignitary at this table." The smirk on my father's face was enough to bolster my spirits. I didn't belong to this world anymore. I felt as if I were running in circles along the edges trying to find a crack where I fit. I wasn't meant to fit here. I was meant to lead.

"Speaking of such, the heir returning is an event of celebration, but we are still at war." An elderly man near my father sat up straighter as he addressed the Collective. "There is a threat looming in the dark, one we cannot ignore."

My father turned towards him, his smile fading. "I'll bite. Speak what's on your mind, Ramir."

The man nodded in thanks and pushed his plate of food from him, using the edge of the table to stand. "I've served this Collective since the second Varius Queen, and now the Kest blood. This Kingdom needs consistency, and we must act urgently to set straight the uncertainty of the future."

"Please, get to the point." My father demanded, an annoyance shone in his soft eyes as he waved his hand in tiresome circles, becoming for him to go on before his patience thinned. He had a patience I never thought I would have. Yet, he was pressed.

The elderly man tugged at the lapels of his jacket. "I would like to petition for a Courtship." My father's lips curled in irritation. The man went on, "We have the obligation to the people of this kingdom to secure the future of the Throne. Kastell is beyond the age of marriage. The kingdom must have a secured future with a King."

"Let's just call it *Queendom* and move on. Was there not queen Ves that served on her own until she was nearly past the age of fertility?"

The delegate huffed, unaccepting the fact that I was allowed to speak here. "Of course, I would not live to see something so devastating again. Not in my time. Queen Ves began the collapse of traditional values of the Ayles and she almost handed our Kingdom to the folk of Tarem without batting an eye."

"She did not rule on an old man's whims." I reminded him.

The delegate rolled his eyes. "I will remind *you* that Queen Ves only had the opportunity to rule alone because her husband died an unfortunate death while hunting. With a secured line of offspring already we did not need to remarry her, though we wished we had later."

"I'm not interested in marrying." I reinforced, nearly choking on the words myself. Everyone around me gasped. My father's eyes widened over the rim of his goblet, and he nearly spit his liquor back into its void. I'd spent years surrounded by women that were very independent and made their own way and were not bothered by it. It was beginning to show.

"I apologize for the frankness. My daughter has not been home for more than a night. Why are we in a rush?" My father asked, clearing his throat and the amusement from his face.

The old man's hand tightened into fists at his sides. "You have no regard for the future of this kingdom when you saddle your steed and ride into a battle at the helm of your men. You must have that same courage with your heir. She must be married. There must be a King to follow after you."

A nod. *He agreed.* My heart stuttered a beat. This was the welcome I deserved. I was absent for so long. They didn't know my worth, my own strength. They believed in the power of a male heir. My ancestors stoked that fire long before me.

I found myself giving into them, appeasing them and gaining favor. Marriage was still a long way off. Wasn't it? "I accept. Who would you suggest as a suitor?"

The man's eyes seemed to soften when he thought he won the battle, but he was confused at my sudden change of heart. "An emissary from my own men."

"His name." My father demanded.

"Kyier Faegerd."

"The *Arvor* emissary. *A spy?"* My father's teeth were grinding in rage. "Explain yourself!"

Ramir faltered a step at the coarseness in my father's voice. Only a king could shake men at their core. My father agreed, but now there was definite hesitation.

"He has chosen our side of the war, fighting for you, his King. Is that not enough?" Ramir finally countered. "He's turned his back on his own kind."

"He's a brute. Kyier is a hardened warrior." I said before my father could lash out again. At the thought of the brute, I remembered his scars and his worn armor, hardened by battle. "What does he offer us as a King? His temper is useful on the battlefield, but can he weather the political storms from the Throne? Not to mention, it's highly unusual for a member of the esteemed Collective to announce approval in favor of an *Arvor* king."

Ramir seemed to be sweating, only using Kyier as a way to test the limits of my father. How much was he like Queen Ves? Was he willing to give his throne to the same kind he so viciously fought against? He was also testing the limits of the Collective, who all seemed to cast their eyes down in shame at the suggestion, unwilling to back the dignitary's proposal. What were they willing to accept in terms of a new King?

Ramir was clearly irritated that I was the one passing the questions, but my father nodded for the man to answer. This was the power I would never have. The Collective demanded a male heir. A man to lead them on the battleground and one in politics.

J. L. Cross

"He is an emissary first." Ramir answered.

"Glorified messenger, a *spy* in our midst. No matter who he's declared his allegiance with, I still have no room for him at this table." My father sat up, straightened his back and addressed the other men. "Any other suggestions?"

Yurdell cocked his head and took me in, his eyes drinking in my gown and the way I didn't shy away, or act as if their conversation bothered me. I stayed poised, exactly as Kendra taught me. I wouldn't let them hurt me this way. I would find a way to use it against them.

His eyes lingered on me a moment more, his head still resting on his hand, entirely disinterested with the older men as they started squabbling and announcing names. I'd begun ignoring it myself. At least if they came to an agreement that Kyier would be their choice, I wouldn't have to be concerned with the formalities. We already grappled through the awkward first encounter.

"You look like a woman with a lot to say." Yurdell whispered to me.

I nodded. "I'm not a prize to be won by a family name. They see this as an opportunity, nothing more. Ramir has control over Kyier, that's the only reason he's offered him. Kyier is one of his men. I would assume there's a level of loyalty owed to Ramir, if only for the fact Kyier retains his life in such proximity to the King. You wouldn't propose yourself?"

He hummed an approval, nodding his head. "You're very interesting, but not quite someone I would choose for myself. These squables are senseless and draining on my mood. Your father is far from his grave, *hopefully*. Should I also mention that these men also hate me? I'd be much worse than an Arvor King, and on that I'd agree with them."

I bristled at the suggestion that I couldn't be his type. He didn't seem like a hard man to please. In fact, he appeared to be a simple man.

I cleared my throat and waited for the men to relax in their seats, some reluctantly. "I would like to propose that Commander Inara would be a great match. To start, he is well acquainted with the responsibilities of the King, and he is Ayl. Secondly, he's well versed in politics. Lastly, he is more capable than anyone in this room in combat. I suppose Kyier could give him a decent challenge." My eyes traveled to Yurdell. It would be a bloodbath between the two warriors, an entertaining one. Especially if they would fight over me and their desire for the throne. An Arvor would bask in the chance to win something so precious for his people and Yurdell would want to prove his prowess in battle again.

Yurdell seemed unnerved by my suggestion, a stark contrast to the disgusted looks of the other members of the Collective. "I suppose though, you are also versed in the ways of the sword. I've been told a few things about your reputation." I said for only him to hear while the others whispered.

Yurdell shrugged. "There are a lot of rumors. Most of them are true."

My father's face hardened, and dull disappointment shone in his eyes. The commander stood just behind him, stiff and pale. "The Commander's life is in debt to the Throne. His life is to serve, *a slave.*

We won't discuss this matter further." His voice was clipped and raw. His demand for the conversation to cease obeyed. The members sat restlessly in their chairs; an unbearable silence followed.

My father stood, straightened his jacket, and glared at the members. The Collective followed suit, it was respectful to stand when the King entered and left a room. He came around the table and offered me his hand. "You're a Queen in the making, if I say so myself."

I took his hand; he guided it into the nook of his arm to escort me from the hall. I held that compliment close to my heart. Yurdell stepped out in front of us after rushing to get to his feet. A sudden decision. "I'd like to request an audience with the princess."

"You've just had one." My father spat. He had no reason to be kind to any member of the Collective after they spent an hour arguing over who should be nominated to court me for the claim to the throne. None of the suitors mentioned had garnered any approval from my father.

I ignored my father's attempt to squash Yurdell's attempts. "Call on me in the next few days. I have more I think we should discuss. As the Executive dignitary, I expect you to have much more to offer on this impending famine."

There was more than one angle to be analyzed here. My father was occupied with the war and prolonging the next rebel attack, he wasn't paying attention to the threat of famine or the onslaught of potential suitors that could be coming. There was so much on his mind now that it would be difficult to keep track of all of it. Something was bound to slip his mind. I could alleviate some of those worries and prove that I was useful here. I wouldn't remain to only be a burden.

Yurdell would give me a good opportunity to exercise my power as future Queen. Too many of the delegates wouldn't take kindly to orders from a woman. With my father's voice behind me I would be able to display my true potential as their ruler. I needed to give them no reason to doubt me. I wanted to be held under the same statutes as a man. I could be challenged in a duel to the death if I assumed the throne. That's the way I wanted it. Forget the suitors and the chaos of marriage. I'd have whoever I wanted when I wanted them. I wouldn't have them fighting for a power that was rightfully mine, though I wouldn't mind seeing men rush into battle over pure greed. Weren't they all doing that already anyways? Wasn't it greed for power and control that kept this war alive?

In the case I received everything I wanted, Yurdell would be my biggest threat. If I could tug on his heart just enough, he may never be able to stomach killing me for something as trivial as power. He was a worthy man, and a valuable dignitary. I wanted to keep him in that position for as long as I could. The Collective proved one thing to me, I couldn't trust them to make a good decision for me. I would need to get the most powerful of them on my side. I'd need him to bend them to my will. If I were going to be smart, I would be readily trying to get Inara on my side as well. Kyier's brutishness would be an added benefit as well. If I could have all three men defending me, it would give me a power I would desperately need when the Collective tried to back me into a decision.

My father was leading me away from the crowded room. "I want to know more about this famine, but I don't have the energy to be everywhere at once. I would have given the order to Commander Inara, but it seems there are other things we've focused on more while the fear of famine has gotten worse."

"What would you like me to do?" I asked. I desperately wanted to prove my worth, even to him. We walked arm and arm away from the dignitaries who still sat, chatting and conversing. Some were even laughing and enjoying themselves. I stole a glance over my shoulder. Sure enough Yurdell felt my gaze on the back of his neck and returned a piercing gaze, a wink, and returned to the conversation he was having.

"Report to me what Yurdell knows about the famine. Find out why my kingdom is on the brink of starvation while I'm dealing with this war."

We walked the rest of the castle in silence. It was a comfortable silence. I leaned into him, enjoying his company. There was so much I could think to ask, but I wasn't sure where to start, or what was more important.

"Is there something on your mind?"

My head lifted from his shoulder when the rumble of his voice met my ears. "Yes- and no. I'm not so sure where to start."

His arm tightened around mine, reassuring me that it was safe to talk to him. "I'll answer any of your questions." He pushed me away, turning me to face him. "Don't be upset if you don't like the answers.

There were so many choices I had to make, and I was unsure of them. Some days I question how I'm still here."

I promised myself I wouldn't get upset with him. I wouldn't let anger be the only emotion I let consume me. I was already angry that he left me abandoned for so long, and for how his letters ceased, and then came in randomly. He never asked how I was fairing in any of them, only wishing me the best. I wanted to understand it. I needed to try to be understanding. I didn't live it through his shoes. I couldn't be so quick to react.

"Why did you leave me there for so long? I was meant to be here."

My father rubbed the back of his neck. He thought through his response. "I don't want to lie to you, but it's difficult. Some days I wished you would run off the way Taria had. Some days I was ecstatic to read in the letters that you were brave and fighting the boys, beating them at their own games, and learning to use a bow. I never wanted you to have to live in fear for your life. Even now your life is in danger here. The Arvors will come to end our bloodline, and the Collective are far from trustworthy. They'll do whatever they can to get who they want in my throne the moment I die. I didn't want you to have to live that way. You had a good life with Kendra."

"Why did you write to me less and less?" Tears welled in my eyes.

He cupped my face and brushed a stray tear from my cheek. "If you began to hate me, then maybe you would stay away forever. You would have been safe that way." He brushed a strand of hair from my face. "There has been so much blood and violence in the last decade. I don't think I could ever explain to you how it feels, right now- to have you home. I wasn't sure I would ever have these moments with you." A single tear that mirrored my own fell from his eye. I wrapped my arms around him and held him. "Every passing day was agony, they threatened to take your life. I had no choice." His voice shook with regret. "I had to give you up." He tightened his arms around me.

I stroked his head. "I never doubted your reasons." I assured him, but that was a lie. I had so many doubts about coming back to this life now that I was here. A part of me wanted the peace of the Sanctuary to hide in again. My father didn't need to know I doubted this life for myself, or that I doubted him and the Aylish traditional ways. He didn't need that from me now. He needed comfort, something I wished I had from him for so long. "You wanted to protect me."

"You're precious to me. My one true weakness." He added as he pulled away from me. "I don't agree that this was the right time for you to return, but my heart has been so much fuller since you walked through those doors."

"I'm glad to be home." I affirmed. "I'll make you proud. I'll get to the bottom of the famine. I assure you; I will hold him accountable."

My father nodded and started to walk away from me. He paused though, and looked over his shoulder, he seemed tense. "If Yurdell touches a single strand of your hair, I will kill him, dismember him, and feed on his agony."

I laughed. "Outrageous!" There was something dangerous and entirely serious in his eyes. My father huffed and straightened shoulders.

He would kill for me.

6 Yurdell

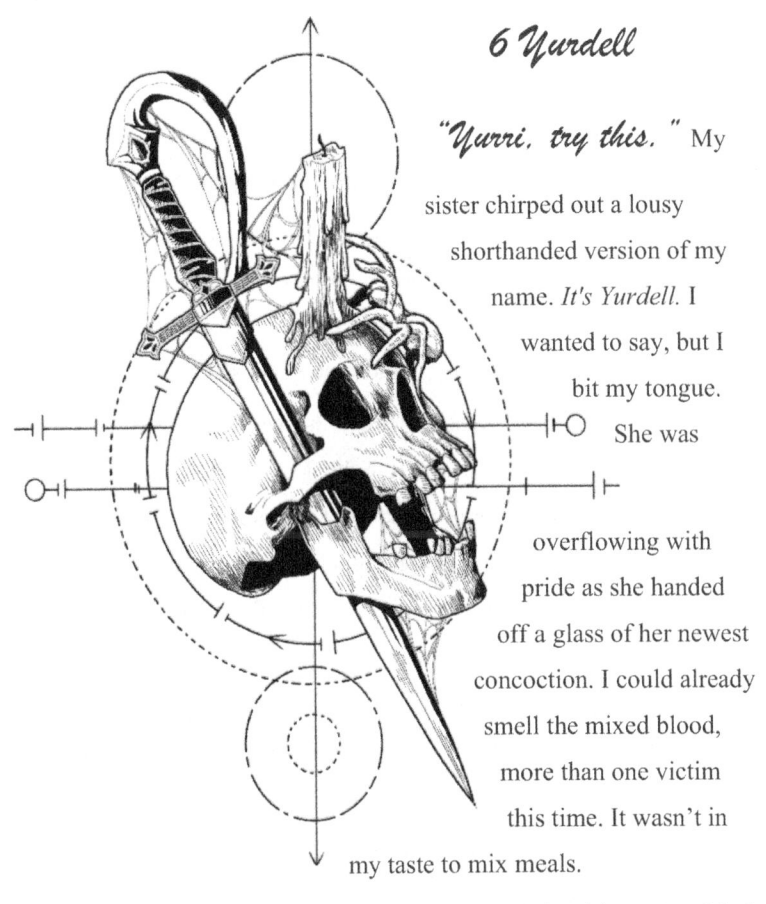

"Yurri, try this." My sister chirped out a lousy shorthanded version of my name. *It's Yurdell.* I wanted to say, but I bit my tongue. She was overflowing with pride as she handed off a glass of her newest concoction. I could already smell the mixed blood, more than one victim this time. It wasn't in my taste to mix meals.

The glass was half filled. Dark red tinted the sides as I swirled the warm blood from one side to the other. I dipped my nose into the glass and inhaled. The scent was sweeter than usual. *A child.*

I passed the glass back to my twin sister. Her hair was clipped as short as mine but combed over to one side. Her dark eyes shot me an offended glare.

"Not even a sip?" She retorted. "Father will love it. It's sweet, young, and fresh."

I chuckled, the sound forced and laced with disgust. "I won't be the judge. Not when it belongs to a child you're bleeding out."

She winced. "Well, I won't be bleeding them out anytime soon." She sipped the glass and her eyes flared to life as the blood touched the insides of her mouth. "Actually," she placed the glass down. "I decided to pay them all handsomely and send them home."

I stared into the crackling fire in the hearth. I leaned into the mantle and watched the flames start to die. I spent years building my home, but it was still as empty as the day I had moved in. Dust collected on surfaces and even in the couches. The sitting room was large enough for ten, but only my sister and I gathered there.

This was one of the times I wished I could stay impartial. I didn't want to be mixed up in my sister's ugly business, but she needed me. She was my only family. I couldn't turn my back on that. That's all I truly had in Aylhm; it was always only her. If it weren't for her, I wouldn't have left the North. Our people weren't treated well here. I was warned before I left, but I thought I'd be able to change them, I only made their opinions worse. I solidified the ones that marked us as vile and unpredictable creatures.

I shifted and turned away from the flames, lifting a brow in surprise after what she had said registered in my mind. "A change of heart?" I pinched my eyes closed and shook my head. Conversations were getting harder to follow and my mind was slowing down. I'd need to feed soon. The blood she offered was tempting, but I could never stomach the blood of children. I didn't have that kind of vile taste in me. I desired to be feared, but I never desired to be a true predator, not the way Yirma so easily was.

    She wagged her finger and tisked at me. She could see the ashen color of my skin. Yirma knew the look of real hunger when she saw it. Her thin red lips pursed. "The opposite. I'm still the dreadful killer. Dear brother, I make more profit from the happy well-fed children. I've taken a new direction with business. I will let the children live for as long as profit continues to climb. When our kin in the North get bored again, I will hire new blood and drain the old dry. I see it as merciful. They don't know when their end will come now."

    "Father never had a sweet tooth. Have you made a separate batch for him?" Her eyes darted away from mine. Guilty. "Take into consideration that you're siphoning children on a regular basis in the attempt to remedy the debts you owe to our father. The King in the North will tire of these games if he does not receive what he really wants. You're only holding him at bay. It's my duty to return you to him, but the more you tempt him with these *gifts* the sooner he'll have an entire envoy to bring us both home. We both know he'll only be interested in taking my head."

    Yirma waved me off. "Father always gets what he wants, eventually."

    "He will come for us if you don't come home. He wants you to return. You were meant to rule beside him. That's why I'm here in the first place, to pluck you from Aylhm and send you back to the North where you belong."

"I ran away." She shrugged.

"*On my trader.*" I snapped. She stowed away on my ship the moment she learned Father was going to force her to succeed him. Yirma was a free spirit. She rebelled. I followed after her days later on a new voyager I had commissioned for longer travels. It wasn't long after we settled in the outskirts of Civith that we heard from our Father. He promised us pardon if Yirma paid him back for what she stole from him. The payment was supposed to be my head; she vowed to die with me before doing either.

Yirma robbed him of his heir. He would never see it settled unless she returned- or produced a new heir for him to seduce with his power. That was impossible for our kind. She would need a remarkably powerful witch or warlock. That magic didn't exist anymore.

Yirma's actions inevitably affected me. I made my way, buying all the farms that slowly deteriorated around the city from the war. It was only after I refused to send my produce to the city that I received a formal invitation - a summoning - to join the King's Collective. I was announced a Governor to my own surprise. The King agreed to pay more for the produce now that the farms were being well taken care of and managed appropriately. In turn I supplied the city with produce and well-fed laborers. It was still plain that the King didn't like our kind. He tolerated my presence. I was a provider for them, a resource, nothing more.

My pockets were overflowing with riches, but no matter the amount I sent to our father he declined to release Yirma of her obligation, or me of my own, but the funds helped to easily sweep his anger under the rug. He held his men on a short leash, and we continued to live across the river in peace.

    I wouldn't rest until I found a way to release her of her duties, but everyday there was something more about her that made me want to shiver. Some days I considered following through with the obligation I had to my father, regardless of my sister's fierce loyalty. The same feeling that struck me in the presence of our father. It was one of the many reasons I had decided to sail across the river and make an independent life for myself. I'm not a saint, nor was I goddess driven, but I deserved my own independence. Yirma truly was our father's daughter. Yirma disregarded life easily, even that of innocent children. It was something I could hardly stomach. Her reputation also affected me. Regularly.

    Other members of the King's collective refused to look at me with respect. I was challenged so often I nearly slept with my sword and shield. Yet now they feared me and the challenges came less and less. I had to kill many challengers to get so high on this pedestal, but it earned me what I needed to become the leading delicate of the King's collective. What was more shocking was that the King never challenged my progression.

    I took the glass from Yirma's hand and took another lingering sniff of its contents. Something was there, something toxic. I tipped the glass and let the warmth touch my tongue. I spit it back into the cup quickly.

"There's something wrong with a donor." I said and handed the glass back to her. Her slim hand grasped the neck of the glass and tipped it in her direction.

"I'm shocked you haven't tasted it yourself. A Soilt's true talent lies within the tongue," I said. I meant that in more ways than one. We were marvelous at seduction and our bite could bring any size man to his knees. We could exert a wicked level of control over nearly any Ayl with our venom as our only weapon.

I walked to the door and gestured with my fingers for her to follow. I knew where she kept her donors. I crossed the muddy path to our barn and stepped inside out of the foggy evening. The thick moisture in the air clung to my skin and made my clothes stick. I shrugged my shoulders and cracked my neck. I hated the wet weather that seemed to hover near the city. Not far enough South to be dry and warm, but not far enough North to be in a constant decay of snow and frost.

Yirma followed and pointed to a boy sitting near the door. He hung against the wall, his feet barely in the dirt. The bottle sat just below him on a stool, collecting every precious drop.

"I smell it. This one." I said as I leaned in to sniff him. "He has something in him." I crouched in front of him and sniffed at his skin, as close as I dared without touching him. That's when I heard it move inside of him.

"Parasite. A deadly one. He needs a tonic to kill it."

Yirma smirked. "You've always had an impeccable set of skills. Your abilities to smell and taste the slightest of things. This is why I need you."

"Well, if I didn't then father would be sending thugs to our door for more reasons than to take back what's his. Feed him this and he'll lose his mind in a week. These toxins eat at our brains."

Yirma laughed. "Too bad he's too smart and too old. He wouldn't be easy to fool into drinking it. At least if he were dead our problems would die with him."

I hit her on the arm. "His people are loyal. They would be here within days to kill you or bring you home to take his place. You cannot escape your fate so easily. Father adored you while I was cast aside, his second best, his unintended heir. Why you discard that privilege so easily is beyond me. You would have a great home in the North."

I worked quickly to take the blood collection system from the boy and lay his shallow breathing body on the ground. When I met her eyes I could see the hurt in them. She wanted the freedom I was born with. She was destined to rule the North, and she didn't want an ounce of that.

"Cure him." I said, ignoring that pain in her eyes. An order, not a suggestion.

"Yes. Yes. Yes." Yirma said mockingly. The pain that was once there absolved into her. She wouldn't wear the mask of her pain for long. She was tough. The truth was tough. "The apothecary will be here in a few hours. He'll be cared for."

"Good. I'll be busy tomorrow. There's an opportunity I can't miss. I'm trusting you to look after these children and send them on their way without harm."

"Yes, brother." She said as she looked at her nails and buffed them against her coat.

"Yirma," she looked up at the sound of her name. "We're not keeping any of them around this time. *No pets.*"

She liked to keep one or two of the older boys around, paying them handsomely until she grew bored and took their lives and all of her coins back from their cold corpses. A ruthless woman.

She groaned but conceded. "As you wish."

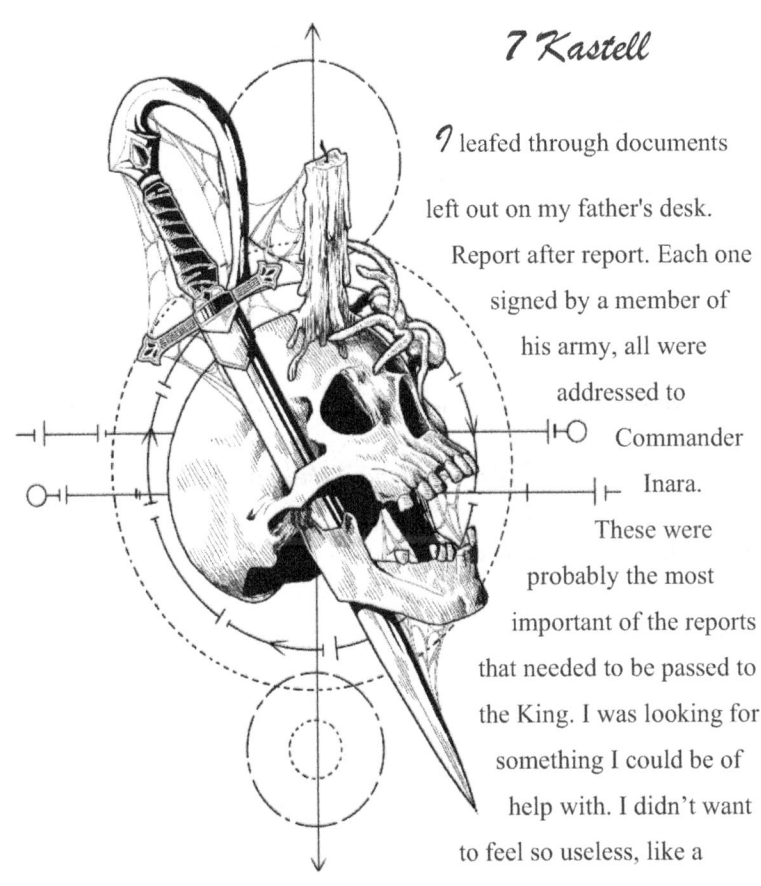

7 Kastell

I leafed through documents left out on my father's desk. Report after report. Each one signed by a member of his army, all were addressed to Commander Inara. These were probably the most important of the reports that needed to be passed to the King. I was looking for something I could be of help with. I didn't want to feel so useless, like a burden. I wanted to prove myself in combat, not just in political endeavors against delegates.

Commander,

A rebel camp has moved inward from the edge of the sea. Thirty men, reasonably confident and unaware that their presence here is known. We must act against this Rebel group. They act as their own. These could be forces under the control of Tarem. The rebels retreat and yet this force presses further. Acting independently from their leader they pose a greater threat. I will listen to them and watch them for as long as I can. I'm afraid they may know I'm here; it won't be much longer before they move to the city to breach the gates.

Waiting for your orders.

Kyier Feagerd

    I smiled to myself, holding the letter in the light of an oil lamp to read the signature a few more times. He even signed his name with an arrogant flare of confidence. Yet, it made me smile. I folded the letter and tucked it into a pocket on my robe.

    This was what I wanted to be a part of. Tarem was sending men here? Arvor men? There was more going on with the rebels than what I knew. Was my father aware of anything else, or was he as equally in the dark as I was? Did he see the small clues hidden in their movements? I could prove to him that I had the strategic mind, that I could handle this. The same way he had proven that he could. Battle was a constant part of Aylish life.

J. L. Cross

I couldn't sleep the first night. Everything was familiar, but not the home I missed. The comforters were too thick, the pillows too plush, and even the room was too warm. All of these luxuries I went without for so long were overbearing now. That's why I was here, sorting through my father's desk in the middle of the night.

I walked the halls of the castle; memories filled every turn. Some of my mother and I, and some with my father. The times I spent with him were usually the harshest, but the most useful lessons I learned.

The memory was so clear. It was in his office that he found me moving between a few shelves of books, a private library of his own. *"If you're going to sneak, girl, then you must not sound like an Orm."* He so casually compared me to a grazing land animal eight times my own size and weight. They were noisy and heavy footed. Most of the time I would be sneaking to avoid Vlad and Inara, but that particular time I was attempting to steal a few books he kept on hand-to-hand combat and political strategies; all of which my mother would never approve of a lady reading. *"It is not our place to do the deeds of men."* I couldn't remember the sound of her voice. Just the notion of wishing I could hear her voice again made my chest ache.

I had to play to my strengths, and to everyone else's weaknesses. My father had one true weakness, *me*. I'd use it against him at every turn to wiggle my way into the power struggle happening within the Collective. I would prove to them all that I was well more than capable.

J. L Cross

The note tucked into my pocket was a one-way ticket into my father's war strategies. If I could convince him I needed to be on the battlefield and not just on the throne, I could be a step closer to proving my worth.

I made my way back to my own room; Inara was storming down the hall in my direction. The tension rolling off of him nearly knocked me back when we came face to face in the darkness of the hall.

"Why would you wander off in the middle of the night?" He barked, his lips curled into an ugly snarl that didn't fit the softness of his eyes, or the worry I saw lurking there in their depths.

I shrugged, ignoring his irritation. "I couldn't sleep." I mused and wiped my hair back over my shoulder from where it fell.

"Don't wander off without telling someone." His tone was hard and unwaveringly cold. This was the voice he used to command his men, but I was not one of those men. Not now, not ever.

"Bite me." I said back equally as cold. He seemed taken aback by my challenge. "This is my home. I'll go where I please. The enemy is not in this castle."

He smirked and advanced until my back was pressed against the cool stone of the wall. A shiver of fear stilled in my spine. There was no one here to save me. I only had my will and my hands.

"I'll check on you anytime I please," he said. His breath was warm against my skin. The scent of honey and something sharp rolled off of it. *Liquor.* "It is my new duty to protect you. There is no freedom from that for either of us." His eyes flashed dangerously drunk and dark, sending a thousand little legs crawling down my arms. "*Do you understand?*" He waited for my silent nod.

The rising panic in my stomach and all those long-ago days when he shoved me around, bullied me and ran me off, pulled my hair, broke my things, and called me names. Every moment that haunted our past between us hovered in the silence between us.

He was thinking of it too. Was that regret I saw dawning in his eyes? I didn't give it another thought. I struck my hand upwards; my palm connecting with his jaw and sent him reeling backward holding it with his hand. I wanted him to suffer the same pain I did. When he glanced up at me I saw the trickle of blood from his lip.

I tried to hold my composure as I moved away from him and to my door. I straightened my shoulders, even as my legs wobbled beneath me. "Don't ever threaten me like that again."

He scoffed and walked down the hall back towards the cellars. He probably needed another bottle before calling it a night. The palm to the face should have at least sobered him up. Did he really come this way to check on me? Was that sweet... or terrifying?

I locked the bolts on my door and tossed myself across my bed. I tossed and turned for what felt like a lifetime. The moon lit up the floor after a while. I looked towards the window and watched the stars, picking out one or two I recognized. Did Kendra miss me as much as I missed her?

I groaned and turned my face into my pillow. I started to drift away into a blissful sleep...

The sound of footsteps outside my door sounded. The bolt rattled and fell away. Every muscle stiffened in fear. My chest tightened at the soft click of the latch that followed. Magic.

It used magic to break its way in. I saw a shadow there, writhing in the air, taking up space and consuming any light around it. It watched me for a moment and then turned away, but then I wasn't so sure it was watching... but calling. The door drifted closed as it turned away. A soft clunk of the bolt resetting.

I let out a long terrified and rattled breath. The sheets were clenched against my chest and my hands were balled into fists. I would never be able to sleep here. Not after the shadow that crept in. I couldn't help but roll out of the bed and run to the door to ensure the locks were reset. Sure enough, they were. Not a single bolt out of place.

I rubbed at my temples as I consumed a flaky pastry in the dining hall. I didn't take the time to change from my nightgown and robe. I just pulled the ends closed around me to cover myself. The hearth hadn't been lit and the early morning sun hardly lit the room through the stained-glass window. There was a chill in the room that settled into my bones.

Sleep only found me for an hour at a time in the night; wrestled awake by the never-ending feeling that I was being watched from the door. Each time I looked the shadow wasn't there only in my nightmare. I promised myself I would talk to my father about the dream and my discomfort.

J. L. Cross

"Princess." The word was clipped and short. An irritated greeting from the door. I glanced over my shoulder to see the Commander stride in. He was in perfect appearance. He was dressed in leather and steel armor, his sword strapped across his back.

He sat across from me and devoured a meal set in front of him by a servant that quickly bustled into the room at his appearance as if they anticipated his arrival at that exact moment. "Commander." I returned.

He looked me over, his head tilting to take in my exhaustion. "Something bothering you?" His voice was more kind than it was the night before.

I straightened myself and cleared my throat. "After we parted ways last night, did you come back?" I had to make sure; was it really a dream?

His easy and blank expression faded into one made of pure concern. "Of course not." His eyes lifted from his plate and met mine. *It was a dream.* "I was only out due to a complaint from a servant that swore she heard someone meandering the castle near the King's office. It was only my duty to inspect. Part of that was ensuring you were safe as well." He smirked. "In the case of an intruder."

"And you never came back?" I pressed. He shook his head in silent confirmation. Definitely a dream.

"I'll have a look around tonight and be sure to inspect every corner of the castle." He held my gaze. "If someone comes again, call for me." He rubbed the back of his neck. "I'll hear you, but if you still feel uncomfortable, I can take a post outside your door."

I cringed at the offer. I wouldn't accept it. *Couldn't.* I couldn't have him so close. I hated him. How could I trust he was telling the truth anyways? "No. There's no need for that." I feared him, but I was drawn to him. Those two feelings didn't mix well at all. Something in my head screamed to me to stay away, to become an ally with him and let the past fall away. My heart was still hurt from all those times. They wanted to fight back.

The thudding rhythmic sound of my father's footsteps broke our focus on each other as he stepped into the room. "Kastell, Inara," he said. "Good morning."

"Father." I greeted with a smile.

Inara stood and took a slight stiff bow. "Your Highness."

"It's time for us to go. I have a party waiting at the gate. We have a lot of ground to cover." My father made to turn back out of the room. I leapt to my feet and stopped him by stepping in his path.

"I want to go." I tried not to back down at the raise of his eyebrow, or to the condecensending look on his face. "I want to be there, like a leader should be. Not to mention, I have very important news from the front. A letter you may have carelessly bypassed. I don't think there's any better time to deal with the threat than now."

A short groan of annoyance passed his lips. "No."

I crossed my arms over my chest. "I will go. I need to be on the battlefield *and* in the throne room."

"Not a chance." He made to slide past, but again I shifted my weight to be in his way.

"Yes. You earned the respect of the Collective and of your army by leading them. I want that same honor. I want them to respect me." Before he could object again. "Kendra taught me to wield a sword and a bow. I can protect myself."

"It's not a good idea, your Highness." Inara chirped from behind us. I glared at him. It wasn't his place to influence these decisions. I wouldn't let him get in my way of becoming who I needed to be.

My father studied my face. "Fine, but you do as I say and remain close to myself and the Commander. No exceptions."

I couldn't help the ecstatic smile that took my face. "Absolutely." I pulled the letter from my pocket and pressed it into his palm. "I suggest this issue be the one we focus on today. It seems urgent. There's something more going on with the rebels. Have you considered that Tarem is feeding the war?"

He peered down at the signature and rolled his eyes. "Feagerd? You think this is pressing? It's hard for me to believe anything he has to say- based on his breeding alone."

"Thirty men are moving without the consent of a King." I barked, not meaning to embarrass my father with a challenge in front of anyone else, but that bridge was crossed now. "If you ask me, that's a call to arms to anyone that can't find a side in this war. If Tarem is digging their hands into it it's because they're weakening this kingdom in favor of their own attack. If you aren't careful, that will include men just like Feagerd. That number will continue to grow the more you leave these groups unchecked. This is where we need to stand our ground and drive their forces into the ground. The rebels will note your quick and apt ability to respond to growing threats, not just the ones that have long existed. Kings need to focus on many things at once. This is one of those things. Recognize Tarem as a threat and send them a message by burying their men in the forest."

Inara nodded. "I agree." He couldn't look me in the face as he said it. "It will prove that you're capable of splitting your focus while remaining in complete control. I can divide the men up from their patrol, groups of two instead of threes, take the spare men with us. Thirty Arvors won't be an easy force. They'll hold their ground well. I'll pick out the men that excel in close quarter maneuvers. I have a few in mind."

My father gave him a nod of approval and the Commander left quickly to gather his men. "If this gets messy you have to run. No exceptions, no heroics. You're my heir."

"I will, but I will fight as well. Don't ask me to succumb to fear." I said, but I wasn't convinced that I was entirely that brave yet either. He needed a compromise to move on. He wouldn't bend without one.

"I haven't seen your skill set. The prospect of you battling beside me is rich, yet absolutely terrifying. If you intend to start accompanying me, then we must start analyzing the depth of your skills. Light training to start and we'll go on from there."

I stared at myself in the mirror. The only leathers that could be dug up for me were the same ones my mother wore. They were a dark green leather with hints of brown. The legs were stiff and tight. She was smaller than me, but they would work for now. Della fussed with the straps on my forearms until she got them snug.

"I's sees about gettin ya somethin that fits ya." She huffed out. She went to my hair and brushed it out. She let most of it fall against my back but created a few braids that met at the back of my head to hold it all out of my face. She crowned the braid with an emerald stone that matched the green of my leather.

The stone shimmered the closer it got to me. "I'vnt seen a mage stone flicker in these walls for many years. The King does a fine job at keepin' the ward strong. Keep all magic out." She seemed mystified but placed the jewel where she wanted it.

"What is it?" I asked.

She smiled as she made sure it was snug. "Was a gift from your father to the Queen. A prized possession. I thought he may like to see you have it."

"Maybe I should ask?"

Della scoffed and shrugged. "Will only go to waste buried in a box as it was before."

My father and Inara stood just outside the gate of the castle. My mare was fixed to be a war horse. She was fitted with leathers and chainmail to protect her from the claws of the Arvors. My father's jaw dropped when he saw the flickering jewel in my hair.

"Where did they find that?" He didn't seem pleased, but not irritated, neutral to say the least.

"I'm not sure. The servant added it." Inara helped me get into my saddle. I ignored the way he stared; he didn't want me here. The leathers defined every part of me, they weren't loose like my average trousers and blouse that hid most of my womanly figure. He wasn't staring at that. He was staring at my lack of confidence, the way I faltered as he tried to help me into the saddle.

"I hope you fight as well as you dress." Inara said with a lift of his lips into a tight smile. "If you can't fight… you die."

I shrugged. "I hope you're not all talk and a little more game." I met his stare. I wouldn't let him make me feel like I was incapable. I knew I was able to fight. I had been in enough fist fights to know that what Kendra taught me with the sword would be just as deadly.

My father and I rode out side by side, the army following at our backs. No one paid any mind to our exit, they only moved to the side to avoid being trampled. Some of the women gasped when they saw me leading with my father. Even the men stared, mostly in distaste. This wasn't the place for a woman. I saw it written on their faces.

We rode through the main gate and started across the vast expanse of valley between us and the Sea's edge. My father didn't so much as look in my direction. I could see the tension rolling off him. It made me wonder if I wasn't being too calm about the danger, I would be walking myself into. I learned some skills with a sword and bow from Kendra. My skills were far from honed and deadly. Just the thought that I may be under equipped in skill made me shiver. Maybe it wouldn't be as bad as they thought it would be.

"You look like your mother," my father said from beside me.

Then I realized he wasn't just tense over the danger we were riding into, but it was bringing back memories he tried for so long to put behind him. Being home would bring back those memories in force for him. He was awkward and stiff near me. So much time had passed that I wasn't surprised. He didn't know me, not like he did when I was a child.

"I'm sorry." I said softly. "I don't mean to bring back those memories."

He rolled his shoulders and straightened, grunting. "I'm worried about you. The memories of her don't bother me, they comfort me. What bothers me is the retching and tight feeling in my gut, the same feeling I've had before when it was your mother and I riding out of these gates. The worry is the same. What if you don't come back with me?"

I glanced sideways at him and offered a short chuckle. "No need to worry." I assured him. "I have you and the Commander to protect me when everything inevitably goes terribly wrong."

The forest in front of us was dense and dark. We slid from our mounts and sent them with a soldier to be tied to posts they pounded into the soft soil. The trees were full of greens and reds; as the nights grew colder ahead of us the leaves turned all shades of oranges, reds, and yellows. Thick vines and ivys hung from the branches of the trees, hugging them so tightly that some were beginning to die. The brush was just as thick.

I tilted my head to the side, listening. My father and Inara had made their way to the opening in the forest, a narrow path leading to the heart of the forest and eventually to the edge of the sea. Not a single bird sang. There were no chirps of crickets or the rustle of leaves as rodents passed from branch to branch. The sound of life was entirely gone from it.

Inara laughed at something my father was saying and gesturing to the cut in the forest. It's darkness from the overlapping trees beckoning them to go in. They were about to start leading the men down the path until I lept in front of them, laying my hand on Inara's chest to hold him back. Even men I hated I didn't want to really die.

His first instinct was to brush my hand away, holding an offense that I would even touch him. My father stopped in his tracks as well. "What is it?" Inara's hand wrapped around the hilt of his balde. For a moment I wanted to stay like that. Away from all the danger that made my stomach knot like a million threads.

"Listen." I implored. They both went still, watching the forest and listening to it. The only sound was that of the groaning trees in the wind.

"They're waiting for us." My father whispered. He heard the threat in the silence the way I had felt it. He took his sword from its sheath, all his men followed suit. His hand held steady as his sword raised, his breathing was even and paced in time to the movement of the trees. He was entirely in tune with his surroundings.

"Your intuition won't fail you."

I nodded. There was one thing I could agree with him on. Did that mean the way I felt about him was something to trust? I didn't want to be convinced that he was really as horrible as I remembered. "We need to take a different route. They're expecting us to walk straight into danger."

"They'll flank us." He smiled, ready to fight.

My father came back to us. "The heaviest ranks will be to the left and right, the flanks. Kastell will lead a majority of men down the center, drawing their attention. We hang back with our best and wait. When the flanks move in we'll hear them. we make our move and strike then."

I nodded in agreement, though I wasn't entirely prepared to be used as bait. I went to take my place at the mouth of the forest, a slew of men followed behind me as they were separated into three groups. My father and Inara argued over the last few men they would keep. The men looked uncomfortable to be the subject of the dispute, but it was settled soon enough with the flip of a coin. Inara seemed to get his way.

I unsheathed my short sword and waited for my men to fall into lines behind me. Inara appeared at my side, smug with his achievement over my father.

"I don't like this," he said. His eyes moved to rest on me. Every fiber of my being was begging me to look back at him, to show him the fear that was rising in my gut and twisting my stomach. I gritted my teeth and refused the urge. I wasn't weak. I could do this. I wouldn't let him see that I doubted myself.

I twirled my blade. "I'll be fine." After building my resolve and swallowing back the feeling rising inside of me, burying it behind my mounting desire to impale an enemy with my sword, I finally looked at him. "Are you afraid?"

He nodded stiffly. "Of course, without fear we don't value life." His hand cupped my chin, forcing me to look up at him. "If it gets bad, fight for your life, if the battle turns- you run away as hard and as fast as you can. My duty is still to protect you."

I jerked my chin from his grip and rolled my eyes. "I will not run."

"Say that now, but in the face of death you will."

"Try me." I spat back. I motioned to the group of men behind me. "On me!" I demanded and started my way forward.

I glanced over my shoulder to see my father resting against one of the posts our mounts were tied to, petting the neck of his own. He nodded towards me to continue on. He had faith in this plan. I wasn't sure I did. Out of the two of them I was the least skilled. They had the best six men that knew their ways with a sword. I gripped my sword hilt until my knuckles paled. I was ill prepared. Hopefully the men they sent with me weren't as useless as I could be.

The forest ate us and shut out most of the light behind us. Everything was suffocating in silence. Not even the sound of the wind was heard in its depths. Every few feet I walked a glimmer of light pierced through the high branches of the trees, lighting the way for us.

One man staggered behind: his attention drawn to something shifting off to our right. *The flanks.* I reined in the tightening in my muscles and focused on getting as far as we could. I glanced over my shoulder time and time again to gauge our depth. The figures behind us became smaller and smaller.

"Keep moving." I encouraged them.

There was a body lying out in front of us, bound and tied at the mouth, wrists, and ankles. I could hardly make out the figure. As we got closer, I held up my hand to hold the men back to running to the prisoner. *Kyier.* My mind whispered. It was him. I could see the scars on the side of his face from where I stood. His skin was rough and cracked from being drug through the mud and across the roots of the trees.

Kyier rolled to his knees and looked up, surveying his rescuers. When his eyes landed on me every muscle in his body tensed. His eyes darted around, looking for my father, or the Commander. Absolute panic filled his face, and he groaned through his gag. A green and black circle rimmed his left eye and his nose looked broken from where it twisted at the bridge.

A man tried to rush around me to get to Kyier. I held my arm out, stopping him in his tracks. "Don't touch him. This is bait. Keep your eyes on the forest."

I turned my back on Kyier and circled, keeping the forest in front of me. He grumbled again. I shot him a warning stare, taking my focus from the trees just long enough. The branches and undergrowth rustled and snapped as Arvors started flinging themselves in our direction.

I turned in to face them, lunging with my sword. A lucky strike, an Arvor fell at my feet. The men moved quickly, surrounding the two of us and fighting off the few Arvors that were getting through the onslaught of my father's and Inara's men to our left and right.

We held the upper hand. I stepped out of the circle and fought beside the men, dodging left away from hungry claws that reached for me and sending my blade down across its arm. It howled in pain as I reeled back and swung again, this time cutting through the flesh. It bit out at me, its jaws snapping close to my face. I stepped back to avoid them and then lunged again, sending my blade through its chest. I never killed, and watching life draining from someone's eyes, even an Arvor, made my insides weak and quivery. I couldn't think of that now.

"Retreat!" My father called from the depths of the dark forest, but I fought on. I was focused and trained on my own advances, my own enemies, while my father and Inara's men were pushed from the trees, slaughtered in a frenzy of blood. Each of them moved back, leaving me on my own in the center, determined to fight on- if only for the loss of ground I thought to retreat. One after another the Arvors baited me further into the forest with nowhere else to go, my men lost behind me in the bustle of the fight and splatters of blood.

Arvors leapt and bit at me, drawing me closer. I swung my sword wildly, attempting to strike anything I could. A tuft of fur here or an ear there. Any bit made me feel more than defeated. I had chosen this battle because I sensed its urgency when my father hadn't. How could I have been naive to think we would be taking them by surprise when they had set the stage expertly. They didn't ensnare the king, but what was next best than the heir herself?

"The King sent his daughter?" A rumbling voice said from the dark. The Arvors striding away from me, enclosing me, but their attacks ceased. "Careless." *Chiding.* "So, *so, so* careless. You smell like fear and innocence. Unruined and exquisite." My stomach turned at his words.

An Arvor much larger than the rest stepped from the darkness, his hair as red as blood and damp from the cold of the forest that embraced him. A snarl set in his lips, his teeth bared and white. His ears pinned back against his head. He stood on his hind legs and strode around me, looking me over. Every part of my skin crawled and itched from the appraisal.

His jaw didn't move naturally as he spoke. "Do you hear that?" Faintly behind me I could still hear my father calling a retreat. Every part was bait and strategically planned to segregate the leader away, but I had gone in his place down the middle. I took the head of the party and marched into death's cold grasp.

"I'm here. I'll fight. I won't cower!" I was impressed by the unwavering tone of my voice, but even my hands couldn't stop shaking.

The beast stalked around me. He towered over me. "You'll die!" He snapped, his jaws a mere inch from my face. I yelped and dropped my sword. "You're scared!" He lashed out, his claws deliberately digging into the ground around me, pulling the roots of the brush from their homes and scoring the mud.

A shudder went through me, and I was filled to the brim with fear. I would die here. I fell to my knees, holding them to my chest and hid my gaze. If I were going to die, I wouldn't look him in the face. I wouldn't watch the animal eat me.

"Pathetic." He mused. "*This* is the heir." This time when he snapped at me his teeth met the flesh of my arm, forcing it away from my face. Pain laced through me. I brought my arm back to my chest shakily. My flesh was torn, and blood pulled inside the gash, piercings left from his jagged sharp teeth. I tried to cover the wound, but I was only met with pain and the useless slipping of my shaking fingers over slippery flesh.

His paw reached out and swiped at my legs, flaying the skin open and receiving a scream from me. I pulled my leg under me as I sobbed and tried to reach for my sword. I'd at least die with it in my hands. Blood pulled around me in the wet crevasse of the ground. My hand curled around the blade as I laid splayed across the ground, my life close to its end.

"Kastell!"

I looked over my shoulder and saw Kyier running up the path, clutching a dagger and rasping for breath as he came to a halt. The Arvors that circled me parted for him. His eyes met the Red haired Arvor and something in him changed. Something in his face turned cold, the worry replaced with anger and hard resilience. His eyes were the burning color of amber.

"It's not nice to harass women." Kyier said, his voice even after catching his breath. He started shucking off his leather vest and clothing. "Pick on someone your own size."

Every breath from the forest stilled as he dug his hands and feet into the mud and started to change. The Emissary. The Arvor. His bones began snapping and morphing. His jaw lengthened and he only allowed himself groans of discomfort as his body changed shape. His entire body lengthened and enlarged. Hair as black as midnight took over his body, and claws extended from his hands.

A growl low and deep echoed from behind me as I drew my sword to my side and pushed myself to my knees, using the steel to balance myself. My damaged arm hung loosely at my side. I couldn't lift my gaze. I couldn't stand to see another one of them stalking toward me, even if this one was on my side. Kyier was close enough that I felt the warmth of his breath on the back of my neck. I wanted to die, to end the waiting. His breathing was loud and heavy, calm and collected as his eyes surveyed my body and took in the damage that was already done.

I spun on my heels, my breath catching in my throat as I let our eyes meet. His were a burning amber, bright and soft as they searched mine, hoping I wouldn't fear him. My face was covered in blood, mud, and tears. I wasn't afraid of him, only of what he was. A massive Arvor stood behind me, his arms on either side of me, a protective barrier. Kyier growled and snapped his jaws. I couldn't help but cringe. He wasn't aiming for me, only sending a warning to the red warrior that seemed to be retreating.

As the Arvor fled into the forest the smaller ones lurking in the trees decided to attack. Their claws dug into Kyier's skin. He maneuvered around me and although I used what was left of my strength to raise my sword in front of me- he had already thrown most of them away and stepped away from me. He growled and bit at a few that fled and yelped to get away from his reaching jaw. I laid under him, vulnerable and at his mercy. His eyes bore down on me, the hate, the chance at vengeance in his grasp. He hesitated. His eyes softened, but there it was again only a second later, the killer. He snapped his jaw, his teeth inches from my face. I pissed myself. I'm sure of it. The smell of it was in the air and I could see him inhaling the scent of my fear as he hovered over me. *Don't ever trust an Arvor.* Kendra's voice whispered in the back of my mind. I shouldn't even trust one that fought against his own kind, chose me over them.

A short hard chuckle rolled out of me as I bleed out into the mud. Then I was laughing, my body racking from the sound coming from me. I laughed in the face of death and silently begged for it to take me, but he pulled away, his eyes clear of the hate that had been there.

The rushing sound of leather boots and steel chainmail met my ears. My eyes were heavy. I'd lost so much blood my skin had turned ashen and pale. I held out my hand to the Arvor, to Kyier, but he reeled away from me as arrows came flying in his direction.

"Stop!" I yelled, but my voice was weak, and my vision was darkening.

"Secure the beast!" My father was there. When I reached, I was greeted with strong warm arms as they lifted me from the cool ground.

"I got you. You'll be alright." I leaned my head against his chest, but I reached out again when I heard the yelps and snarls of terror from him.

"Help him." I rasped.

"No." There was no room for argument in his tone. I laid my head against his chest and let the dark and warmth consume me until I felt as if I was falling.

My body ached when I woke up. My arm and leg were secured in tight bandages. Scratches on my knuckles, elbows, and knees had a soothing concoction spread over them. A pounding reverberated through my head. I wanted to lie back down and rest, but I needed to move. Stiffness laced my limbs as I moved. I wasn't sure how long I'd been resting already, but from the looks of my wounds it could have been a week or two.

I sat up and surveyed my room. Della was sleeping in an armchair not far from my side. I reached for her. She bolted upright when I grazed my hand over her own.

"Kastell! Yer awake."

I nodded. "How long?"

"Four days. Yer father wanted us ta keep ya under until the bones in yer arm healed. The healer has been here three times a day since, strengthening the bone. The first witch he's let in this here castle since ya left. That arm is good and set, jus' as new."

I rolled my eyes. "He drugged me to avoid me. He feels guilty for letting me go out there."

"Ye must understand, Princess. He loves ya. Yer all he has. He was a wreck when he came back. He only left yer side yesterday when the healer cured the infection in yer leg."

"Infection?"

"The forest is a nasty place." She drawled. "Yer heart had a hard time. It's good to see ya awake."

"I'm just glad to be alive. What did my father do with the Arvor he snared?" I asked. I needed to see him. Even if it was only for a moment to thank him.

Della shrugged. "The jail. Down by the gate I presume." Della patted the bed beside me. "I'll let ya sleep awhile. In the morn, I'll send yer father."

I tossed and turned in my bed. I never saw an Arvor shift before. It wasn't something that could easily be forgotten. The sound of his rage as his body morphed and towered beside me was something I had never heard from a man before. Every hair on my neck pricked upward and chills ran over my back. Even after the event I was shaken.

In the heat of the moment, I wasn't sure I could trust Kyier. His eyes were filled with rage and a thirst for blood. His hair stood straight and rough. The dark black hair blended into the darkness of the foliage and trees where the Arvors waited for an opening. Kyier took a threatened and defensive stance, though for the most part he advanced on them. He never allowed them to make the first move. He never let them get to me.

The first Arvor that moved in on his dark looming figure was torn in half. Kyier's claws clenched around the Arvor and his teeth dug into his scaled chest. The sound of bones snapping, and crunching made me gag at just the memory. After the first, others followed. He never paused or hesitated in his advance to claim their lives.

    I sat up and took a deep breath. I broke into a sweat and my heart raced. I was afraid of him. Kyier didn't allow any of them the chance to get near me, but for a split second I wasn't sure he even knew I was there. When he moved in and stood over me, I was sure I saw hate in his eyes. Yet, he hesitated and allowed my father's men to take him. That wasn't what anyone else saw.

    No. They saw a blood bathed beast leaning over me, teeth bared and death on all sides. He stopped and stared down on me, the entrails of one of them tangled in his claws. Recognition and regret came to his eyes as he stared at me. Was he afraid of what he became? Did he recognize me, or my fear?

    My father took him into chains and dragged the beast behind horses after penetrating him with spears to bring him to his knees. I'd awoken a few times from the bumps and rattle of the wagon to see him being pulled behind us like a weathered trophy. They rode with him beaten and bloodied behind them until Kyier thrashed for his freedom. He whimpered for mercy, but it was ignored. When they stopped, Kyier was no more than a rag doll. The men beat him with their feet and fists even as his body gave in and shifted back. Again, those bones popped. He screamed in the agony of it that time.

    I tried to stop them on one occasion, but no one listened, and the darkness swallowed me again. Did I try hard enough? The Commander landed the final blow to the head. Kyier was rendered unconscious and thrown into a wagon with his arms, neck, and legs chained to the wagon.

    I rubbed the sweat on my neck and forehead. I couldn't stay here, so close to comfort, but so far from sleep. Guilt swallowed me. If it weren't for me… it was very possible that my father would have been rational, or that Kyier would have never shifted in the first place. Kyier fought for him, pledged himself. He was loyal and a thorough emissary. After reading his report I knew what made him so valuable. Kyier was detailed and direct. None of that mattered now, not after I pissed myself watching him tear into his enemies and then turn on me.

    I should have been more reasonable. The skills Kendra and the other witches offered me in swordplay was just that, *play*. I wasn't near ready for a combat experience, but I was cocky and stubborn. I embarrassed myself and my father when I was baited so easily. I have a lot of work to do before I could prove my combat skills to the warriors and the Collective. I would be lucky if my father ever allowed me to step foot into a battle again.

    I swung my legs over the edge of the bed, desperate to be stretched. My bare feet on the stone floor stung from the cold. I welcomed the pain, the numbing sensation that filled my heels and soles. It took me only a few moments to put my green leathers on and crown my head with the emerald stone. It glistened at my touch. I didn't fuss with my hair in the same manner Della did. Instead, I tied it back into a tight braid. It wasn't traditional, but it was the way I liked it. I tightened the laces on my boots, my feet welcomed the sudden warmth.

J. L. Cross

The halls were empty and quiet. The only sound was the crackling of a fireplace in a small living area off the entryway. I peered in around the corner to see my father slumped back in his armchair staring into the dying flames. Another crackle and then a snap.

I cringed and straightened my back and held myself high, committed to where I was going. "You waited up," I said. Even with his back on me I could see the way he clenched down on the arms of the chair at the sound of my voice. Was he wishing I would have chosen to stay in my bed? Or maybe that I hadn't come home at all.

His head turned to me; exhaustion written all over his face. He waited. "You've always done exactly what you believed to be right, no matter the consequence. I wanted to be here for you when you were awake."

"How did you know it would be today?" I moved to stand beside him, drinking in the warmth from his fire that was dwindling to embers.

There was a knowing grin on his face. "You called out for me to save him the last few days. I knew you'd wake again soon. We're a lot alike. I wouldn't have chosen to spare this one, but then again, you're more like your mother in that way. She saw a bit of good in everyone, even our enemies." He sat up in his chair and leaned back into the cushions. "You defended him, even when he towered over you, intending you to be his final victim."

"You don't know that." I challenged, taking the seat beside his own. "I trusted him to choose differently." Didn't I already prove to myself that giving him that chance was a gamble, and I would have lost had it not been from the hesitation he gave me before my father's men stepped in? I'd seen the hate in him, the rage, and the vengeance he desperately craved. It was all there in the depths of his eyes, written in the scars that tore his face in two.

I pissed myself. He's dangerous. Why is my father always right when I don't want him to be?

I was reconsidering. Going to Kyier now could be a mistake. Sparing him could cost me my life. Seeing him chained up in the constraints of our prison could give me the reassurance I needed to sleep. I spent my whole life without seeing someone shift into an Arvor. I was more frightened of the process and the sound it made rather than the result. The beast was beautiful and majestic. It was pure power. Seeing him as a man again could put my fears to rest. He wasn't the threat. Was he? Somehow, I knew that he wasn't. It was a fact, but there was a world of those beasts just outside the city. If there were more like Kyier the battle was already a defeat.

My father grunted, pulling me from my thoughts. "Couldn't you see the carnage he left in his rage? Everyone is his enemy. Despite his declaration to fight for me- it does not absolve his prior associations. He was formerly the emissary of our enemy. Kyier is the reason we know the Rebel King has gone missing. They're either leaderless or he's returned, or maybe the emissary has lied his way into our midst? How should we know the truth? Kyier came to me when their men started fighting for power. He claimed he didn't want to be a part of their chaos." His eyes glared into my own, attempting to compel me to take his side. "I've never trusted him. It must be a ruse. He's only here because the Collective thought he would be an asset. They demanded he be pardoned of his crimes against the Ayles. I still don't trust him. Neither should you."

"If it's not fake?" I asked.

"I'll apologize to the hole in the ground- where I decide to bury him. For now, he's the enemy. All his men were butchered. Though I gave him only a few, a loss is a loss. Then he cornered my daughter. You didn't see what I saw." He stood from his chair, rocking on unstable legs from exhaustion or from the alcohol. Maybe both. He staggered out.

I stared into the burnt embers of the fire. Should I stay or should I go? My heart pounded. Every shadow in the room was immense and unwelcoming as I was left alone with my thoughts. I stifled the swallowing of the lump in my throat that grew. Sweat beaded on my forehead as I stared into the void of the fireplace. My eyes unwavering from the spot I marked in the dying fire. I could feel their eyes even though I knew they didn't exist. I feared them, even though they were only shadows. Somewhere in my mind, *they're watching. They're here. You'll die,* whispered faintly. The fear bubbled over. The sound of his morphing bones; then the quiet rumbled growl that had come from him. That's all I could hear, the silence, and then the affirmation that he was there. The sound of it etched into my mind. The silence echoed my fear in my desperation to live. His bones snapped, pure terror in thier faces when they regarded him. Kyier was terrified, too, but only when it was my father's men he faced, those he was supposedly loyal to.

I pulled my leathers down from the uncomfortable way they settled from sitting, banishing the recount of those events. Now that I wasn't smothered by the looming shadow of death, I remembered so clearly. My legs begged to run, but I would face this. I would face my fear. If I left Kyier to rot in the prison my fear would win. If I killed him, my fear would haunt me. I'd see his face for the rest of my life. He would be the face of my fears and doubts. I never stood and fought. I laid on the ground under him in the hopes he wouldn't shred me, that maybe the Mother would let me live. I had sat in my blood and piss without the notion to move my weak and tired limbs. I should have died. Kyier was something I feared, but he was also my savior.

There was a middle ground. He wore the face of what I feared, but he was the heart of a man that saved me when he didn't need to. I could wield him like a shield, or a weapon. Kyier valued his life above anything. He bore through the hate and ostracizing he received here in the Aylish army and when he could have run… he stayed.

My feet carried me into the darkness outside the castle. I locked my gaze on the floor that sped under my feet, afraid to look up into the dark and see those fears, the hot breath of the red Arvor cascading over my body. The warmth brought on by my own anxious thoughts. Though the moon lit everything like a dim glowing torch, that darkness still hugged me.

The moon's lightful embrace chased away the fears that were lurking, lingering, in the shadows behind me. Trapping them in the dark swells of the castle. Kyier may be in a real prison, but this was the prison that held everything from my fears to my delights. The castle beckoned to me, those fears whispering through the cracks in the metal and stone.

My eyes moistened as I took a deep breath, arching my face to the sky. The trembling in my hands stilled and the uneven rapid movements of my chest eased. The sounds of growling Arvors, the blood, the guts, the clashing and slicing of swords through flesh behind me, *his* growl, *his* bones snapping to create the beast, *the terror in his eyes afterwards;* those thoughts stilled and were muffled somewhere deep inside. I locked them there, throwing every ounce of the good things in my life against it until the rattling for their freedom stopped. They would come again, but for now there was peace. The cool air filled my lungs, pushing down further. I let my mind still in the moment.

My lips tilted into a smile. I knelt in the dirt and let my hands caress into its softness. With my head pressed to the ground I thanked the Mother for the comfort she gave me and for the pain she helped to push out.

I only stayed there a moment. Ayles didn't believe in these things, and I wasn't sure I wanted to be questioned about it later. There are no deities to them, such things were the creation of men for the answers only they desperately craved. Ayles were comfortable accepting that we are, and life didn't need an explanation. I never believed the way Kendra had, but without her I felt incredibly closer to my faith than ever. The Reflector would be proud. It was something that helped to fill the emptiness left with the absence of the sisters in my life.

J. L. Cross

The walk to the prison was short. Not so far as to be close to the civilians and not so far as to be close to the castle, but still within the closed gates of the castle grounds. It appeared mostly unused and ancient, just a door that led into the depths of a small hillside and well beneath it. The ground around the entrance was laced with weeds, thornes, and the dirt path I stood on that led through it all. The door could have been hundreds of pounds, requiring the strength of a warrior to open it. The hinges were rusted enough to hold the door stiff and fixed in its spot, but I could smell the scent of wet dog and abandonment. Kyier was here.

I stopped short of the door. The guard was picking at… *her*… fingers and nearly nodding off to sleep. I cleared my throat and she jerked to her feet. I tried my best to shake the look of shock on my face. A *woman*. A warrior? She was dressed and armed like one. She was also hidden in the thick overgrowth of the grounds, huddled in the dirt and moss just outside a typically barren prison, a post she looked comfortable and familiar with. The rock she sat on was fixed in its place. The small fire at her feet was well used and indented into the ground as if it'd been there as long as the prison.

"You're a woman." I said, pointing out the obvious when I couldn't think of the right words to buy myself passage into the prison without a lengthy encounter. "There aren't many female warriors." I said, noting the soft smile on her face as she let me soak it in.

The small woman nodded shyly. "I don't have any family." She held her spear close, leaning her weight into it. "If you're curious about how I've made myself here. A warrior, I mean." She corrected herself. "Plus, I'm a halfling. Mostly old witch blood. My father was Aylish, though. Ostracized for my mere existence. They took me, a payment for his debt to the crown for breaking the rules but executed soon after."

"*Hm.*" A million more questions about her status as a warrior and her life rang through my mind, but I had to remain focused. I gestured to the door. "Do you mind?"

Her brows furrowed. "The King said the prisoner isn't allowed to have visitors."

I nodded. "The King and I disagree on many levels. I like breaking his rules. What will it cost me to get in?"

A wicked smile came to her eyes. "I heard you were in the battle. That you carved your way through the Arvors until the tide turned against you and their numbers grew." She huffed. "I know who you are."

I nodded again but looked away. How could I meet her enthusiastic remarks and the eagerness in her voice if I couldn't cope well with the Arvors I killed and my failure in the face of evil? More importantly, I pissed myself in terror when I was confronted by the red Arvor. That was enough to embarrass me for a lifetime.

The guard put her hand on my shoulder, bringing my attention back to her. "I want to fight with you. Lead your own unit and I'll follow. That's all I ask." She huffed a short breathless chuckle. "That's the cost to get into the prison."

"You probably see enough battles on your own." I said, taking in her clean armor and perfect chainmail. I knew it was a lie. She was no better than a slave in my father's army, but not worthy enough to fight beside his men.

She shook her head. "Not at all. I've never left the city. I was sold into the army by my relatives not so long after my parents passed. I have the easy posts, here mostly, but I want to be out there on the front line, *fighting like you.*"

I stuck my hand out for her to grasp. She didn't hesitate. "We have a deal…" I didn't recall if she'd given me a name or not.

"Safrim." She added for me.

She turned and unlocked the door for me, pushing the heavy metal barrier open with both arms and a grunt. Her strength was impressive. The metal was thick and nearly unyielding. Once it began to swing it opened with ease.

Safrim smiled and motioned for me to cross the threshold. "If you need anything, call for me. The door must remain closed in the case the prisoner attempts to overpower you. I'll be listening."

Hello Kastell, am I as horrifying as your thoughts make me? Am I so terrifying? The dark called out to me in a deep masculine rumble, drawing me in before I knew my feet were moving. It was his voice. I remembered the sound now imprinting on the inside of my head. Safrim didn't hesitate more than a second before sealing the door and slamming the arm back into place across it. How could I hear him in the back of my head?

Your fears are quite endless. They're calling me.

I could feel him, the beast I had seen the other day, lurking somewhere in the dark. The walls were moist with condensation. Each droplet that fell to the stone floor echoed in the emptiness.

The rattling of chains and the sound of rusted metal dragging on stone came from the last cell in the chamber. When I stopped, I took a moment to take in the sight. *A man. Nothing more.* I reminded myself.

I'm a beast. You know I'm a beast. You've seen it! The darkness around me screamed within the walls of my mind. It spoke to me in his voice. Someone I feared. It harnessed my very thoughts against me. *I would kill you if your father wouldn't have come. I'm an animal!*

He lay naked and curled into a tight ball, his knees against his chest to ward off the cold. Kyier shivered. I squatted down and surveyed him closer. He did everything to avoid my gaze. He was equally afraid of me, or embarrassed. On this side of the cell, I had all the power.

Don't let me fool you. I cower until the moment to strike is perfect. I'll kill you!

"I can smell the River Root on you." His voice was a soft whisper, nothing like the angry voice in the darkness. He avoided my gaze. Bruises lined his sides and the place my father had speared him in the shoulder remained untreated. Nothing more than a bandage was added to cease the bleeding.

"Look at me." He refused. "Kyier, where is the beast that made me piss myself only a few nights ago?" His eyes darted to me then. "You fought then as if all the rage you bottled up had suddenly combusted. Now..." I nodded to the corner in which he used to relieve himself. "Now you have nothing but your shit for company. You still won't try to fight your way out?"

I deserve to rot. I'm nothing. You have the power over me here. It's everything outside that should scare you. The voice crooned inside my head. *No one can be trusted.*

He grunted as he moved, pulling himself into a kneeling position in front of me; he cradled an arm to his chest, the bones snapped in the center and a bone protruded from the skin. "I'm broken. The beast is afraid."

"Of what? The battle only turned against you when you faced my father, when you turned to me. You could have gotten away." I pointed to the stone in my hair. I had seen his eyes lock on it before my father had taken me. "Why did it affect you? You stared at it before they took you." Kyier looked away from me to the ground. "I was soaked in my own piss! I waited for death, and somehow, I escaped while everyone around me was torn to pieces." I grasped the steel rods of the door separating us and leaned closer until my forehead touched the steel. I took a breath to steady myself.

Kill me before I kill you. Silence the animal! The darkness shouted. I agreed. In my heart I knew I would be safer in the world with one less Arvor to face. Kyier was the largest and most terrifying I saw that day. One less Arvor his size, with his might, and I could save hundreds of Aylish lives. *Have me executed.* He egged me.

Kyier used his one good arm to crawl closer to me, the chain connected to the collar around his neck grew taut. I pulled away then, the fear inside me reigniting. Even though he was just a man, he was still a beast on the inside.

He chuckled under his breath. "You adorn your head with a sliver of relic and don't know it. Your father has your wounds treated with River Root to ward off vile magic spirits and you're oblivious to it." He laughed, low and deep. "You're ensnared in lies and secrets and are entirely unphased." He paused for a moment, "You don't know. Only oblivion can leave someone so calm. I've been searching for pieces of the relic for *years* now, running myself in circles just to feel its power. You don't even know what it is." He let out another breathless chuckle, followed by a grunt of pure agony. "I'll make a bargain with you."

I lie. I have no answers. I have no future. My fate is death. Cleanse the world. Cleanse my sins and destruction from this place with my blood. I shook my head, trying to force the voice away. "I don't bargain with beasts that can't be controlled." I stood up, my back straight and my head held high. I was on the winning side of this. I wouldn't let him get what he wanted. I wanted answers, *all of them*.

Kyier smiled, his eyes flashing a dark amber, the beast was here with us. I reeled backwards. I couldn't face it again. *It kills. It hunts. You're prey in the sight of it.* The cruel darkness whispered. As much as I wished I had the nerve to face the beast… I knew I wasn't ready. I could face the man, but not the beast today. The fear in me settled when the burning amber in his eyes receded. Even the voice seemed to wither away as his eyes became that of the man.

"You really are afraid." His voice was low and soft. An effort to sooth away my fear, but my bones and muscles were ready to fight, *or run.* I would run. I knew I would. Bile rose in the back of my mouth at the thought I was more of a coward than I was the day he towered over me. At least then I was so fixed to the ground in my fear I didn't think clearly. I didn't think about running then, but now, even with the advantage, I wanted to run.

I cleared my throat, swallowing the bile, fear, and panic that was welling there. *You should fear me. Don't release me. Use me. Kill me. Kill yourself.* The voice in the dark turned on me. Every part of my body wanted to tense and cry, scream for it to leave me. My gut fluttered, the panic rising. My skin was moist from the sweat, the sudden urge to run, and the mounting fear that Kyier would try to kill me. The voice winning. My fear was tangible, a thick salty moisture that hung in the air of the prison.

I could finish what I started. The voice was laughing. He spent years looking for what we had? A relic? A mage stone? Why was he so desperate for it to spend so long looking for it, surrounded by the same people that hated his kind? I never heard legends or whispers of any relic. Only mage stones, they detected the presence of magic. Della told me that much. Kendra even told me about them a few times. They were rare slivers of stones that belonged to the first witches and given to magicless mages, blessed with the power of the witch. I'd never seen one before, not until now. I even thought to argue once with Kendra that they were just stones that reflected light. I knew better now.

"Tell me what you know." I demanded.

Kyier laughed and held up his broken arm the best he could and motioned to his naked body with the other. "I won't tell you anything. Not like this." That smile came back to his face as he stood meeting my confident demeanor with his own unwavering one. Even with a broken body he stood stronger than other men. "Make a deal with me, seal our bargain with the Relic and in the event that either of us attempts to break the bargain, the Relic will…" he trailed off and waved his hand. "The oathbreaker will die. It's a simple bargain."

Only a fool would try to trick you! I'm disgusting! The voice barked, attempting to drag me back into that consuming feeling of anxiousness and fear, just as I was gaining control of it. My breathing evened.

There was that wicked smile on his lips again. The one that beckoned me to fight and not run. The same smile that made me fear him the first time we met. His smile pulled at the scars on his face, a reminder of the traumas and dangers he fought through and won. If I denied him this, then I came here for nothing. I wouldn't leave settling my fear, only locking it away with the answers I wanted.

"I can hear the darkness whisper to you." He said, gripping the bars of his cell. My breath caught in my throat. He was in desperate need of stability. He wobbled on his feet slightly. The blood loss gained on him. "It's the spirits of the dead. In this place, evil lives in the hearts of every man. Even the stones weep with its power here.

Aylhm is home to many secrets. The voices here aren't mine and they're not you. Don't listen to them."

"River Root." I said softly.

"That voice…" He stuttered. "It tempts you into horrible things. It's vile. It drives men mad. I can hardly keep it out now. It's only been a few days and I feel helpless. Your father knew you would come. He's been treating you. Protecting you."

"He's a good man."

"He beat me and had me tortured after returning to the city. You can call him whatever you like, but he's not a good man."

I swallowed hard. He was always a good man to me. "Maybe if you had children of your own to protect you would understand his anger."

He chuckled. His eyes closed as he leaned into the cool bars, his brow steady against its rusted surface. "Make a deal with me and I swear you will come to know all the things I know."

"Fine." My voice cracked on the word. Every part of my mouth was dry. From the fear or from the panic inside of me that was rising again. I couldn't help but think I was making a horrible mistake. I was hashing a whole new problem for myself. Something deep inside me told me this was right, but what if I was wrong? I couldn't let the fear and panic take away the fact that I felt in my bones that what I was about to do was best.

No. This is wrong. He is death. He is hated. He is an animal. He will be the end of all things good. He will bring suffering. That voice was softer, and it spoke differently, not pretending to be him in my mind. It was further away in my mind now. It tried to climb to the surface, to get a foothold in my mind again in the panic that was there. *Your father will never respect you. You're hated by everyone. The Collective will never support you.*

Kyier gestured to the stone in my hair. "Hold the stone and speak of the condition of the bargain you want to place. The stone remembers everything. Don't say anything to the stone if you intend for it to be taken lightly."

Bargain for his death. Make him die. No one loves you. You're a prize to be won.

I fumbled trying to get the stone from my hair. Silent tears ran down my cheeks. I wanted to leave, the voice inside the darkness was heavy and bitter. Its hooks dug into my mind. I knew what I wanted though. I'd be fast. The stone fell to the ground from my trembling hands.

You're an idiot. You should have died in the forest. He would have killed you then. A fool.

As I snatched it from the ground my grip was tight. Kyier reached through the bars with his good hand, stilling them as his hand fell over my own. My heart raced at the touch. My nerves twisted into a million knots. The touch was gentle, reassuring. I half expected him to use the strength he had left to strangle me, but it was comfort I found in the very person I feared.

J. L. Cross

"Everything will be fine." He soothed. "Ignore it. The darkness is heavy, but you'll be fine. Steel your mind against it. Think of good things. Think of someone you love, and the voice will recede."

I did as he said. I thought of Kendra. I thought of how her hands would soothingly comb through my hair when I was sad, when I missed my father. She would hold me when I cried. I tried to think of the times she would walk with me. The dinners we ate together and the secrets we shared. The voice was a muffle, the heaviness was lighter than it was before. It wasn't more than a thick fog holding on now.

"I want all that you know. Every secret of Aylhm and elsewhere. All the secrets you know." I said to the stone. I watched it flicker and hum at my words. Its soft light shining on the palms of my hand in my face.

"Give me the stone before it's light fades." Kyier demanded, holding out his hand. "I'll say my condition."

I placed it into the palm of his outstretched hand. "I'll have my freedom. That includes from the bonds of the King's army and to any debts he thinks I owe the crown." I knew what he would ask for before it left his lips. I was prepared. I knew what I would counter with. I wouldn't let him leave here with his freedom and nothing to hold him responsible for it.

I held out my hand for the stone. He placed it there gently. It was glowing brighter than it did before, the light filling the chamber. Its surface was warm now. "I'll have your service as my protector. You will not threaten my life or attempt to take it. When I call, you will answer."

He smirked. "In that case I need something a little more intimate from you. With my freedom I'm made your slave. The endless cycle." He held out his hand. I nearly refused him the stone. "A bargain is only finished when both parties are satisfied."

I placed it there in his palm, fearing the worst. Would he demand for me to stand before him naked as he did now for me? Would he ask something even more intimate? A union? Something I'd never be able to forget about?

"You come for me. When you call, I'll answer, you will do the same for me. No questions asked."

"That's it?" I countered; my eyes wide with releaf that he didn't ask for some of the things that were running through my head. It could have been worse. There were worse things for someone to ask of me. If all he demanded was my presence, how could I deny it? I'd get my answers and my fear of the beast could rest.

"I'm satisfied. Are you satisfied?" He asked, a spark coming to his eyes. He was close to freedom now. It was seconds away for him. I nodded my agreement. He bit his lip and rolled his eyes. "Say it." He stepped closer to the bars, his hand outstretched with the stone in the center of his palm. My breath caught, but I didn't reel away this time. *The beast was mine now.* My life above all others, even his own, was safe.

"I'm satisfied." I touched the stone and the relic glowed until it started to tremble in his hand. A crack filled the air and then there were two pieces in his rough hand. Each splinter of the stone had what looked like an ancient Aylish symbol on it. If I wasn't wrong, it was an emblem of servitude or binding.

"Take one. A symbol of our bargain. When the bargain is fulfilled the two pieces will come back together."

"This is such a load of shit." I said while rolling my eyes and reaching for the stone. Even though I saw the magic in the stone swell with my own eyes, I was ready to deny it. When my hand touched the smooth surface, they tingled with an electric pulse and the stone began to glow again. I wrapped my hand around the small sliver that was now mine. The bargain replayed in my mind like I was watching it with a pair of eyes staring through the tinted color of the stone. Every word was there in the stone. It wouldn't forget it. Just as Kyier had promised.

"Safrim." I called for the guard. My voice was steady and the tears that were once on my face were dried and undetectable.

The door swung open, and the woman came barreling down the stairs with her sword drawn and her helmet slammed into place. She bashed her sword against the steel rods of the prison door, making Kyier take a step back. His hands raised in pure defeat.

"Stand your ground, my lady!" She hissed out. "He's just a man!"

"Safrim." I smiled and placed a hand on her shoulder. "All is well. Open the cell. The prisoner is free."

"My lady?" Safrim whipped her helm from her head and stared blankly at me after lowering her sword. "Only the King can give those orders."

"Do you want to fight with me Safrim, or would you like to remain here, guarding an empty prison?" I made the threat lightly, just enough for the woman to groan and hurry to find the keys in a fold of her armor. I shrugged. "My Father will understand. The prisoner is mine now. Come to the castle. We'll have a guest room prepared. A bath will be drawn, and a healer will be called." Safrim still stared at me without blinking, her face drained of color. "Without delay." I stressed and pushed on her to move her towards the stairs.

After she left, I turned back to Kyier. "Tomorrow, you will make yourself presentable. We will talk then." I took the handle to the cell door in my hand and retched it open, rust falling to the ground in a red mist. "I don't want to be kept waiting."

"When you call, I will answer." He said, the wicked spark in his eyes only growing. He wouldn't make himself readily available. He was going to force me to call on our bargain just to keep him under some semblance of control. We both came out victorious this time, but eventually I would have to face the beast he hid within himself, the same beast I was still terrified of.

I felt his eyes on me with every step I took. The voice was there again, warning me not to turn my back on him. With every step I felt it pressing on me, pulling on me to stay in the depths of the prison. Thankfully, Kyier's cell was the first down the stairs and it wasn't a long walk back to the surface. I couldn't imagine the power the darkness held below us.

I couldn't sleep. Every time I laid my head down a surge of fresh energy spiked through me. I yielded to it and found myself outside in the garden in a loose pair of trousers and plain shirt before the sun was ready for me. I dug at weeds that surrounded one of my favorite benches and tossed them into the path to be cleaned up later. With every root freed from the ground I felt one more worry silenced in the back of my mind.

Kyier was somewhere in the castle being treated and taken care of. He only cried out once, loud enough to wake the dead. I assumed his arm was set back into place and a bandage was applied. It was by far his most gruesome wound to tend to. Since then, the castle has been cold and silent.

The sun came over the hills and valleys, crested the city with its light. Watching the colors splash through the sky was beyond words. I remembered watching the sunrise with Kendra every morning over tea and biscuits. When I was young, she made goals for me every morning. One day I would be learning a new phrase in the Elder Aylish tongue, and some days I was practicing something as simple as my patience.

As I stared at the sun and soaked in its morning warmth, I set a goal. "I'll convince my father I'm right. This was a good decision."

"Am I interrupting?" The voice was as smooth as silk. I didn't turn to look at him. My lack of sleep was starting to beat on me. A stiff reminder that I still had a long day ahead of me. "I can go if you'd like." He said again.

I shook my head and moved to sit on the bench, patting the spot beside me, inviting Yurdell to sit. His movements looked stiff, unsure, but he sat. "Good morning."

"You're filthy. Have you slept? Your eyes are heavy," he said. I could feel his eyes searching every crevice of my face. There was true concern in the way he surveyed me, not entirely as if I were prey.

I shrugged. "I had a lot on my mind to keep me awake."

"I can tell. I can smell the wet Arvor on you from here. Or is that just reaching my nose from the castle? I'm unsure. To say the least, you've been busy this last night."

I nodded. "I'm afraid I'm making horrible decisions."

He chuckled. "And here I thought you were going to roast me about my lack of responsibility and capability of handling my duties as a leader and dignitary. I wasn't sure I was ready to see you."

"That reminds me. What is causing the famine?"

Yurdell bit his bottom lip, mulling over the things that lay there on his tongue. "I'm not sure. I know there's a few undesirable things happening in the villages to the north and west, but that's expected from territories closer to the Rebels. I'll have to go out there myself, inspect the mills and the caravans that are supposed to be transiting the food. I'm not sure where things are going wrong."

He seemed upset, his brow furrowed as he thought through all the possibilities. "It could be stolen or destroyed." I offered.

"That's my fear. Good food is destroyed to draw our attention and focus us on something trivial in comparison to a direct attack, leaving us weak and ill prepared. I'll get you answers before we suffer permanently from these actions."

I smiled and stood, changing the subject. I didn't want to talk about the things that bothered me. I wanted a deep breath away from them. Even though they followed me into the peacefulness of the garden, regardless of my desires. "You came sooner than I expected."

He rubbed the back of his neck nervously. He twisted to face me, his knees spreading. Yurdell tugs at his embroidered and finely crafted jacket and stared up at me, his eyes held a deep red down in the depths of the browns. They were mesmerizing. I had to tear my eyes away, but then I was looking at his succulent lips. I felt the flush come to my cheeks. I cleared my throat, swallowing my shame.

"I came the very next day, but you had left with your father. Then the next day, but you were bed ridden. I was here only yesterday, but the answer was the same. I thought you were avoiding me, that your offer was merely a taunt. I see that wasn't the case."

He took my hand and turned it over, lifting the sleeve of my shirt until he could see the healing claw marks on my arms. "Disgusting beasts," he offered as his fingers touched at the scabbing wound gently. "You're a very brave woman."

"It's nothing," I said. "I wasn't ready, and I allowed myself to be lured into a trap. I got what was waiting for me there. I learned from my mistakes, and I won't make them again."

"With every success, there are countless failures behind it. Don't be hard on yourself. You lived, and according to the reports, that's impressive as well. All of the men that went into that trap with you weren't so lucky to leave with their lives. I'm appalled that your father would have allowed you to be so foolish."

"It was a lesson."

"Lessons don't end with your child cowering in the mud, nearly flayed to pieces by mindless beasts. Only men like *my* father would call that a lesson." Yurdell retorted, rage flaring in his eyes. There was unrest in his family. It didn't explain much, other than why he'd come so far from his own kind.

I pulled my hand away from him, but I enjoyed the comfort of his fingers stroking my arm. It made me consider what it would mean to pick him as a suitor, to suggest him. He didn't offer himself readily the other day. He wasn't interested in the games the Collective was playing.

"Can you get me a few answers about the famine? I need something to saite my father. He needs answers. It would be even better if you found a solution in your endeavor as well."

He tisked, a smirk coming to his face, his eyes brightening. "Only if you promise to let me call on you again, and not for matters like these."

I shrugged. "What else would you have me do?"

J. L. Cross

"Do you trust me not to lead you into danger?"

I nodded. I didn't know what made me trust him so easily. Maybe it was his smile or the way his eyes held me in a trance so close to bliss.

He stood and bowed slightly. "I'll plan something for my next visit. Something you may like." Yurdell turned on his heel and sauntered off towards the gate, turning his nose away from the castle in distaste. He turned again, moving backwards flawlessly on his heels as he faced me. "Don't get killed while I'm away?"

"I don't make those kinds of promises." I shouted with a laugh in my voice and a smile on my face. I was looking forward to a meeting separate from all things political and dangerous. Yurdell lifted my spirits, it was a presence I needed.

I slept the first part of the morning and the first hours of the evening, well past what I'd demanded of Kyier. I was supposed to meet him in the morning, but instead I'd left him waiting for me. I climbed out of my bed realizing I hadn't washed after digging in the garden. I didn't bother removing my boots either. Della bustled into my room carrying a pitcher of steaming water.

"I heard ya woke."

"Who told you? The walls?" I said as a chuckle left me. She somehow knew exactly when her service was needed.

"Hush." She retorted and filled my wooden tub with the water. "The Arvor man wants a word with ya when yer finished dressing. He seems rather impatient with ya."

I groaned inwardly. "No, I beg you, go in my place. I just want quiet."

Della laughed as she tossed a hand towel back over her shoulder and shoved the empty pitcher she used under a desk. "He claimed you demanded an audience with 'em this morrn."

I remembered it. I'd suffer through it, get a few answers and let him be on his way. He couldn't stay in the castle. I'd call for him when I needed him, when I was ready for more answers.

I stripped out of my clothing and dropped into the water quickly. "Tell the *Arvor man* that I'll be out in a moment."

"Ya must me quick." Della warned. "Yer father and the Commander are plottin' to kill the Arvor man."

I couldn't help but laugh. I made this choice. Was I surprised they both hated it? Della slammed the door and left me to scrub the debris from my scalp and the smudged dirt from my skin. I scrubbed and laced the water through my hair. There was something infused in the water, not the lavender like before. No, this was something that smelled like fresh soil and rain. *River Root.* I groaned again. The smell was enticing and rich, lovely even, but I wasn't excited that they felt the need to use a spirit repellent on me. I heard Kyier when he mentioned the properties of River Root even though I choose to ignore most of it. If the smell was so strong, then my father wasn't just using it to dress my wounds but infusing it in the water used to clean me those days.

I wrung out my hair and pinned it to the top of my head. Della had taken a moment to lay out a dark pink dress on the bed that flared below the waist. A dress fit for a princess. The sleeves were taut on my arms and sheer. The neckline plunged to my belly button. Thankfully she didn't leave heels on the floor for me, but instead a dainty pair of plain pink slippers.

My long golden white hair only took me a few minutes to braid and slide a comb through, the rest I left to hang down my back. By the time I was finished it was nearly dry. I stepped into the hallway, unsurprised to be greeted by the sounds of men shouting. I ignored what they were arguing about until I stepped into the dining hall, drawing all three of their attention and the room fell silent. My father and Inara were hoovering closely to a chair Kyier was seated at, his feet propped on the table as he rolled what looked to be herbs between his fingers.

"I was just about to come to you. I was beginning to tire of waiting." Kyier announced.

"You'll wait as long as it takes. Your freedom does not give you the right to be rude." Inara said with a curl in his lip, the hate seething off him.

I waved him away. "I can deal with Kyier." I motioned to the door. "If the two of you don't mind?"

My father grumbled, kicking a chair's foot. The chair toppled at the force of his rage. He stormed from the room, Inara on his heels.

It would take him a while to accept my decision. He'd lived a long time with only his own to deal with.

"I was truly wondering if you intended for me to tolerate them any longer. I'm not sure I could have." His eyes turned that menacing amber. "The beast doesn't like to be trifled with."

"I want some answers. Only a few to start."

"The meaning of life, existence, and the one true God?" He said sarcastically, biting his lip waiting for me to retort back to him, but I only shook my head. *Only one god?* I brushed the thought away. Soilts and Arvors believed there could be many gods.

"Actually, I just want to know about you first, then the Relic." I pulled a seat out beside him and made myself comfortable. "Where do you hail from? Tarem? Aylhm? Gorgon? Veitich?"

"None of the above. I'm very, very, very old."

"How old?"

"I've lost count." He retorted, looking down to his herbs and rolling them again between his fingers. He held them to his nose and took in the scent that they released.

I groaned in irritation. "Then where are you from?" I repeated.

He laughed. "How about I tell you what I think you're ready for, and then we talk about the rest later?"

I nodded in agreement and motioned for him to go on.

"I'm descended from a very long line of Arvors where I'm from, but when I was just a young man- I, and a handful of others, were taken and made captive by the Aylish. First, we came here to Aylhm with the Ayles. We were their slaves. Many years later an attack came from Tarem. Some of their people stayed here after a semblance of peace was made, the others returned to their side of the sea, taking a group of Arvors with them to Tarem as a gift from the Ayles. In Tarem they pitted us against each other for entertainment. I was never killed in the fighting rings, mostly due to the size and power of my Arvor. I've been indebted to a powerful position, passed through generations of their government. About a decade ago I was released with many my people, but there's still many more of us in Tarem, facing the consequences of my actions. They came here seeking a new life. Alcux was our King, and then his son after him was to succeed, but things changed. Since Vlad destroyed our village no one has seen Alcux. The boy returned recently, a proxy King in place of someone else named king, so rumor has it. I was an emissary for Alcux, we were very close before, during the age of war between Tarem and Alyhm, and after. When I accepted his disappearance, I came here and pledged myself to your father. I vowed to fight for the Ayles. Of course, my debts to Tarem have gone unpaid in the meantime."

"You're a coward. You thought the Arvors were going to meet their end, so you switched teams like a slithery coward."

"Take that back." He snarled, his eyes burning amber, but I wasn't afraid.

"Accept the truth." I countered.

"The truth of why I came to your father is so much deeper than the surface of what I'm giving to you now. You're not ready for the rest."

"Do I just wait for you to tell me when I'm ready?"

He chuckled then, the amber sizzling there, but not ebbatting. "No. You'll know when you're ready. You'll know when you *need* the answers."

I changed the subject, back peddling the details he had already given me. "The war you spoke of, that was before the great war."

"Yes. The great war erupted between the Ayles and the witches, mages, and all those affiliated with magic. Ayles never saw magic like theirs before. They feared it. With fear and power comes desolation. The magic folk wielded something darker and much greater, the darkest magic *The Mother* offered. They created the Soilts, a weapon to yield specifically against Ayles. Every ounce of their bodies and power are designed to attack and kill Ayles. The Ayles harnessed what was left of my people against the Soilts and magic folk, nearly wiping out the last of the Arvors in Aylhm. Of course, the magic folk and the Ayles came to some very tense, but mutual peace agreement. Here we are today."

"And the Relic?" I asked as I processed the information about Kyier. He was centuries old now, and so old he had lost count. What made him so different from everyone else? Why had he lived such a long life and unaffected by time and age?

"*They,*" more than one… "were brought here with the Ayles when they first came to Aylhm. There were first two, but one was destroyed and broke into many pieces. They hold a lot of power when they're whole. I've been looking for its pieces, and now I've found another. The other Relic, it was lost, and so were the stories and the legends about them. I don't know where the whole Relic is, but it's filled with power and magic."

I pointed to the piece that was hanging around his neck, wrapped in wire and clipped onto a thread used as a necklace. "You made the bargain with me because you knew it would split?"

He nodded. "We both got what we wanted. You will have answers and I will have a taste of freedom. I came to your father because I felt the Relic here. I know you have the other half, so now I can move on. I don't need to stay here."

"You'll come when I call." I said in warning.

"Give me a few weeks at least. Give me time to stretch. *To run.*"

I saw the need in his eyes. Kyier needed this freedom and space more than anything. He bounced from one hand of slavery to the next throughout his existance. His only freedom was short-lived. Then he was a soldier for my father. A hated one. I decided then as our eyes were locked on each other that I would give him freedom. Real freedom.

"Alright. You can have freedom, but I will call for you and when I do, you *will* answer."

Kyier shuffled from his chair, kneeling in front of me with his head bent, his hair pulling around him. "Yes," his face lifted, and those amber eyes met my own. "*My Queen.*"

When I had first met him, I never suspected the Arvor under his skin, his ears were pointed but short. Aylish like, but not really

Aylish. His blood was pure Arvor. It was so old that he looked the genetic part of who he was. This is what the first of their blood looked like before Aylhm. Who would have guessed that in that moment of our meeting I would have broken Kendra's number one rule: *Do not associate with Arvors;* To add, taking advice on how to wear my hair from a stranger?

The next few days passed slowly, dragging on and on. Inara lurked in the shadows, pretending to be unnoticeable, but the lurking was obnoxious. Since the battle and my constant state of insomnia, my father demanded he keep a close eye on me. It was unbearable.

    Yurdell sent a short letter two days after our last meeting. A young boy delivered it into my own hands, saying that Yurdell deemed no one else worthy to read it. He wasn't a man to be trifled with and the order was followed. I pulled the letter from the book I was reading. I used it as a bookmark. I spent most of my day discussing strategies with my father, playing games of dice, and just enjoying his company again. We missed so much time together that he was eager to let me into his daily life.

    I tore the seal from the letter and unfolded its edges carefully.

Kastell,

    I fear there's no good news regarding my intent to find answers. I'll spare you, save the knowledge I've gathered for when we meet again. I've written to inform you that the mission has required me to spend much more time away than I hoped. Please, forgive my absence.

    Yuri

    I sat by a window in my room looking down at the garden I tended only a few days ago, longing to be there. The garden was messy and unkempt. That would be where I focused my attention after getting what I needed from Yurdell. Roses were growing wildly out of control and over the stone fences, the gates were being ambushed by creeping vines and wildflowers. There was an ancient oak in the center of the garden; it had been cursed by witches a long time ago, at least that's what the legend says, and it caused the leaves to turn pink and then the color of red just before they would fall. The story says that it's the blood of the witches that cursed it to turn the leaves such a dark red. For now, the leaves remained pink. When they turned red, we knew snow would be just over the mountains.

    I played with my hair as I passed time lost within my thoughts. There was a steady pour of rain and all I wanted to do was enjoy the view. I had been sewing a new dress in the late evenings when it was far too dark to meddle in the garden. The Collective had threatened again to find the best suiter for me. With Kyier far gone, his scent a dying touch in the castle, he was no longer a viable option. Nor would my father ever condon a match like that. One man propositioned his youngest bachelor son. He was five. Everyone gagged at the proposition, not just me. I could thank them for not being that low later when the ordeal was over. Inara was still not in play due to his debts to the crown. I was relieved knowing he couldn't be considered. I'd nearly mentioned Yurdell, still not recommended by any member of the Collective. He would be suiting. He was extremely kind to me and bearable to be around, but no one wanted a halfbreed for a King.

 Yurdell was a noble, mannered, masculine, elegant, graceful, and downright suave. The Collective would have to think of a new argument that didn't include his breeding. I'd ask him first myself before mentioning his name. I closed my eyes, thinking about how his wicked smile that barely hid his fangs was sensuous. He had such smooth and flawless skin, pale and vibrant. His hair and eyes were a welcome contrast that made him even more alluring. Why was I suddenly feeling so torn with him away? I didn't think I'd miss a man like this. I had gotten excited about our next meeting; he promised something special. With his trip extended, who knew how long it would be.

 A halfbreed was bad news for the wellbeing of the Kingdom, or so the Collective thought, but it would bring in a new era. What did I really want for the future of my people? Who would be the best King, that's what my decision needed to be fueled with. Yurdell knew the collective and commanded authority. If there were a better match, I'd have to find him soon before the Collective caved in and married me to an adolescent boy.

Just then a heavy knock echoed through the room, impatient, another two followed swiftly after. I bolted up and crossed the room, swinging the heavy door open. Inara was fuming with anger. I jolted back from him in fear. I knew then, after seeing the darkness in his eyes, his slender and sharp features framed by his brilliant straight hair.

"You've heard then?" I asked smugly. The Commander was not amused in the slightest.

"How can you make light of something like this? The Collective will never allow this. The more you're seen with him the more rumors that will arise."

I shrugged. "They're not rumors. I've thought it over. Yurdell would be a great King."

"He's-"

"Mention his breeding to me one more time and I'll have no more reason to converse with you as I do an ant."

He bit his lip in frustration. "It's not just his breeding. If you want to be factual, his father recklessly kidnapped the blood of an Ayl against her own will. He paid handsomely for a witch to use the same spell their old elders used to create Soilts. Yurdell is not really a man, he's a puppet. He will only live if the magic in his veins wills him to live."

I stepped through the door, closing my chamber off to him and gestured for him to walk with me down the hall to the sitting room. "What's your concern about how he was given life? It doesn't make it less true that he already commands authority where it'll be desperately needed."

Inara clutched at his sword as if he'd have to protect us from an inbound threat. "Your father is far from his death; I can promise you that. Anyone can earn the respect of the Collective if only given the time."

"Do you count yourself among that number? It's been how many years? Twenty, since you came to be with us. Still, they don't stand in your defense against the King. You should have titles by now, not just guarding him from the shadows."

There was a look of defeat in his eyes. I didn't want to dwell on it for too long, so I took a seat in an open armchair as soon as we made it to the room. He was quiet now, as if I'd stolen the foundation of his argument, but I could see he had much more to say. "Just say it. Tell me how you feel now before you've lost your chance."

He sat heavily into a chair across from me, setting his sword to the side to lean against the velvet arm of the chair. I didn't ignore the way his hand idly brushed along the hilt as if silently admiring its craftsmanship.

"Yurdell has authority because he's killed every man that's challenged him. He commands through the lives he's taken to remain in power."

I shrugged an idle shoulder. "That's the way of our people. My father fought off a handful of men to claim the right as the superior suitor to my mother. You know this. You know we live by the sword."

He nodded in agreement. "It's more than that. He works in the darkness against everything the King stands for. He's never stood with your father. Not once. He's challenging his way to the top and he's always plotting new ways to get what he wants."

"As is everyone in the Collective." I huffed out a breath of irritation. "Inara, you're describing all the elders, aside from their skills with blades. They wanted to marry me to a child. If I don't claim, there's a better suitor soon I'll end up with a boy-King."

"I would be a better suitor." Inara said calmly, his eyes focused on mine. He dared me to challenge him then. We both knew he was right, but the Collective would never have him if he remained a slave.

I sat straight, laying the edge of my dress flat. I didn't realize, but my eyes shifted everywhere but to his. I felt him watching me. "I've already announced you as a suitor. You didn't seem keen on the idea then. Everyone denied you; even my father denied you. Now you want to make your case?"

He nodded stiffly. "I have no interest in bedding you. My only interest is to refuse Yurdell the chance at ruining this kingdom. My interest lies with the Kingdom, not in selfish power hustles."

"How would you convince my father?"

"I don't need to. Your father despises the halfbr- *the man*." Inara corrected quickly under the skewer of my eyes. "He'll let me fight him in the arena."

"You'll need to practice then." I remarked cooly, the corner of my mouth twitching into a smile. "I'd hate to miss the opportunity to be married to a man that will never seduce me into his bed. Especially if it's someone I hate equally as much in return."

Inara made some unintentional huffing sound as he stood, grasping his sword in his sturdy hands. "Give me a year… or ten, maybe I'll want to bed you then." I didn't miss the humor, the smile that traced over his face and brightened his features as he left. "Or, until I'm snug in my grave." He called over his shoulder.

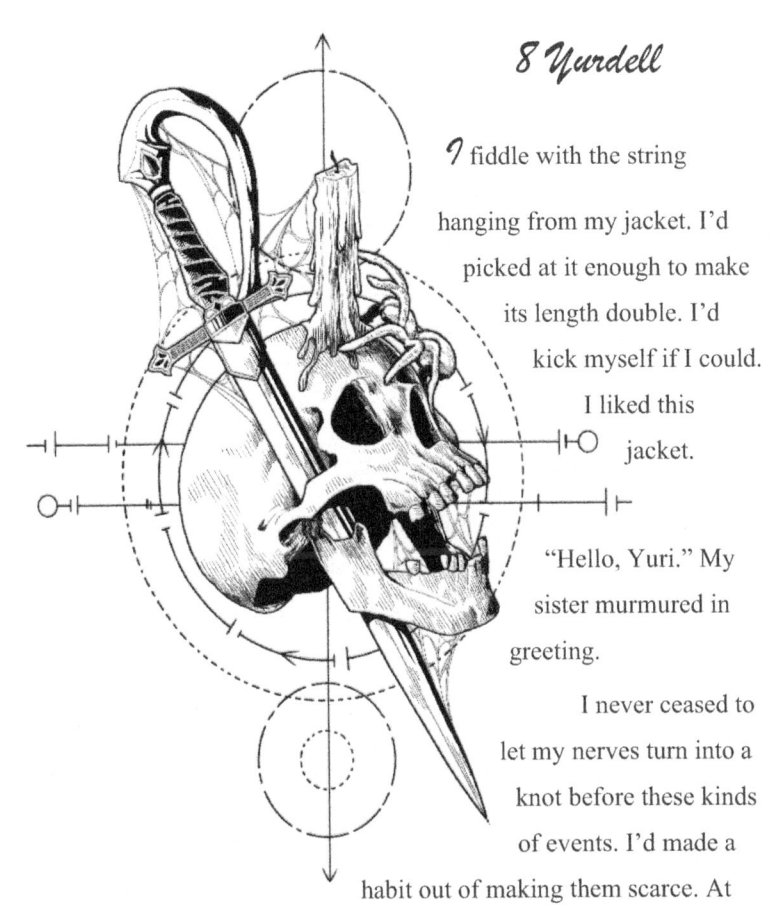

8 Yurdell

I fiddle with the string hanging from my jacket. I'd picked at it enough to make its length double. I'd kick myself if I could. I liked this jacket.

"Hello, Yuri." My sister murmured in greeting.

I never ceased to let my nerves turn into a knot before these kinds of events. I'd made a habit out of making them scarce. At one time they happened regularly, but that meant I was consistently shoving my own head under the water. Finally, my life was under control. The water of my demise had sunk to my waist, and everything was impeccably under control.

"So many familiar faces." I purred as I strode into the office. My sister sat straight on the arm of a chair; an unfathomably dark man was in its center. The tension between them could be felt across the room. I tried to refrain from remarking on my sister's tastes. Though, I wished she would do better. The men she normally frequented were temporary and fleeting pleasures. On more than one occasion they brought her heartache. I wished she had the sense to seek permanence, but she enjoyed the endless turning wheel of new companionship.

"We've been waiting." She croaked, tilting her head and studying me as if my face was saying more than my mouth. She could read me like a book. It was the curse of being a twin. To have someone that knew your mind as thoroughly as they knew their own was sometimes unsettling.

I tried to survey the room again, discreetly. These were people my sister had chosen. These were people she thought would bring us the most fortune. A proxy from our father, the Soilt King in the North, another proxy… I could smell Arvor on him even though the smell of pine and burnt embers in the fire were equally distasteful in the air. I didn't recognize him, but I imagined he was representing something far larger than just a few rebels that branched out away from the King, no… this was more. He sat as if he were someone of real power. A member of the Royal Collective I recognized. He's an elder who looked far too uncomfortable in this place. I recognized him right away, Ramir. He was the man that spoke frankly about marrying Kastell to the emissary. Little did they mention that the emissary was an Arvor. It seemed the Collective was positively bursting with the urge to embrace a more forward-thinking approach. However, Ramir was only one of the men. Yurdell would have to win them all or force them to follow his lead.

I stopped in front of the mantle, bracing myself a moment. Yirma had convinced me this course of action would gain us favor in the light of our father, but something inside of me screamed at the top of its lungs that this wouldn't bring anything more than pain. I recognized some of the men here and I wondered if they were spies for the King, or traitors, like myself. I couldn't trust any of them.

"Thank you for coming." I heard myself say, an involuntary habit. "You've all heard the news by now, the female heir to the throne has returned. Kastell is due to be married to secure the throne in the event of the King's death. This is not the only reason we meet. Many of us are at odds with the King. With that said, we propose a solution. We rid the Kingdom of the King and we go in a different direction."

Yirma nodded and then stood. "I've invited a guest."

From the shadow of the doorway a slim man entered, compensating his weight from one leg to the other as he moved. There was a lurch to his step that made everyone aware of the unnatural way he moved. When he removed his hood, I should have been shocked, but I wasn't. My father's pet strolled in. His long white hair is an emblem of his heritage.

"This is not what I planned." I said, my teeth grinding towards my sister. "This was not the way."

She only chuckled, her voice cracking. "No, brother, this is father's way."

"He only brings with him everything I've tried to uproot from the very beginning. This is counterproductive and you know it." I wanted to reach for her, strangle her. I knew what this appearance meant for myself and for Kastell.

"Please." His voice was hoarse, coated with the blood of Soilts. He'd become powerful and bent with magic from the day my father took him. "I come to amend the wrongs in Aylhm. Every ounce of my being was meant to rule here. Whatever you had planned was punitive in comparison."

Vlad moved to the chair that was tall in comparison to the rest. The chair that was originally left open for me. As he sat, he groaned. The weight removed from his deformed leg gave him ease. The snarl that was set onto his face relaxed into something calmer and cooler, menacing.

"My sister is not meant to rule this great Kingdom. The King in the North has finally released me to take what is mine. Will anyone argue?"

I rolled my eyes. "He should have left you on the bank of the river to freeze or be eaten by the monster that mangled your leg."

Vlad chuckled as if it weren't an insult. "*Brother*, you've never liked having your playthings taken. Have you?" Vlad had lived with us so long he was a brother; A brother I hated with every ounce of my own weight.

"Kastell is not a plaything." I corrected it evenly. I was annoyed to hear myself protesting him, giving him what he wanted. I couldn't control it.

Vlad lifted his shoulders, straightening himself. His face looked pensive and consuming. "I was talking about the Kingdom and it's fickle Collective, but if you'd like to include my sister, it gives me pleasure knowing that someone is playing with her. It also gives me a great juncture into the plans I've laid forth. Ramir, a member of the collective, as you may know, is interested in returning the traditional ways to the Kingdom: That a pure Aylish bloodline lays claim to the throne."

"Were you not the man that announced that Kyier, the Arvor-emissary, would be noble enough to become the next King of Aylhm?" I pointedly stared down the elder, hoping to see him squirm under the pressure, but surprisingly he only cocked the corner of his mouth in entertainment. "Did I miss hear you?" I probed. The man was increasingly restless under the scrutiny of the rest of the eyes in the room staring at him.

The man nodded in confirmation and then held out his hands in submission. "To be fair, I was testing the King's resolve to the traditional ways."

"Were you satisfied?"

"Very." He announced with a smile. "The King refused every suitor we mentioned, aside from the five-year-old Aylish boy. I'd take that as victory."

Vlad waved our bickering away, silencing the both of us. The red tinted swirl that came from his fingertips hinted at the power granted to him through the Soilt blood, but reinforced by something in his own, a secret I guarded closely. Vlad was offered our blood regularly to amplify his power. It made him a worthy foe. I wouldn't have stepped up to him the first years he was with us as I saw the power manifest in him. I wouldn't do it now. I was a coward to say the least.

"The Northern King senses a power awakening in Aylhm, one that has long since been dead." Vlad started, "He's concerned that this power may have its own plans, but I have convinced him to rest his search for its owner. Of course, the power is much like my own, I take my own interest in it. Instead, I've convinced the Northern King that focusing our plans on the throne when it becomes vulnerable is much more effective. We will uproot the King. Once he is dead, Ramir will be sure to have won the rest of the Collective over to my return as King. Yuri, I would expect you to follow me as my Commander."

His offer was tempting. Being the Commander would relieve me of my obligations as a delegate, it would give me a hungry power. Controlling legions of Ayles at my call, an army at my back. It would be hard for me to argue with such an offer, to deny it at all would make my chest hurt. "Tell me what will come of Kastell." I finally asked.

"If she does not interfere with our plans she will be gifted to a friend of mine. Until then, you can do as you wish with her. I'd prefer if she was kept safe. If she dies, I will have two solom men to dance around. You know I'd rather kill you than dance, Yuri."

"What will you have the Arvors do?" The red headed proxy of the Arvors seemed comfortable and unbothered by Vlad, despite what the man had done to their people before his banishment. It was a shame that his desire to win the war outdid his need for vengeance. Or maybe he knew that he would never have the power to defeat the abomination that sat before him.

"You will continue to cause disturbances just beyond the city. Make the King uncomfortable. Before we know it, the King will be moving his men there, leaving the palace ripe for the taking." Vlad looked hungry and eager, as if his victory was only moments away.

"Have I told you the Arvor King has returned? On the heels of the Princess no less." The red head added. "He surfaced against us only a night ago. We suspected that he'd returned from Tarem years ago and buried himself in the heart of King Vor's men. He's always been good at deception, but it was hard to believe with my own eyes when he chased my men away with his jaws." The red-haired man looked pained, mildly betrayed. "My uncle is unruly at best when he becomes the beast. Not many of us can stand against him. I hear whispers that the Arvor King still has followers and loyalists in my midst. It will only be a matter of time before I've weeded them out. However, I disagree heavily with Vlad, an untimely death of the Princess will settle well, maybe swaying those loyalists to back me instead. King Vor will become disoriented and the throne that much more vulnerable. Why spare her?"

"*That...* is not up for debate, the Princess will live." I scolded.

Vlad held out a hand, silencing me. "I take it back, Yuri. I might be tempted to dance around your shattered heart." I was a breath away from announcing myself as the Princess' personal protector if I had to be. Why did I care so much? *Innocence. You've always protected the naive and innocent.*

I couldn't continue to protect her, not here. Vlad was dangerous. I would never be strong enough to battle him. He wasn't a man I wanted to cross. I'd have to bottle up those helpless emotions that would torment me after her death. Vlad was right, I'd have a shattered heart, if only because I knew I could have done more for her.

I turned the conversation back to the red head, accepting Vlad's decision. "The Arvor King, has he taken a side in the war? Or is he content serving as his own best spy under the nose of King Vor?"

"I take his defense of the Princess as his decision to side with King Vor. However, my King has spent years playing both sides of the fence to get what he wants. I'll never be sure of his next move. I think he's running from his responsibilities now, or he has other obligations he isn't comfortable sharing with me."

"Then his decision has been made." Vlad confirmed. "It seems to me that you are no longer a proxy. I'll recognize you as King of your peoples if you follow me to my victory."

"I'll play my role." The red head confirmed and stood. "You'll see my men in action soon." The man didn't hesitate or wait for his promotion to somehow be rescinded. Instead, he left with his victory intact.

"This is wrong." I added to Vlad as the other men followed suit to leave. They had their directives for now.

Vlad stood and straightened his long coat used to cover his deformed leg as he sat. The twisted leg was grotesque, but Vad wore it with pride. The stern set of his jaw and the twist of his lips confirmed the pain as he moved.

"I will not have my birthright kept from me." He'd kill every member of his blood if it meant having what he believed to be his. It was all he said before he hobbled away.

9 Kastell

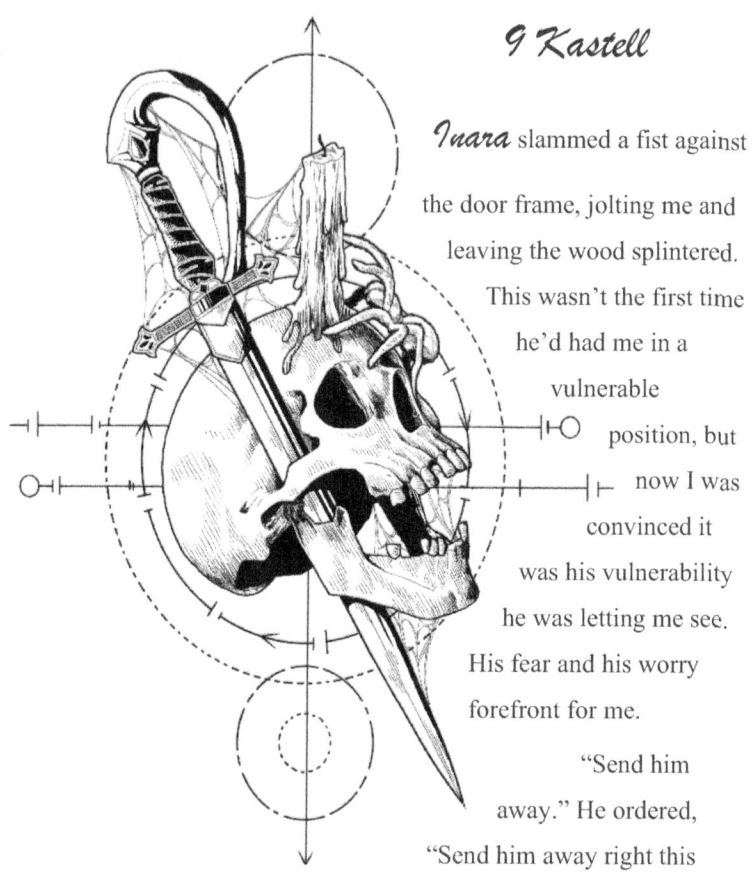

Inara slammed a fist against the door frame, jolting me and leaving the wood splintered. This wasn't the first time he'd had me in a vulnerable position, but now I was convinced it was his vulnerability he was letting me see. His fear and his worry forefront for me.

"Send him away." He ordered, "Send him away right this second." Inara made it clear days earlier that there was something about Yurdell that he didn't trust. It wasn't until now, locked between him and the dead end of my bedroom that I felt how nervous he'd truly been about this. It radiated off him in waves of tense displeasure.

I huffed and pushed on his chest to move him away from my door. "Absolutely not!" I shoved him. "You'll have no part in making decisions for me. Yurdell is extremely powerful, well mannered, and above all - he's not ashamed to admit that he wants me despite not wanting the throne. You want me for platonic nonsense, I won't be an accessory for a man that wants the throne. Believe it or not, that is what you want, you just don't have the balls to say it out loud. You can't even give me a sound reason as to why Yurdell is so awful. If it's your intuition you want me to follow, then you'll be sorely disappointed with me."

He crossed his arms. "It could have been anyone else! I can feel it in my bones. Is that not enough for you? I'm a seasoned warrior. I know how to judge men."

I pointed at him. "It should have been you then. You should have defended yourself. I will not marry a child. Yurdell offers me a companionship that you won't."

I walked off down the hall, but I could hear the Commander following after me. Frankly, it made me feel much more secure. I needed Yurdell to get to the bottom of the impending famine. If I spent too much time alone with him my curiosity would get the best of me. I wouldn't want to spend our time talking about politics.

Yurdell was standing just inside the castle doors. When I got to him, he bent in a deep bow and kissed my hand gently. "Divine, my lady."

"Thank you." I gestured toward one of our entertaining rooms off of the main hall, somewhere we could sit, have tea, and get to know one another. Although, I had more plans of suffocating him in talk of politics first. He didn't send word that he was returning. Only three days passed after his letter. I was surprised, but he seemed like a capable man. He wouldn't have returned early if he hadn't found the answers he needed. Would he?

I looked over my shoulder at Inara. He snarled and gripped the hilt of his sword as he stood in the entryway to the room. He wouldn't leave us alone for a moment, not until I demanded it. I knew he didn't want me to hate him, not any more than I did already. He'd concede and leave us if only I asked.

"Where did your travels take you? You weren't gone for long." I noted, sipping from a cup Della suddenly placed on the table beside me, then one in front of Yurdell.

He chuckled. "Actually, I sent out a lot of letters and waited for replies. Most of the farmlands closest to the city I could manage traveling to, the rest it would be useless to travel there and back. I reach a large audience with my quil, all at once with many curriers to do the leg work."

"Have any responded?"

"One. They said their fields are riddled with rot. Something contagious that's jumping from field to field, but the field hands aren't getting sicknesses. Most often when a rot like this spreads the field hands get sickness as well. There's something foul about what's happening."

"Sounds like magic." I added. "Kendra and the witches I was raised with were capable of raising a rot that could spread if they wanted to, but it was dark magic. They didn't appreciate those kinds of acts. They taught me about them, but never participated in them."

"Why would anyone do that?" Yurdell looked horrified. "They're taking food from children."

"If it's anyone, it's not any of the magic folk I've ever met. The sanctuaries are home to the most skilled witches and mages, warlocks come and go, but many never obtain the power on their own to do this amount of damage."

Yurdell nodded in thought. Staring out a window into the overgrown garden. "I'll keep an eye out for more. I'll listen and watch for this magic folk. Whoever is doing it is trying to weaken the Kingdom."

"It could be the Arvors." Inara said, entirely uninvited to the conversation.

"How so?" Yurdell asked as he moved to the window, watching birds move through the bushes. Content to be here. He didn't let Inara's presence disturb him any, or the hate that was in the man's voice as he spoke to him.

"The one writing the letter could be lying. Arvors have attacked our farms for their harvests before. It wouldn't be a stretch that the farms are now bartering with them to save their lives. Give them food and there's a semblance of peace."

Yurdell smiled over his shoulder. "That's a great perspective. I'll have no choice but to investigate now." He read the short-lived disappointment in my eyes. "Only a few days, there and back." Yurdell went back to staring out the window. "You've trimmed the bushes." He noted.

"Yes. I was getting bored of feeling like a hostage."

"Surely you're not a prisoner here." His eyebrows were furrowed when he turned, searching my face and then Inara's. "She is free to leave?"

Inara looked as if he were biting back a million replies, each of which would justify why they preferred for me to stay put. "Of course." He finally said, the words a curse.

"I have plans for us. I promised them to you, if I recall." Yurdell said, striding to me in only a few sure steps and offering me his hand. "Follow me?"

He led me outside, our hands together as if they belonged that way. My mare stood in the gravel, restless from her wait. I ran to her and hugged her neck and stroked her. She was just as excited to see me as well. She nickered in delight.

"How did you know?!" I beamed at him. I had tried to leave the confinement of the castle the last few days, but my father had been increasingly relentless about keeping me a prisoner, despite Inara trying to convince Yurdell that I wasn't. It was only Inara that would not be able to disappoint me further or humiliate himself with a debate with Yurdell over the matter.

"The stable boy has been trying to get through the gate since you arrived; he came to me yesterday. They were denying him. No visitors outside of the Royal Collective."

"Why would you do something so kind?" I asked as I took her reins and started to walk the excitement out of her. He kept up beside me.

J. L. Cross

"I couldn't part with my own. I knew you would want to see her." Yurdell touched her jaw. "She's very strong, built like many of our work horses."

"She's rather lazy." I added. "Commander Inara," I beckoned.

"Yes," he said sternly, anger still pinching his face.

"Would you mind taking her to the castle stables?" He nodded, taking the reins from my hand. He was probably relieved to have an escape from Yurdell. Just as he began to turn towards the stable, Yurdell was there to stop him.

"Actually, I hoped to put the mare to use." He looked sheepish, unguarded with the way he gently took the reins from Inara, walking the mare back to me. "If you accept, I thought I would take you out of the city for a while. For fresh air."

"That's not a good idea." Inara said sternly. "Your father will be angry."

I shrugged then, unafraid to stand my ground. "Let him be."

Yurdell snapped his fingers and the same boy that accompanied him during our first meeting was there, hurriedly pulling a steed behind him. It was only fitting that Yurdell owned a sleek, tall, black steed resembling midnight.

"Thank you, Famir." He patted the boy on the head and tossed him a few coins. Famir was about to hurry off with his score of coins when Yurdell called after him. "Some for your mother." This time tossing him a sack of coins. The joy in the boys' eyes made the both of us smile.

J. L. Cross

Yurdell offered me a hand as I saddled my mare, adjusting my dress and legs. Within moments we were riding away from the castle. Inara was displeased and the anger was tangible at our backs, but we both paid it no mind.

"I hate to mention it, but you seem to be making everyone very angry." Yurdell commented as we moved at a lazy stroll.

I nodded. "It's a habit I'm making. The Commander and the King are very opposed to us meeting like this outside of the Court gatherings." I remarked.

"*Hmm*," He grumbled. "I am a *dirty half breed.*" He declared excitedly. "I may have heard him shouting while I waited." He rolled his shoulders. "I'm rather accustomed to such judgements. You must be more interested in the authority I have at court." It could have been a question, but I knew to disagree would be a lie.

Again, he knew how to skip the niceties. "Well," I chuckled. "I am, but I want to know why you have no intent to succeed to the throne. You never declared yourself a suitor."

He shot a nervous glance at me. "I don't believe a woman should head the Kingdom. There has always been a male heir. The royal Collective will eventually propose someone more suitable before allowing you to reign alone, or with a boy." He let out a nervous grunt. "The time will come for that. I don't normally rush into those kinds of arrangements. To be honest, you weren't what I had expected when I heard the feast was in honor of the returned heir. I didn't expect you to know anything about the war or strategies to combat the issues we're having with this famine. To be frank, I didn't expect you to take the lead in the issue. You forced my hand when you opened the conversation. Without which I may have prioritized other things. Your father is lucky to have you as a daughter." He turned his head to look me over. "Should I mention that it's out of the ordinary to see an Aylish woman in trousers with her hair braided very loosely? I was told there was a new boy taking to the garden, then I was properly informed that it was you."

"I only do as I wish when I wish to do it. Including braiding my hair whichever way I want and wearing trousers as I please."

He laughed then, the sound carrying. For a moment it was musical before it died. "I like it. It's different."

We rode side by side until we reached the city gate. Yurdell called for it to open and they obeyed. They seemed skeptical when they saw me riding beside him, but not one of them made a move to stop me. After we passed the gate another sack of coins emerged from Yurdell's coat and were tossed into the hands of an unrecognizable guard.

"Are you proving something?" I asked.

Yurdell answered with the lift of an eyebrow. "I'm not sure I know what you mean by that."

"Paying the guards for their silence." I pestered further. "Are you proving to me that everyone around me can be persuaded into doing the deeds of someone else apart from the King's will?"

He grunted. "Your skill at observation bests you on its own. You think I'm proving something by being obvious when in reality I have no need to hide things from you. You're already aware your father prefers you nestled away in the arms of safety. You already know the dangers that lurk beyond the wall, and your recent encounter with death. It's clear that you're intelligent to deduce that all men can be bought in some way or another. Even Kyier, the ruthless Emissary, was bought by your beauty alone."

"Why did you come back so early?" I dismissed what he'd said about Kyier. I wondered where he'd run off to, or if he was safe. The reality was that he was bought with the temptation of freedom, or the illusion of freedom and that was something only I needed to know. I continued then; "Why did you change your arrangements? I thought you would be traveling to each farm. You would have been gone for weeks."

He shifted in his saddle, his eyes barely meeting mine. "After your run in with death, I felt I was more needed here… for you. I wanted to see you. It's selfish, I know, but the letters will carry enough weight to get answers. I was confident in that decision, don't make me second guess myself."

I couldn't help but look away from him as the heat lined my cheeks. He changed his arrangements for me. "That was kind of you."

"It was selfish." He said again. I wasn't too sure about that. He wanted to be here for me. How was that selfish?

We spent an hour riding out away from the city to a hill with a dying tree. Just below there was an elaborate estate. It was well cared for and well-lit in every room. Yurdell helped me down from my horse and took a seat at the base of the tree, overlooking the estate. I could feel his eyes boring into me from where I stood. I was marveling at the view he had here to both the estate and to the city at our backs.

"Yours?" I asked, indicating the estate.

"Yes."

"How did you come to be here? Everyone talks about your breeding so casually, but the Soilts all went North after the great war ended. Why did you come back?"

He motioned for me to sit beside him, offering me his cool hand as I lowered myself to the ground. "It was one of the few times in my life I was truly selfless. I came here for my sister. She's my father's heir in the North, but she wanted nothing to do with it. He told me that I should kill her if she refused to return with me. I can't tell him she's refused to return because I've never asked her to go back. She knows why I'm here though. We both know that it's because of him."

"You love her very much."

He grunted. "Hardly. My sister is a horrible being, just as my father is. She does things I don't understand for reasons of her own. Mostly, she's trying to gain favor with our father to attempt to be in his good grace again. If she can manage that, she may manage his leniency in letting her remain a nobody. She begs for him to choose a new heir. I've come in his stead, and I can guarantee her that her efforts are futile. She will never manage to squirm her way out of her duties."

J. K. Cross

"You've not offered yourself? Is that a habit of yours? First your father and now the Ayl throne."

He chuckled then. "It seems to have become one. My father wouldn't have me. I was the unexpected child of his labors. Yirma rose from the magic first and I merely stumbled through after her. We're both half empty. One needs the other, that's why I can't kill her. I don't favor my sister, but I could never kill her as he's asked."

I turned to him. "I think you were a delightful surprise." I reached for his hand. "Your father is an idiot for not recognizing you."

"I fear he, the Commander, and your father would say the same about you for recognizing me."

I elbowed him gently. "I try to see the best in people despite where they came from. The witches saw the best in me."

"Speaking of, why would you come back to this kind of life if you had such freedom there?"

I couldn't help but realize that even though Kendra kept a steady hand on my shoulder and guided me in the right direction, she never held me prisoner. I came and went as I pleased. Everything she did was to be loving and protective, but my father's rule over me is nearly tyranny. He'd lock me in my room if only it benefited him. Since the battle with the Arvors he never mentioned the training, he felt so keen on before.

I braced myself with the fact I may regret returning to this life. "I ask myself the same question. I think I did it because this is where I belong. Living amongst the magic folk was hard. They scrutinized me and made fun of me, but none of that compares to the way my father treats me. He's made it clear he loves me, but he's not ready for me to grow up yet. I'm tired of feeling trapped here. I want to be useful."

"You've driven me to prioritize the famine despite my conviction that it was only a rumor, or that the fear would pass, or that the late harvest would be more plentiful. I'd like to think you have a use. Not many people make me question my intuition."

I watched the sun drape down over the estate, spilling pools of pinks and ribbons of red throughout the sky. I leaned forward, embracing every moment of the sun setting. The tree above us glittered with the wings of night flies, small delicate things that lit up the night by catching the rays of the moon on their wings. As the sun disappeared, they started to wake and flutter around us.

"Are you ready to go back?" he asked. His hand made its way to my back. He brushed up my column, touching each knot gently that held my dress in place. The touch made me shiver with delight.

I stood as quickly as my body allowed, igniting a short-lived moment of dizziness. "Yes. My father will be upset as it is. I think I should head back on my own."

"No." The startling sound in his voice surprised me. "I'll accompany you to the city gates at least."

"You're much kinder than they give you credit for."

Yurdell laughed and helped me into the saddle. "You're very wrong. I'm only selfish." Something about the way he said it made me believe him. It made me blush knowing that he was selfish for me. I wasn't so sure it was entirely a compliment, but I wished to think it was.

My father waited for me as I walked through the door. I'd taken my time stabling my horse and brushing her out. I wasn't ready to confront him just yet. We'd gone days without looking each other in the face. He was upset about my decision to free Kyier, and now that anger was amplified by my choice in men. I was tired and wanted to crawl to my room and soak in a bath to erase the traces of sweat from my evening ride with Yurdell, but there was no way to put this off further.

"I thought you'd be more responsible than this." My father was standing, an arm braced on the mantle of the fireplace as a fire roared, filling the room with the scent of fresh pine and a burning warmth. "You have made one pour mistake after another. You wanted to prove yourself to me in combat and instead you nearly lost your life. What honor is there in losing a battle and your life? The Emissary that turned to his true form and hovered over you, *freed*. What consequences will he ever suffer? Did he know they were setting a trap? Was it his idea?" My father went silent for a moment, "then you have the audacity to entertain the attention of a half-breed that has only one intention, *power*. He will use you to get to me. To get what he wants."

I placed my hand on his shoulder. "Let me make mistakes. How will I learn without them? What if this time, you're wrong?"

"I don't want you to get hurt." The look in his eyes was agony. He'd lived so long forcing us apart that now that we finally had the chance to live our lives together, he wanted nothing more than to protect me from everything that could hurt me.

"I must be trained for combat. Inara, anyone that's available." I let out a harsh breath. "I thought what I learned from the magic folk was enough, but their techniques aren't going to measure up. I need to build on them. My lack of skill wasn't what bested me, it was fear that did. I never saw them up close like that. I was horrified. All the things the townspeople say about them came to life for me out there. I wished it were a lie, but it's not. Kyier as a man is not someone I fear, but as an Arvor he horrifies me. I need exposure and training. I need to control my fear. I've bargained with him. He's in my service. I'll use him to become familiar with their transitions if I must. I won't let it bother me again. Next time I will be prepared."

"And the half-breed?" My father asked. He wouldn't concede until he had an acceptable answer to all of my actions. He won't loosen his reign until he knew he could trust me.

"Yurdell reports of a rot in the outer farmlands. Inara questions whether it's a lie to cover up the trading between Alyish and the Arvors, or fact. Yurdell will be hearing from the farms, to put the claims Inara makes to rest, and to confirm the rot. He's an ally, but he is selfish. He does things on his own terms. I think if I ask him for more, I can get more from him. He seems to bend to my will, but he still puts himself first. He refuses to announce himself as a suitor. I will ask him. He may not be your choice, but you're not dying anytime soon. When the Collective deem him suitable, we can focus their attention back on this war Where it belongs..."

My father grasped my hand. "We need to open food trading routes to the East and South to ensure we sustain throughout the winter; we need to minimize the effects of the famine before it's too late. We also need to focus them on driving back the Arvors further from the city. We'll need to call on their men from their districts, a draft of sorts. We need to move on from the silly games they're playing. It's distracting them from the danger out there."

"Not having a male to ascend the throne is more dangerous to them. Do this and let them refocus."

"You will not marry him. Promise me."

I laughed, covering my smile with my hand. "I won't promise, but I won't rush either. I can promise that the war will end, or you will die before I marry."

"I hate that man. He's a snake in the grass."

"Sometimes, if you stand behind the snake your enemy gets bit by the snake first."

"The Collective isn't your enemy." He said with a soft smile.

"They are if they keep trying to marry me to a child."

I was panting, pulling on the roots of a thorn bush with all my might, my feet braced against the ground. I'd never wanted to work so hard at something. This one bush was in the way. It crowded the entrance of the gardens and made them look unwelcoming. All I wanted was for it to be gone. I felt oddly the same about Inara. The Commander seemed like he was always in the way.

Three days had passed since Yurdell had taken me from the city. I wanted to go again, but I thought I'd appease my father and stay where I was safe. That first time I was accompanied by Yurdell, that was still more safe than venturing out on my own. I spent each day grooming my mare and tilling the garden. The front walkways were mostly clear, and the roses were trimmed back to resemble some control over the rapidly spreading plant.

I loosened my grip on the root and sat back, checking my nails. They were caked in dirt. I groaned as I brushed them up and down my trousers to separate the dirt from them. There was no mistaking the sound of pristine and well-polished dress shoes as they came closer to me. They stopped just in front of me.

When I looked, I was half expecting Inara to fetch me for my father. Instead, I was looking up at Yurdell with a wicked grin on his face. "Do you commonly find yourself doing the work of your laborers?"

I hurried to my feet. "I prefer it. I hate feeling useless."

"As you've mentioned before." He waved away the comment. "You're far too beautiful to be working yourself this hard in the sun."

"Have you come for another reason other than to remark on my lack of laborers, or the fact that the sun may stain my skin a shade too dark?" I shot him a pointed glare and he only returned it.

He couldn't help but chuckle after a moment. "I wanted your company again. I thought I'd ask you if the Collective has decided on a man for you yet. Oddly enough, they have not asked for my opinion. I doubt they will, being that I'm entirely uninterested in the matter." He shifted his weight uncomfortably. "Anyways, I wouldn't want to steal someone that's been promised away, stirring rumors and such." I could see the wickedness in his eyes. He would do just that if they had chosen someone already.

"Don't play coy, Yurdell. You know they haven't." I sighed. "The royal Collective will have no say in who I marry. I like to paint the picture that they do, appease their appetite for power if it's only by a little." I shrugged. We started to walk through the rest of the overgrown gardens I didn't have the time to get to yet. I took in every branch I wanted removed.

"I will ascend after my father." I continued as I stopped to play with a petal that was falling from a delicate white flower. This was the moment. I would ask him, now or never. "In that case, you can either court me as a suitor and usher in a new era of kingship, a benevolent queen and a *half-breed* king. Or you will fight me to the death. I won't accommodate your presence when you've been so forthcoming about your greed." He hesitated and fell behind in shock at my words.

He laughed abruptly. "You would throw away your own life?"

"You have plans to take the throne. Once my father is gone you will attempt to be voted in by the Collective while the throne is vacant, or you will have to challenge me to take it. Don't hesitate now to acknowledge your selfishness and how far you would take it. You will challenge my right. Not now, but later. You are selfish, just as you said. I've been warned you're ambitious. Why would it be so hard for you to be a suitor? Why do you wait for the fall of my father's dynasty to exercise the weight you carry with the Collective?"

My forwardness raised a darkness in his eyes. It wasn't ordinary for women to challenge men. It wasn't ordinary to be forward, but here I stood. He was a proud man. His eyes leveled as if to extinguish the fire that I started behind them. "I wanted to make it on my own accord. The Collective will not stand with an unmarried heir. I'd announce myself as having a claim. I'd fight to the death to take it. I'd fought for the power I have. I'll fight again, even if it has to be you. Although, my skills would make it an unfair fight."

"When we meet in combat, you will regret not taking my proposition seriously." I turned on my heel and proceeded back into the castle. The game was now his. He would determine the outcome. He never openly lied to me. He told me on a few accounts that he was selfish. I should have known that it came from his need to have power, especially because he was once denied that from his father. My own father was right.

A courtship with Yurdell would prove fruitful for the whole kingdom. There was no guarantee that I would follow through, but I could learn to find more things alluring about him. I could learn more of his secrets. It would take a few apologies from him for me to really forgive the way he had knowingly decided to backhand my right to the throne while simultaneously seeking out my companionship. He was the epitome of a double-edged sword.

Just then a hand touched my shoulder as I was about to walk into the Castle. Yurdell was standing one step lower than me on the front steps, our eyes even. His whole demeanor confirmed that he was in an unusual place of discomfort. Yurdell wasn't accustomed to being in the position he was in now.

The look of a man that knows his mind came to his face, as if he had to own this decision. "I will accept your offer of courtship. Any death would be a pity." There was something different about him at that moment, as if maybe he had decided he was finished pretending. As if the reality struck him, to gain power his way there would be more death. He seemed relaxed and less worried about the fact that I had ordered him to make a decision.

"Lovely, where should we start?" I had never courted anyone before. I had never been so attracted to a man before. What was I really getting myself into?

"I want to take you to the market." He suggested. "I want the Ayles to see us together."

"You are such a powerful man already, but your concern lies with showing the people you have the favor of the crown through my hand?" I said in irritation. I may have let my mind get carried away. Maybe I saw too much promise in his submission. He was still a selfish man and I would do my best to remember it.

J. L. Cross

He shook his head. "You don't quite understand. No one really has." He let out a long uneven breath. "It's never been about power. I'm not equal to any of them in mind, they want a new dignitary, but I have defeated my opposers. I retain my power not only because I make good decisions, but because I must battle for it. They think I'm a no-good *half-breed,* like everyone else. Seeing me with the next in line to the throne will show them who *you* really are. It will also make them think twice about how they treat half-breeds. We're no less than them. We have value too."

I nodded. "Fine, if you don't parade me around to prove something more malicious. You do not control me, nor I you."

There was something in his face. It was like looking into half a mirror. The maliciousness and darkness inside of him sang to me, pulling me in. It showed me a strength I was once too afraid to show others. With Yurdell I made demands and he followed.

"As you wish, my lady."

He walked me to the gate arm in arm, where he called for the guards to allow us to pass. I couldn't help to remember my dirty trousers or my mussed-up hair from working in the garden. There were probably smudges of dirt around my face as well. I didn't want to embarrass him by looking so careless, but he didn't pay it any mind.

The sound of the creaking gate never dulled. It was like the music to freedom. I used to be able to leave the Sanctuary as I pleased, but now I'm nearly a prisoner to my own kingdom, all in the name of safety. As the gate opened it reminded me so clearly of the Sanctuary that I wanted to be back there in their fields tilling the soil and caring for their gardens. That wasn't my life anymore. The sooner I accepted that the easier this life would be.

We were walking together in the heart of the market when he broke the long silence between us. "How have you come to be so forward?"

I answered without hesitation. "My caregiver, Kendra, was not a shy woman." I rubbed my arm. "Plus, I've learned not to hold my breath around here. I realized that not everyone wants to be kind to me. However, with you it was easier. It was strange, but I felt like you pulled me in. My voice is free with you."

"What do you mean?" He asked. He stopped in front of me, placing his hands on my arms. "Has someone hurt you?"

I laughed. "No!" He took in a breath. "I met a guard at the watch tower on my way into town, he seemed strange and made me uncomfortable. I later found out who he truly was, Kyier, the Arvor Emissary. After analyzing that experience, I realized I need to be forward about my intentions or else I may be tempting others to think I'm vulnerable. He learned that I was as vulnerable and weak as I appeared to be, but I shouldn't have to prove myself to anyone. I feel like I'll need to. With him it was mutual, he saw me at my most vulnerable and saved me, not long after it was him that was vulnerable and needed me. I don't want to be in a position of weakness in front of anyone."

Yurdell took my hand and brought it to his lips. He let out a warm breath against my skin, giving me goosebumps. "Initially, I was put off by your candid nature, but it was so alluring. I just wish I could feel more useful when I'm in your presence." He rubbed my hand against his cheek and took in a deep breath, his fangs tickling the skin of my wrist, making my blood hot. "My masculinity was stripped the moment you asked me to sit as your guest at the feast, when you commanded attention at the table in front of all the dignitaries," he paused and looked up at me from under such heavy lashes, "I wished for you to look like a fool then, I wanted to put you in your place, like every woman." He flashed his fangs at me, "I was mistaken. Then you demanded me to call on you in front of the King, and then again when you blatantly offered a courtship in the garden. It's like you're threatening my position as a man. I felt suffocated by your presence. Yet, when you walked away and the weight lifted, I couldn't breathe. I want that suffering as you emasculate me. It's such a breath of fresh air compared to the average woman here."

    I laughed then, covering my mouth as I giggled, and my heart raced. What was he doing to me? "If you think I'm emasculating, you should spend more time with the elder witches."

    "Oh no," he chuckled as he let my hand drop. "I can only handle one enchanting woman at a time."

    Our intimate exchange had drawn the eyes of a few stragglers just outside the market. There were haphazard stalls lining the gravel streets everywhere. Some were trying to sell cloth, others food, pottery, flowers, and even wines.

    Yurdell let my hand fall from his arm. "Enjoy the market, I have someone to speak with."

I enjoyed walking around and looking at the wares. "Have you ever had perfume, my lady?" A young woman approached behind me with a vial in her hands. "Rose water." She said,

I uncorked the small vial and brought it to my nose. It was such a soft and dreamy smell. I handed her a coin and kept the vial.

I wandered through the crowds, bumping into strangers who didn't recognize me. I was still so new in the city, and so locked away that there were hardly any glances thrown my way. I stopped to admire a bright teal colored fabric.

"Have you felt it?" An older man asked. "This is Till, a common fae fabric, it's traveled many miles to come here. You can feel it if you wish. It is very rare." He held it out for me, and I ran my fingers over it. It was so soft, smooth, and delicate.

"Where is it from?"

He smiled and shrugged. "These come from the Fae, but they don't tell us their secrets." He chuckled. "Would you like a dress fashioned for you?"

"*Mmm*. A woman of fine taste." A husky voice said beside me. It was not Yurdell, but it was familiar. I stool a glance to my right. It was the stranger that had given me a coin my first night.

"Oh! I've been meaning to find you." I said, but the truth was I forgot about his small act of kindness. "I wanted to thank you for your kindness."

He laughed. "It was not kindness, it was pity. You were timid and naive."

"Pity?" I questioned, aghast. "What makes someone like you pity someone like me?"

He shrugged one shoulder. "Well," he paused, "I know who I am, where I come from and what my future holds. You, on the other hand, looked entirely out of place and lost that evening. I'm glad though, fate decided to be kind to you."

He took a purse of coins from his robe and tossed it to the salesman. "The teal scarves for the Princess, they bring out the green in her eyes." He quickly left before I had the chance to ask him his name. He was lost to the sea of people.

10 Yurdell

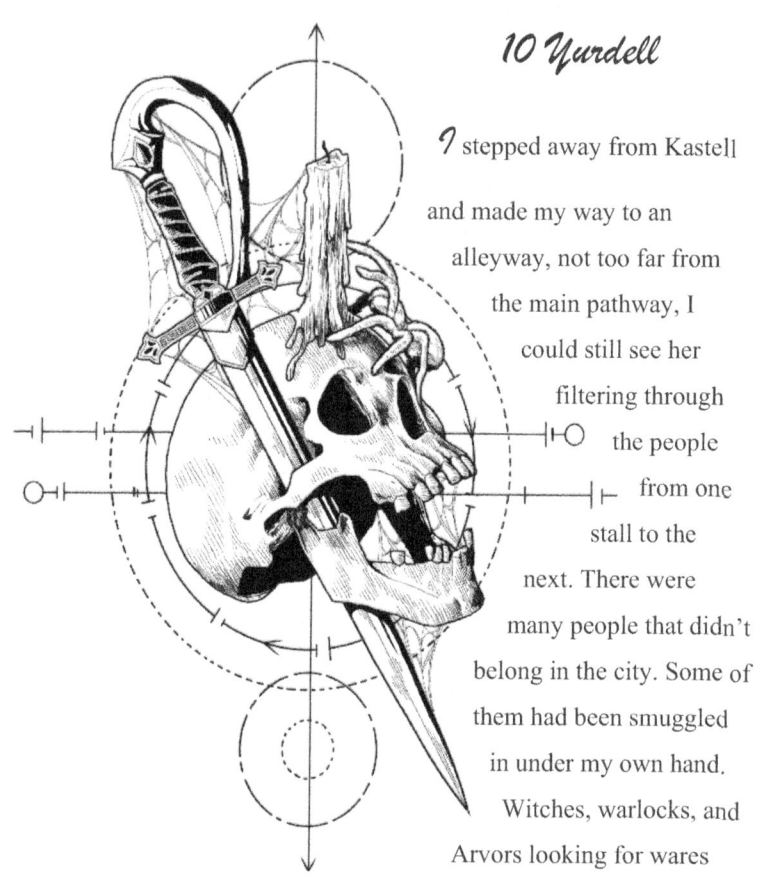

I stepped away from Kastell and made my way to an alleyway, not too far from the main pathway, I could still see her filtering through the people from one stall to the next. There were many people that didn't belong in the city. Some of them had been smuggled in under my own hand. Witches, warlocks, and Arvors looking for wares and foods to take back home. All did a fabulous job of blending in with the Ayles.

The Ayl I intended to meet was tucked into the shadows. His long slender shadow draped down over the gravel and dirt path. He was a very impatient man. As I approached, he threw a heavy purse of coins to me. I snagged them out of the air and hung the bag from my waist.

"Do you have any other demands?" I asked as I brushed my hand against my coat. "I'm bored with this already."

"Your job is not yet done, if you fail to keep her occupied your head will be the next on the ground." The Ayl threatened. "If you want her to live, this is the way."

I groaned. "I am not a slave. I am a paid hand. Your next coin purse should be heavier, or she will discover you, *brother*." I ran a hand through my short hair. The day was hot. "She is very clever. I like that about her. You vow that she won't be hurt this way?"

"She's splendid, and her death could have been quick. I won't make you any promises, Yuri, my sister has a habit of being overbearing and incessant. She tends to get in the way." He commented. A dark sound on the tip of his voice. "Is the assassin prepared? The King will be first."

I nodded. "He's in the stable awaiting your commands. The princess and the King are both occupied. I had Arvors stage a small disturbance near the forest earlier in the day. The way is clear for you. Upon the King's death I expect that coin purse, else the Princess and her new war-beast-pet will be next for you to contend with. While she may be easily displaced, he is another great warrior." I threatened. A small tilt to my lips made my threat weak. Kyier would be the least of Vlad's problems. There would be and the Commander that would lash out as well if something were to happen to her. "However, I pray the Mother blesses her, gives many years to live, if only to have another look into her eyes after she's been made vicious by your return."

He laughed darkly. "With the death of the King, it will be only hours before the demise of his followers. I am in your debt for clearing a path."

"You're welcome." I spat as he hobbled away from the crowd rather than through it. "Tall bastard." This would be the last light for the heir. Something about the air of Vlad convinced me that he was nothing but lies. He would take Kastell's life without remorse. Vlad would decimate everyone that came to her defense. I watched her move through the market with teal blue scarves around her neck and a small vial of perfume in her hand.

I felt a sting of guilt as I watched her. She was filled with the meanest desires, buried within her mind. When our eyes met over the crowd, I saw her desires like they were mine. They streamed across my mind, an ill intrusion. I tried for years to suppress my Soilt traits, but I learned to embrace them for the coins they brought into my pocket. And now as I saw her desire to dominate men that got in her way, I trembled. I knew from the projections that she was a master hunter, though not a master with the sword yet. Her threats at armed combat with me made me laugh. She walked with such confidence despite her lie that she could best me. Maybe she hid more than what I was allowed to see.

Once the death of the Princess and the King rang throughout the Kingdom, I would propose myself to the Royal Collective and all the dignitaries in hope that they would follow through with custom and elect the executive dignitary to the throne. It would be a test of time and urgency. Surely, I'd have to make my election quicker than Vlad's own claim. Then we would have to fight. I would have to face him. There would be no choice. Maybe the Mother would be kind to me as well. I would have to play my hand just right. When I was contacted to set the stage for his elaborate plan, I was horrified that she wouldn't be safe, but was it that far off than what I would have done? All I wanted was the throne. With the Collective at my back, I would do all I could to drive Vlad from the land before he had the chance to reach for the power he thought was his birthright. If I learned anything in my life, it was that birthrights were never meant to be honored, they held no standing. My father taught me that much.

    I took a long, deep breath. Being so close to Kastell made me feel her even more. She was strong, a brilliant pulsating aura flowed from her trying to consume me. It was seductive and equally horrifying. I wanted to lean into it. This was by far the hardest job I would ever do. Vlad said one thing, but I knew her life would be a dim light snuffed by his darkness soon enough. When I stood shoulder to shoulder with her, or eye to eye, I wanted to protect her as fiercely as myself. She was such an innocent woman. She had made herself so easy to compel into my will. With the venom in my fangs and a small glide across her skin, I infected her with a wicked desire, but I had infected myself with her just as much.

    What I had done to her was cruel, but I wanted her to enjoy these last hours before Vlad turned her world asunder. I interlocked her finger with mine and twirled her into my arms, putting my lips near her ear. "You're truly a profound woman."

    She inhaled sharply at my actions. I twirled her and placed her on her feet. "You're a very tactile man." She gushed with delight.

    I held her hand in mine for a moment longer. "Tell me, Princess, are you enjoying yourself?"

She nodded excitedly. "Far more than I had intended."

"You thought I would make this unpleasant?" I showed her my fangs to reignite the venom under her skin. Just the sight of them made her flush. "I think you like me much more than you're admitting to me, *my* lady."

I stroked her cheek with my thumb and coaxed her face near mine. "You're being very seductive." She giggled. I could hear her heart racing under my touch. *Thump, thump, thump.*

"Would you allow me to kiss you?" I asked with my lips only inches from hers.

I watched her stare at my mouth before I smiled. Aylish were so vulnerable to the powers of Soilts, although that's exactly how our kind were made to be.

"Yes," she said breathlessly.

I pressed my lips to hers and pulled her body against mine. She fit so nicely against me. How could I be staging the scene of her ruin? How could I have been the one to coordinate this? Now, even my heart began to race against the cage of my chest.

Her mouth opened to mine, her tongue demanding and soft on my own. She had no mercy in her passion. She took what she wanted. Her hands burrowed into my jacket, holding me against her as if something would force us apart. I broke our kiss and stared down into her perfect face. "How have I become so lucky to have such a wonderfully demanding woman come into my life?"

"Fate is strange." She whispered. Her fate would have her fade into the darkness of Vlad before her life truly began, like a whispered plee in the wind.

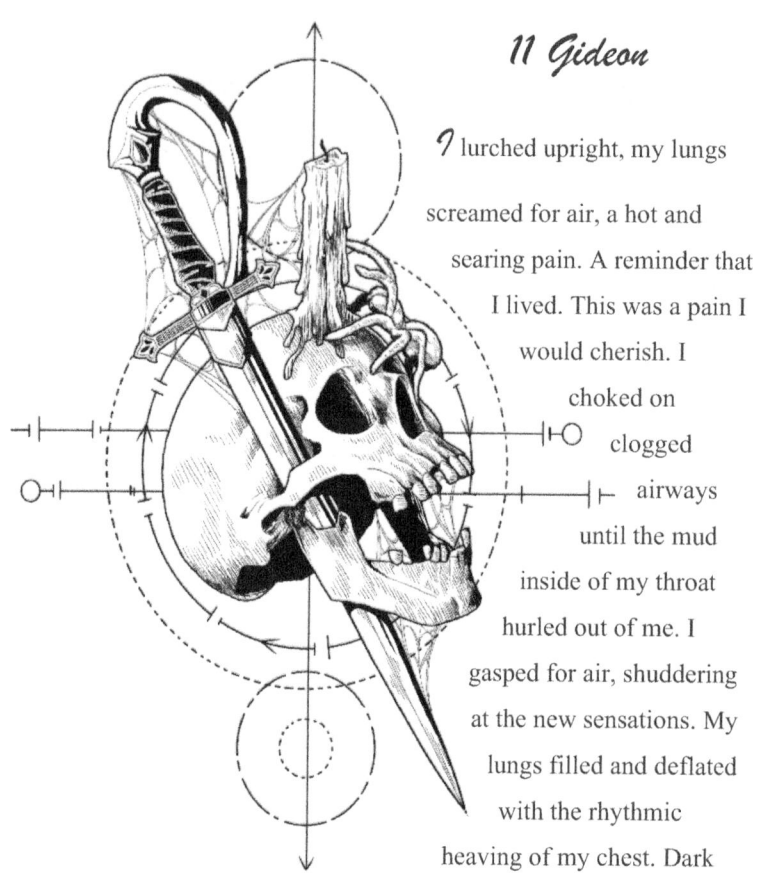

11 Gideon

I lurched upright, my lungs screamed for air, a hot and searing pain. A reminder that I lived. This was a pain I would cherish. I choked on clogged airways until the mud inside of my throat hurled out of me. I gasped for air, shuddering at the new sensations. My lungs filled and deflated with the rhythmic heaving of my chest. Dark mud and clay clung to every inch of my body. It weighed me down as the rising sun made everything increasingly hot. I sat up surrounded by the tall trees on the edges of the meadow and tried to brush as much of the drying mud from my skin as I could while still trying to consume the sounds enveloping my senses. Birds. Crickets. The rush of the river. The last physical memory I had was burying myself in the dirt, struggling to bring air into my lungs, pleading for my plans to work.

J. L. Cross

The sounds around me made me shiver and tremble. It was like hearing for the first time, seeing for the first time, smelling for the first time. The dew smelled fresh, woodsy, and wet. The damp made me cold and covered me in goosebumps. The sounds of birds all around me, calling to each other throughout the treetops. Every color was so bright, the green of the grass and the vibrant blue of the sky washed over me. I blocked my eyes from the sun until they adjusted to the intrusion of light. The croak of carriage wheels and the chatter of travelers met my ears from not far out of the meadow. *Voices.* It was magical to hear their voices. Voices sounded so far away, muffled and distant as if held under the rapids of the river as it rushed. They always sounded broken, but now it was clear and magnificent.

It was the end for me when I died. There was nothing left for me, and I'd gone to my death with pride and without remorse, but now it was a whole new life and a new beginning. I would cherish it. I was a warlock skilled in compulsion and manipulation, showing minds what I wanted them to see and hear. I had never been able to use physical magic, and I was mocked for it day in and day out. That was the beginning of my journey to seek Claret Magic, the most feared magic of our people. Now, with the power of Claret Magic I would live an immortal life, more powerful than anyone could have imagined. I was the wrong man to mock.

I stood up and got my bearings. I never had any sense of pressure and weight as a spirit, everything had been light and airy, breathy even. My legs trembled under me and my knees nearly buckled. It felt like trying to walk for the first time and through a bog of dense water and weeds. After a moment it became natural again, like I'd never forgotten. Yet, with every step I felt awkward and felt as if I'd sway too far to one side. One foot in front of the other. I naturally had a heading. I could feel the presence of my blood nearby. It pulled me and called to me.

First, before seeking out Ethal, I needed to bathe and don fresh clothing. I buried a chest in the treeline, filled with a coin purse, clothing, and a dagger. I had done so before committing myself to the magic I was going to do, hopeful that I would live again. I walked the line of trees until I saw the marking I left. Another remnant of my prior life. The gouges in the tree were way up the trunk, much further than I had expected. The wait had been much longer than I had expected. I wasn't prepared to see that so many years passed. Just how long, I would have to ask Ethal. Was the war won? I assumed it was well over with. I'd never planned to be stuck in the Inbetween for as long as I was. The world changed.

After digging up the small chest I took it to the river just south of the meadow, close to a Witch Sanctuary. The pull of the vial was in the same direction. I had a heading and clothing, but nothing to cease the tumbling of my nerves or the unending ach in my core. Hunger. I remembered hunger, but this wasn't for food. My life was tied to something else now, not something as trivial as food or water.

I cleansed myself in the cold clear water of the river and quickly surfaced before the cold reached for my bones. There was no time to waste. I could feel the vial getting weaker and weaker as I slowly transformed. Ethal had taken blood from it, and once the blood was gone, I would be reduced to nothing. It was all that I had left. As long as the vial existed there would be breath in my lungs and life for me to cling to.

The robes against my skin were scratchy, a sensation I didn't miss. I strapped my belt and dagger around my waist and positioned it on my right side so it would be easy to reach. The worst that could happen is I would have to kill Ethal to live. Claret Magic was very addicting and consuming. She would most likely fight me for it. No one I ever met had the control to stop using such potent magic. I'd take her life as long as it meant keeping my own.

I kneeled by the edge of the water and peered into my reflection. I was the same as I was the day I perished, except for the marks on my chest. I hadn't been able to see them that day. I felt every bit of them as they seared into me, but they looked more grotesque than I imagined they would. Before I closed my robe I examined them. They were large scars made of raised and pale skin. Each one of them left me with a memory of a warlock or Witch that had lived and been consumed by the Claret Magic. Each one of their faces and agony I held dear to my heart. They had paved the way for me to become who I was, leaving remnants of Claret Magic across the land. Without them I would have never been such a success. Some of their experiments had led me in the right direction. Every one of my peers laughed at me, but if they could see me now, they wouldn't be able to look me in the face and deny my power.

I used my finger to comb my beard straight into a presentable manner, and through my hair so it didn't look as messy. I didn't look a moment over twenty-seven. I had remained just as I was. I chuckled; I would be handsome forever if Ethal wouldn't use up my life force before I found her. The ache was constant, the urgency didn't increase throughout me. Unchanging. Something in me calmed, if the magic was idle then the blood was't being used. I could get away without taking her life, if she was able to separate herself from the power it offered.

I tightened the laces of my brown plain boots and tucked my trousers into them. I needed to move quickly to find her. I went off in the direction from which the pull was coming. I came across a main road of gravel and stopped. This hadn't been here when I died. A pair of Aylish guards on horseback patrolled the roadways, the banner they carried was different than before. The men looked down on me as they strode past. The colors were a dark blue, not the Varius greens.

"Ayls!" I called out to them. They stopped and grimaced at me, not pleased by my interruption. "Which banner do you carry?" I asked. Their helmets made their faces look slim and hidden. Both helmets had plumes of long hair coming from the top, decorating each in the blue colors of the Aylish house. These were both officers of higher ranks.

The guard that was listening to me knocked his hand against his partner's light leather armor, who hadn't been paying attention. "Did you hear that? The warlock doesn't know which banner this is!" They both laugh at me. "Have you been living under a rock, Warlock?"

I shrugged and rubbed the back of my neck. "I've been unavailable for some time, now that I think of it." I paused. "The banner." I demanded.

"Kest." He answered. "The Varius banners were stripped after the death of the Queen. King Vor controls the Kingdom, from the farmlands, to the rebel Forests, all the way to the edge of the river. The Witch's valley is between those, if you didn't know that either." He laughed. "It seems the poor man has lost his bearings!" The men laughed, mocking me.

Every part of my chest recoiled at their laughter and tightened with the rising of their mocking tones. I'd changed to stand against these people, but the time wasn't right yet. I'd have to cripple my need for justice and stifle my pride. There were other things that needed to come first.

I did know where the valley was, but it sounded like the rebel forces had been pushed from the valley into the forest and the witches and warlocks were being watched by patrols like a flock of sheep.

"Thank you for your time." I started walking in the opposite direction from the patrol.

It wasn't long before I could see a sanctuary out in front of me. It was nothing but a small village surrounded by walls with one main gate. It hadn't changed since the last time I'd passed it. For the most part only women lived in the sanctuaries. This is where a lot of the witch and warlock history is kept, and they were mostly protected from any attacks during the wars. This particular sanctuary had towering walls made of stone and mortar. The gates were made of thick iron bars that coiled through each other with sharp edges and fine points. There were bushes and flowers growing around the walls to make it look more inviting, but it wasn't meant to be an invitation to anyone. These places were sacred. Only a few men ever stepped onto these grounds and came back.

    I walked to the gate and gave it a fierce rattle. There was an elderly woman standing just on the other side tending to a stallion. She looked like she had just returned from a brief journey. Sweat was dripping from her short black hair and her brown skin glistened.

    "We don't like your kind around here, Claret wielder." She commented without looking in my direction. "Say what you will and go."

    I cleared my throat. What a lovely woman. I could feel her strength in magic from where I stood. She was matriarch here. I closed my eyes and focused on her until pictures of her life had snapped into my mind. I stopped on a fresh memory of a young woman that she had parted with not so long ago. "Kendra," Her name came to me through her memories of conversations, the way it sounded sweet when someone said it to her. "You were the caregiver to Kastell, how fortunate." There wasn't one part of her memory that was guarded. The look on her face invited me to keep searching as if she didn't have anything to hide. The memories came faster and more intense, the emotions and pain. I couldn't quite place where it was coming from and reached out for small details as I receded from her mind. She didn't fight in the way I'd imagined, by closing off her mind. She overwhelmed me and made me suffer the agony of it.

Her head snapped around and she glared at me, siphoning the pain she'd caused like fuel. "What is your purpose here? Why do you dig into my mind and intrude on my privacy without a second thought? There's no regret or remorse for what you've done. You've tainted those memories with your presence, souring them."

"I'd say fate brought me to a good place, Kendra." I smiled, the whites of my teeth contrasting against my bright red eyes and reddened lips. The pain receded. I didn't allow it to bring me to my knees, not the way I knew she wished to see me. "She was the Princess and she's special."

She came to the gate then, leading the stallion. "You can't come inside, but I'll hear what you have to say." She opened the gate and came out to stand beside me. "Now, we're equals. Here I'm not protected by the walls and the power they give me."

"Very well." I gestured for her to walk beside me as I strolled down the path. "I came here looking for a young woman, a slave by the name Ethal, but I think my original intentions of visiting may be suppressed by something even more pressing for us."

She glanced at me, making eye contact. I could tell she was nervous. Her eyes looked worried, but she didn't let the flicker of it appear in her face. Usually, all accounts of Claret wielders were negative, gruesome, and bathed in death. I didn't come here to harm her or to take anything. I was different. "Go on."

"You were the caregiver to the heir of the throne, the Kest dynasty. Magic folk have been very angry with the Ayles after the Soilts turned from the war, and we were defeated. Ever since our lands have been pushed back and confiscated by the Ayles. Even here they make their presence known. The Ayles are our greatest enemy."

She shrugged. "Despite what the Magic folk have compromised over the years, we have peace. There has been no blood shed here."

"Yet, you're treated like garbage. You aren't even allowed into the Aylish City without the threat of death." I added. "I saw you part ways with her. I know how hard that was. It shouldn't be like that."

"You gathered all of this from my memories?" She asked, skeptical. "You must have been a very skilled warlock in compulsion. I'm very skilled in my defenses, yet you've come away with memories to suit your agenda. It's impressive."

I nodded. "Even more," I went on. "I know the special friendship you've had with the king." I was going to keep that memory as a weapon later, but she entertained my need to converse and be civil in the shadow of my intrusion. I'd found the memory of them and grasped it with what felt like my fingernails and dragged it out with me. I didn't want to weaponize it, but now she could see the game I was already playing.

She grunted and shooed me away. "That's enough." She started walking back to the sanctuary. Kendra thought she could escape me; all that I would come to know and the power I would wield? No. There was no turning back for her.

I watched her walk away from me. "You told him his daughter was returning. You warned him. Why? You knew he'd need to prepare."

"That's none of your concern." Her tone was sharp and demanding.

I focused on her as she walked away. "Get me an audience with the King. Within the week we can have our lands, the witches won't be threatened like this."

She turned to me and waved her arm in the air. "When has a Claret wielder ever cared for anyone other than himself?"

I pointed to the guards picking on a few children in the road, taking their ball and tossing it into the weeds. "When my people were subjugated to a man that doesn't do anything for them. Yet, they pay his taxes and let him confiscate their lands, even take their children as slaves."

Kendra touched her face as she watched the guards continue to push one of the children around. "Fine. You will have an audience with the King, but you better be prepared."

It would take me only a few moments in the room with the most important people to be prepared. I would find their weakness and use it against them as I found hers. The end of this dynasty would mean a new age for witches and all species alike.

"I won't disappoint you." I called after her.

"Gideon, is that you?" Ethal stepped out from behind the gate and into the road. She looked healthy and alert. She was far more beautiful than I remembered. "I didn't think your spell worked." She was breathless at the sight of me.

She stopped in front of me and laid a hand on my chest, feeling that I was real. The touch sent a pleasing sensation down my body. The warmth of her hand and the weight of it against me nearly made me collapse. I hadn't felt a touch in so long. My body ached for it. The vial was dangling against her chest. I instinctively reached for it, but I couldn't take it. "Odd."

She touched the vial with her finger, and it felt like my soul had warmed up on the inside, sparking with life. "I'm bound to you." She said as she touched the vial. "I felt this awful pulling sensation. I knew the vial would take me to you, but I stayed here, knowing you would come for it."

"How long did it take?" I asked. I had no control over my fate. Ethal controlled life or death for me now.

She smiled. "Only a few weeks. I was having trouble resisting the blood the first few nights after I left that meadow, so I came here. They helped me fight it, now it's just a pendant."

I laughed. "*No.* That is not *just* a pendant. That's my life in your hands. You tip the blood out and I will die." I paused and took in the features of her face. She looked soft and her face was slim with sharp features. Ethal's hair hung loosely all around her and grazed against her shoulders. I wanted to touch it.

"Isn't it good that I have no intent to kill you?" She joked. a small smile played across her thin dainty lips. She reached for the vial again, this time in a more protective manner, or just to reassure herself that it was there. *I'm bound to you.* The way her lips formed those words and the way they resonated in my soul was consuming. I'd like to hear her say it a thousand times.

    I dropped to my knees in front of her. "Come with me?" I was so entranced by her; I knew it was the pendant and the magic binding me to her. The longer she wore it the more control she would have. As desperately as I tried, I couldn't influence her mind either. It resisted every prob. "Come with me, don't leave me."

    She took two fingers and tipped my head back, so I stared up at her. "I'll follow you to the end of the world, Gideon. I waited for you, didn't I?"

    We barely knew each other, but the magic was holding us together, fixing us to each other. We could have been the same person. Deep within me I thought I needed her. I knew this was a lie and that I was being manipulated by the Claret Magic holding us together, but if I had to take someone, why not a vengeful and dark little mage?

    I took her hands in mine and pressed them against my lips firmly. "This is a new genesis for Claret Magic, what I've done has never been done before."

12 Kendra

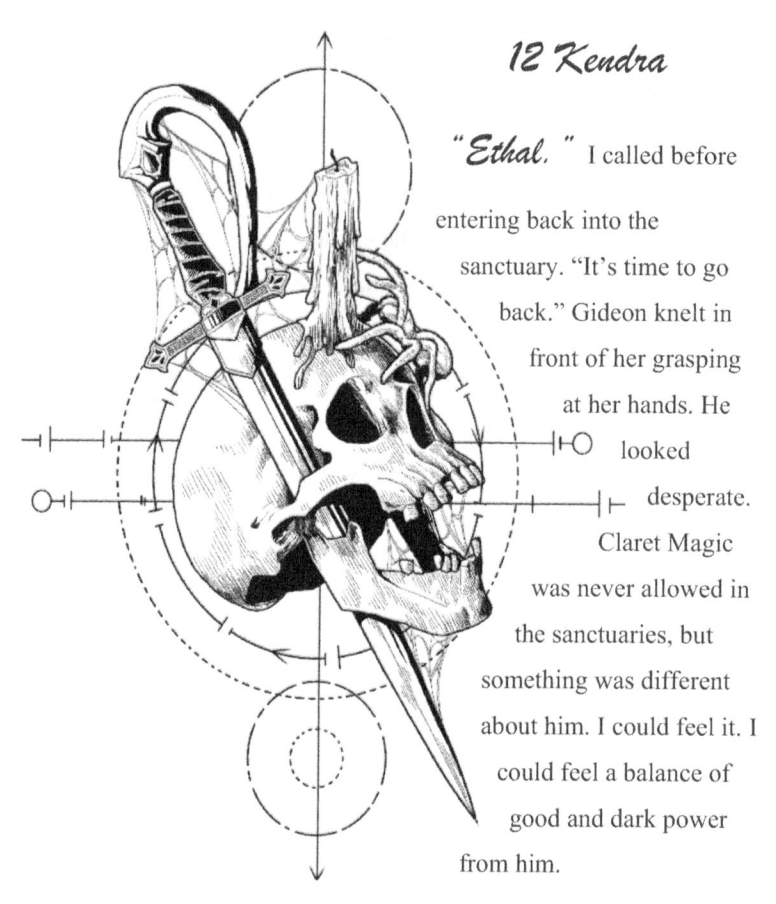

"*Ethal,*" I called before entering back into the sanctuary. "It's time to go back." Gideon knelt in front of her grasping at her hands. He looked desperate. Claret Magic was never allowed in the sanctuaries, but something was different about him. I could feel it. I could feel a balance of good and dark power from him.

"Bring him inside, quickly," I said.

Both followed me in through the sanctuary's large iron gates. Some of the other sisters that were out tending their gardens or practicing magic turned their eyes to us as we walked past them. I kept my focus and ignored their stares. The council would have plenty of questions for me later, but I was willing to face their scrutiny.

The roads in the sanctuary were dirt and the grass in some places was wildly overgrown. We tried to maintain it as best as possible, but most of us were getting too old to work so tirelessly in the fields. One of the sisters was planting flowers in front of the dormitory as we passed. It was just on our left off the main path.

I motioned to the dormitory. "This is where Ethal is staying. She will continue to stay with the other sisters. Men are not permitted in the dormitories." Gideon nodded, confirming he understood.

I continued down the path until we came to a small brick building. "This is my personal abode. I live separately from the others. I'm currently the Mother Superior here. I speak and perform for Mother."

"Where should I stay?" Gideon asked.

I lead them into my home. "You will occupy my guest room for now. I'll send word to the King and hopefully you won't be here longer than the moon's full cycle. I can't trust the other sisters. Many of these women come from very troubled backgrounds, some have even played in dark magics before. First, they'll be afraid, then intrigued, and sooner rather than later your powers will be a temptation to them, ruining the sanctity of this place."

"You can lock me in a cell if it makes them feel better," he said.

I had them follow me into my office space. It was small and cramped, but there was just enough space for the three of us.

"No, you're my guest. I want to take notes of your power. I want to document your story for history." I gestured to available seats in my office. I encouraged them to sit with me. "Those are my terms. You have the right to stay if I can study with you during that time. Maybe I can also help you answer some of your own questions."

Gideon sat and crossed one leg over the other. "Where would you like me to begin?"

A smile crossed my lips. "Tell me about your childhood."

"It was the fifth generation of the Varius dynasty. I was schooled by my mother, and I was constantly bullied." Ethal placed her hand on his shoulder to comfort him and took the seat closest to him. "I was never able to do physical magic and I was struggling to master compulsion."

I took a notebook from my desk and started to make notes. The fifth Varius dynasty was more than fifty years ago, but he didn't look a day over thirty. "Has the Claret Magic preserved your youth?"

"No. My youth was preserved in my blood, and in my death." He answered. He pointed at the vial around Ethal's neck. "My blood."

I looked up from my notes, confused. "Your death?"

"I would tell you the spell, I would explain it in detail, in length, but my worst fear is someone taking this power and using it with the wrong intentions. I'm the first to do this. I wouldn't part with the knowledge even in my final breath."

"Can't anyone say the same about you? What if your intentions aren't so pure? What if this is merely a facade?" I pointed out.

He shrugged. "Only I can know for certain my intentions. It's up to you to decide if I'm telling you the truth. Nothing I say can convince a woman like you. You question everything, Kendra. I encourage you to stay that way."

Images of taking Kastell in as a child flashed before me, saying goodbye to her father, the lessons I had taught her in Earth magic, the day I left her at the tower, and the moment I had allowed Gideon into the Sanctuary. I pressed a hand against my aching forehead. The intrusion into my mind was painful, like a needle piercing through my skull. I rubbed at the spot until it faded. This was just one demonstration of his power. His powers were strong and overbearing.

"Aren't those the memories you question the most? Haven't you wondered throughout your life if you've done the right thing?" He leaned forward. "I can't show you my intentions. I can only show you moments of my life, and yours, that have convinced me I was good enough to do something."

"Please, not again." I begged. "You're much stronger than you think. It's painful."

"I apologize. I'm still learning to manage."

"Let's move on. You mentioned that you have died, do you have a grave?" I asked.

He nodded. "I would like to show it to you sometime, but I'm afraid it should just be the two of us."

Ethal's head snapped to the side, staring him down. "I already know, why can't I go?" She tightened her grip on his shoulder.

He placed a hand over hers to ease the tension. "I think I'll just need a few moments alone with Kendra. I'd like to tell her more about my circumstances." Her gaze dropped in disappointment, but she seemed to rest with his answer.

"We'll go tomorrow morning, and we'll stop for today."

I showed him to the guest room. "The sheets might smell stale, but I haven't had a guest in a long time." I fluffed the pillow and opened the window to move the air around. The breeze made the curtains drift gently into the room. "Let me know if there's anything you might need to settle in."

I took Ethal's hand and guided her to the front door. "Let's give Gideon some time to rest."

We walked side by side until we got to the dormitory. Ethal sat on the front step of the wooden stairs that lead inside. "It's difficult to be away from him." She rubbed her arms, goosebumps raised all over them. "I don't know why I feel this way, Kendra. I barely know him."

I sat on the step beside her. "Well, I'd say it's the vial around your neck. I have never seen such a powerful creature drop to his knees in front of a woman and beg her for anything. You have an undeniable power over him."

"I shouldn't have used his blood and the magic connected to it. If I wouldn't have then I wouldn't have this connection to him." Ethal seemed afraid of this new connection, but she couldn't help being drawn to him.

J. L. Cross

I shrugged. "That's not entirely true. This kind of magic is dangerous and rare, we don't know anything about it. You can't be sure that the vial alone is your connection. Did anything else happen when you found the vial?"

"I just picked it up and he was there. He appeared from nothing. It was like talking to a ghost." Her eyes were filled with tears. "I don't want to be this connected and drawn to someone. I didn't know this would happen if I brought him back."

I put my arm around her for comfort. "I want to know that story when you're ready to tell it. Something must make him vulnerable. If he doesn't have good intentions, we need to know how best to weaken him. Anything could help."

She pushed my arm off her shoulders in disgust. "No!" She stood up in defiance. "I wouldn't ever want to hurt him. I just don't want to feel so responsible for him."

"It's okay." I tried to calm her. "I don't want to hurt him either. No one *wants* to hurt anyone. Now," I patted the space beside me, and she sat down. "Tell me what happened when you picked up the vial."

"It was like lightning in my fingers, and he scared me. I thought I had just found a lost piece of jewelry. But once I touched it I didn't want to leave it there."

I rubbed her back. "I think I know what happened. Old tether magic is very fickle, and rare. It's unpredictable. When you touched the vial, his spirit must have attached to you, and even after putting him back together the way you did, his spirit has permanently attached to you. It sounds like he may have several weaknesses."

"I'm a weakness?"

I laughed. "His spirit is yours to command. It's imprinted on you. You could be more than a weakness; you could be a puppet master."

"Am I dangerous?"

"Maybe. It depends on how you use this gift. Everything is a gift until it's abused." I patted her back and stood. "Try not to fret too much. This is a place of peace. You don't have to be scared here."

I started walking back to my home. I wanted to check in with Gideon and make sure he was settling. There needs to be clear definitive rules and boundaries set as well. My feet were dragging in the dirt as I shuffled down the path. My knees and joints ached. Getting older was taking a turn for the worse on my body. Now, more than ever before, I spend most of my days at my desk or in a chair. Standing was tiring. My whole body was aging quickly. It was another reason I had sent Kastell away. I had lived a long life. I didn't want her to be here when it ended. I didn't want her to see me get weak.

A younger council member came running up to me. "Mother Superior!" She called.

I tried to ignore her approach, but I couldn't walk as fast as I used to. "Yes?"

"You've brought a *man* into the Sanctuary, it's forbidden!" She gasped. "What is the meaning of this?"

"Are you questioning my decisions as Mother Superior here?" I stopped and turned to the tall young woman. "It's okay if you are. Just be honest." I prompted.

She signed. "Not at all, but the sisters will ask questions. Shouldn't council members be prepared to answer them?"

I smiled and touched her arm comfortingly. "You will tell anyone that asks that he is a very powerful guest of mine, and the council is studying his abilities as a warlock. We are documenting history and he won't be here for very long. There is no need to concern anyone. If they have a problem, you can tell them to speak with me."

The woman nodded and left, satisfied with my answer. Most of the time I could easily intimidate them with my position to stop asking questions, but the new young women were more curious and unfazed.

I pushed the door to my home open and closed it behind me. I needed to sit. I went to the couch in the living area and sat down hard. I rubbed my knees as I rested. The fireplace across from me was dusty and needed to be swept, but I didn't have the energy to get up and do anything more for the day. I sat back and closed my eyes, enjoying the sounds of the birds just outside the window behind me.

The pain in my knees and joints slowly faded and I felt more limber. I opened my eyes to see Gideon kneeling in front of me with his hands hovering over my knees. His eyes were closed, and he was focusing. Red mist was floating around the joints, his magic lingering against my skin as the pain went away. It was warm.

His eyes opened and he looked up at me. "You're starting to feel your age."

"A hundred and fifteen is pretty old." I chuckled. "I'm losing my connection with my magic and my body is starting to fall apart."

He sighed. "Everyone dies at some point. You've lived a very fruitful life. You were giving, you were kind, you were accepting, and you were compassionate. Every life you've touched has been blessed. I'm glad I lived to get to know you." He paused for a moment. "You've met me before."

I cocked my head to the side, confused. I didn't recognize him. "I don't remember ever meeting you."

"It was in passing, but you were kind to me. You were delivering blankets to some of the people that were suffering from the Aylish invasion of our towns, it was tax season. My mother was worried that we wouldn't have anything to offer the guards. You gave her all the money you had, and you told the other children to stop bullying me the way they were. Everyone listened to your demands. No one dared to defy you."

I laughed. "I remember." I poked his arm. "You were such a flaky little kid. You were small and couldn't fight them back. I worried about you, but I forgot to check on you again." I caught myself starting to feel guilty. "I'm sorry I didn't come back."

He shrugged. "I think this is good enough."

The next morning my desk was cluttered with documents, blank paper, and custom spell books. I took my time tidying up. I was trying my best to keep my distance from the other sisters and their incessant questions about Gideon and his mysterious powers. They know there's more to what I'll give them, but they couldn't know the whole story. They couldn't know that he had cheated death, or that a dark part of me wanted the same. Our duty as Witches at the sanctuary is honoring the Mother, where all pure magic comes; Gideon was not honoring the Mother of Magic, he was cheating her. I'm selfish for the knowledge he has. I wasn't able to escape my own curiosity, and they couldn't know my weakness.

A soft knock at the door made me look up. I picked up my journal and pencil. "Are you ready?"

Gideon gave me a smile. "Of course. How are your knees feeling?"

"I can walk faster and more upright, and sometimes I want to run. I'd say those are both good signs."

We walked out of the house, and he offered me his arm before we started down the path. His presence awakened a defensive and protective instinct throughout the sanctuary. He still had *good* things about him that I could sense, regardless of what the Mother whispered into my head about him through the other sisters. They knew I'd allowed this, and while they were hesitant to accept him and respect him, they accepted his presence would remain.

Gideon's skin was cool and papery to the touch, and he was ghost pale. There were so many questions about him that I hadn't gotten to ask yet.

"There's something on your mind." Gideon noted as he pushed open the iron gates of the sanctuary and closed them behind us with a wave of his hand.

"Do you ever feel cold?"

"Actually, now that you mention it, I do. It's a cold wet feeling, but when I touch my skin it's drier than the desert." He answered.

The main road was remarkably busy. There were families of all sorts traveling to and from the city. Most had chariots and carriages stuffed with wares they could sell. Even the town nearby was buzzing. The weather had been good for gardening and traveling. One large wagon brisked past us creaking and jingling glass against glass in the back. The old man in the front with a permanent hunch shouted for us to get out of the way. Not everyone could be in good spirits all at once. Not much farther down the road he was stopped by a party of Aylish guards looking to inspect his wagon. Instead of stopping him to inspect, they stole bottles of his wine. When they were finished, they kicked one of the back wheels that was wobbling until it was excessively loose. The man pulled his cart to the side and tightened the loose wheel before going on. The old man grumbled, but never raised further quarrel with the guards.

J. L. Cross

Gideon watched the interaction and waited until the guards came closer. He was about to approach. I shook my head, a silent plea for him to avoid them. I grabbed his arm to hold him back. The four guards passed on their horses carrying the banner of Kest. They were all young and cocky. They sipped the bottles of wine as they passed, pleased with their laborless victory.

"Your time will come." I said to Gideon as I followed him through the brush to a thin path hidden by years of growth between the trees. It looked unused except for the tracks of animals.

He pushed a few prickly bushes out of the way. "Just through here."

I passed through to an open meadow. The trees surrounded it in a less than perfect circle. I let the long pieces of grass brush through my fingertips as it waved in the light breeze. Patches of wildflowers were growing throughout the opening in various colors and the trees were starting to bloom light pink flowers. The sun casted bright beams of light into the small grooves between the shadows of the trees. Rushing water sounded just beyond. I could see light bouncing off the ripples through the surface of the river from where I stood.

"I didn't know Westfil Grove was so beautiful, or that it was so close."

Gideon picked a thick red flower and offered it to me. I took it between my fingers and held it to my nose. It wasn't fragrant, but it smelled fresh, like wet grass and dew. He led me to a pile of mud in the center, it was starting to harden from the sun and turn to crumbling dirt.

"I died here." He knelt on the ground in front of a large boulder and dug his fingers into the ground. The dirt jammed under his nails, but he kept digging until the white of bones was beginning to show. I saw the tears on his face as he dug, lifting each one of his bones from the ground and putting them to the side in the tall grass. The last that he removed was his skull. Gideon was shaking with sobs and resting his forehead against the cool chipped white surface.

"What did I do?" He cried out to me. "I don't feel normal anymore." His voice was cracking through the pain and his chin trembled. "I'm so lost. I know what I'm here for, I know what I need to do, but everything is foreign and strange. The Mother has given me a life beyond my time, a war beyond the one I wished to end."

I knelt to the ground beside him and pried his skull from his fingers and set it down. "Tell me what spells you used here." I asked as I rubbed his back. "If I could understand the magic, then maybe I can help you accept the fated path you're walking now."

"I used a sacrificial chant, the ones the elders use before harvest." He leaned back onto his legs and hugged himself. "I feel wet, and disgusting... and cold." He took a deep breath, steadying his voice. "Ethal used a birthing spell. The one used for the Soilts."

I nodded in understanding. I pulled my book out and started making short notes I could use later for research. "I'm surprised Ethal is alive. I suppose it's your infested Claret that let her live. The Claret Magic probably has some unknown claim on her. I'll have to do some research. Both of those spells are usually done by elders. They're rather taxing on one's magic. You've both been blessed by the Mother."

"I can't leave my body here." He said as he started reaching for the bones. I stopped him by resting my hand against his.

"Gideon, I'll bring your bones to the Sanctuary. I'll have them locked away. We can't afford to lose these to anyone. They're a vital part of your existence, even now." I pulled my overcoat off and used it to bundle the bones. "Trust me to take care of you, like you took care of me." I said as I stood.

He nodded and rose to his feet. "I knew I'd have a hard time here. I couldn't let Ethal see me that way. I can barely accept what I am now. I can't let her have all my weaknesses."

"It never happened." I said as I started walking out of the grove. I heard him shuffling after me. "Let's go home."

13 Kastell

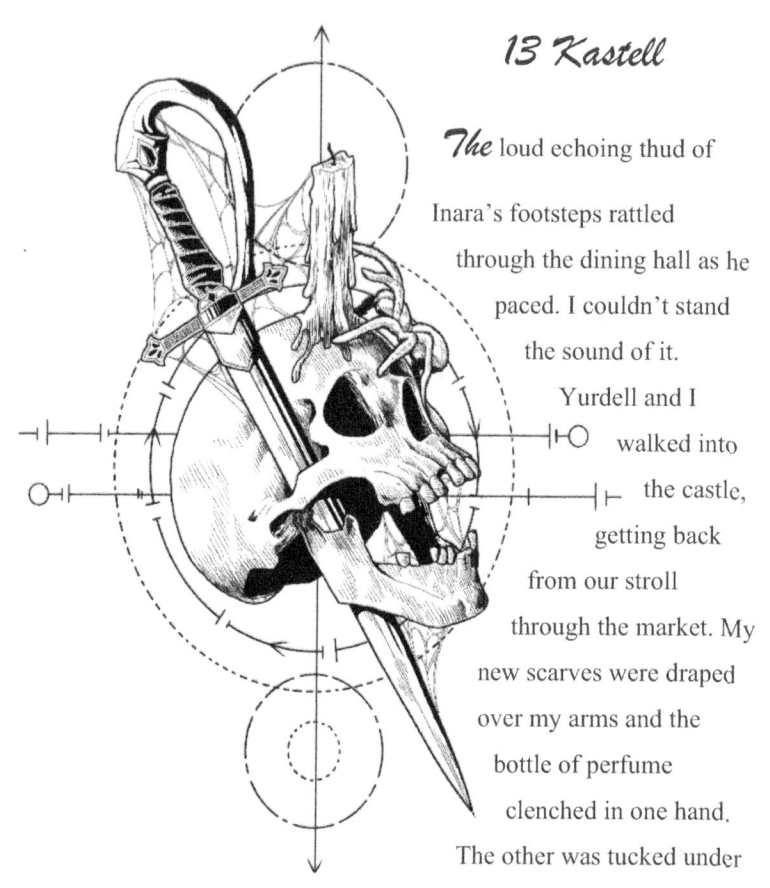

The loud echoing thud of Inara's footsteps rattled through the dining hall as he paced. I couldn't stand the sound of it. Yurdell and I walked into the castle, getting back from our stroll through the market. My new scarves were draped over my arms and the bottle of perfume clenched in one hand. The other was tucked under Yurdell's arm.

I was finding myself more and more attracted to the young Collective member with every moment that passed. I never received so much attention before. It was my young heart that was to blame for my feelings growing at an unprecedented rate. Even though I knew I shouldn't feel this way. Just a glance into his eyes made my skin hot and my cheeks flush. He brushed his free hand against my knuckles, making my heart jump through my chest erratically.

"I think I've worn out my welcome for one night." Yurdell relinquished my hand and tilted his head at Inara's aggressive stare. My skin burned from the separation. I wanted to stay close to him.

I reached for his hand and stepped closer to him. I pressed his hand to my cheek. "Will you come again soon?"

"Of course," He answered quickly. "I would never keep a woman waiting." He pressed a light fleeting kiss to my forehead. Without any hesitation he retreated down the hall and out the main door.

I could feel Inara's eyes glued to the back of my neck. "Do we have a problem?" I asked without turning to make eye contact with him. If he became any more enraged by my cold shoulder, he would have erupted into flames.

"No," he said with a haunting chill in his voice, as if suddenly he didn't care at all. "Should I escort you to your room?"

I shrugged and went off towards the stairwell. My room was on the second floor. "Do as you please. My father thinks I need protection, but I'm opposed. Do as you wish."

There was a stiff silence and then his heavy footsteps followed me up the stairs. I didn't want to make eye contact. I didn't want to let myself feel any sorrow for him. His anger and hate made him this way. Yurdell was a smart decision, a contested decision, but a smart one. He was of two races, he was intelligent and moderately cunning, and he could irrevocably hold his own in combat. His skills in combat alone secured him his seat in the Royal Collective. No one would object to his ruling, not without losing their own life and honor. He would put them in their grave and had done so to others a few times before to maintain his control. The fear he projected into anyone that would contest for his position has guaranteed they wouldn't act on their ambitions. Paired with his control over the trade in the market he had full control over the Collective, regardless of their disapproval. He would make a perfect King, especially one I would choose myself. What suitor would stand against him in combat? *None.*

    I stopped just outside my room; the door was partially cracked revealing the flicker of a lit candle. Though, I knew I hadn't left it that way. Della was probably in and out throughout the day cleaning and setting a bath before I returned. It's becoming normal now, something that would just *be* in my life. My bath was drawn usually just before I returned to my room. It was like she knew exactly when I would be ready. She was a very attentive woman. We weren't very close, but her tender care reminded me of Kendra, and sometimes, paired with my return to the castle, I almost think she's my mother barging in to give me demands. Not much different than when I was a small child.

    Per usual, Inara was about to step in front of me to check my room for intruders. I stopped him. "Not tonight. The threats aren't inside this castle. This is my space, my private space, and I'm tired of having it violated."

    He sighed in frustration and rolled his eyes. "Please." He prompted.

    "No." I repeated firmly. "I'll be fine. Della has already set my bath; I don't need you."

    He nodded. "Will you be down for dinner?"

"Yes, but let my father know I'll be late, if he's even returned himself. The sun is already setting. I didn't realize the time was passing so fast."

"I suppose I can run your message." He said snidely. "Although, last I checked, I'm not a courier." He gestured towards the wardrobe. "Your mother's clothing was moved here this afternoon. Your father thought you may want more of her things. There's new dresses and attire as well, Della has chosen them."

I opened the door and without saying goodbye I closed it behind me. I listened through the hard wood. He grunted. He was frustrated with me, as if we had always been friends and I was suddenly shutting him out. *Good.* We could have been friends, in a different life. Maybe it was my easy nature and kindness that led him to believe we were. Maybe it was my ability to converse so openly with him. Maybe I brought this on him.

Della pushed open my bedroom door and held it open so I could pass through. She had helped me don a burgundy dress after my bath. My eyes and hair stood out against such a dark color. It wasn't one of my mother's old dresses. Instead, it was much more flattering and form fitting. It was more modern and daring. I was partly ashamed at how much cleavage I was showing, but I knew it would bother Inara and my father, so I chose it anyway. Della paired the dress with a white pair of flats, they were new and rubbed against the backs of my feet uncomfortably as we made our way down the stairs and through the hall to the dining area.

Inara appeared from a smaller corridor on the left and offered me his arm, forcing me to stop and acknowledge him. "I'm not playing this little game with you anymore." He remarked. "You can push me aside and be a stone-cold woman, but I will not leave your side. I will be here for you."

I chuckled. "I didn't start this game. You did that to yourself. You're just upset because I'm winning and you're losing. I'm getting exactly what I want and you're not. You were so sure that there was a suitable man, and I chose the only one you and my father truly detest. Now, there's more competition to find me a husband. Yurdell has earned my complete affection. He will not be the next King, but no one will challenge him. Every suitor that will be suggested will cower at the idea of battling Yurdell. I will claim the throne, no one else."

A small half wavering smile crossed his lips then dropped. "There are better men to find and a better match in titles. You don't have to do this alone." He offered out his arm again. "As a friend. I may disagree with your choices, but I will still call you friend." He insisted, raising an elbow to me again. *Friend?*

"Fine." I huffed. Yurdell was a great choice, and my plan to use him until my claim was made was even far more superior. It would take a miracle from the Mother to convince Inara of that. "Promise me not to challenge Yurdell in any way. You'd lose."

"I will make no such promise. Your safety will be my utmost concern. If that in itself is a challenge to a man that has already won, so be it, I will fight him to remain loyal to my duty." I stiffened at the flattering comment. I had asserted that he couldn't compete with Yurdell, but it felt as if he were still making an attempt all out of spite. *Or duty.*

Inara was not the man I should have thought to try befriending to begin with. He's a slave, but a Commander, not of any high station, and he was right about that. His station is dependent on the whims of the throne. Soon, those whims would be my own. He held no lands and had no family name after becoming a slave. His only position was as Commander, his freedom would be bought by fulfilling his oath of service. I should be cautious finding a friend in anyone close to the throne. Inara was right, my father and the Collective wanted to marry me to secure my bloodline. If it was my father's decision, I probably wouldn't like my new husband, likely a pure Aylish child, someone I could easily control and manipulate into my will. He would probably be the son of a boring territory owner or a district governor. Meeting Yurdell had given me the opportunity to make the decision on my own terms. To attempt to bend the Collective to my own will and secure my claim without a husband.

As we stepped into the dining room, I was surprised to see my father *and* Yurdell waiting. I quickly released my hold on Inara's arm. I could feel the irritation seeping off of him. Yurdell pulled out a chair for me beside him. He was dressed in a fancy customary black overcoat with red fringes, the same color of my dress. Something about the way he moved was rigid and uneasy.

My father took his seat. His annoyance and anger were tangible; he had arranged this. There weren't many times he didn't greet me. After the three of us were seated he motioned for the servers to bring in the first course of our meal, a light healthy salad mix. My father didn't touch much of his food, instead he let it sit and stared down the long table at the two of us. Was he analyzing us? After the last course was served my father didn't touch it and pushed it off to the side. I had seen him this way before when I was a child. After any inexplicable act by Vlad, he would be the same. He wouldn't eat, he wouldn't drink, he wouldn't remove his eyes from the offender, but I wasn't the focus of his overbearing gaze. He watched every move of Yurdell as he finished his food. He used this time to determine his exact words and his approach to the situation.

My father stood and walked down the long edge of the table. Slowly he dragged his knuckles across the rough antique surface. He made his way until he was standing just to the right side of Yurdell, making him stiff. Did he fear my father? Of course, Yurdell was in a more compromising position and far from armed to protect himself.

"Kastell, remind me what I said if this man were to touch you." My Father placed his hand flat on the table and leaned over Yurdell.

"You said-"

"I said, I will kill him!" He interrupted. Quickly he snatched a knife from Yurdell's place setting and held it to his throat. "You make the worst decisions regarding men." He directed at me.

Yurdell's forehead was beading with sweat as he tried to hold himself away from the blade, but there was no escaping him. My father gripped his shoulders, holding him in place.

"Yurdell would be a great choice." I countered sternly, trying to ignore his childish reaction. "He carries considerable leverage over the Collective and owns the most demanding districts. He determines the food trade; he determines the worth of our currency in the market. Don't you think my choice would have been made on grounds of facts, not just that of my heart?"

I was treating my father like any of his diplomats did. I could see the steam in his eyes when he noticed my ability to treat him like a King, and not like my father. He was regarding how I could separate the times when one versus the other was needed, weighing his appreciation for me against his anger.

The *King* didn't stay his hand at my reasoning. "Soilts are tricksters. They poison people and things with their venom. They're not to be trusted." He said in Yurdell's ear. "Tell me," He urged. "Did you use your venom on my daughter?" There was a pause, a silence other than the telling swallow of panic from Yurdell. "Please, don't lie to me, *rat.*"

Yurdell snarled and bared his fangs as the knife pressed harder against his skin, a droplet of blood escaping down his white neck. My heart leapt in my chest. How had I missed it? Why was my father always right? Regardless, I wanted to protect Yurdell, "Does it really matter? He's the choice I've made."

"Through a vile poison to make you think it's your choice! He's been luring you in!"

"What if I told you I would never do something like that to someone so... *precious*?" Yurdell said through clenched teeth.

"You lie." My father snarled back. Pressing the knife and drawing more blood and leaving a deeper wound.

"That's enough." Inara took my father by the arm and pulled him away. "You can't kill anyone in the Royal Collective, not like this. A public challenge must be made, and your reasons validated. The Collective will consider you an unjust King if this were how you handled it."

My father shoved Inara away from him. "Don't touch me, *slave*!" He spat, his hair falling to the sides of his face, giving him a menacing look. "You're all burdens! All of you!" He let the knife clatter to the floor. Clenching and unclenching his hands in anger. He was attempting to keep his emotions under control, and visibly failing. He came to me and offered me his hand. "Come with me." He demanded. He made it clear I didn't have a choice in the matter.

My throat was tight, and fear raced through my veins. It had been a long time since I've seen my father this angry. Was this the man he had to become around the people he was supposed to trust? What had Inara done to deserve such cruel candor from him?

I took his hand, unable to bear more of my father's fury for one evening. His grip was tight and cold. His palms were clammy. Was he nervous and scared? What made him act out so harshly?

My mind was filled with questions. The first I wanted answered was if Yurdell was truly using his venom against me. Something inside of me was telling me my father wasn't wrong. It would explain why my feelings for him progressed so quickly. If he was, when did I get the first dose? Was it the first night I saw him in the dining hall, or was it the afternoon we spent at the market today, or before? How fast does venom really work? Was it the time he visited me in the garden, or when we rode to the edge of the city overlooking his estate?

My father ushered me into his office and slammed the door behind us, shoving the lock into place as he muttered to himself. "Snakes, they're all snakes; predators and monsters." He began to pace through his office. "The castle isn't safe for her." He wasn't talking to me. He turned to me, locking our eyes for the first time that night. "It's not safe for you here."

"Tell me what's going on." I begged. "You're not sending me away again!"

"They want the throne, both. I see the way Inara's eyes follow you, and Yurdell watches you like a rat in a field. He's hunting you. They may not want you, but they want the power you promise them."

I laughed. "You're absurd. Yurdell isn't hunting me. I asked him for our courtship. He was nearly as surprised as you are. Although, his surprise was purely because I'm a woman asking for what I want."

"No! He's dangerous. Yurdell has paid for his control over the food trade. He makes money by letting districts starve. He's promising you answers when I've already gotten them myself. Inara and I believe he's behind the inbound famine. We're almost certain. Who else would be routing our supply away from the city?"

"Have you ever considered that it's being stolen? That it might not be him?" I asked, desperate to find a way to make Yurdell favorable in his eyes.

He smacked his lips. "Stop defending him. It's disgusting."

"This is nonsense, I'm not under any kind of spell. I'm fine."

A loud thud on the door echoed through the office, ceasing our debate. My father went to the door and opened it. Inara stood glaring on the other side.

"*Slave*?" He grumbled.

"I'm serious, Inara, you're *nothing* here." My father confirmed without hesitation, reminding Inara exactly of where he belonged.

Inara met my eyes, peering over my father's shoulders. "Are you convinced now that I would never be worthy? I still can't believe you announced my name in front of the Collective." Inara paused, turning his attention back to his King. "The only way to free someone of a Soilt's venom is to kill the Soilt. Challenge him at the next Collective gathering, *or I will*." Inara bit at his lip in the seconds of silence between them. "I will not let him dishonor her this way. Neither will you. We can call an emergency gathering. Sooner rather than later."

It was a threat. If Inara called Yurdell to combat over my honor and lost, my father would lose his finest Commander. If he called Yurdell to combat and won, Inara would inherit Yurdell's lands, districts, and territories upon the King's vote of confidence. My father would not be able to call him unworthy in the light of such a victory. He would suddenly have the worth to offer me a Courtship in my father's eyes and to the Collective, offering a more stable solution to my need to supply a King for them. To avoid either of those occurrences, my father would have to challenge Yurdell directly, but the consequences of a failed combat were much greater as a King.

"Fine." He conceded in irritation. "Commander Inara will challenge Yurdell Revaine to combat." He wrung his hands together, letting some of the tension seep out of him. "We will not rush the Collective into a second gathering so soon. They will be suspicious. I will not let them know my daughter is vulnerable. Not while they're hovering like Vultures."

"This is ridiculous!" I shouted and shot to my feet. "You have no proof that Yurdell has done anything to me!"

Inara shoved past my father and grabbed my arm. I fought back against him until finally I gave in, and he turned my wrist face up. "How did you get this?" He asked, pointing at a small scratch on my wrist with red swelling around it. Originally, I assumed the scratch was from my time struggling with thorns in the garden. It never crossed my mind that it would be anything else.

"Who knows and who cares?" I snatched my arm away. "A scratch from in the garden."

"It's infected, Kastell." Inara took my hand and pointed at the red swelling around the cut. "It doesn't hurt?"

I touched it then; warmth swelled and tingled throughout my body as it moved from my wrist to every extremity. "*It feels good.*" I whispered.

"It's venom. I noticed it when you came in earlier, but it's been there for a while. Long enough to become infected. When Yurdell continued to appear at your call, I knew something was wrong. I told your father. Yurdell was getting a little too confident he won you over. Confidence betrayed him, so your father invited him tonight. A recognition of the courtship. We decided we would confront the issue and let him know he doesn't not belong here."

Inara rubbed his finger against the red swollen skin, and it felt like it was lit on fire. The red inflamed skin began to ache with an unbearable throbbing rhythm. I dropped to my knees and cradled my hand to my chest as it slowly seeped away after seething throughout my arm. My eyes were glazed over with the making of tears, but I wouldn't cry in front of them. Pins and needles racked over my skin as if the blood was cut off from every limb. I wouldn't cry in front of them. Slowly the pain ceased.

"Why does it hurt so bad?" I gasped, letting air back into my lungs. I held my breath as the pain passed.

Inara showed a vial he had tucked in his pocket. "Our healer gave me an herbal tonic. She told me to touch the infected area with it, if it causes excruciating pain, then it's venom." He shrugged. "She has a history with Soilts in the kingdom."

J. L. Cross

He helped me to my feet, avoiding the infected area. My father took a seat at his desk, seeming calmer than he was before.

"I doubted you. I should have trusted you." My father said, he then reached into a compartment in his desk and withdrew a tall bottle of liquor and one glass. He poured himself a glass of the strong, sweet, dark honey colored liqueur. The scent wafted into the air enough to make my nose hairs tickle with its strength.

"If you defeat Yurdell, I will give you a vote of confidence to retain his seat and titles. You will have earned it then." A gift, granting a slave the right to obtain titles was not ordinary. If my father wished, he could easily deny his slave the right and appoint the titles elsewhere. Technically, titles earned by a slave belonged to the master.

"I also want the right to Courtship if Kastell will agree." The power grab. Inara didn't want me; he wanted the throne.

I snapped my head to look at him. "You renounced your interest with a look of disgust and shock when I thought of announcing you as a suitor. What's changed?"

"I couldn't compete with Yurdell's position. Once I kill him, and have his titles, I will no longer be a slave. I will only be a Commander," he gave a twisted half smile, "and a district governor, and the territory owner of the Silversage Farmlands, should I go on? I *will* be worthy."

"A worthy man to wed." My father interjected. He swallowed a shot of his liquor. "Your right to Courtship will be granted." He took another sip of his liquor. "Kastell, this means you will have an equal Aylish suitor and the approval of the Collective. This is an opportunity not to be missed." Although we both knew what it meant for my happiness. Both Inara and I would be miserable in our union. All we would both have is power.

"What if I object?" I said in a snarky undertone. Inara and I were hardly friends. I was even trying to distance any kind of friendship that was growing. How could I live with him for the rest of my life as a husband?

"I'm not playing this game." My father said, "You will wed who I wish you to, when I wish you to do so. You will be a good wife and a better queen. I expect no less from my daughter."

Inara gave me a half smile that looked rather disgusting to me. "I doubt there will be objections when the day comes. I'll respect you and I will not walk on you with the power of the throne. Your life will be comfortable."

"I can think of a few objections already." I countered. I stood and approached him, keeping my gaze direct and even. "You stink, you're way too tall and you're always changing your mind. You're so unsure of yourself. It's the ugliest thing about you. You have no confidence." I struck him where it would hurt the most. "Can you even be called a man when you never have the courage to take what you want? You denied yourself when I announced you, and now, as you scheme for a victory against Yurdell, you think you will get all that you want, but you won't win."

His mouth dropped as I pushed past him to go to my chambers. I had enough of these men for one night. I touched the swelling area on my wrist. It released a warm and hot sensation throughout my body, making me shiver with excitement. I smiled as I held it close to my lips, the warmth radiating through my skin and clinging to my lips. I licked the spot, and my mouth was filled with the desire to be kissed by him again.

When I came to my room, I opened the door and snuck in quickly. I closed the door behind me and lit a lantern hanging from a bed post. I sat on the end of my plush bed pressing my wound to my mouth, groaning at the intense feeling cursing through my body. Warm lightening pulse through me igniting me in a desire I'd never felt before. Flutters in my belly and heat rises with an ache between my legs.

I put my shaking hands into my lap, ashamed of the feelings and sensations trembling over my body and through my flesh. Was the venom getting stronger? I looked around for anything to distract me from the power of it. My wardrobe was slightly hung open. I went to the wardrobe and nudged it all the way open with my slipper clad toe.

The clothing was probably in rough condition for as long as it was locked away, but to my surprise they were decently cared for. There was a small chest at the bottom, still sealed. It had *Varius* seared across the top. This was my mother's. I opened it to reveal several pristine outfits, including a riding outfit. The embroidery was amazing, and the colors were vibrant and beautiful.

I stood in front of my mirror to admire myself. I didn't take very much time to view what I looked like in my mother's red dress earlier that night. I continued to look at myself. Kendra was right; I was returned to the Kingdom as a woman. I continued to admire myself.

J. L. Cross

Why not? Through the mirror I caught the distinct movement of a shadow in the corner behind my bedpost. I stood still and unwavering. I reached for my vanity as if I would grab another pin for my hair but instead, I took an old, rusted letter opener from the cold marble surface. It was long and heavy in the hilt.

It was common for dogs to sneak around the castle in search of food, but my room looked undisturbed. Whatever was hiding in here was probably hiding for good reason.

I controlled my breathing as my heart started to race against my ribs, *thump, thump, thump.* I was sure they could hear it crashing against my chest. I could hear the echoing of it in my ears. My breathing became more rapid even though I attempted to control it. I grasped the hilt of the dagger tightly, my knuckles turning pale against the dark of the handle.

I had my gaze locked on the swaying shadow. I knew it was staring back at me, its eyes glistened ever so slightly. A sliver of the moon was uncovered from the clouds outside my window, casting a ray into the corner, exposing the ugly man with amber eyes. His eyes were black in the darkness and then lit like candles. His hair was unkempt and uncombed. It looked matted and grimy, a shimmer of grease on the surface. His skin was covered in black smudges, and he was missing teeth. This man was an Arvor, a starving one. Just as my own people would be if I didn't find answers to the famine.

He let out a guttural cry of fury as he launched himself towards me through the air, reaching with his hands and nails. He was attempting to shift as he lunged, but he was too slow. I saw how they shifted firsthand. It could be fast, or it could be slow and torturing. This man was weakened by starvation and sleep deprivation. I turned and flung the blade at him, piercing his neck and sending him to the ground grasping at his gaping wound. He slid across the floor and stopped at my feet. Another second of hesitation and I would have been pinned under his weight, missing the opportunity to throw my blade. In the process I ripped the hem of the dress up to my waist as I maintained my balance, exposing my legs.

"Shame, I ruined my dress." I stood over him, fingering the frayed material. He was grasping his neck with his dirty hands trying to control the bleeding, but he was gasping through blood that was choking him. He coughed, sending blood out from between his lips. Blood was staining the hem of my dress.

"*You* ruined my dress." I corrected through clenched teeth. I reached down and pulled the letter opener from his neck, causing the blood to gush out faster and splash onto me. An unknown excitement coursed through me at the warmth of it on my skin, and the sight of its vicious bright color.

My door slammed open. Inara's jaw dropped when he saw me standing over the bloody intruder with my dress ripped open and blood covering my hands and face from retrieving the blade from its target.

"Give me your hunter's knife." I demanded. I had slaughtered enough animals at the Sanctuary that death alone didn't disturb me like it once had. I was surrounded by it in the woods. I knew that killing a man should have shaken me more, but I was unwavering, and I didn't question my cold resilience. Kendra had taught me well. I'd meditate about killing a man later, but for now I would revel in it.

"No." Inara said defiantly and tried to cover the handle of the blade from me. "Don't do something you'll regret."

I sauntered over to him and shoved his hand from the weapon and took it from him. He barely resisted after my skin touched his. I don't think he would ever deny me if it came to it. He was trying to take me in with his eyes, consuming me like a predator, as if for some reason he had to think of me as a challenger. So much of my body was exposed and I had forgotten, but I didn't care. He wasn't looking there. He was studying the calm in my face and the undisturbed light in my eyes. I wasn't to be trifled with. He was seeing me for the first time as a woman that truly didn't need his protection.

I turned on my heel and took the blade to my intruder's neck. He was still struggling to bring air into his lungs. The light was just starting to die in his eyes, and I enjoyed every second of it. I took him by his hair and yanked on his neck until I heard the definite snap of spine. His hands became limp and his dark eyes vacant. I used the knife to separate the head from the body, spraying blood onto my dress, arms, and face. It wasn't as easy as a single stroke. It took many, and ample applied pressure to separate the spinal column and cut through the cartilage.

I stood up and offered the blade to Inara. He was still staring at me, but his eyes looked clouded over with intrigue, the interpretation of a threat vanished. "You are your mother's child. Just as crazy as they say she was." He took the blade and sheathed it after wiping it against his pant leg. The red stains on his brown trousers dried dark.

"My mother was not crazy." I clarified. "I told you; I can handle myself." I said and pushed past him, the head of the man dangling from my hand. His scalp was cold.

Heads turned as I walked through the castle holding the head of the invader. Women audibly gasped and turned away. Most women would not leave themselves so uncovered either. Everyone's attention was primarily resting on the head dangling from my fingers, but some took in the sight of my bare legs, covered only by specks of blood.

Inara was following me with his head held high, proud. Had I finally proved my capability to him by taking a life and without any regard for the shock of others, carrying it through the castle? Was he somehow proud of my indifference? Was my outburst in my father's office suddenly forgotten?

I crossed the yard and demanded a double headed spear from a passing guard. At the sight of me he dropped the spear onto the ground and backed away. Inara quickly picked it up and passed it to me, falling back into step behind me.

When we reached the gate, he shouted to the guard. "Open the gate!" The gate instantly started to swing open at his demand.

He waited in the arch of the gate. In an open spot of grass just in front of the gate I slammed the pike into the ground and mounted the head to face out into the market. The intruder's jaw was slackened and broke from the force of the spear, even his eyes bugged out, the lids stuck open. I turned to see women who screamed and covered the eyes of their children and even men that held their hands over their mouths in shock.

"Let my enemies know my strength!" I shouted. "I am not a victim; I will not concede. I will fight like a man. I will rebel. I will kill." I paused, scanning the market for someone to speak against me. They were holding their breath, afraid of me; afraid to end up like the head I'd placed in front of them.

The stranger I ran into at the tavern and again at the market was near the back watching me closely, absorbing my words. He had a wicked smile as if he enjoyed my rage. I ignored his amusement. "Attempts on my life will prove futile!" I turned on my heel and headed back towards the castle.

"Close the gate!" Inara commanded after we passed through.

The walk back into the castle as the adrenaline wore down was awkward. I finally felt all the eyes on me. I still held my head high. I couldn't allow them to know I was bothered. I only slightly regretted my actions. I thought I had been spared the hellish tendencies of my mother's family, but I was just as much a victim as Vlad. I even had that same rage and aptitude to kill without hesitation. Was Inara right about me being like her? Was he right about us being crazy?

I stood at the door of my room while Inara checked for threats that continued to lurk in the shadows. He leaned over the body that remained, sniffed the air and cringed. "*Arvor.*" He spat. "I shouldn't have let your words affect my duties. I should have escorted you and inspected the room. I won't let you interfere with my duties again."

He was angry with himself. I went to his side and placed a hand on his tense arm. His jaw was clenched, and he ground his teeth in anger. "You only gave me what I needed." I said, "I wanted space, and I wanted you to know I can defend myself. Now you know I can, and you can give me the space I need."

"My only duty now is to protect you. I failed."

I clenched down on his arm and waited for him to meet my eyes. "Do you trust me when I tell you I can handle myself now?" He nodded. "Then don't beat yourself up about this. I wouldn't have come home if I was afraid of the shadows."

Suddenly he wrapped his arm around my waist and pulled me into him in a giant hug, squeezing me and inhaling my scent. He let out a breath on my neck. There was a smell of vanilla enveloping me, but while it should have pleased me, I was instead disgusted by it. I put my arms around him and stroked his hair to comfort him. I couldn't be rude and shove him away like I wanted. He needed me. I couldn't place his reasoning, but I could feel it in his arms and through his chest. He was communicating that he truly cared in the only way he could. His hair was incredibly smooth and silky between my fingers, the only good thing I'd noticed about him since I had chosen Yurdell. All the things I've come to hate about Inara were because of the venom in my blood, or just amplified from it. I knew I'd enjoy his company, the warmth in his arms, or the loyalty in his eyes, but the venom made it all vile. It twisted everything. I pushed his friendship away, but if he won in his challenge, my father would force us together. I could accept him. I could forgive him for our childhood. *Couldn't I?*

I wanted to scream in anger. I should have been enjoying this embrace as it mended some of the hurt feelings between us, but I couldn't wait for him to let me go. My skin started to itch from the touch, but I wanted to be held by him, because I knew he was true to his word, and he was loyal to me. I needed someone like that, didn't I?

He pulled away from me and took my chin in his hand. "I will teach you how to fight, hand to hand combat and with a sword. I will give you the tools to protect yourself. No matter how much your father protests. We should have started after you were nearly killed, but this cements the obvious. We cannot protect you like we thought we could."

I jerked my chin from his grip. "I'm already proficient with the bow, knives, and swords." I retorted. I was only being difficult.

He shook me slightly to get my attention. "No." He whispered fiercely. "That is not enough here. Your skills aren't honed like they need to be. I will teach you to command, and how to battle like an Ayl. I will not leave you defenseless in the face of adversity."

"Alright then." I conceded.

He took my arm and guided me from the room, shutting the door behind us. "You'll stay in a guest room until it's cleaned. I'll bring your things to you."

"Should we see my father?"

"Mm," He grunted. "I don't think an appearance with your father is necessary. He's rather drunk right now. I'm sure he's already heard." I shuddered free of his hold on me. "You've left a lasting impression on the people. What should I call it…?" He cast his hands over his head as if labeling a banner over me. "The Executioner!" I giggled at the thought that anyone would think that, but that's exactly what they saw of me. It was much easier to enjoy his company without his touch. "I'm sure all the women hate you now." He continued with a slight uptake in his voice, filled with unrivaled pride. "I've never seen a woman command attention before saying a single word! Every man was staring in your direction; even they were consumed with fascination and yearning."

"*Yearning?*" I mocked. "I'm nothing." I said with a blush coming to my cheeks. "If only they could have seen Kendra in her prime."

He chuckled. "Every man wanted a taste of you." He said, taunting me with a husky tone. I backed away from him. It was odd to hear him this way, his intent unguarded by the acute annoyance and irritation, as was usual for him. He was being himself, and it looked comfortable for him to be this way with me.

"How would any man even have those thoughts? If I were a man, I wouldn't have the nerve to look in the direction of a woman escorted by you." I shoved his arm. Despite my overall disgust of him, I knew other men were intimidated by him. "You know, this is hard for me. I'm not used to you being so… *different* around me. The venom is making it hard to enjoy it. I think of you and bile rises. I'm in your arms and the warmth is burning my skin with an insatiable itch, but I should feel comforted."

He looked more serious now. "You know that I hold no station? The only title I hold is Commander. If I ever lose that title, I will be nothing to everyone. I know now, if I do die, I will still have room in your heart, even if it is hate. Men have no fear of confronting a man like me. I may be large and scary, but I hold no true value." He paused, his head dipping. "If I lose in combat, it will mean death. I need you on my side. I must defeat him, for you, and for me. I don't want you to feel this way about me forever. I want you to have the will to feel something for me, even if it is hate, but I want it to be from your own desire. I don't want him mastering you from behind your blood like a coward."

My heart ached at the thought. "That's not all true. My father's army would fall apart without a capable Commander. I'm sure he would stop Yurdell's hand before the death blow."

"A commander can be replaced. I'm disposable." He backed away from me. "I'll do my best to defend your honor, and the freedom to love, which that man stole from you."

"I don't want either of you to die." I said in a hurt whisper.

He touched his knuckles to my cheek. "We will cross that bridge when it comes. First, I need to train, so do you. Yurdell is not to be underestimated."

"It's hard to say this, but my body is screaming for Yurdell to defeat you, but my mind needs you to win. You can't fail me." I brushed a stray strand of hair from my eyes. "Do not fail me." An order from his future Queen. I'd fight for myself, but the Collective would never allow a woman onto the sands of the arena. Inara would be my warrior.

J. L. Cross

He nodded and gave me another half-smile. "Anything else I can do for you, my lady?"

I shook my head and turned from him. One of them would die. My father was a stern man, he wouldn't break the traditions of a challenge, not a proper challenge. The Collective would get what they wanted, two suitors fighting for the right to the throne. I wanted to fight for myself, but my heart skipped, I wasn't sure I could, not in my condition. Not when every part of me yearned to please the man that was probably plotting and cowering in his estate far outside the city.

I sat at the vanity in the guest room staring at my reflection. I was covered in blood. What was so attractive about this to any man? It was dirty and unfeminine. Most women don't get so disheveled, maybe that was the whole allure to it.

I began unclasping the buttons down the front. Inara would be returning soon with clothing for me. I missed our horrible bantering when it was slightly less laced with hostility and hate. I wanted things to be more like they were earlier when he felt no need to hide himself behind his stern set jaw and clouded eyes.

Every time I closed my eyes, I saw Yurdell and the flash of his fangs. With every fiber of my being, I had to resist the urge to put my wrist to my lips and drown in the sensations it gave to me. Were these images he was sending to me from so far away, or was it just a condition of the venom?

The door to the room burst in. The disturbance in the silence jolted me out of my seat. My breasts were nearly exposed entirely as the material was pulling away after the buttons had been undone. I crossed my arms over my chest to hide some of the exposure.

"Couldn't you knock first?!" I shouted.

He swallowed his surprise and quickly closed his gaping mouth and tried not to let his eyes wander. "I apologize, I suppose I should have knocked. It was quiet, I was afraid something happened to you."

For a moment I was angry, but I tried to suffocate that feeling as I buttoned myself back up. When Yurdell died I would be released of the feelings I was being drowned in, allowing me to feel something new. I turned my back to him and started taking the pins out of my hair, the golden white locks fell to my shoulders with a light bounce.

"Would you need anything else from me?" He asked.

I laughed. "Why? You're not a currier, but suddenly you'll do anything at my beck and call?" I peered over my shoulder, but I didn't make eye contact. I didn't want to feel the venom rush through me like a hot molten lava trying to consume me.

"Not at all." He left the door open behind him and walked to me, laying the clothes he had brought on the vanity table. He walked away from me, standing a bit away, reconfirming his platonic intent. "I admit, I could leave, but that would ruin my evening. I enjoy your hostile company. I don't really have much else to look forward to recently."

"Why is it so hard to fight the venom?" I asked.

He chuckled. His eyes didn't linger over my body or try to seduce me. He made no move to touch me, and I still had the urge to run from him, reinforced by the venom in my blood, but I fought it.

Inara mulled over what he was thinking, chewing at the inside of his lip before answering. "Venom is like a brand, but more intrusive. It tells you what's good for you, what's bad for you, what you can and cannot have, and above all it's a stamp of ownership. It's connected to him and as long as he's alive everything will be hard for you."

Inara sat heavily into a chair that was positioned next to the balcony. He was watching me, waiting for me to go on, to confide in him more. This is what friends do, isn't it?

"I hate this. I want to be free to feel the way I want to, to make the choices I want to. I thought I was. I thought I chose him with logic, not because some infection inside me convinced me to."

"It could have been a combination of both. We make mistakes. We choose the wrong paths to follow. I chose Vlad once, and here we are. I want that man to be struck dead by lightning, or by my sword."

I shrugged. "I think everyone here would want that. It's hard to believe you, that you think choosing to follow Vald was a mistake. He was ruthless, and I can still see that same bit of him in you now." I sat into the chair at my vanity and brushed out my hair as we talked. Surprisingly, this kind of friendship was nice.

He chuckled. "And… with Soilt venom inside of you and taking the head of an intruder, you think you're nothing like us? Your mother's blood is strong in her children. You can't deny that you and he are very similar, even if you bury it. I'm just like him because I've been around him too much."

"Do you think your *ruthlessness* will give you an edge against Yurdell?" His face seemed to drop when he was forced to think about it. "I doubt any man will stand long against you." I lied. I wanted him to feel that I was behind him, that I supported him. Part of me really did, but the fact remained, Yurdell hadn't lost to any opponent in all the years he was seated in the Collective.

"Bite your tongue. There are plenty of fine men in the Collective that can hold their own against me. I'd be foolish to doubt them. Yurdell is a very skilled warrior." He affirmed my own thoughts. "But I can take him. Negativity won't get us anywhere."

"I think after this trial you will have your head so far up your own ass that I'll have to pull it out of you."

He laughed. A sincere smile crossed his lips. "We'll see about that." He joked back and closed the door behind him as he left. The only sound remaining was of the wick in the lantern crackling.

I dipped myself into a bath that a servant prepared for me. They had infused the water with fresh lavender, mint, and salts. My body started to relax as I leaned into the comfort of its warm embrace. I closed my eyes and as I sat there, all I could think about was Yurdell's smile, his smell, and how his laughter was more satisfying to listen to than anyone else's. I was consumed by him. I still wanted him despite the knowledge I had of him and the betrayal he'd left me with.

14 Yurdell

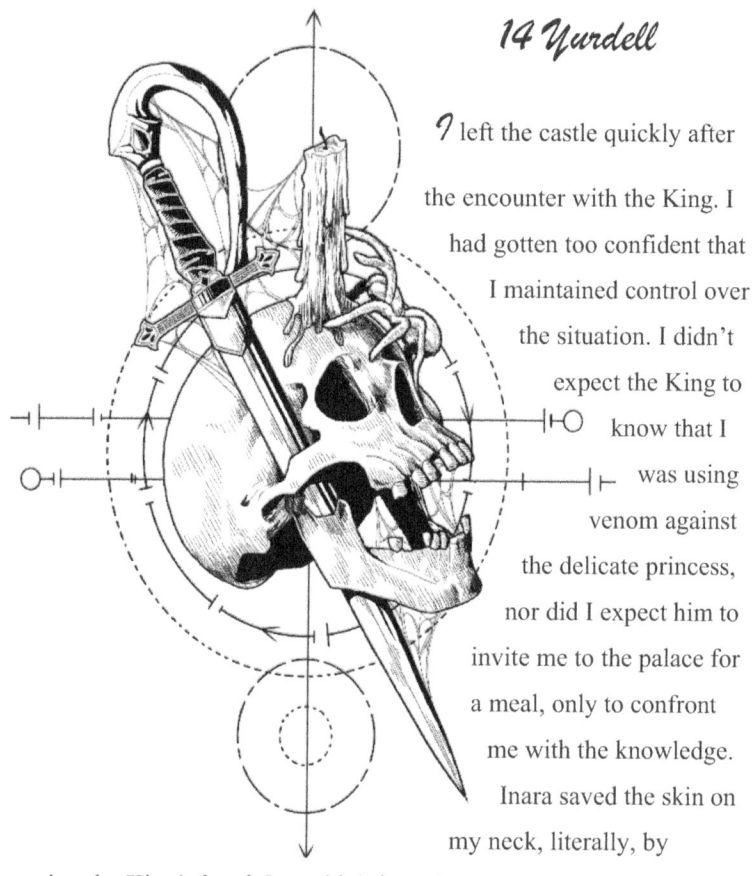

I left the castle quickly after the encounter with the King. I had gotten too confident that I maintained control over the situation. I didn't expect the King to know that I was using venom against the delicate princess, nor did I expect him to invite me to the palace for a meal, only to confront me with the knowledge. Inara saved the skin on my neck, literally, by staying the King's hand. I wouldn't have long before I was confronted legally in front of the Collective. I made the wound discrete. I knew Inara was looking for it, inspecting her for it to know it was there. He needed a way to turn the King in his favor, it interrupted the love his daughter was finding. I was betrayed by who I thought was my ally. The very man Vlad would have us trust, but even Inara put himself before Vlad's plan. He was willing to disrupt it only because he didn't want to see Kastell with another man, ploy or no ploy.

J. L. Cross

I passed through the gate and went to the tavern. I wiped the back of my arm across my neck to get rid of the blood dripping from the healing wound. I needed to feed. The anger and the desperate need to feel control again was making me uncontrollably hungry. The streets were busy tonight during such a cloudy night. It was strange, but the lively atmosphere guaranteed I would be able to catch a meal if I needed to. I would first call those I had infected, bringing them to me with only the sound in their ears and minds.

The tavern was busy, flowing over the brim of the door with locals. My Arvor contact was playing a daring game of chance with dice surrounded by gamblers. His opponent was slowly catching him in the race to victory. A pile of coins in the center of the table was growing. I tugged on the arm of his cloak to catch his attention. He gave me a lighthearted smile, only weavering a heartbeat when he recognized me.

"Excuse me gentleman; duty calls." He took three coins from the center. The men went into an uproar of protests as he walked away from the game. He threw an arm over my shoulder as we shuffled our way out of the crammed tavern. I could smell the heavy scent of cherry alcohol spilling from his breath over my face. His red hair was disheveled, and his beard had wet droplets of either sweat or beer clinging to the ends of its roughness.

I dragged him out into the street and threw him in the dirt. "You're a disgrace." I said and kicked him. "What're you doing here? You haven't paid your dues, Aluxious; if you want, I can put the Aylish guards onto your trail, and we both know how much you hate running from those bastards."

"Give it a rest, *Yuri*." He placed the three coins into my outstretched hand. "I always pay."

I rolled my eyes. "What are you doing here? You've been here several days in a row; it's not a very safe practice for you these days." I couldn't help but sound as tired and annoyed with him as I felt. I needed to tell him my plot with the princess was discovered and that the safety of the city for his people would soon be gone. They wouldn't even be able to pay their way in if I was removed.

"I came to see if the old Arvor I sent your way actually did his deed." Aluxious laughed sarcastically. "I bet he shakes to the bone and trembles with disgust. There's no way he can do what he was needed for. He gets lost looking for his own cabin." Aluxious was chuckling as he rubbed his beard. "He was a disposable addict, and I would be surprised if he succeeds in his quest." He glanced me over and took in my distress. "We both know that mutt failed. No need for us to dance around the conversation I suppose."

I groaned. "What the hell!" I kick his leg again. "I gave her venom! I risked everything. Yet your profound mistake has secured the King's life and the Commander has rooted out my plans against them."

"Oh." Aluxious sucked in a breath through his teeth. "*Thss*", he laughed out through gritted teeth. "You're going to die, or worse, you'll win, and the King will have to surrender his sword in a duel with you, forcing you to do Vlad's job, killing the King, cementing his future as King. Anyhow, why would you use venom?" He asked, dumbfounded.

"She's very stubborn, and she thinks she could take the throne without a man. I needed to turn her attention solely on me, convincing her that she needed me. I did my job," I sat beside him, "and you failed to do yours. The King should be dead." I kicked a few stones out from under my heels. "I heard them, I'm going to be challenged."

Aluxious put a hand on my back as if to comfort me.

I grimaced. "Why couldn't you pull through with someone more capable? You could have done it yourself. At least then the part I played would have been of more use."

"Well, because I won't send someone to do my dirty work for me. Vlad lost my respect the moment he contracted everyone with fear and coins. For the means to win my war I won't let Vlad do it for me. I don't need him, no one does." He stood up, looking down on me. "She doesn't deserve the war her father and I have, nor does she deserve that hideous brother of hers. When I make my move to end this war it will be of a more diplomatic nature."

I stood up beside him and accompanied him to the main city gate. "What now?"

He pulled his hood up over his head. "You can win your trial by combat. We'll find another way. Maybe Vlad will send your sister's goons to kill us now that we've failed him, or maybe life will go on and we will remain the lost losers. Assassinating the King isn't the way. Whose idea was this again? Oh, that's right… a half mangled angry child." Aluxious didn't know the first thing about Vlad, or the power my father had given him over the years in his banishment. He was truly meant to be feared and Aluxious would never understand.

I smiled. "You know he planned this. Don't be delusional. I wouldn't have dared to take on this plot if I would have known you wouldn't follow through."

Aluxious laughed with his chin turned to the sky. "I'm the proxy King of the Arvors! When would I have ever followed through with an Aylish plan, especially an Ayl I don't know? I have no interest in his war."

"We thought you wanted to win the war." I pointed out. "If you're not on Vlad's side by the end of all of this he'll be after you and all of your people. Don't dismiss me! You know in your gut he's going to get what he wants, and when he does, we need to be on his side to live."

He nodded. "I do want to win… but I like the princess and I like fighting my own battles. She's grown on me. Ask her if she admires the teal scarves. They cost me a fifth coin and a double shot of liquor at the tavern. Not to mention, I think blood red and teal are rather complimentary."

I slapped him on the back of the head lightly. "What the hell! Stay away from her! You're going to blow your cover here. Stop being so careless. I wondered who bought them for her when I had my back turned. I should have known." I snapped.

Aluxious rubbed the back of his head. "Listen Yurdell, she's lovely. She's hard to resist. Not everyone is a *fairy*."

"Eat your words." I said with spite. "I'm not just into men. I kind of like her. I'm tempted by everyone all the same. The venom makes it worse."

"*Oooo*," Aluxious chuckled. "Well, be careful, too many men vying after her and she might explode!" He gestured with his hands, his head exploding. "*Poof.*"

Aluxious started to walk away down the path leading away from the city. "Aluxious!" I called after him. He stopped his staggering walk to look back at me. "You can't have her, it's impossible."

Aluxious started laughing like a madman. "Fate might say otherwise!" He shouted as he started running down the muddy path like a child, twirling in circles. I knew he said it to irritate me, if for no other reason. After a short while into the darkness, he let his hood fall and walked slowly off like an average man. For a man with a war, Aluxious was a free soul.

A masculine hand touched my shoulder tenderly, making me turn around. "Thane." I said softly. He was one of my *familiars*. I wasn't confused about my sexuality; I just didn't care for gender to define how I picked my suitors.

"You look hungry." Thane said as he took my hand. "Would you like to feed? I heard your call."

I couldn't say I wasn't hungry, I needed to feed. I nodded eagerly. "This will be the last time. I need to start cutting my ties." I said bluntly. I had to start letting them go, all of them. Inara would defeat me in combat, and there was no way I could win against him. I'd fought my way to my success over the years, but none had been

Commanders or trained in the art of the sword. My death would free them of me, or I could do it myself, freeing them of all their miseries. I could free them with death, leading them into the afterlife to be with me.

    I pulled the small fragile man into an ally between a few worn down homes in the lower district near the gate. I turned him away from me and brushed his long gray hair away from his neck. He was an older Ayl that was desperate for affection, which led him looking for Soilts to fill his void. Of course, I was happy to oblige.

    Aylish blood was powerful and lasted longer than a human's or a witch. Most of my familiars were small Aylish men. I laid my forearm across his upper chest and held his shoulder. The first puncture always hurts the worst. He let out a small yelp as my fangs pierced a soft spot in his neck. I filled his mind with pictures of the wildflower fields outside of the city, and the horses in his barn. I let him see my memories inside the castle, how the walls were decorated, and the carpet was laid throughout the halls in blues and reds. I let him see the banners in the dining halls hanging proudly from the ceiling. I showed him the overgrown gardens and the roses that were spilling over the walls. Thane always wanted to see the inside of the castle.

    As he became weaker, I had to sink to the ground on one knee to hold him in my arms tightly. His life force slipped out of him and the connection I had with his mind faded into a dark void. I released him and let his body fall to the ground.

J. L. Cross

"Very nice of you." *It was him.* My once ally. He betrayed me and set me on a path to my death and here he came, to seek counsel with me. I wished he would disappear into thin air.

"I won't let him suffer the agony of my death, I will let him die the peaceful way, remaining in touch with my mind to take to the next life," I said.

"Yes, because death is better than a period of mild pain." The Ayl taunted. "They'll live through it, you're just greedy and want to take them with you, like old human Kings. Disgraceful and greedy."

I nodded. "I think that's part of it. They're so willing."

Inara moved closer to me. I backed away slightly. I couldn't trust him. "Your contact gave us a sorry excuse for an assassin. He reeked of bile, sweat, and dirt. A total disgrace to the Arvor name. I think that's the exact reason why we think so little of them. Now that they failed, the princess is alive, and I must alter my plans. If I simply assassinate the king then she will ascend, so now I must force her to ascend with me at her side. I wished to keep her platonic, and when Vlad becomes King, I would have been gifted her as a pet, but now things must change."

"The Arvor King proxy seems to think he has a chance with the Princess as well. Although, I think he likes her to some degree, or only for her courage. How about you? Do you deserve her?" I placed Thane's arms on his shallow chest with his hands folded and closed his eyes. He was a victim of the famine that we were bringing to the city. The famine we had planned to weaken the Kingdom for Vlad.

Inara laughed. "No. I don't deserve her, but she's so attractive it's hard not to be a savage with her. I'll hold back, until the time is right. I might learn to genuinely care for her. Once the trial is over and your death is set, there won't be much in my way anymore. I'll be training, so you might as well."

I walked over to him and bared my fangs. "Don't be so cocky, it's unattractive on such a handsome man."

"Are you flirting with me, Yuri?" He smirked. "You're a tiny little man with nothing to offer; except for a corpse for the princess to cry over."

I grabbed his arm and jerked him forward and planted my fangs into his arm. He pushed me off and drew his sword. His mind was starting to fill with images of me. "How dare you!" He yelled.

I laughed at him as I used my finger to brush the blood around my lips into my mouth. "You taste like a sweet plain ordinary Ayl to me, nothing spectacular." I moaned as I sucked the blood from my fingers. "You're nothing special. You're a traitor to those you've allied with for only your own gain."

He sheathed his sword. "You'll meet your end."

I shrugged. "*We all die some time.*" I smiled up into the sky as I repeated the words Aluxious had said to me. "Better go find the healer before the end of an hour or she won't be able to get all the venom out. *Tic-Toc, Tic-Toc.*" I taunted him.

The more I feed the stronger I become. I could use this strength, but it was daunting to think I'd have to fight to the death with Inara. He was a powerful man, and large. I could hope for the best and feed until I was plump with blood, but the outcome of our duel wouldn't be easily swayed in my favor. I'd need to train.

15 Gideon

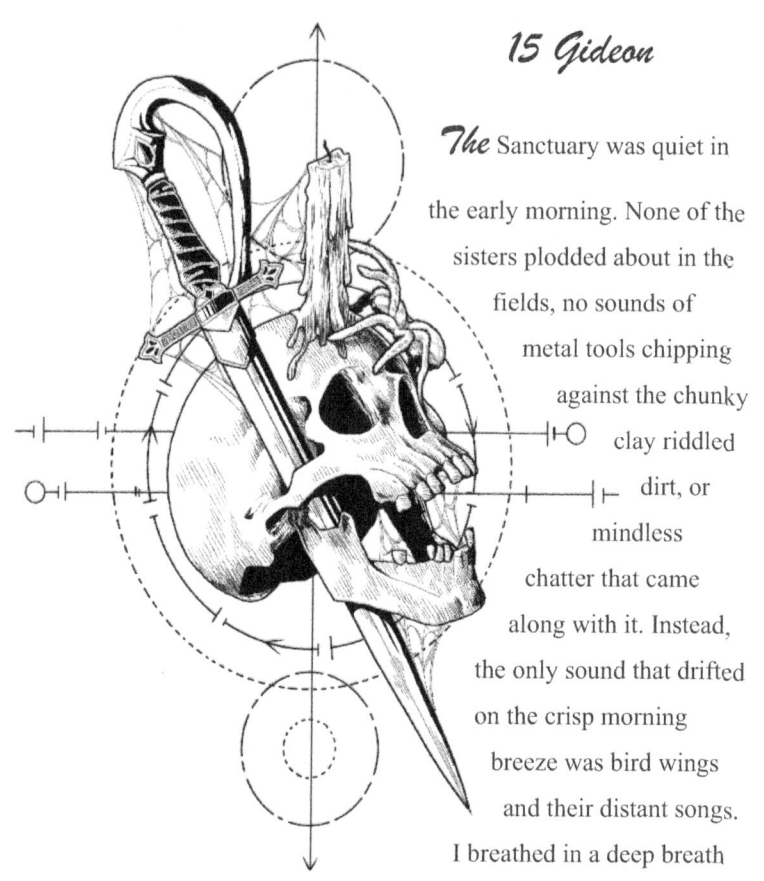

The Sanctuary was quiet in the early morning. None of the sisters plodded about in the fields, no sounds of metal tools chipping against the chunky clay riddled dirt, or mindless chatter that came along with it. Instead, the only sound that drifted on the crisp morning breeze was bird wings and their distant songs. I breathed in a deep breath and turned my face up to the warm opening morning sky. I enjoyed the sun more than I did before my death. I appreciated its radiant presence more than ever. These were the times I felt most alive. I listened faintly to the sound of rustling tree branches and cascading leaves.

I've learned to settle during my meditation routines. Kendra taught me true meditation to help become more present, to feel myself in this reality, despite not being more than an empty shell. It aided in separating my consciousness from the Claret Magic. The clammy texture of my skin and the wet feeling that clung to me would slowly disappear while I meditated. It made me more ready for the day to come. Most of the time I felt like half a man. I was barely able to struggle through. I was clinging to Ethal, trying to siphon her energy as my own, and for a few days it wore us down to the core. She tried to keep her distance from me. It was difficult to see her, but I had to stay away. We both needed time to repair ourselves. I found myself staring after her and following behind her, listening and feeling the tension, gauging if she would ever need me. She wouldn't need me here. I was silly to think she would. Her presence relaxed me, but I couldn't get close. The meditation helped to allow me to exert full control by centering myself. More than anything, I wanted to be close to her again.

A small dainty hand combed through my brown wavy hair. "Good morning, Ethal." I took her hand into mine greedily and pressed my lips against the pale skin on the back of her hand. It was as if the gravity in my heart pulled her in and summoned her. I would not let this moment slip through my fingers. I would touch her and listen to her, soak it all in while it lasted, down to the last drop she had to offer me. "How are you feeling?" She must miss me as I've missed her; why else would she have come to me on her own without me begging for her? It was as if she could have heard my thoughts and felt my longing. I held her hand tightly, afraid to let her go.

She shrugged with a soft smile. "I feel more accepting of our situation the longer I'm in it." I could hear the *but* hovering between us.

"*But...*" I prompted her.

"I'm not sure about you, Gideon. Something inside of me longs for you so much I'd move a mountain. Another part of me fears you." She touched her cheek gingerly. "I needed to be near you today. It's been too long. I feel incomplete without you. Thank you, for giving me the space I needed. I know you've tried to stay close, to keep me in your sights, but you still stayed away from me when you could have come. That's all I could ask."

I gestured to the spot in the grass in front of me. "Meditate with me." I wanted to show her I was changing and learning about myself enough to make her comfortable and safe in my presence. My power would never cease to put fear in others, even her.

She sat down and crossed her thin legs and gave me a small smile. "I've never done this."

"I would tell you how, but I'm not a teacher like Kendra. She's one of a kind." I closed my eyes and projected an image into her mind. It was the way I saw her. The first time in the meadow holding the vial. She was scrawny and boney then, but still just as beautiful. She was glowing, and now she was even more radiant. I let her see herself through my eyes, projecting my feelings onto the memory for her to feel. I let her feel my loneliness and emptiness in the days I spent distancing myself from her as well. I needed her to know.

"What was that?" She asked quietly with a bright smile in her eyes.

"I want you to see yourself the way I do, and there's no reason for you to fear someone that loves you the way I do." I threw loose grass at her playfully. "I feel like I was born to love you in this new life. If it were magic or not, I'll gladly accept it. I was alone for a long time after my mother passed away in my first life, now I have you in this life. It's like the spirits of the Claret Magic knew I would need you. Hopefully, we never need to find out why." I threw another handful of grass at her. "Try to worry less."

"Easier said than done." She giggled and tossed a clump of dirt into my chest, leaving dusty stains on my top.

She got up and ran off giggling as I stood to chase her. She was quick but she wasn't quicker than magic. I snapped my finger and appeared in front of her from a puff of red smoke as she was looking back to where I was standing. I grabbed her and slung her over my shoulder. Ethal laughed and beat her fists against my back as she demanded for me to put her down.

"Gideon." Kendra said sternly from the porch of her cottage. "There's someone here to see you."

I came to a slow walk and placed Ethal on her feet and offered her my hand. "Would you join me?"

"This seems like official business. I should leave you to it." She tried to pull away.

I snatched both of her hands and pulled her to my chest roughly. "We're one. We're a package deal. We'll do everything together now. I won't leave you out, not for a moment."

"Fine, only if you control your anger, it can get the best of you. I feel it." A blush creeped up her little cheeks and ended on the tips of her ears. She cast her gaze down to the ground and looked up at me through her lashes. I swore my heart crashed against my ribs and tried to leap out of my body into her hands. *Impossible*, there wasn't a heart there in the first place.

"Whatever my lady wishes." I stuttered out. I placed a kiss on her delicate lips, tempting her for more. They were soft under mine. I wanted to hold her there in that moment for as long as I could, letting our breath and emotions mingle. The connection I had into her mind was pulsing as I let her take in my arousal. I cupped the back of her neck, trying to pull her up to me slightly. Her body pressed against me in all the perfect ways. I wanted to see into her mind, but I couldn't. I could only give her what was inside my own.

She broke the kiss with a heavy breath. My heart fluttered like a naive little woman's as I stared at her in awe. I bowed in front of her, a humbling position by warlocks to those that were superior and pressed my forehead to her dainty cool hands. "As long as you're by my side, I will do as you wish." I committed.

Ethal took my chin in her hand and tilted it up to look at her. "I'm flattered by the power I have over you, but we're equals." She tugged on my arm. "Stand up."

"Whatever my lady wishes." I said again as I stood straight. She giggled, a precious sound.

We walked into the cottage together and sat where Kendra told us to. I thought we would be meeting with King Vor, but a tall red headed man came into the room. I probed his mind gently, trying not to alert him. This man was an Arvor hybrid, not the type of person I thought I would be meeting today. He was scruffy looking and smelled like stale beer and bread.

J. L. Cross

"This is DeLuca Aluxious. First proxy King of the Arvors." Kendra announced.

"Do you mean to say '*rebels*'," I asked mockingly. "When have the rebels ever been organized enough to be anything better than just that?"

"Mind your manners!" Kendra snapped. "Please, we're on the same team." She said more gently.

"Except his team doesn't play by anyone's rules. At least not from what I've gathered." Aluxious bantered back as he slammed his muscular body into a chair. "It's been a very long while since a Claret wielder has walked. It's a dangerous and volatile magic that's usually all consuming. My mother had a very hard time with it in her early years, thankfully she was spared."

I scoffed in disbelief. "Cases of women using Claret Magic are rare, and even more unheard of - ones who survive it. You're also referring to a hybrid, who would have even less affinity for magic than myself."

Kendra sat next to Aluxious. "He was an orphan at a neighboring Sanctuary. Aluxious was raised by the witches after his father left him off there. We could be trusted, because I was the one that aided his mother's battle with Claret wielding while she was pregnant. She left the magic to save her child."

"How crass, abandoned by your father, a mother with infinite ability and self-control dies in a brutal attack by a prepubescent rage filled child." I mocked. "Did your father abandon you because of the witch's blood in you?" It was a likely cause. Most Arvors didn't like to interbreed, even back then. It was taboo and awkward for the children. "Some Arvors think the impurity is disturbing. I know you can shift; I can see it in your eyes." I raised myself from my seat, staring down on him as his face twisted in anger. I turned my hungry eyes on Kendra. "Tell me why his father left him Kendra, because Aluxious' mind is pushing me out of those traumatic moments."

Aluxious slammed his hand on the table, making Ethal jolt. I placed my hand on hers to calm her. "My village was viciously ransacked by King Vor's army, led by his beloved son, Vlad. I hid in a cellar, waiting for him to return for *two days*. When he came back for me it wasn't safe anywhere to be an Arvor, much less a hybrid so close to the city. He brought me to the sanctuaries to make sure I had the best chance of survival. The other packs wouldn't have a hybrid in their ranks. I was raised as a Warlock. I know a few fun tricks. Magic runs in my blood, but not nearly as strong as the Arvor." Aluxious snapped his finger, a flame ignited in his palm. He waved his hand sharply and the flames died into smoke.

I kept probing his mind, but this time I probed harder until he was bent over grabbing his skull and groaning in pain. Aluxious fell from his chair and dragged his nails against the wooden floors. When he looked up at me, I could see the Arvor inside of him, his eyes large and red around the rims. His face was shaking with rage as he held back the animalistic urge to shift. His nails and fingers were beginning to lengthen. His nails dug into the hardwood floors, splintering it and splitting a few of the boards. The hair on his head was getting thicker and longer as it sprouted from the pores of his chest.

"Stop it!" Ethal yelled at me suddenly. I released him and turned to look at her, fear for his life swimming in her eyes as she started to leak tears. Ethal clutched to one of my hands, pulling at me to return to her. I was losing myself to the power the Magic had inside of me. I had to remember the promise I'd made to her.

I brushed my knuckles across her cheek and down her neck, catching the tears between my fingers and trying to brush them away so I didn't have to see them. She was so warm, tempting me back. "I'm sorry..." I apologized, seeing her fear for his life reminded me of what I was really missing in this body. I couldn't control my loss of empathy or sympathy. That's why I needed her. The missing reason dawned on me. "As you wish." I said as I dipped my head in regret. She called us equals, but she was my Queen. A word from her could stop me in my tracks.

She stroked my arm. "It's alright." *but it wasn't.*

"Tell me what you saw." Kendra demanded after I took my seat again, almost losing my balance as I sat. I was still shocked by the lack of care I had for anyone apart from myself and for Ethal.

"He wouldn't have seen anything I wouldn't have told you on my own!" Aluxious released a growl toward me. As he calmed his animalistic features started to recede.

Kendra waved him off. "Arvors are compulsive liars, 'specially rebels. I need to know your story is true, every word, before you have a chance to lie about it." She said sternly.

I placed my hand on Ethal's thigh for comfort. I needed to feel her warmth on my skin. She continued to draw shapes on my hand, the warmth of her fingers filling me. I gave my attention to Kendra. "I take it you want the important bits?" She nodded. I started from the most recent memories I found. "He's come directly from the city, a staggering walk. He accepted a deal with an Ayl. He's spoken to Vlad, who has returned, and there's traitors within the palace, but the man's face was difficult to see, probably because they're assumptions and not memories of who the traitor is. His contact, the governor of the market district, Yurdell, knows his identity. The Ayl was plotting the slaughter of the Princess, and then the King. Fortunately, our *friend* provided a poor asset, ensuring that the deed wouldn't be fulfilled. I think he has a small crush on the Princess as well." Aluxious blushed slightly with embarrassment. "He followed through with his bargain, but the Princess lives. She's under the influence of Soilt venom and the Ayl adversary dwells in the walls of the castle, his plot to destroy the King is only thickening. He fears for the life of the Princess the most. He wants to guard her. Mostly… Aluxious is looking to bring the war to an end." I paused, moving my eyes over Aluxious. "It seems he'd like to resolve the war before the true Arvor King returns to take his throne."

 Kendra smiled. "A Arvor with a burden of truth to bear. Thank you, Aluxious. I'm honored. Though, we have taken it by force. I know powerful men will use power in poor ways."

 "We're not all compulsive liars. Half the time they're lying to feed their families. Recently though, I've paid Yurdell to send more food to the Northwest, and we've been collecting. Starvation is closing in on Civith as we speak. Of course, Yurdell will be dead soon and I'll lose that leverage over the Aylish. I'm in desperate need of a more diplomatic solution to this war, and I'm seeking the aid of a Warlock before I succumb to my enemy. Unfortunately, I've lost too many of my men to the Aylish and there's no way I can send them back onto the battlefield."

Kendra smiled. "Aluxious needs a more *diplomatic solution* to the war. I've told Vor you're seeking counsel, he's agreed, and he's also seeking an end to the war, but he's asking for you to use your powers to vanquish the Arvors and rebels. Apparently, his commander has convinced him this is the way to end the war. I told him we will negotiate the ideal end to the war when we have counsel. Now, we can take Aluxious' agenda and knowledge with us."

"His commander sounds like an idiot." I scratched my head. "If I convince the King there's a *diplomatic solution*, will you accept the cost, even if it's unfavorable?"

Aluxious nodded aggressively. "I need this to end. I didn't realize how out of hand it was getting until I met her. She would be a good Queen. Peace is all this Kingdom needs. It's what we all deserve."

I combed my hands through my wiry beard. "I'll find a solution. Be patient and heed my call when it comes. I need you to be open minded. You may need to sacrifice something personal."

Aluxious laughed and clapped his hands together. "What a wonderful Idea! This war and this position have cost me everything. I can lose a bit more. I cling to a remnant of my freedom. The King and his men do not know me in this form, only the beast. I'll continue to use that to my advantage."

I leaned forward and grabbed his hand in mine and pulled his wrist to my nose to inhale his scent. "Unbelievable!" I shouted and tossed his hand away. "You're not any hybrid. You're a science experiment."

Kendra put a hand against my chest to calm me. The Claret Magic was floating around the room in a swirl of red mist. When I breathed in the rage the mist retreated into me.

"Tell me what you know." Kendra urged.

I flicked my hand at Aluxious. "He's playing the long game. He's been waiting for an opportunity. He knows something we don't. I can't put a finger on it, and he's so guarded." I sat back down. "He's a Tribred, three very lethal breeds mixed in a perfect little experiment. His father was a hybrid. Soilt and Arvor." I said coldly. "I don't know his end game, but I don't trust him at all."

"Impossible." Kendra said with a short chuckle of disdain. "That can't be true. He needs an end to the war. I couldn't care less what breed he is."

Aluxious shrugged. "I was thinking about telling you, but you already seem prejudiced against an Arvor-witch. I need a diplomatic solution to *our* problem. I want to be a father, have a family, and live the rest of my life in peace."

"There hasn't been a Tetrabred in centuries. The only ones I've heard of were slaughtered by Claret Welders during their time." Kendra said. "You're a perfect result of great bloodlines, strong ones. Please, tell me you won't be attempting to create a child pushing all the strongest races into one?"

"I never really thought about it before." Aluxious started, "I knew my parents well enough to know why I was special, but I never thought about continuing in such a toxic family legacy. I don't know a single Ayl that would procreate with an Arvor like me anyways. I have no interest in the experiments of my dead ancestors."

"Thank the Mother!" I cursed. "They're powerful. If created just right, in the perfect sequence of combining the four species, it can create a very powerful being. Not only can they shift into their Arvor forms, but they can also hunt like a Soilt born with fangs and venom, they can cast spells and incantations like witches, and they're nimble tall beings, stronger than most average Arvors with the agility of the Ayles, not to mention the intellect they're born with. Aluxious' father was born Arvor and Soilt, a deadly combination, he found a powerful witch who could wield and *survive* Claret Magic, and Aluxious was born welding magic. With more training Aluxious could master his power like any Warlock. If you give him the strongest and most deadly Aylish bloodline to mix into that, you'll have an army of Vlad's running all over the Kingdom."

"Gee Wiz!" Aluxious jokes at me annoyingly. "To be honest, I've never considered that kind of life. I can tell just the prospect of it terrifies you. Are you afraid of their power, or are you afraid of a new species coming of it, like the Soilts? Or something stronger than you?"

Aluxious paused and locked eyes with Kendra, leaving my thoughts racing and abandoning the thought of mixing his genes with Ayles. Was I afraid of something stronger than me, or something that could be more destructive to our way of life?

Aluxious tapped his finger on the table, snaring Kendra's attention from her thoughts. "By the way, I went back when I heard the shouts. The rebel sent to assassinate her needed to die, and she did a magnificent job. He was a waste of fresh air. Did I mention she chopped his head off and mounted it in front of the castle herself? I've never been so impressed." Aluxious bit his lip like an animal imagining its prey. "Of course, I've spoken to her, and she's also a very delicate but strong woman. She's kind, and naive, but I think she might be starting to grow out of that. Betrayal will do that to her."

As I probed his mind, I could tell he was obsessing over the Princess. He was hiding his infatuation for her in a box in the corner of his mind. My racing worries eased slightly. He had no intention of making a move for the throne. He knew his place with the Ayles and knew not to challenge it with such an unfathomable crush. I feared a Tetrabreed the most, they would be too powerful. If a breed like that became acquainted with Claret Magic they would be less likely to fail with so much natural power occuring in their blood.

Kendra scratched at the surface of her wooden table for a moment, leaving us to sit in silence. "Gideon, this is a good idea. Don't you think one diplomatic solution could help unite all the races? This sounds good to me. Fearing something that hasn't been determined yet is absurd. Tetra-Breeding has never been successful, even if it was, it doesn't mean it's evil and bad. Look at yourself for an example of that. You're one of a kind. Aluxious came here because we both know that someone of your power can convince the King and root out the evil in his midst. Both sides of this war desperately need you. Even if they don't want to admit it."

"I shook my head. "I want to, but I need to be cautious. If I would have it my way- Aluxious wouldn't leave here with his head."

"Couldn't we at least attempt peace before we take the life of the Proxy King because of some irrational fear you have?" She was teasing me. For a moment my mood lightened, but the fear still sat in me. "We can deal with that kind of problem much later, *if* it arises."

I lifted my hand and gestured for the back door of the cottage to open. It slammed against the back wall and the hinges creaked. "Fine. You're right. His procreating is rather unstoppable unless I kill him here, but then the war would rage on until the Arvors have been exterminated, which is a waste of a magnificent species. Not to mention, the lives of the King and the Princess will be lost. No need for innocent blood to be spilt any more than it already has. I'll convince the King into a diplomatic negotiation. Look out for a courier from me."

With a sudden flick of my hand Aluxious was shoved forcefully from Kendra's cottage and dragged to the gate and cast out of the sanctuary. I watched him fall into the dirt through the window, carried by the Claret Magic. "He's so rude and obnoxious. He's a drunkard, too." I sniffed the air. "How are we going to get that gross wet dog smell out of here?"

Kendra laughed and stood up. "Just open the windows."

"He has a crush on her." I looked over at Kendra. "He's tucking his infatuation for her away in the back of his mind. I hope he does that with every Aylish he encounters."

Ethal sat back in her chair and giggled. "That's just ripe, two abandoned and hurt little souls off to fall in love. He's a man, he'll chase that infatuation to the ends of the world after the war ends. He'll have nothing to fear then. If Kastell is half the woman I expect her to be, she'll hate him. This war was fought by two people," she held up two fingers and wiggled them, "her father and Aluxious. He has Aylish blood all over his hands. She'll never spread her legs for that monster." Her words were reassuring to hear. She could be right. He may chase his infatuation, but the Princess wouldn't fall for someone she thought was a monster.

"Then maybe there will be no Tetra-breeds to worry about," I said. "My day has been ruined by unwelcome visitors. I think I'll take the rest of the day off from your whims, Kendra." I offered my hand to Ethal. "Would you like to go to the meadow with me, my love?"

A blush creeped across her soft sharp cheeks and a smile lingered on her lips. "Yes." She took my hand and shot up from her seat.

The meadow sprouted blooms of purple wildflowers all over with sparse groupings of similar blue ones. It was more beautiful than I could have ever expected, and even more so with Ethal in the center of it. Decades passed since I last laid in the grass and enjoyed the tranquil atmosphere in this place. My neck was tickled by the grass and the smell of the rich wet soil was calming. I wanted to stay here for an eternity.

Ethal caressed my cheek and ran her slender fingers through my hair. She combed the strands as I lay with my head in her lap, staring up at the passing clouds. She smelled sweet, divine rose petals drifting past your nose. The clouds passed slowly, and birds were gliding across the sky above me, some sang songs in the trees.

"Gideon," she asked softly. Her voice was a melody in my ears, accompanied by the birds and the constant rustling of leaves by the small creatures around us.

"Mmm?" I grumbled. I enjoyed those small moments in comfort and silence.

"Why did you come into Claret Magic? Didn't you know it would kill you someday?"

Leave it to a woman to ruin a good moment. I sat up and dusted the grass from my robe. I wanted to ignore that she had even asked. *How does someone get involved with something so utterly consuming and dark?*

She grabbed at my hand, the regret for asking in her eyes. "I'm so sorry, I shouldn't-"

"No, no." I gripped her hand gently. "I'm just trying to find a good enough answer for you."

"Were you that naive?" She cast her eyes down, saddened. "Was your life so awful?"

"Oh, was I?!" I laughed and then I lied. Maybe she would pity me. Or maybe she would know that I lied. "I wanted to bring my father back to life. Thus, I was brought to Claret Magic." *What a ridiculous lie!* I honestly couldn't tell her what either of my parents looked like anymore. After they died the details of their faces seemed to slowly fade in my memory. Yet, I could still hear my mother's voice calling to me during the darkest moments in my life. That would never fade. Her voice was torture on the ears, high pitched and annoying.

Ethal gasped, "How could you lie? You're so horrible at lies. Now, be honest!" I couldn't actually tell her the truth, could I? I should. I knew I should. Ethal was such a pure woman. How could I tell her the truth about my nature? I'm not an admirable man. I knew she would catch my lie; it was almost like we were so connected- she could know anything.

I made my decision. She's a pure woman, what could I fear? "I'll be honest now. I turned to Claret Magic because I was told I could never do real magic. I wanted to prove myself, and I outdid myself if I'm going to be frank. Not only did I prove that I was capable of so much more, but I lived longer than some of my bullies, so now I have no one to prove anything to. If they are still alive, they're old men and not worth a breath of time."

Claret Magic was not meant for a living and breathing man, it was an unholy gift bestowed by witches upon the Soilts. Their emptiness and darkness feeds Claret Magic without it taking their lives, as they had no life force to be drained in the first place. Magnificent creatures. Claret Magic was used by witches to create the ill-tempered beasts. And now, they're powerful creatures of their own volition, procreating and living in the shadows of life. After they were created by Claret Magic, it was as if it had given them real life, flowing through them like a soul. They weren't puppets to witches as they thought they would be. The history of Soilts was cruel to witches.

I waited a moment, but there was never any judgment on her face. "You could have practiced pure magic, through the Mother. Why did you choose such a dark path?" She asked.

"I wanted power over those that had shown me doubt." Then it was out. The truth was bathed in the light. A horrible truth. One without any real explanation. I was greedy for power. I lusted for the ability to exercise my strength on all those that told me I would never do real magic, and now they feared me. They would fear for their lives when I came around. "The fear they'll have when I walk into a room… It's tantalizing." I paused, a dirty smile coming to my lips. "I feel that same fear on some of the sisters at the Sanctuary, and I don't feel a shred of guilt over it. This is what I always wanted. That fear satisfies my desire to be powerful, strong, and lethal. I have no other reason apart from the greed that festered inside of me."

"Then that's that. What was done can't be changed and we'll move on now." Ethal stood up, took my hand and kissed it lightly.

How could someone as rage filled, power hungry, and vile find something so *pure*? She was the sun in my otherwise dark afterlife.

I took her face in my hands and kissed her. Her lips were full and soft. I held her close to me, afraid that she would slip away within my moment of bliss. My finger went through her hair and to the back of her neck. Her skin was radiating with life and longevity.

I separated us for only a moment to look into her eyes. "I love you, Ethal." I let the words sit there for a second, playing off the tip of my tongue. Words I had thought I would never say to anyone. "I love you." I repeated. I wrapped my arm around the small of her back and brought her close to me again.

"Hold onto me. You don't have to return the words; just hold me." I whispered into her ear desperately. The only fear I faced was her sudden disappearance, as if her existence was a joke to taunt me with. She wrapped her arms tightly around my neck and held me, just as I needed in that moment.

"Your escort will be arriving shortly, and I don't think you'll be very pleased with it." Kendra dropped her journal down onto the dining table and sank into a chair. In the weeks that passed I helped her sand the splintered floor and started to till in the fields to contribute to the sisters. I could tell Kendra's body was starting to ache again. I wanted to do what I could to ease her pain.

"I thought Vor would show a little more hospitality. I don't know him the way I used to." Kendra said as she rubbed her knees.

"I wasn't expecting hospitality from an Ayl anyways." I said as I picked at a cornish hen I was eating. Ethal was crunching on raw carrots across from me, I haven't noticed if she actually ate meat in the time we spent together.

Ethal was wearing a basic dress, gray, like most of the sisters in the sanctuary. She was starting to wear her hair down around her face as it got longer and more vibrant. The brown of her hair was the same as her deep eyes. I couldn't help but admire her for a moment. I couldn't help but attempt to see inside her mind, but I only ever found glimpses of my own memories there. Today I was seeing the shore of an ocean in the images, nothing more. I've found myself wondering about where she came from before she was enslaved.

I pushed my plate away and folded my hands on the table. "Should I pretend to be compliant?" I asked Kendra. Ethal was reading a book she had found on Magic and various other things. She could ignore the world around her so easily with a book in her hands.

Kendra touched my hands softly. "We both know that whatever chains they put you in are a futile attempt to make them feel like they're in control." She paused. "Control your anger, and be patient with Vor, he won't be easy to convince. Being King has been terribly rough on him."

Over the weeks we've spent with Kendra, it was apparent she was losing most control that she had with her magic. Her mind was weakening just as quickly as her body. Her mind was wide open for me, giving me opportunities to see her life, her memories, and her thoughts. I hated being so intrusive with her, but there were so many things she wouldn't tell me about the King, things that could potentially turn the tides of our negotiations. She knew him better than anyone, I needed her insights now, more than ever.

I used the Claret Magic to embrace her until she was caught in a trance, unaware of everything happening around her.

Ethal slammed her book on the table. "What are you doing, Gideon?" She asked rhetorically, scolding me with her tone.

I positioned myself behind Kendra and touched her temples with the tips of my fingers. "I need to know the King the way she does. I need to have all the information available to turn him to a diplomatic solution to this war. I need her memories to use against him."

Ethal sighed irritably. She didn't like this method either, but the escort was arriving, and this was our last chance. "I've been wondering; why hasn't she met with him about this already? She says his name so casually, what stops her from going to him?"

I motioned to Kendra's journal on the table. "I've been a very busy man. I've taken the liberty to read her journal. Something happened between the two of them and he won't even write her back. There's a collection of old letters in the front, and every other entry seems to be a letter. *Dear Vor* this and *Vor* that. She misses him, and he's cast her aside."

Ethal took the journal and opened the cover and pulled out the first letter at the top and read from it. "My Dearest; You haven't written to me in months. I've stopped sending my letters to guard what remains of my heart. I send my sincerest regards; your wife was lost at such a young age; the sisters are praying to the Mother to ease her passing into the next life. Have faith that all will be well. My thoughts are always with you and so is my love.

 Be kind to the slave boy I've sent to you, his mother was the Queen's servant, and your beloved's murderer. He is a gift that I send to redeem the mistake I've made by sending his mother. Her actions have cost you your wife and have cost her son his freedom." Ethal folded the letter and placed it back in the journal. "Sounds like one of the servants in the castle had a very homicidal mother and Kendra is bearing the punishment of her lover's dead wife." She clicked her tongue and tossed the journal onto the table. "You have a lot of leverage in that alone. If the King never reads her letter, that very servant boy is probably a grown man, walking through the halls, and he has no idea."

 "No. He would have questioned the boy as a gift... Wouldn't he?" I asked, contemplating.

 Ethal shrugged. "Slaves are gifted to people every day. What King can have too many slaves?" She challenged me, but I didn't answer.

 I focused on my connection with Kendra and toned out the world around me until there was nothing but silence. The red mist of the Claret Magic slowly funneled in through her ears, opening her mind entirely to me. I could hear the voices of people in her life, and her voice. Some of the memories I was trying to reach were cloudy and fragmented. Kendra lived such a long life, and with those years came forgetfulness, but some memories clung on strong in her subconscious.

I found a memory of her as a young woman bathing in sunlight that poured in through a window. Then I saw *him* there with her.

"Come sit with me. You're always in a rush to leave." Kendra motioned to the empty spot in her bed. Her dark skin stood out flawless against the cream-colored sheets. She tugged a thin sheet up under her chin and sighed in content when Vor took the spot beside her.

He was a strong young Ayl, tall and muscular. His hair was braided tightly down his back with only a few strands that came loose. "I need to leave. I have to stop seeing you."

Kendra laughed. She was a daring young woman, not willing to play by the rules. "Is your Ayl bride waiting on you again while you spend your time with me?" She threw a leg over Vor and cuddled closer to him. The sun danced on her youthful skin. Her black hair was filled with tight curls and flowed down her back and over the pillows.

"This isn't fair to her. I'll be facing combat with all of her suitors at the end of the week. I'll either die, or I'll become the next in line to the throne."

Kendra laughed and rolled away from him, staring up into the ceiling. "Well, should you die, then our time spent together wouldn't be wasted. If you live, my love will go on unrequited, and you'll become the next Sovereign leader of our great Kingdom. You have the chance to make a difference." She turned toward him, grabbing his hand in desperation. "Promise me; promise that if you live you won't waste this opportunity."

J. L. Cross

Vor turned on his side and propped his head up on his hand, his elbow digging into the bed. "I won't waste it. Every day that goes by, I will think of you when I fail to heal the Kingdom."

"I'll hold you to it." She touched his cheek gingerly and moved closer to him until their lips were sealed.

I broke away from the memory. Her love for him had been strong, but her love for the Kingdom even stronger. She gave him up so that he could go to either his death or become the next King. She wouldn't have known then that he would be victorious. Kendra sacrificed the man she loved in the impractical idea that he could make a greater change for all the Kingdom. To this day she lived with the regret of giving him up, because the rifts were growing wider.

I let myself drift in and out of memories until I found another. This one was red and filled with dread and despair. This one was buried in her mind, as if she never wanted to remember it, but it stayed here. It was an unforgettable moment.

The streets were packed with citizens attempting to get into the arena. Kendra was shoving her way forward through the crowd, determined to get in before the gates closed off to the overflow. She had her hair pulled back tightly and a hood over her head, witches weren't allowed into the city, but the Arena was north of the city, and everyone showed up to these formalities. Everyone wanted to know who the next King would be.

Kendra found a seat on the highest balcony. The view here was poor, but it would do. She grasped onto the rail in front of her as people shoved past. They were attempting to fill every inch of space.

Creaking sounds and the clash of iron gave away that the gates had been closed and the ceremony would begin soon. There were five suitors for the Princess, and they would fight to the death for the right to marry her, a common practice for an heiress of the throne. There was no telling how many of the suitors had gotten close to the Princess like Vor had.

The crowd was buzzing. A lean old Ayl walked out into the grass of the arena wearing a suit of ceremonial armor. He stopped in the center. Kendra couldn't hear what he was saying, but the Royal Collective and the attendees on the ground level would be able to hear him clearly. He didn't spend a lot of time with formalities and quickly left the field. He was most likely commencing the ceremony, detailing its purpose to the Collective, as was usual.

A moment of silence passed and then all five gates to the tunnels under the stands opened slowly. A few agile men slide out with the gate barely open and instantaneously engaged in combat. The clash of steel rang out across the open air followed by the eruption of the crowd. One of the contestants used a short sword and the other used a dagger and small shield.

Kendra searched the arena floor for Vor, two of the contestants had him pinned against a pillar without room for escape. She wanted to turn away and hide her face, but she had to watch. If he would die, she would experience every moment of it. Vor was a skilled warrior for his age, he was young, but older than most of the contestants. He didn't rush into the thick of the fight like the younger men did, he bided his time and let his competition come to him.

Two of his competitors paired together to defeat him and began circling around him. This was a good strategy for fighters that were smaller or less skilled than their opponents. One contestant shot arrow after arrow in his direction, and another lunged in with his sword. Vor used his shield to catch the arrows and parried the swordsman with ease. With a quick step he shoved his sword through the chest of the young man. He sank down onto one knee, using his shield to cover his body from the archer's arrows. As every new arrow hit the shield it became too heavy for Vor to lift.

The archerer advanced, zoning in on his kill. Vor waited, sunken and still like a snake. The archer lowered his bow and pulled a dagger from its hilt. With the ceasing of firing arrows Vor stood and leapt over the shield; it was planted in the ground and the weight of it held upright by the multitude of arrows jammed into its front. The archer tried to evade Vor, but he tackled the man to the ground and used his own blade to shove through his chin and up into his skull.

Vor stood, covered in blood, dirt, and grass from the arena floor. One contestant remained, a small Ayl with a dagger who triumphed over the other swordsman. The shorter Ayl started to circle around Vor, decreasing the space between them a little at a time.

Vor stood, unmoving in the center, statuesque. His head was bent, listening and feeling his surroundings. Anyone with a right mind could have seen the predator within him at that moment. Kendra never saw this side of him before that day. Vor was trained, and well trained. Farmers often had to fight off Arvors and others attempting to steal their harvest or kill their livestock. Vor's training came from defending himself, not pitiful sparring.

Kendra covered her eyes for a moment, horrified that somehow this little man could defeat him. Then there was a guttural cry of rage and the man lunged for Vor from behind, but he side-stepped, evading the man and taking the advantage. Vor moved quickly and grabbed the man, lifting him by his neck and choking him. He didn't hesitate to drive his blade through his heart.

It was over, Vor had secured his position, covered in the blood of his competitors. He moved to the center of the arena and stabbed his sword into the ground and dropped to one knee, he waited for the King's blessing.

I lifted myself from within her memories and glanced up at Ethal. She was staring out the window, watching the approaching wagon and guards. "Gideon, you need to hurry, they're almost here." She said softly.

"I'm almost finished. I need more. There has to be something about him leaving her. I can't just use my own presumptions."

"Find it quickly." Ethal insisted.

I let myself back in, probing harder this time. It wasn't safe for Kendra, but I needed information she would never give to me. Her memories were guarded. I found one, filled with pain and glimpses of Vor's face.

"That woman was a pest for my family!" Vor said angrily. He was with Kendra in her cottage. He was clothed in dark messed robes; he was visiting her in secret.

Kendra was on her knees in front of him sobbing. "You asked for her, she did only what we wanted."

Vor lowered himself to be face to face with Kendra and wiped some of the tears from her cheeks. "I've lost my wife. The servant was a rebel, I'll have to cover it up. The servant girl tried to kill my children after my wife. That wasn't part of the deal we made with her."

"It's not my fault..." Kendra pleaded. "I didn't know she would try hurting children."

Vor placed a jar on the table, there was a hand floating in a brownish green liquid. It was putrid. "This is the hand of your rebel servant. She killed my wife and made an attempt on my young children while they slept in their beds." He walked away from Kendra towards the door. "I won't be coming back. This is the last time we will meet. It's for the best."

I withdrew from Kendra entirely and used my magic to wake her. Her eyes pierced mine, angry, because she knew what I had done to her. Kendra would have felt my presence in her memories like a watermark. She tried to stand, but I forced her back into her chair with a hand on her shoulder. "It's all a lie." I accused her. "Vor lied to the entire Kingdom to protect you!" I sat down, stunned. "Here, I thought he may have been the bad guy, but now I see how he truly stopped a war between the Aylish and witches. He's been protecting the Kingdom from further divides."

Kendra let her head fall, unable to look me in the eyes. "I've lost him. I'll never get him back." She looked up, her dark brown eyes meeting mine. "We met with a witch from the far north, I think she lived with the dwarves in Hagan. The dwarves were being overtaxed for the import of their jewels by the Varius dynasty. She came here looking for work, but she was aligned with the Rebels. Vor and I made a contract with her. His fee was his farm, promising her she could own it if she followed through with her end of the bargain. It was years after his crowning. He came to me because his wife was suffering from hearing voices in her head, and he didn't think he could save her. I sent the rebel as a slave. A common gift to royals. No one would have thought twice about it, but she attempted the lives of his heirs as well; he murdered her brutally for her choices."

"He loves his children more than anything in the world." I sat in front of her. "He told the entire Kingdom that his wife was insane, that she committed suicide and killed her servant, but you sent that servant to him to kill the Queen," I said. "You thought you would be queen."

She shook her head. "I just wanted him back! It was his idea, and I still lost him. We were foolish in our youth. He blames himself just as much as he blames me. This isn't just my punishment, but his own."

J. L. Cross

I peered out the window, my chariot awaited. I chuckled to myself, knowing that there was no way this would end well. "I take it the King doesn't trust your recommendations."

She shook her head again, looking up at me, her eyes were filled with tears. "I can't have my own children. It's why I've dedicated myself to this place."

I chuckled as a guard rapped his knuckles against the front door. He was impatient and came again before I had the chance to take in a steadying breath. "I have all that I need."

Kendra went to the door as quickly as she could. A tall muscular guard with short hair pushed past her roughly, knocking her to the ground, trying to get to me. He was a menacing looking man with a grimace on his face. I wasn't pleased to have him here and he wasn't pleased to be here. One of his ears looked like it was bit off near the base, a nasty result from battle. The healed length was jagged and raised, a dull pale white scar.

I studied the man in front of me as Ethal assisted Kendra to her feet. She groaned in pain. I couldn't do much for her pain anymore, it returned twice as strong with every attempt I made.

Finger pointed at Kendra; I regarded the guard with a flare of hatred in my tone. "Was that necessary?" With a sharp jerk of my finger the red mist poured out of my hand and twisted around the large guard, holding him firmly. My eyes were glowing, I could feel the intensity of the Claret Magic pumping through the blood vessels around my eyes.

He shook his head; his eyes were wide. "I'm sorry... I shouldn't have!" He yelled as the mist squeezed him continuously, a little tighter and tighter by every passing second. "I- I- I-" He stuttered until his larynx and throat were crushed by the force I applied. I smiled viciously. This was more satisfying than I thought it would be. Every cell of my body was buzzing with power and strength.

"No, it wasn't." I said sternly, responding to my own previous question, as his body lifted from the ground and hovered towards me. I closed my hand into a fist and with it the red mist closed around the guard, crushing him like a scrap piece of tin. The mist ate at his body, devouring it, leaving nothing but his clothing on the floor. His blood had tried escaping in every direction but was consumed; not a single drop went to waste. The mist sped around the room erratically. I felt warm and full. Before that moment, the only time I would feel so complete was within Ethal's touch, but now nothing could make me feel more whole.

I laughed when another guard ran into the building, his jaw slacked. He was filled to the brim with fear. I could smell it on him. "Would you like to try as well?!" I challenged the younger guard. He was much smaller than the first. Kendra and Ethal were huddled in the corner. I had tuned out the sound of their cries.

Ethal was cringing inwardly to Kendra for comfort, her face turned away from me. I crossed the room and bent at the knees. I lowered myself to them. I felt a tinge of regret as I watched her. Kendra attempted to loosen Ethal's hold on her, but it was futile. I surfaced the fear she had once had of me, and this time it was much worse than before.

I brushed my hand through Ethal's hair, whispering a short spell to calm her down. "I'm sorry." I stammered, realizing how caught up in the power I had been. "I'm so sorry." The glowing in my eyes dimmed.

Ethal tilted her head back, the spell taking effect. Her eyes were puffy from the tears spilt, but there was no more fear or distress coming from her. "Don't be sorry, I'm weak." She said and let her head drop. My spell was too strong, sending her into a deep sleep. I took a deep breath, absorbing the slowing mist around us until it was contained within me.

"You're a monster deep within." Kendra raged, meeting my eyes over Ethal's loose body in her arms.

"The monster is on your team." I pointed out. "You might want to keep me on your team." I stroked Ethal's hair. "Keep her safe while I'm away." I ordered. She nodded in agreement.

The young Ayl led me outside. A small party of Aylish guards on horseback with a jail wagon approached us. I could smell the sweat on their necks and see the fear in their eyes. They knew what I was. I smiled inwardly; they would soon know that their companion was forever lost.

I waited for the envoy to come to a stop before I approached them further. I walked to the wagon, and it was opened for me. I placed my hands out to be cuffed. I could feel the weight of the magic casted on them as soon as the metal touched my skin. It seared my wrists and brought me to the ground. I felt a tear inside of me, widening, turning into a gorge. I was splitting into two, maybe I was falling apart entirely. The power I had felt a moment ago was gone, replaced by an emptiness. A large dark pit for my consciousness to fall into. Where I once felt my bound to Ethal, there was nothing.

Looking down at my feet, I tried to draw in another breath, but my lungs were filling with water and clay. I choked, gasping and clinging to my neck. I craned my neck up to search for help, but they all stood idly by, smirking and laughing at my agony.

The door to the cottage sprang open. Ethal came running out, her hands at her sides and engulfed in flames. Her brown eyes were glowing like the last embers in a fire pit. I tried reaching for her, but as my hands raised a whip cracked against my knuckles.

A scream tore from Ethal as the red mist tore through her and out through her hands and mouth. It soared around us, carrying Ethal's flames with it. The burning red mist dragged the last of the elven guards to the ground and absorbed them like food. Ethal was harnessing the full power of the Claret Magic through our bound while I laid on the ground losing my battle to the creeping darkness and the lack of oxygen.

There was little effort remaining inside of me, such little motivation to live. I wanted to return to the dirt where I came from. I was cold and wet, empty and distraught. My consciousness was detached and scrambling to put coherent thoughts together. I was weeping. I feared death more than anything in the universe. I had gone out of my way to avoid an eternal death, and selfishly granted myself immortality. If this were the day I would die, I would be taking Ethal, a poor innocent girl, to that fiery doom with me. She didn't deserve any of this cruelty. She never deserved such an unbreakable tether to me. Yet, she endured. With every moment she tried to be happy with it, she let me in, she showed me unconditionally care. There wasn't more I could have asked for. Since that first day I came to her she protected my life force, clinging to it, and keeping it close to her heart. Now, it wasn't fair, she would perish into this darkness with me.

J. L. Cross

16 Kendra

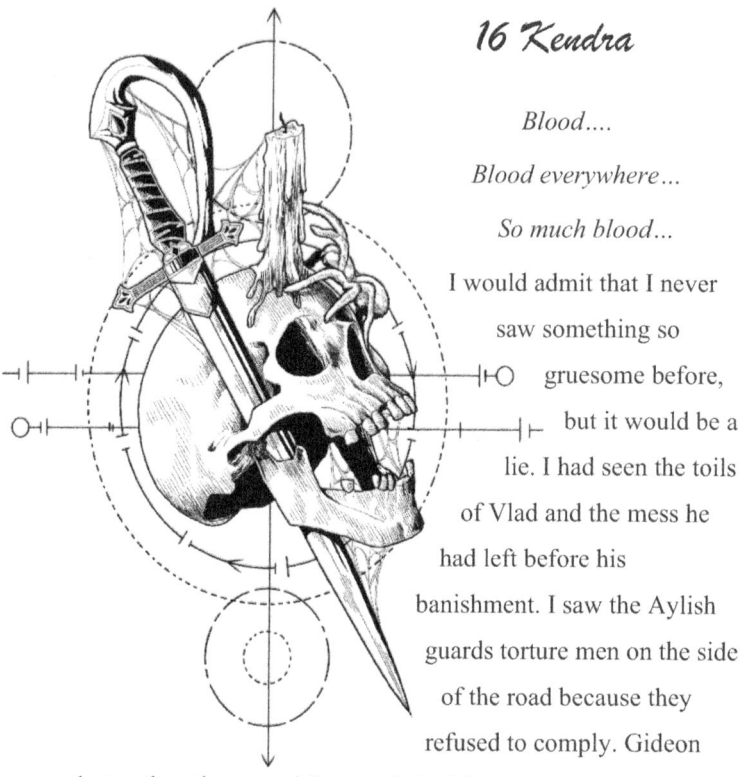

Blood....

Blood everywhere...

So much blood...

I would admit that I never saw something so gruesome before, but it would be a lie. I had seen the toils of Vlad and the mess he had left before his banishment. I saw the Aylish guards torture men on the side of the road because they refused to comply. Gideon was no better than the rest of the people in this war.

I held Ethal in my arms, her eyes black and wide while her body remained motionless. She laid limp across my lap. Sisters walked towards the scene and collapsed as they realized the horror in front of them. Some of them cried and some just sat in terror, silent streams of tears falling from their eyes. Many of them began to pray to the Mother. I could see the sadness in their faces and the anger... at me. I allowed him here and he soiled their sacred and safe land.

Mother Reflector made her way past me, bending over what was left of a few of the bodies, waving her hand over them, absorbing something from them.

"They must have peace." Her voice was nothing more than a rasp, unused and sharp. She went to each body and performed her ritual. "I see their last thoughts. They are free now." When she finished, she stood in front of me, her face covered by her hood. "I will be the next Mother Supreme. You will not be welcome here once you leave. You've brought unrest in the twilight of our service. The Mother will frown upon you." She stood straight and strode off, her cloak pulled tight around her, the hem stained by the blood she had to walk through.

This was once a good and clean place, and I let in destruction. I had high hopes for Gideon's powers. If he used them the right way everyone could be free from war and tyranny. After what I saw, I doubted there was much I could do to keep Gideon from falling off into the void of Claret Magic. He's gone too far, and for most Warlocks that have gotten so deep into the magic they were soon consumed with its intensity.

Ethal's breathing was shallow and weak. I set her down and walked to Gideon. My shuffling feet tripped on a limb of one of the soldiers that was cast aside, sending me to the ground. I struggled to regain my footing. Dirt and blood mixed into a dark burgundy paste between my fingers as I hoisted myself up. Most of the guards were decapitated, their heads taken clean off and their bodies mangled. For some of the victims their bodies weren't even left. The Claret Magic fed on their flesh and blood, leaving guts and clothing scattered on the ground for some of the unlucky victims.

Gideon's body was stiff and laying just beside the open door to the wagon. He was going to go freely, but the endowed cuffs were meant to sever a welder's connection with all their magic. I should have seen this coming. I should have known Vor wouldn't trust him to allow him his power. There was no way I could have known the endowment would have severed Gideon's connection with Ethal as well.

I sat beside him and pulled at the cuffs, but they were solid steel, there was no way I could get them to release on my own. His skin was becoming chalky and ash-like. If I touched it, it would drift into the air like dust. All life was leaving him.

The sounds of horse hooves beating into the ground echoed in my ears. The rider was approaching quickly. I took Gideon into my lap, pulling him close. He didn't mean for this to happen. He wouldn't have wanted this to happen. I didn't want them to take him. I looked up to see a small rider, a pale woman with short brown hair that barely whispered across her shoulders as she moved. She floated elegantly down from her stead with a lightweight cloak cascading over her figure, even before he came to an abrupt stop. When I saw her move to Ethal I moved to be there as well. This woman moved with a purpose, and I knew in my gut to trust her, to listen to her.

She was a lean short woman with multiple blades strapped to her. A brown satchel was loosely slung over her shoulder. The woman knelt in front of me. WIthout hesitation she dug through her bag and pulled out a miniscule tube with a cork in the top. It looked like salt, but it was denser and looked more reflective in the sun.

"Hold her upright!" The woman instructed. "Turn your nose away." She ordered and I did as she said. I recognized this woman, but from a very long time ago. She didn't age a day. *A Soilt.* I drew my conclusion when her dark red eyes looked back at me.

"I know you…" I whispered, not realizing I spoke aloud.

"Keep her still." She said and nudged my arm back up from where I was loosening my grip on her weight. She handed me the vial. "When I say, you will uncork this under her nose and let her breathe it in. She's still breathing, so we have to be quick."

I nodded. She rushed to Gideon, knelt and took the steel cuffs in her hands, she pulled on each and the metal bent to her will, making enough room for his hands to slip through. The strength of a well fed Soilt wasn't one to challenge. She tossed the cuffs away from him.

"Now." She commanded.

I opened the vial; the smell was so strong I couldn't help but take in some of its scent even though I wasn't trying. It was grotesque. The hair on my arms stood. I felt my heart beginning to race.

Ethal shot upright out of my arms, gasping for air, but as she wrestled to get her senses and baring back, the Claret Magic didn't return to infest her; instead, it seemed to seep through the air from her body to Gideon's. It was returning to where it belonged.

The flakey and ash-like look on Gideon's skin started to fill with life and color. I breathed out a sigh of relief. I feared I was going to lose both so quickly.

The woman helped Gideon to his feet, he shook her away and was weak, but he stumbled his way to Ethal who was staring out into the mess of bodies and blood around them.

"I don't remember..." Ethal said, touching a small pool of blood and observing the red running between her fingers.

Gideon fell beside her and nestled into her side, seeking comfort. "It was me. It was all me." He sobbed into her. "Don't fret." Gideon whispered into her. She obliged and wrapped her arms around him. She was desperate for the same comfort.

"What happened?!" I demanded from him.

"When they placed the cuffs on me, the bond I had with my life force was severed, yanking me from my body. The only place the Magic had left to go was to her. I used her to try to free myself. The Claret Magic would have killed her."

He was breathless, his lungs heaving as if they were ready to give out at any second. Ethal didn't have anything to say. The mystery woman stood in front of the three of us unphased.

The woman perked up slightly, taking in our surroundings. "I think it's time for us to leave." She quickly mounted her horse and turned him towards the gate. "I'll be waiting outside the gate. I'm not a fan of blessed places."

"We're not welcome here anymore." Gideon said as he struggled to his feet. Ethal was in even worse shape, clinging to his side. She didn't even have the least bit of energy to stand on her own. "I got you." Gideon scooped her into his arms and steadied himself after a slight wobble and the threat that he might collapse passed. Ethal swiped away what was left of tears on his face. I could feel his guilt. It was something we would share in this memory.

    The sisters were all closing in on my cottage, flame in hand. Mother Reflector led them. This was it then. There would be no goodbyes and no bittersweet memories shared between myself and them after so many years spent together. I ruined the peace they established here and because of that they would drive me out. I was the disease they let in. I knew that much about myself when I caught myself plotting the death of the queen so long ago. I would never be spared from my bad decisions, and I would constantly make them over and over again. It wasn't until I faced the consequences that I knew the weight of everything I was losing.

    Gideon and I walked to the gate side by side as the sisters pressured us from behind to move faster. They weren't the type for violence or vengeance. They wouldn't act out upon us, which would be expected of anyone else. The sisters would serve a period of mourning for the fallen guards and thank the Mother that they were all spared from the destruction that occurred and move on with their lives as if I never existed in them. A new sister would step into my seat and lead them. The Mother Reflector assumed that person would be her. I wouldn't be surprised, but they would still elect her formally. They would never again offer their aid to us as long as the memory of the incident lived on inside of the Monarch.

The stranger was waiting just outside the iron gates for us. She leapt down from her horse and helped to put Ethal in the saddle.

"Should we do introductions?" She said jokingly as she cinched the girth tighter around the belly of the stead.

"This is Vivian." Gideon said, irritated with her lighthearted tone. "She's a Royal Assassin."

"Don't be so crude." She said in that same joking tone. "I'm a *spy* for the King."

Gideon laughed sarcastically then. "She was hired not much longer after the death of the Queen."

"Once King Vor made contact to send his daughter into the West, I was constantly on a mission. I watched you raise her into a fine young woman." Vivian said.

Ethal grunted, rubbing her face. "Vivian sold me to Dawson and Tilda."

"You were unremarkable then, was I supposed to allow you to follow me around and drink my blood so that I could teach you compulsion and mind magic?" Vivian asked rhetorically. "Look where you are now; while you're still rather pathetic in my opinion, you're also the deadliest woman known alive."

"Doubtful." Ethal scoffed.

"As long as you hold the power over Gideon that you do, you will be a mighty foe to whichever side loses you in this war." Vivian casted her eyes over her shoulder at Gideon flirtatiously, the light dancing in them. She guided the mount out in front of us. "I'd say I'm on whichever side you take. Just to be safe."

"I'm not taking a side. Although, if I can't secure this diplomatic solution for Aluxious, I may be facing him as a foe no matter how much I try to find a better solution. I have a feeling that I'll unite them in their hate for me."

I chuckled then. His perception of Aluxious was all wrong. "He's not a bad man, Gideon. He may not have pure intentions, but I would say your prejudice against whatever children he wants to create are unjust. We want to stop the war. When we do, love will spread throughout the Kingdom. Hybrids, Tribreds, and Tetra-breeds will be all over. Aluxious is doing it more so as a King looking to unite his people to theirs, but he's already told you he's not interested in continuing whatever experiments his parents were a part of."

"I don't think his people are aware of his breeding." Gideon said angrily. "He was burying it deep within himself. He's afraid they'll retaliate in hate, like everyone else does. It's better to be known as an Arvor than as a Tribreed."

"Actually, they are." Vivian chimed in. "He's the proxy King of the rebels more than he is of just the Arvors. Do you think all the rebels are Arvors? His forces are diverse. He didn't want *you* to know."

"Well, it's a war between the Arvors and the Ayles." Gideon said pointedly.

"Sure, because the village that was attacked by Vlad was mostly Arvors." Vivian glared over her shoulder at him. "Yet, there are so many people out there who want vengeance against the King and his Collective. They all hold grudges, and most hybrids with even an ounce of Arvor in them can turn occasionally, but others like Aluxious, can turn whenever they want because the gene is so strong in them."

"Doesn't King Vor want peace?" Ethal said in irritation as she rubbed at her temples. "It's hard to understand why this war has gone on so long. Aluxious wants peace on behalf of the Arvors, and Vor wants peace and agrees to a negotiation. Why haven't they done this sooner?"

I scoffed and kicked a rock out of my path. "It's complicated. Vor is the King, but he's still held accountable by the Collective. At his age he can't afford to be challenged. He's been trying to ease them into agreeing to a peace agreement, but some of them hold generations of hate from their ancestors. Of course, he's walked away from peace on his own as well. Years of the Arvors being relentless and attacking his villages and guards have made him just as angry with them as they are at the Ayles. He knows the Collective pushes themselves on their subjects. He knows that they're greedy and hard on us, but it was much worse during the Varius dynasty. No one seems to understand that. The Collective is still many miles from peace agreements. Why do you think he's treating us like prisoners and not guests? They would question him incessantly if they caught him entertaining Warlocks. Mages, and witches."

"Why am I negotiating with him if he's not able to end the war? If the Collective will revolt against him, then why now? Why try?" Gideon waved an irritated hand.

I smiled then, knowing the truth. I knew why he chose now, why he would so suddenly agree to this. "It's his daughter. He'll face their challenges as long as he finds peace for her. He doesn't want her to rule in a world like this. He'll exercise what he has left in power to end this before she succeeds him. He's a tired old man now, much like I'm a tired old woman."

Ethal leveled a glare at Gideon. Sensing her eyes on him he turned his gaze up to her. "Convince him. Whatever it may take. Convince him to end the war. This is your chance. If we need to target and kill every member of the Collective to end this war, then we will. And if that scarce King of the Arvors wants to object then he better step up and face us like a man. We'll acknowledge Aluxious as the King until peace is agreed to."

"As you wish." Gideon responded. He had a jolt of excitement in his step to have a heading from his handler. It was something not to be missed. Vivian was right, Ethal held the power here.

"What did you put up my nose?" Ethal snapped, changing the topic and centering her glare on Vivian. We all glanced at her. She was troubled and clung to the horse's mane, her knuckles paled against the dark black hair of the horse.

Vivian snickered. "My Apothecary calls them Salts, because of the color and texture. It's a rather rare adrenaline stimulant."

"I've never heard of such a thing," I said. "Where did the Apothecarry find something so strong?"

Mmm. Vivian hummed for a moment. "She's very well-traveled. She's also deformed from her experiments. *Anyway*, she got the ingredients from the Volcanic ash in Gorgon and she fired it under intense heat mixed with crystals I've brought her from Votich. She's been there, but it seems fitting that I bring her what she needs and receive some of the bounty of her creation. I mostly like to use it before I start a brawl." She shivered and whimpered with excitement. "Oh! I love that racing feeling it puts in my heart."

Ethal grimaced. "Well, no surprise that I hate it."

I tried to keep pace with them, but Gideon had to fall behind with me to help me forward. He stayed beside me with an arm around me.

"We have a long walk; we should try to get along." I said to Ethal. Silence fell between us, and it made the air thick.

Two days of travel, *without* horses. We stopped at the tower where I said goodbye to Kastell, that memory flooded through me. It hurt to remember her, but excitement coursed through me knowing that this time I would be seeing her again. I couldn't wait to see her and hold her again. She was the closest thing I had to a child. The first few weeks without her were the loneliest times of my life. She always brought so much life and joy to my home. That time was equally consumed with studying Gideon.

I stood looking out over the city the way I did with Kastell so many weeks ago. "I can't believe I'm here again." I said out loud.

Gideon turned to look at me, a smile on his lips. "Destiny has a funny way of bearing down on us all."

Vivian approached us with a heavy rope in her hands. "I'm glad we're all on our own feet again for this leg of the journey." She directed to Ethal. "This isn't going to be easy. I'm taking you in under the pretense that I've collected you as a bounty for the King. I'll need to restrain you all. From here on out it will be a long walk, and a dark one. I'll place a hood over each of you." Vivian took the hood from her saddle bag and handed it to each of us. "Once we get inside the City, I need you to be prepared. You will have things thrown at you. You'll be spit on and heckled at." She went to Gideon and took his chin in her hand and forced him to lock eyes with her. "You *must* always keep your cool. There cannot be devastation in the walls of the city."

"Is there another way?" Ethal pleaded.

"No. You're a fugitive as it is. At least six guards were torn apart at the Sanctuary. If the sisters haven't sent word for your arrest already, I would be shocked. The only way for witches and Warlocks to get into the city will be in these bindings."

Gideon looked between me and Ethal, making his decision. "I trust you. Don't let me regret it later." He thrusted his hands out to Vivian and she quickly tied them tightly around his wrists, making him wince in pain.

"Keep your heads down."

Ethal and I were hesitant to let Vivian tie us up. This would be Ethal's second time in this predicament with Vivian. I could only imagine the resentment she harbored.

The bonds were tight, almost too tight. I had to keep moving my fingers to make sure that blood flowed through them. If I moved my hands too much the binding would start cutting through my fraile skin. We were all tied off in a straight line. First Gideon, then me, and then Ethal. Ethal was supposed to help me keep up if I started to lag too much. Vivian came one by one to us and slipped the hoods over our heads.

"Keep your heads down and remain calm. Once we get to the market, I'll pick up the pace. It won't last more than a few moments. Be strong."

I heard Vivian mount her horse and give him a light kick in his side. After a second my bindings pulled tight in front of me, and I lurched forward. I tried to move my feet fast enough to keep up, but it was difficult. Ethal placed her hands on my back, giving me a light boost forward as we moved. We still had a long walk to the city.

It wasn't long before my arms were aching from the force of being pulled forward. I whimpered with every step. My eyes were filled with tears and my shoulders were screaming in pain.

"It's okay." Ethal said as she came closer to me.

"It's not much further. We're going to pass through the gates soon." Vivian said softly, only for us to hear.

The sounds of running children, wagons, and chattering people caught my ears. I tried to focus on the sounds and smells around me instead of the pain searing through my weakened body. I could smell fresh baked bread, pies, and more. As we moved further there were the noises of small livestock like chickens and goats around us.

Thud-Whack. Ethal let out a cry of pain, someone was throwing things. Soon enough a rock struck my back, making me lunge forward, forcing me to try to keep myself up right. If I fell, I would most likely be dragged all the way to the palace gates. This wasn't the way I wanted to see the city, behind a black bag and bound, with hatred being thrown at me.

"Go back to the woods you hag!" A young boy shouted.

"Slut!" Someone else shouted. Ethal was getting the worst of it from what I could tell.

"Die! You old lard!" Another shouted

I started to tone out the shouts and concentrated on each shuffle forward I took. *One-two-three- four THUD,* another piece of garbage thrown at me, hitting my neck. It was wet and gross. It smelled like rotten vegetation, accompanied by more slurs.

One-two-three-four, I continued to count. I made it to twenty without any interruption. I lifted my head and listened. We came to a stop. It was quiet here.

"Open the gate, I've collected bounties for the King."

The crash of steel rang out as the gate was opened enough to allow us through.

I heard someone approaching. "I'll have them taken to the dungeons. I sent word to the King of your arrival." A man said.

"Thank you, Commander Inara. Be gentle with them, the King will want them unharmed." Vivian stressed.

"As you wish." He responded shortly.

852

J. L. Cross

17 Kastell

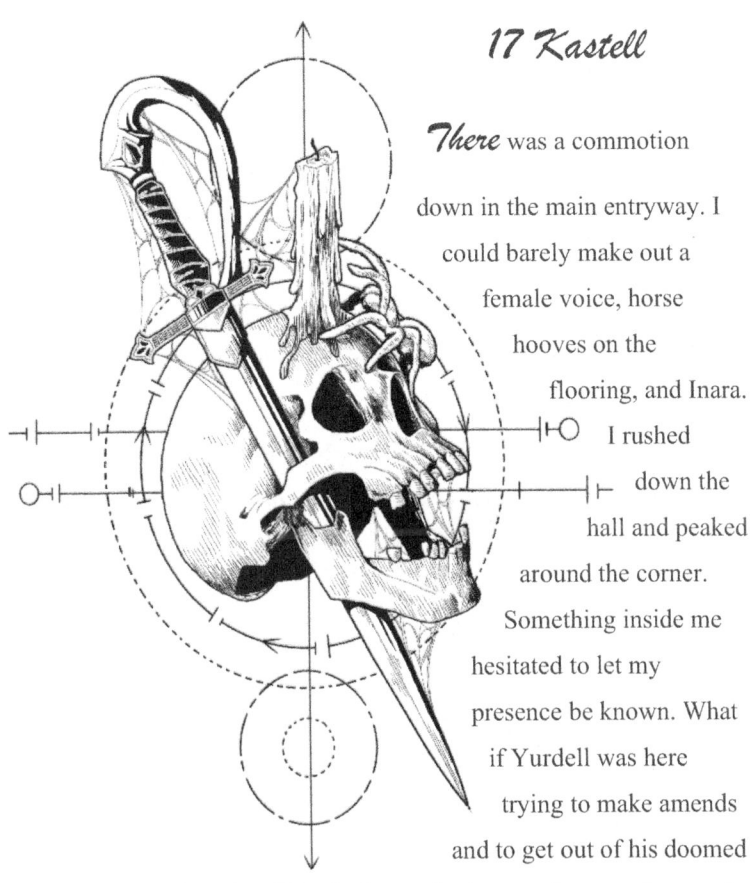

There was a commotion down in the main entryway. I could barely make out a female voice, horse hooves on the flooring, and Inara. I rushed down the hall and peaked around the corner. Something inside me hesitated to let my presence be known. What if Yurdell was here trying to make amends and to get out of his doomed fate? The mere thought of him had me gripping my forearm close and touching the tender spot. The more distance between us the more it began to let off a painful stabbing sensation through my body. It was uncomfortable, but not unbearable. It soon would be. Inara said it was probably due to the minimal amount of Venom I had been exposed to. It was leaving my body quickly, but only killing the Soilt would sever the bond we were given.

Slowly the time away from Yurdell was making my body crave the Venom. I just wanted another moment with him. It was shocking how often my mind wandered to him, lingered on the image of him, the sensation I had when he stood so close to me while his lips fluttered against mine. I wanted him, but the truth was that those feelings were fake, and I had to resist the urge to sneak away and seek him out. Of course, Inara took his guardianship very seriously. He posted outside my door every night and followed me through the castle throughout the day. It was hard to believe he was getting any rest himself. I admired his devotion.

Some nights the only danger he felt the need to chase away were nightmares. Nightmares as simple as the door opening and a shadowy figure stepping through, or the ones with the Red Arvor hovering over me and eating me from the feet up so he could see the pain in my face with every slow bite and every inch the slow sink of his teeth lighting up my entire body with a searing tearing feeling I couldn't shake even when I would be awake.

"I'll have them taken to the dungeons. I sent word to the King of your arrival." Inara said, breaking through my thoughts. He unwound a rope from the horse's saddle. The mysterious woman had ridden right in through the front doors with her bounties. Her hair was short and burgundy and brushed over her slime shoulders with a light bounce. I recognized her slim figure from my childhood. She hadn't changed a bit from my memories so long ago.

"Thank you, Commander Inara. Be gentle with them, the King will want them unharmed." She stressed, *unharmed*. Was he known for taking his anger out on prisoners because he couldn't do that to his own men? I wouldn't be shocked if that were the case. He was *ruthless* in his own ways.

"As you wish." He responded. He took the rope in his hands and pulled them forward. I didn't take any time to regard the prisoners before. The hunter was clearly cashing in on a job or bounty my father had sent her on.

A short older woman was in the middle, the sack over her head covering her shoulders as well. She was a plump older woman with dark skin. She stumbled at the tug on her wrists and let out a sharp cry of pain. My heart leapt into my throat and crashed into my gut. The plummeting feeling filled me, and tears started to fill the corners of my eyes, but I tried to hold them back.

"Stop!" I yelled as I hurled myself around the corner. I would know Kendra's voice anywhere.

Inara hesitated, but then ignored me to take them to the basement. The distance between us was growing more and more with each day that passed. We had turned a stone over, and then it flopped right back into place. He was distancing himself again. He was focused on protecting me and preparing me for threats. He treated me like any other soldier. The friendship we were building suddenly crumbled. That was comforting for me, I didn't want to always be treated like I was special, and I wasn't sure I was entirely ready for a friendship that was as fickle as his. He was so focused on his duties he would be too tired to want to speak. The trial by combat would be soon, but until then we both had to suffer the side-effects of the venom cursing through my veins. It made me equally as distant at times.

"They're criminals." Inara said sharply with another pull on the rope.

Kendra fell to the ground, I tried to support her as she went. I softened her fall slightly. She groaned up at me in awe. "Kastell?"

"I'm here." I whispered. I pulled the ropes from her hands and the sack from over her head. She had a bruise on her chin and her left eye was darkened by a bruise. It was going swell. My heart ached for her.

"The Princess commanded you to stop." My father's voice echoed from down the hall followed by the sound of his heavy footsteps and soft thump of his thick boots on the floor. His arms were crossed over his chest as he stared at the prisoners. He remained emotionless. There was only a slight curiosity on his face when he approached the first prisoner. He walked a circle around the lean man, taking him in. My father was keeping his distance from me as well. There was no mistaking his disappointment. I should have never given Yurdell a second glance. It made me ache knowing that originally my only goal was to make a decision best for me and the throne, but I got ahead of myself with the absurd thought Yurdell could have really been the perfect route to get what I wanted. I let down everyone around me, and their distance from me was proving it.

It was evident that my father had been expecting this person's arrival. He moved around the one in the back, making his way past me. His stern gaze met mine for only a brief second. He continued to study the tiny thin woman for a second and then shrugged. He looked Kendra over with the briefest bit of concern and lifted his gaze from her so that no one else would see it, but I saw it.

"Vivian." He demanded. The woman stepped forward and gave a short bow, "tell me what happened. I sent an entire envoy. I heard that there was a slaughter." Word traveled fast here.

She smirked slightly. Vivian tried to turn her face away from him so he wouldn't see. "The warlock has a bond with the small mage. It's how he holds so much power. If you hurt her, you hurt him. The steel endowed cuffs practically reduced him to a pile of ash and dirt. Her life force, and the magic that binds him is how he retains his eternal life. Faced with an inevitable threat, the Claret Magic reacted of its own accord, routing itself through the mage. None of the guards survived. She is his weakness."

I held Kendra's weak body in my arms. Watching the short conversation my father was having. He had yet to acknowledge Kendra at all. She was resting against me with her eyes closed, breathing deeply. Kendra clung to my blouse, trying to hold me close to her. This wasn't the way I intended to see her next.

"Your Highness, he's extremely dangerous." Vivian affirmed.

"*Very Dangerous.*" The hooded man mocked with a shake of his shoulders. Was he laughing? How could this possibly be funny?

With a quick jerk of his hands the rope burned from around his wrists. The flame followed the length of the rope freeing the three of them and turned into ash, floating in the air around us like snowflakes. He lifted his hood and dropped it on the ground. He was lean yet rather muscular. He looked sturdy and strong. His jaw was sharp and covered in an even beard. His brown hair hung loosely and barely covered his ears. There was a cocky glint of confidence in his dark eyes.

The man held out his hand to my father. "My name is Gideon."

For a moment I thought my father would refuse, but instead he grasped his hand. "Welcome, I'm Vor Kest."

"It's nice to finally meet you." Gideon gestured for the little thin woman that was with him to approach. She rubbed her wrists. They were red from the rope. "This is Ethal, my companion." I could tell he meant that they were much more. His arm was around her waist protectively.

"Why were you brought to the castle like this?!" I shouted, bearing down under Kendra's weight. "Why is she so hurt?!" I pleaded for an answer.

Vivian came to me and knelt, helping to lift Kendra to her feet. "I'll take her to the healer. There was no other way to get them into the castle. Witches and Warlocks aren't allowed into the city. This was to protect them from the Collective. Word has probably already reached the other Soldiers that their brothers in arms were slaughtered at the Sanctuary by a powerful Warlock. They're all safer this way."

"I know you." I said to her as she shifted all of Kendra's weight onto her shoulders and lifted.

"I've worked for your father since the death of your mother. You've seen me around." She smirked and strode off with Kendra over her shoulders like it was nothing to shrug about. Her short cape swayed around her as she moved. Vivian was a strong independent woman, everything I wished people would notice about me.

My father looked over Gideon and Ethal again for a second, taking them in. "Commander Inara." Inara stepped forward. "Take them to the guest tower. Post guards. I don't want them leaving their room." My father directed his attention towards Gideon then. "We'll meet in the morning."

My father came to me as the others walked off and offered me his hand, bringing me to my feet. "Kendra will be well cared for."

"Why were you so cold with her?" I asked.

"We don't have anything to speak about," he said. "We've long since parted ways."

"Don't lie to me."

"Fine," he rubbed his prominent jaw. "I'm not sure where to start. The last time we spoke I was so angry, now, it's as if that anger has faded with time. It still doesn't excuse the things we did so long ago. It's complicated now."

I rubbed his arm. "It's okay to forgive, she's a good woman."

"What's spawned your interest?" he asked.

"You're awkward when she's around, or if she's mentioned. I could tell something was there." I pinched him. "Don't let this time go to waste. I love her, but I think it would mean more if it were you there when she wakes."

He nodded. "I think you're right." a small blush crept up his cheek. I could tell there was still hesitation in his voice. "I'll make sure she's taken care of."

Inara's heavy footsteps echoed from a staircase nearby. I groaned audibly. I needed my space from him today, especially after the way he had no sympathy for Kendra. I rushed off to my room before he could find me in the parlor again. I heard him approach and post himself outside my door. It would be another long night.

My arm was in constant pain. I sat down heavily on the bed and rubbed the infected spot. It was more swollen than before and it had small lightning shaped marks forming around it as the venom penetrated deeper. It was embedded in my blood. Killing Yurdell would effectively put an end to my pain, but I knew I would suffer as well. There wasn't any way around it. Soilt Venom is a tool used to subdue their prey; it wasn't meant to linger in living beings. Soilts had full control of its release as well. Unique to only them, venom was a magical bond between the Soilt and its prey, like a tracking beacon.

Della entered and started drawing me a bath. "What's on your mind?" She asked bluntly as she came to me. She took my hand in hers and twisted my wrist to face up. "It's getting worse. I'll bandage it again before I leave."

"Please, don't bother." I said as I rubbed the spot. As time wore on the physical emotions, I felt from touching it wore away and replaced with a painful throbbing and longing to find him to sedate the pain.

"Kastell," she said sternly. "Covering it will protect the wound from other infections. Let me take care of you." She insisted.

"Alright." The air on the wound felt nice after she cleaned it, soothed by an ointment she added beneath the bandage. The ointment settled against the red skin, cooling the area. I wouldn't fight with her about it. She only wanted what was best.

The grunting of men drifted from the courtyard. I was dressed in a pair of old brown trousers and a beat-up red blouse. I had my hair pulled into a sloppy ponytail. Today I didn't care to look like a royal. It was tiresome, the dresses, the hair styling, the painted lips and the heavy black around my eyes. I was confident enough in my trousers. I didn't need beauty and finery to fill an empty void.

I had to rise before Della to avoid her fussing. I needed a break. Just before the sun came out, I was able to exercise my mare in the ring behind the castle and take my time to groom her. I didn't sleep well, not for many nights. The early tasks of going through the motions with my mare weren't just calming, they were grounding.

I'd bear the chastising from Della and the other ladies later before lunch as they rushed to make me more presentable for my father. Not that it mattered, he cared less for a dress or a blouse. He was only ever concerned about my progress in unearthing anything about the famine through Yurdell, but those notions were over. I was useless to my father. I failed to learn anything. My emotions, my gender, my hormones… it was all used against me.

Inara trained me every day at this time. Just as the sun crested the highest point in the sky. I held a wooden sword in my hands as I opened the doors to the courtyard. He shouted commands at a large formation of men, steel swords drawn and at the ready. He ran them through basic form and balance drills.

My skills increased with every moment we spent training. I enjoyed the balancing and the form training the most, they leaned on my strengths as a woman and hunter. I was small, lean, and strong. My center was much easier to find. These men wouldn't ever have that luck. They were rock solid, large and refined warriors. Practice made them deadly in combat.

It was one of the few enjoyable moments Inara and I were able to share. I found myself able to admire his skill in teaching, and his fluid techniques. Some unique to him and only the men he trained. He allowed for me to distance myself from him, but in the heat of our training we would be tangled in a spare or at a standstill, breathing the same few inches of air. Or worse, our bodies would be pressed together in uncomfortable holds. These were the only moments we had now. Neither of us wasted the time with complaints.

Inara slowly increased his presence around me after a week of training. Sometimes we needed companionship, and most of the time we both liked being left on our own. Even as the power of Yurdell's venom faded leaving only pain behind, I didn't need to tell Inara about it, he knew. He saw the pain every day. I was poisoned by a Yurdell, targeted by him. Inara gave me plenty of space and I still felt smothered. The feelings the venom seeded in me somehow turned into my own and I loathed them. Yet, every day in the courtyard he set his hurt feelings aside and treated me like everyone else. I could tell that when he wanted my company, I wasn't there for him. I enjoyed those moments during our training. It's as if nothing else mattered.

    I moved through the ranks of the men. Some faltered as my gaze lingered on them and their movements. I made them uneasy. It was cruel, the way I walked amongst them with the intention to intimidate them with my station but satisfying.

    Then it was me who faltered a step, turning my eyes back to a man. I stepped back in front of him, surveying the scars on his face. His mouth twitched at the corner when he took me in. With every motion called he moved with confidence and precision. His sword stabbed to the left and to the right of me, sparing me only a feather of space. He didn't waver and neither did I. His eyes were locked on me, daring me to move or flinch a muscle. I wouldn't give into him.

    "It's nice to see you, Kyier. I thought you would have left by now, but here you are." I cleared my throat, hiding the rough wooden sword behind my back. I was slightly embarrassed. Kyier was a skilled warrior, beyond many of his peers. I wasn't sure I wanted him to see me as a trainee.

    "Are you here to train, or to watch me?" His voice was soft, nearly a whisper. Men didn't talk while taking commands from an officer, but from the scars on his face, he probably didn't follow many rules. Inara wasn't his officer anymore; Kyier was only here because he wanted to be.

    I gave him a stiff shrug. "I don't see why a lady of my stature can't have both. Good training and leather clad men to gawk at. Seems like a satisfying day."

    A rough smile came across his face. "If you stare for too long the Commander may be jealous. I don't have time for jealous men."

    I moved to his side; the men moved to make space in their ranks for me. "I don't have time or patience for it myself. He's not jealous, he just hates Arvors." I said as I flipped my wooden sword a few times, comforting myself with the reminder of its weight.

    Kyier's gaze didn't follow me. He didn't pay any mind to me as we both followed Inara's commands. Occasionally he offered a soft correction. *Widen your stance. Raise your sword. Don't look at your feet.*

    The weight of the sword versus my smaller weight meant I was compensating for the sword more in my steps and form. Sometimes my legs needed to be further apart to maintain my balance. I was so much shorter than the rest of the men in the formation. The corrections from Kyier were useful reminders, keeping me focused during the training.

    "Thrust!" The Commander called.

    I threw my sword forward in a violent thrust and then back again to my chest. Inara watched my every move. Judging my capabilities from the front of the formation.

"*Vi-bitas!*" He called in a booming voice in the Elder Aylish. It was rarely used, but our warriors still used it, more than most.

I swung my sword from below my waist, twisting my hips and planting my feet, guiding the sword into the air over the left side of my head. These large motions normally left me off balance, but today I held myself and followed through with the downward motion, bringing the sword straight down in a sweeping motion of pure power. A powerful swing like this would penetrate the skull of most men. A killing blow.

"*Wasay.*" Reset. Inara walked through the formation after his command. He stopped in front of me. Everyone sheathed their weapons. He stared down at me in admiration. "Very good." He said quietly.

"Dismissed." He called out over the formation.

Inara tilted his head towards Kyier who sheathed his sword and started to stretch out his muscles. "Being friendly?" The hate in his tone was tangible. This was the side of him I detested the most.

Kyier nodded curtly. "I may have given her a hard time." He didn't divulge that we both knew Inara would be this way. He was short with Inara. We both saw that flame of hate fanned in Inara's eyes. Kyier looked towards me and raised an eyebrow. "Remember what you don't have time for, and what you do. Stay focused." He tapped his chest where the green sliver of stone was set into a beautiful silver necklace. "I'll be listening for you." Only I was supposed to understand.

I gave him a brief nod and rubbed the back of my neck. Under Inara's pressing stare everything felt itchy and unnerved. I didn't intend to explain to him how the bond of the relic worked between us. It was none of his concern, friends or not.

Kyier started to move past us. Inara stopped him with a hand on his chest. "I think you should be on your way soon." It wasn't a suggestion.

A deep breath and Kyier looked to me for confirmation. He didn't answer to the Commander like he once did. I shook my head, leaving him the choice to do as he wished. "I will no longer be available. I'm heading to port to travel across the sea." Kyier replied. "There will be plenty of distance between the Queen and I. Holster your hate, *Commander.*"

Inara only rolled his eyes. He tried to use his position over Kyier and it failed, "very well."

"Will you hear me from that far? What if it doesn't work that way?" I said, panicking. What would happen if the Stones had a limit? Could they erupt? Could we die?

Kyier smiled and rested his hand on my shoulder for a moment. "Don't worry, I will hear you."

Inara crossed his arms over his chest. "The port is closed. We don't travel the sea to Tarem. You know it's forbidden. It's against the accords we reached with them."

"That's why I won't be using an Aylish port." Kyier retorted. He gave me a dip of his head, "My *Queen.*" Then to Inara, "Commander."

The other men left, chattering amongst themselves. I handed the wooden sword to Inara, breaking his focus from Kyier as he sauntered off.

"When will you promote me to steel?" I asked.

"I have a better idea, and a gift." He said taking me to a large bag lying on the ground by the door. His encounter with the other man was entirely forgotten. "I had these custom made for you." He withdrew a gorgeous pair of small axes.

The axes shone in the light. The handles were dark wood with golden designs of leaves, trees, and flowers etched in gold through it. The head was pure solid steel, sharpened to dangerous points.

"Thank you…" I whispered as I weighed them in my hands, I flipped the one in my right hand and caught the handle perfectly. They were balanced enough for throwing. "What are these for? I've been training for a sword." I asked.

"Well," He took out his sword. "You're small and agile. I felt like the sword was getting in the way, but it helped to teach you balance and self-awareness. You've thrown axes before, and you're deadly accurate. These weapons are more familiar to you than the sword. I thought this would enunciate your strengths." He put distance between us, preparing for a spare. "I made the request through an old friend. They were crafted by the hands of dwarves, and the gold etched from the hands of a fae. He says they're magic."

I stared down at them in awe. "They're beautiful." The magic in them called to me, whispering my name. I heard the magic. Could anyone else?

J. L. Cross

He smiled, arrogant and pleased that he impressed me. "A beautiful weapon for a beautiful Carver of Men."

I couldn't help but chuckle. After mutilating the Arvor intruder I was being referred to as the *Carver of Men*.

"I've never battled close combat with axes." I said simply. "That's what the sword was for." I let my smile fade and set my mind to our lesson.

Inara laughed with excitement. "We'll continue to train, but this time we will train with the axes." He tapped my arm with the flat side of his blade. "*Starting today*."

I backed away from him. My muscles were already sore from the formation training. Every muscle ached as he instructed me into my stance. I was low to the ground, one ax over my head and the other in front of my chest pointing outward. At first it was new and awkward, but after a few drills of moving, like a dance from side to side and around in a circle, the weight was perfect, and it felt natural.

"Now, swing the one at your chest and allow the momentum to spin you forward, and follow through by bringing the one over your head down. The first blow will be powerful and knock your opponent back, the second will either force him backwards a second time and make him lose his balance, or it will slice through him. Either or will give you the upper hand. A quick victory."

We practiced the movement repeatedly until my hands started to numb from my grip and my head was spinning as fast as my body. He was right. These movements were better for my size and speed versus the overbearing weight of the sword. My speed alone could make me lethal in combat.

"Good!" He applauded and backed away from me. We were both covered in sweat as we sat down in the center of the unkempt yard. "I have one more lesson for today."

"I don't think I can do much more." I complained.

"Nonsense! This is the last one." He said, offering me a hand and lurching me to my feet. "The axes make you quick, small, and even more deadly. But I want you to try to protect yourself this time." Inara paused, circling close behind me until he was close to my ear, whispering. "See me as the ultimate threat."

"You haven't taught me a defense." I said curtly, ignoring his boring attempt at intimidating me. I couldn't encourage him to use his pathetic attempts at my childish heart, once easily affected by his temper and deep tone as he whispered threats during our training. I wouldn't let him start treating me like he did when I was a child. I was resistant to that now. I needed this training.

He tapped my arm. "Ready position." Inara's dark demeanor drained away. I groaned and lowered myself into my ready position. As long as I ignored his attempts, I would be safe. The moment I let him get to me would be the moment that ruthless monster started to surface more and more on me. He'd find new ways to torment me if it meant getting my time and emotions riled.

"I'll try to overpower you because you're small. I'll try to use that alone against you." Inara said as he pulled me away from the thought of his aggressive nature, "as I follow through on the downward strike, catch my blade with your ax above your head, use my momentum to spin as usual, but slide the beard of the ax into the hilt of my sword and throw it away from you. I should naturally want to hold onto my sword but also move backwards to avoid your attack. Whichever I chose will seal my fate. If I try to cling to my sword, I will be left in the line of your second ax, with all your might throw it into my abdomen. If I back away, follow through with a second attack as we've been practicing. I'll be unarmed and you'll win the battle."

    I shrugged. "This might work in training, but combat is unpredictable. Wouldn't this call for knowing my opponent's next move?"

    Inara nodded. "What was my first rule of defense when we practiced with the sword?"

    "Watch my opponent." I repeated back to him.

    "Kastell," he scolded. "Watch your opponent. Watch my feet, my shift in weight, the direction of my eyes. *Watch me.*"

    I nodded sharply in understanding. "I'll be able to see when you decide to go for a power swing." I muttered to myself. I've been practicing for long enough to know his habits during combat.

    I watched him as we went into our ready positions. I used my axes to push off a few light attacks. He stepped to his left, I followed suit and took a step in the opposite direction. Combat was a beautiful dance between enemies. A small smirk played on his lips and his eyes flared when he tried to out step me and attack me from the side with the short, determined, thrust, but I matched him and kept him centered in front of me, thwarting his feeble attacks. He attempted the same maneuver, but this time used a sweeping motion across my midline. I dropped to the ground, the sword swishing over me as I rolled away. I kicked his legs out from under him and sprang to my feet, I had the advantage. My heart pounded as I threw my ax powerfully over my head and downward where his head would have been, but he was quick to move, trapping my ax into the ground. I yanked it free and stepped back a few paces after he got his feet under him.

"You're being very forward with your attacks," he pointed. "Don't be overconfident."

I laughed. "Don't be so cocky. The teacher doesn't always win. I can see you breathing hard." His chest was heaving, but I remained calm. The light weight of the axes made combat a steady and flawless dance, despite the screaming of my muscles as I moved them.

It was then he decided to make his attack, the one I was waiting for. I saw the grip on his hilt tighten, the shift of his weight to his dominant foot, that telling bend in his knees so he could throw his weight behind his attack. Even his mouth twitched slightly just before he started.

I grinned as I made the motions, he instructed me. As the beard of the ax caught the sword it loosened his grip, and I easily used the ax to fling the sword away. Inara hesitated, unsure of which fate he would choose, but I was so quick I had my ax an inch away from his abdomen before he decided. He fell backwards and tried to stand as fast as he could. He thought he would be given the time to decide. *Wrong.*

The teacher was defeated. I could see the embarrassment creeping on him, but it didn't stay. The teacher longed for the day the student didn't need to be taught. We still had a lot of training to do, but my skills were adequate for combat.

"That was perfect." He was out of breath now. He straightened his hair and brushed the dirt off him.

I was smug. "The teacher has been defeated." I said aloud.

"You're very skilled now. Although, there is still plenty to learn."

I set my axes down and sunk down beside them. "I wouldn't be so capable without you." I patted the spot beside me.

He sat. "Just because I've given you weapons doesn't mean you should start seeking out trouble," he said. "I worried that giving you these would prompt you to make bad decisions."

"Ye of little faith." I said with a smile. "You aren't prompting any thoughts I haven't mulled over a thousand times before."

"You're impressionable. Please, be cautious." He flicked his hand in the direction Kyier had gone earlier. "He isn't the type to be friendly with. He's sour and rebellious, he hardly listened when we needed him to. Kyier has gotten into his fair share of nasty duels. I'll admit he's capable and a fine warrior, but I wouldn't hesitate to take his hand off if he leads you down a dark path. Kyier is lucky to be alive. You gave him that mercy."

I scoffed. "I'm impressionable, but I'm not stupid. You need to trust me. Trust me to make the best decisions for myself. Stop underestimating my ability to take care of myself." I chuckled softly, a sweet but menacing sound. "If you ever touch his hands- I'll take one of your own. Kyier answers to me. Me alone."

Inara swallowed hard, his throat bobbing. I was the one intimidating him now, but he knew to take me seriously, I wasn't saying it for entertainment, but as a fact.

"Understood." He pulled a leather harness from his bag and handed it to me, moving our conversation away from Kyier. "Carry them on your back. I still think of that rebel that tried to rip your throat out. You were lucky to have something to use as a weapon then. Now, you're never defenseless."

"It doesn't matter." I said with disdain. "I'm trapped in this castle. My father won't let me leave and you're constantly nearby. I doubt I'll ever have to defend myself again."

His head dipped. "You never know." Inara was right, an attack could come at any time. The Arvor intruder had proved that to all of us. We weren't as safe as we believed we were behind those walls. The heckler would have a field day if only he knew the threat was truly within our walls. Or maybe he wasn't so far off that first day.

"You have other things you should worry about." I said, taking his mind off of the past. There was nothing either of us could do to change it. He couldn't have changed the way things unfolded. Why bother worrying over it and feeling guilty?

"Like what?" He asked, leaning back onto his elbows.

"You're trial by combat. I hear Yurdell is a killer in the arena, he's nothing but pure power and strength."

Inara rolled to his side and looked up at me with a playful smirk. "Are you worried about me?"

"Aren't you worried about yourself?" I prodded back.

"I think everyone should be afraid to die, but I haven't met anyone with the skills I have. I'm confident he'll fall at the tip of my blade."

I scoffed and stood to my feet. "You're so arrogant. You may have taught me all I know, but you still lost in our spar."

"Don't be so high and mighty." He stood and squared his shoulders, meeting my gaze. "I let you win." His voice rumbled with amusement.

I rolled my eyes and picked up my things. "When the Collective convenes in a full moon's time and sets the date of your duel, don't expect me to look on with pity when Yurdell takes your life."

I left him then, clenching my axes in my hands. I had to find some way to save him. He was an arrogant and confident man that didn't know what was best for him, even when he stared death in the face. There had to be something I could do for him.

I laid on my bed staring up into the empty wooden ceiling. My life was passing, trapped in a castle with nowhere to go. I shot up straight. No one could really keep me here. My father thought he could when I was young, and now he thought the same. I was an escape artist then and I could be now. I was done living by their fear.

I tied my hair up in a ponytail and harnessed my axes. They were light and fit just right across my back. I went to my mother's old chest and took out an old faded black cape. It only hung to my waist, but it was long enough to conceal my weapons.

The window was wide enough for me to fit through with a bit of a squeeze, but it wasn't much different than when I was a child. The breeze brushed through the open frame, disturbing the flat curtains and carried them into the room. I was about to leap out onto the roof below, but first, I ran to my vanity and picked up the old, rusted letter opener and jammed it into the mouth of my boot. I couldn't leave without my first true weapon. It held sentimental value.

The slope of the roof was steeper than I recalled. I balanced myself on the frame of the window for a moment, judging my likely fall. A short giggle left my lips suddenly as I let go and had to catch myself before sliding down the slippery surface to the fall I'd considered. It wouldn't kill me, but it wouldn't be pleasant. The surface was slick, but not impossible to traverse. *One foot after the other,* I chanted in my head. Another little giggle as I made it over to the latis that climbed the side of the steel castle wall. Not many of the walls were steel, but most of them faced the mountains on the other side of the river. The walls reflected the light back to Voitich, a symbol of our perseverance over the powers Soilts had during the great war.

Ivy crested over the edge of the roof and had started creeping to the ridge of the roof. The latis was thick wood, but it was getting weak with age. I grabbed hold and swung my legs over. It was like second nature. The harder part was getting my footing on the way back up, especially with the roof wet with condensation.

My feet slapped the ground lightly, letting a small splash circle my feet. I wanted to run and jump through the puddles brought by the short rainstorm we had earlier in the day. I gathered my childish excitement and locked it away in my heart. I still had to make it to the other side of the wall into the town below. I followed the wall of the castle, keeping myself tucked into the shadows. I looked for guards making rounds before I dashed into the overgrown garden and fought my way to the very back. I didn't get that far into grooming it. It would take months to make it remotely presentable.

I placed my hand on the back walls and felt for a break in the solid concrete. I searched for a moment until I found the hole I looked for. It was much lower and smaller to crawl through than I remembered, but I was a small child the last time I used it. The opening in the wall had gone unfilled and unchecked through all these years that passed. Surprisingly, it was also easy to find. I always went from the fountain in the center of the garden and straight back. Bushes covered the small hole from eyesight.

I moved the branches and twigs of the bush out of my way and lowered myself onto my belly and pushed my way through. A small thorn from an uncut rose bush scratched at the right side of my face. I felt it snagged in the skin and tear.

"Ow," I grabbed my check and whipped away the blood dripping down my cheek bone as I stood on the other side. After crawling through low and dense bushes I was relieved to be back on my feet again. I wasn't far from the guards on the wall and the gate to the castle. Small buildings were scattered in front of me and provided the perfect cover in the full moonlight to get to the tavern.

The alleys were muddy and littered with empty wooden storage crates and buckets of waste that needed to be taken outside the city for dumping. I turned my nose away from the rotting food and putrid smell of Aylish waste. I missed these disgusting things about the city, but that didn't make them anymore pleasing.

I stopped just outside the tavern. It was buzzing with life. Men surrounded a small table lit in a bright lantern light. They were all arguing over a sketchy dice game. At the center of the chaotic arguing was the red headed man that bought me the scarves. I regretted not wearing it on my visit, but it was an obnoxious color. I didn't want to be easily recognized by guards, or anyone.

"I've won!" The red head shouted and clapped the other man on the back. "There's no guessing. You've rolled one too many and your luck has run out!"

The game was easy to cheat with a set of trick dice, but it was the most common game to play. Opponents would agree to any given number and roll a single dice. A die would be added with every passing turn. The goal was to get as close to the agreed number without going over. The red head was five points from the number carved into the surface of the table next to the chart tracking their game. The surface of the table was littered with other game charts.

"You're a cheat!" The man spat at him. "You've never lost a table yet!" The older, more ragged, desperate man grabbed his wrists and pushed up on his sleeves. He was disappointed to see that there were no trick dice up his sleeves. My friend won fair and square.

The red head took the coin from the surface of the rocking and unstable table and handed five of the eight pieces back to the losing man. An act of generosity not shown by many gamblers.

"I don't play for the coin, but for amusement." He said as he passed the coins.

The older man was left in shock. He jammed the coins into his pocket and turned away and left quickly, most likely fearing the generous man was only playing tricks and cruel pranks on him.

The table cleared. The red head fell into a chair with a wobble and placed three coins on the table. A barmaid came and collected them, leaving a tall foaming beverage made of cheap wheat and barley in front of him. I could smell it as I approached.

"Another, please?" I asked and handed her three more coins from my own purse. The coins I flashed were clean and bright. She smiled brightly and placed another one down for me. She knew I had the coin to spend on the condition of my currency. It wasn't dirty and mucked with age.

As I sat the man smiled up at me from ear to ear. His cheeks were rosy from the heat of his debate and the alcohol he had already consumed. He straightened himself and waited for me to settle into my seat.

J. L. Cross

"Look what's dropped in! Are you enjoying a rebellious night out against the wishes of our benevolent King?" he teased.

I nodded, a crooked grin playing on my lips. "It's exciting, really. I was getting so cooped up. The air was getting stale, too." I took a long sip from the rich alcohol and sighed. "It's been so long…" I was almost speaking directly to my mug of beer.

"Don't fall in love so fast." The man said jokingly. "Why did you choose my tabel?"

"I want to know your name." I blurted quickly.

He rubbed his beard and tisked. *Tsk Tsk Tsk.* Then clicked his tongue once. "You see, I don't think it matters who I am."

I reached across the table and shoved his arm. "It matters to me. From the first day you were kind to me."

"DeLuca Aluxious." He said shortly. "Call me Aluxious. It seems everyone else does."

I bobbed my head in approval. Finally, a name to put to the face and red trimmed beard. For a tavern rat he was mostly well groomed. His smile was contagious. I couldn't help but return it.

"You're such a character. Why are you always gambling for the pot if you don't want it?" I took another long sip of my beer and gestured for the barmaid to bring me another. She was a pretty woman with well-rounded breasts that were pushed tightly into a plump position by her bodice. Women here made money from their bodies. It still made me chuckle at them. I never had to do such things for money, but maybe I would have if I needed to. I guess I'll never have to know.

"I usually like to take what I can and give to who I want to. I'm not a greedy man. But I don't think anyone would play with me if it weren't for what's in my pockets." he grunted, moving his mug to his lips. He watched me finish off my own quickly.

"It seems like money makes the world go around down here. I don't hear much about it where I'm from. I'm always shocked to see what people will do for a small piece of metal to shove in their pockets."

Aluxious' smile dropped. "You don't understand their hardship either. If you did, maybe you would be less likely to judge. There's nothing wrong with nakedness. It's only Ayles that have a sense for modesty. I come to look at the *almost* naked and bouncing tits. Where I come from women don't always cover themselves and it's normal. I like the curiosity of this way a bit more."

"I hope I'm never in the position to find out what it's like to live that way. I prefer my nakedness to be very covered." I put my mug down on the table, the condensation running off the glass in droplets until they met in a wet rim around the base. "I think once I'm Queen I'll try to change these things. I don't like seeing people so hard off. It shouldn't be this way. She should expose herself because she wants to, not because she must."

He nodded. "Enough of that. You're supposed to be enjoying a rebellious night out. I see you didn't wear the scarves." He pointed out with a wink.

"I'm sorry, I really wish I would have worn one, but I'm trying to blend in here." I joked.

J. L. Cross

Aluxious laughed and reached across the table, but hesitated. "Do you mind?"

"Wait, what?" I said frantically pulling my hands through my hair. "Is there something on me?"

He laughed and took a leaf and twisted it from my hair, and then a small thorn. "I see the travel here was treacherous."

"Surprisingly so! I didn't remember the route being so low to the ground, but I was smaller then."

A loud chorus of fast paced songs broke from inside the tavern and spilled through the doorway as three men staggered out. I lifted my beverage to them and sang the last few words. "*...and here the Aylish come to drown!*" I slammed the bottom of my mug on the table and tipped the beer, spilling its contents into my mouth.

"Chug, chug, chug!" Aluxious and the others chanted in unison.

When my mug was empty, I dropped it to the ground and lifted my arms in victory, turning my face into the moonlight, bathing in the freedom I felt coursing through my body.

The men staggered off continuing their songs and laughter. Aluxious was entirely amused with me. "You're a unique little Princess."

"You're an elusive and mysterious hybrid."

He shrugged. "I guess, I do my best to maintain the mystery." He stood and motioned for me to follow. "Let's go for a walk."

I laughed and shook my head. "I don't think so." I said as I stood and waggled a finger at him in defiance. "I hold my alcohol very well, and no one will be taking advantage of me tonight."

He chuckled and shrugged, continuing to walk off without me. "Enjoy your lonesome night; All by yourself." He chuckled. "*Alone.*" He added.

"Fine." I said and followed him. "Where are we going?"

He pointed to the gate. "There's a nice little spot just inside the gates that gets a great view of the sky. What's even better is that it's one of the few places covered in grass."

We both plopped down to the ground. His arm almost brushed mine, so I moved myself away, putting a liberal distance between the two of us. He was still a stranger. The grass was soft between my fingers. I combed it through my hands over and over again. I wanted it to calm my racing heart and the ball of nerves growing inside of me. There was something strange about this man that made my instinct to run or fight simmer.

Aluxious noticed my movement away but ignored it. He pointed at a constellation in the sky. I couldn't make out what it was at first, but I haven't spent a lot of time staring at stars recently. Not like I used to at the Sanctuary.

"That's the constellation of the Lone Arvor." He said simply. "Legends call it the Devil's guide, because if you follow them over the sea, they take you to Tarem, treacherous oceans. Only a few trade vessels have made it to Tarem. Ironically, what is it your father calls the Arvor King? The Devil, isn't it? It's odd, the Devil is a human term and a human idea."

I shrugged then. "We don't have deities or gods. Even the Mother was named by mortal beings, but in her right she's still our goddess."

He didn't look surprised. "No matter the origin-, that's what the Arvors think of Vor, too..." He let out a deep breath, his chest rumbling a soft growl. "This war is wrong on both sides. It just depends which perspective you take once you're a part of it. No matter which side you're on, you feel like the good guy fighting the good fight, but you're always someone else's villain."

I saw it then, an Arvor with its head bent. "I guess he's referring to the souls the Arvor King has collected from the war, that's all. I don't think he means it in a literal sense. Why does it matter anyways? I'm sure the rebels have used some choice words to describe my father in return."

Aluxious shrugged. "I don't know if it matters at all. I just think it's misleading. What if the Arvor King isn't as bad as you're told he is?"

"He has killed a lot of Ayles."

"Or is that just what they tell you? Come on! You're a deviant. Challenge the system! Tell me what you really think of him." Aluxious was staring at me now instead of up at the sky. I could feel his eyes on me. I couldn't tear mine away from the stars. They were beautiful.

"Well," I started. I hesitated for a moment. "I think it's a huge misunderstanding. My brother started this war, not my father. It wasn't his decision to kill off that village. Vlad is a sick poison to our family name. I think it was the Arvor retaliation that made my father realize there was no turning back; plus, most of the Collective thinks the same way Vlad does. There was no use in fighting them. I don't think he's a bad man, I don't think my father is either, but they both have thousands of deaths on their hands. For that I can't forgive either of them. It's what divides my father and I to this day. It's overwhelming, our different opinions on the war. I can't always look at him the same. Not after knowing what I do about the war and seeing it firsthand. Yet, I still love him."

Hmmm... Aluxious grumbled. "I like your point of view. You see them both as toxicities that should be removed."

"I do." I agreed. "Why did you bring it up?"

Aluxious leaned close to me, his eyes turning a bright abnormal amber. A soft growl passed his lips making the hair on my arms stand. "I'm part Arvor."

"What else are you?!" I snapped, moving slightly away from. I was shocked that anyone of his kind had made it into the city walls. Hybrid or not.

He laughed at my reaction. "I'll give you two guesses of my breeding."

"Soilt." I blurted.

"Mmm. Do you think I'm a violent hybrid attempting to pull you into the dark and seduce you for your blood?" He wiggled his

eyebrows and his eyes glistened. Was that really what everyone thought of Yurdell's kind? They couldn't all be that way. Yurdell proved his ability to fool me and be cunning in his own right.

I couldn't help but chuckle nervously. "No. I just think that's where you get the pale skin, and the *I-don't-give-a-shit* attitude you have. My recent suitor was like that, and he's Aylish and Soilt."

He nodded. "Very well, you're right." He confirmed. "You have one last guess."

"You said you're a hybrid." I pointed.

He gave a curt bob of his head and then lifted a shoulder in guilt, biting his lip. "*I lied*, I'm a Tribrid. I don't like to tell many. It's frowned upon to be so mixed."

I nodded. "A secret I'll take to the grave. I'm honored."

He shoved me lightly. "I'll hold you to it!"

"Dwarven." I said with a laugh that I tried to hide.

Aluxious sucked in a sharp breath and groaned. "How dare you! No one has seen a dwarf in ages."

"The beard. You're clean cut. Only the dwarves cared that much about their facial hair."

"You're so *very* wrong. Have you ever seen an Arvor with unkempt hair shift? They're all mangled and tangled, downright disgusting to look at. I promise you, the beast inside of me is spectacular and gorgeous."

"Okay, so what are you?" I asked.

"Why don't we strike an accord?" I agreed impatiently. He continued, "you come again in three days' time, and I will give you one more guess. That's a fifty percent chance of guessing it right." I stuck out my hand and he grasped it, shaking it gingerly. "Great." He stood and dusted off his pants. "Although, I must be going."

"So soon?" I asked, disappointed. I was enjoying myself in his company. Why was it so easy to take company with the same beings I was being told to avoid?

He pointed to his nose. "I can smell a rather vile being coming to collect his dues for my presence."

"Yurdell?" I shot to my feet when Aluxious confirmed with a sharp nod of his head. "I can't be here. You can't leave me alone here!" I panicked and grabbed at his arms.

Aluxious quickly turned over my wrist and saw the bandage. He brought it to his nose and inhaled deeply. "*Ahh*..." He dropped my wrist. "I thought it was a lie. He used venom on you. He told me about the confrontation."

"Yes, and if he finds me it'll be like starting all over again. I don't think I can control myself. I need your help." I begged him. I couldn't stop the swelling of tears. Even if I ran, Yurdell would be able to find me. Without the safety of the palace walls, I was someone else for him to hunt.

Aluxious pushed me behind him.

"Made a friend I see." Yurdells husky voice said. I heard his footsteps crunching in the dirt and rock. I kept my gaze downward, afraid that looking him in the eye would ignite a stronger pain induced by the venom. I could feel it in my chest and in my veins, pulsing and racing at the sound of his voice. He called to me in the darkness of my subconscious, pleading with me to come to him.

"You're not wanted here." Aluxious said, a low growl coming out of the back of his throat.

Yurdell laughed. "Pay your dues or leave. I don't care about the girl. The Collective will convene soon, and I will fight the Commander. It's a shame, really. I thought maybe she would have the guts to fight for her own honor. Or maybe just have better character judgment."

His insult struck somewhere deep inside me that the venom couldn't touch. *My pride.* I pushed in front of Aluxious. I squared my shoulders as I met his deep endless eyes. The venom lept and bounded through me, attempting to send me into his arms. I clenched my fists and fought back against the urge.

Yurdell beckoned for me to come to him. "Don't fight it." He coaxed.

Aluxious placed a hand on my shoulder and held it there firmly. He leaned forward and whispered in my ear. "You're stronger than him."

"This is not the time, nor the place." A shadowy figure stepped from out of the Tavern, a bag slung over his shoulder. *Kyier.* A dark whisper in my mind echoed that I'd be safe with him, that as long as we were bound by the Relic he would be my safety. A part of me wanted to cower and run to him.

Yurdell scoffed. "Of course, the King would have his soldiers watching her. I'm no fool. Take her and go before I seal my fate and hers. I've nothing left to live for anyways." He gave an awful flick of his wrist and walked past us to where a horse was hitched. "Maybe another time, *Princess*." Yurdell said to me, looking down at me from his stead. There was pain in his eyes. Was he fabricating hate for me to justify his decisions?

My body had tensed so tightly, and my knees locked. Freckles of darkness splattered my eyes until the tension in my legs eased away. Fear swelled throughout me as much as the desire to run to Yurdell did. A constant battle with his venom, and the real thing was worse than the everyday pain. I could go to him now and end the pain that licked its way along my veins and over my skin. I could be rid of the numbness inside my chest and the itch on the back of my neck. I shook away those thoughts. I wouldn't let a man like him control me. I wouldn't be subdued.

Yurdell turned his horse to the city gate and kicked him into a steady trot. When he was a fair distance away, I felt the tension leave my body entirely. A swimmy feeling came over my head and behind my eyes. I wouldn't pass out. I wouldn't let him even have a small victory over me, even one he wouldn't witness.

Kyier came to us and shoved Aluxious on the shoulder roughly, knocking him off balance slightly and forcing him to stagger until he got his footing. "You're an idiot. She wouldn't be able to win in combat against him, yet you fanned the flames!"

He moved to me, forcing me to look up to meet his gaze. His hand came to my chin, forcing me not to move. "Next time, *call me*. What good is our bargain if you won't use it?"

I jerked my chin free of his grasp. "I don't need a protector."

"No, you need someone to rely on. Let me be that person. You can and will fight him, but you're not ready." He lifted my chin again, but this time his touch was gentle, and his eyes were pleading. "Be safe while I'm away. Be smart. Bide your time and make your move when he's not expecting it. Don't let him set the scenario. Can you do that for me?"

"Yes." I couldn't help but agree. Kyier was right, Aluxious encouraged me to walk right into the fight Yurdell was setting. He would have had the upper hand.

I stepped away from Kyier and got my bearings, tugging my cape around me tightly. "Be safe on your journey." I left them both standing there without a proper goodbye. I could still feel the warmth of Kyier's finger on my chin. I itched at the spot wishing that he wouldn't have touched me at all. I didn't need him. He needed me. He secured his life with our bargain, and I was only merciful, guaranteeing he wouldn't come to take my life; that was the only part of the bargain that mattered to me. I wouldn't ever call him. He could die alone for all I cared, like all the men in my life. I didn't need them.

Crawling back to the roof and in through the window was the difficult part. I had slipped on the roof a time or two before getting to the window, both times I nearly fell. It could have been a messy death.

I tossed my cloak onto the vanity and kicked off my boots and trousers. I gently set my axes against the bed frame and plopped down. I needed to clear my mind. Every part of me was still buzzing with anger and pricks of pain from the encounter with Yurdell. I should have known better than to go there. It was still his land, *his* territory. I should have known he would bait me into a duel. For him there would be satisfaction in killing me before he had to die. For a man that fought endlessly for his titles and lands, I was surprised to see he was more apprehensive than Inara about the challenge. Both men seemed convinced they would lose to the other. Or was Yurdell only accepting that if Inara didn't take his life, my father surely would? Yurdell lived on borrowed time.

I closed my eyes as I folded my legs under me and cleared my mind, opening it the way Kendra had taught me. I needed to center myself. If I could focus through the pain, I could find my center and separate the venom from my mind. I needed to stop being so reckless just because the people around me wanted to protect me. They didn't mean any harm. My father only wanted me to be safe. Kyier wanted me to be safe. Inara wanted me to be safe. Wasn't that enough for me? Why did I have to get into my own head and make such reckless decisions? Why was I angry with them all?

My breathing evened as I sat, focusing on my center, a small light in the dark abyss I imagined was the shell my body provided, pulling the energy in my body to my core. I could feel the heat of the venom radiating out from my wrist and along my veins until it got to my chest, flooding my heart. The pain was crippling. I held my chest and used my energy to push it back out. The light inside of me got all the dimmer. A chill came over me as I controlled that pain, letting it only move throughout my hand and wrist. I'd cut it off if only that would solve all my problems.

Every part of my body was sapped and weary. As my mind and strength began to fail me the pain spread again. It would take an immense amount of focus for me to control it and to fight at the same time. Yurdell would have called to the venom and used it to cripple me in a duel tonight. I wouldn't have won even if my fighting skills were superior. They weren't.

I laid my head back onto my pillow and let the warmth and comfort of the mattress swallow me into a blissful sweaty sleep where the pain couldn't reach me.

18 Kastell

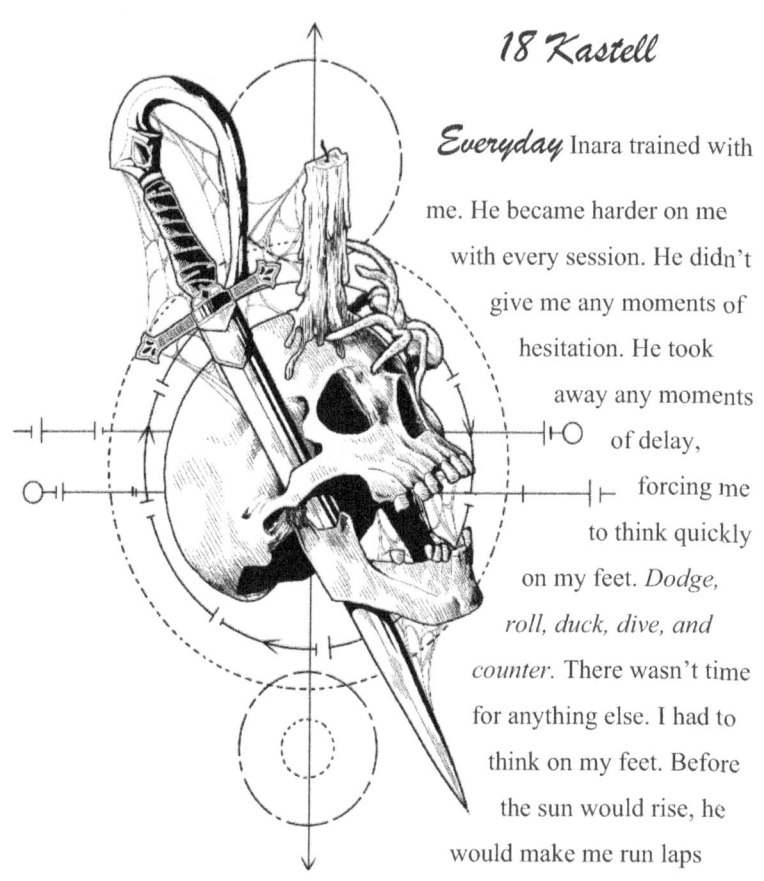

Everyday Inara trained with me. He became harder on me with every session. He didn't give me any moments of hesitation. He took away any moments of delay, forcing me to think quickly on my feet. *Dodge, roll, duck, dive, and counter.* There wasn't time for anything else. I had to think on my feet. Before the sun would rise, he would make me run laps around the palace until I couldn't keep going. Then it was time to train my muscles and my combat skills.

In the meantime, the Collective had gathered, Yurdell never showed his face, and they voted in a unanimous decision that Ianar would duel the delegate for his titles, and for my honor. What Yurdell had done to me was treason against the King and against the honor of the crown. No one debated. The decision was final and the Collective left as quickly as they had come.

J. L. Cross

"You're almost as good as me." Inara grabbed my arm and yanked me to my feet. We were both breathing heavily. The sun beat down on us as we practiced. "You still seem distracted. What's on your mind?" Somehow, I'd allowed myself to open to him again in the last few weeks that passed. He wasn't just a lurking guard following me around on my father's orders anymore. He was a friend, but I was still tentative about putting a title to it. It was more comfortable now, as if we were children again that could banter, but he wasn't the bully anymore. I could accept the fact that he changed, but I wasn't positive I could trust him yet, not entirely. It was hard to trust anyone.

I fidgeted for a second and then strolled to the shade to sit and drink from a jar of water. "It's the venom." I chugged the water until my stomach was full.

"Careful, you'll make yourself sick." Inara took the jar from my hands and drank deeply. *Hypocrite.* He sat beside me and leaned back onto his elbows. "Does it hurt?"

I nodded and stared at the ground. "It's hard to fight through it. I can control it if I focus, but it takes so much energy. I've been practicing for weeks now. I think I can control it long enough for a single fight, but I'll never know until I'm faced with it."

"I think you're doing very well. For the first half of our fight, you seemed focused and aware. Our spars run longer than the average duel. I think you can hold your own. Can you endure the pain though, and fight with it? I'm more concerned about you going into a battle."

"I can. Soldiers aren't nearly as skilled as you, my father, or Yurdell. They know what they need to make it by. That's not enough against us. A battle would be far easier than a skilled duel."

Inara chuckled and asked sarcastically, "are you planning to duel?"

I didn't indulge him with an answer. We sat in silence for a long moment. Some things were for me alone to know. I wanted, and fully intended, to back Yurdell into a duel before he saw the arena. This was my fight anyways, wasn't it? The Collective named a date after the passing of the full moon. Surprisingly, even the Arvors kept off our lands during the time. Less food was being stolen. It all seemed to be fitting together, like life could be easy and the war could just fade into history.

The doors to the training ring burst open and my father was there. We shot to our feet. Inara offered him a slight bow.

"Grain houses are being burned." So much for peace and quiet recently. "Assemble five men to ride with us." My father was about to walk back out after Inara took off to do as he was told, but he stopped and looked over his shoulder. "I had new leather armor made for you. Get ready, you're coming with us."

My heart leapt. It wasn't a question or an offer, he was demanding that I go with him. I fumbled for my axes and made my way to my room to dress. On my bed was a full set of leathers in my father's colors. The blue and browns melded together beautifully.

I dressed as quickly as I could and strapped my axes across my back. I was waiting in the courtyard in front of the castle on my horse before any of the men arrived. Soldiers trickled in with their horses, my father was close behind them with Inara.

When they stopped, he only took a moment to look me over and nodded his head in approval. He turned his attention to the men. "Grain houses are being lit on fire just outside the city. We've lost two already, and by the time we reach the farm it could be doubled. We need to save the rest."

My father jerked his horse in the direction of the city gates and kicked it into a quick trot. When we passed through the city gates and the road opened up to us we were moving as fast as we could. The horse hooves beat into the ground, carrying us with the wind. The nearest farms were in the valley outside the city, close.

As we surged over the first hill I could see the smoke rising into the sky in front of us, black and thick. Farmers were rushing to three grain houses that were burning with buckets of water, tossing them onto the flames and scurrying back to the well for more as quickly as they could.

My father motioned to the four soldiers to dismount. "Put out the fires, quick!" He yelled and turned his horse away. He beckoned Inara and I. "We make a pass around the farm. Scout for Arvors or warlocks. I want whoever's doing this in chains or dead!"

Inara took off around the left side of the farms and my father to the right. I kicked my horse and started through the center of the farming village. I didn't have to go far before I was face to face with an Arvor. He tucked himself back against one of the farm buildings, a bag of grain dropping from his jowls, half empty from the puncturing of his teeth.

I slid from the back of my horse and pulled an ax from its sheath. The Arvor dropped the bag and lunged on its long-extended legs, missing me as I darted out of its reach. I couldn't help the satisfied smile that came to my lips. "*Surrender or die.*"

The Arvor lashed out with its paw and without any hesitation I swung my ax through its arm, blood soared from the wound as the arm fell before me. It howled and wailed in pain. There was no way around me except through combat. The Arvor saw its death and still charged clumsily in my direction. It tottered off balance as it naturally tried to use its wounded arm to run towards me, but the pain hindered it and it fell into the dirt, trying to kick its way back to its feet. I wanted to see the Arvor suffer. It took our food and burned the grain houses. Our people would starve. With a single downward swing of my ax, I buried it into its spine and gloated as its howl broke into a screech of agony.

Inara rounded the corner behind me and brought his horse to a stop. The Arvor died at my feet, bringing a silence back into the air. I kicked the body over for him to see. "Arvor."

He grunted. "Only one. Your father didn't find others and neither did I. This is the kind of damage they can do on their own!" Inara was angry and shouted as he motioned around us to the smoking grain houses as if to make a point to me.

"We're both upset about it, Inara." I put my hand on his shoulder. "I'm not the enemy, they are. Shouting won't bring the food back."

J. L. Cross

The two of us met with my father in front of the grain houses that the smoke was dying from. He looked proud to see me, as if he knew already that I'd killed the guilty. Was he doing this so that I could get my revenge for the intruder, or for the trap they baited me into in the woods?

"What would you have us do to stop this?" My father asked with his arms crossed over his chest.

"Post guards throughout our farms. Kill Arvors on sight."

My father looked to Inara who nodded in agreement with me. "You heard her. Assemble guards and distribute them throughout the farms."

"Yes, sir."

The next morning, I sat alone in the training ring. I had only a week to decide when to make my move against Yurdell. Only a few days to plan. There wasn't much to plan, just the fear I needed to control, and then the venom. I had to be mentally prepared to fight him. When I awoke that morning, I knew this was the day. It was now or never for my vengeance. I couldn't keep putting it off like I had been.

I knew Inara would arrive after me, but I wasn't expecting him to be in a relaxed set of trousers and a button down that was barely tucked in. He looked clean and wet as if he'd just stepped out of the bath.

"You're dressed for a war." He said as I stood. "I figured I'd let us take the day off from training."

"That's why I'm here." I pulled my leathers back into place from where they had started to bunch up. "I'm going into the market."

"Your father would want me to come." He quipped.

"My father isn't here, and he doesn't need to know. I want to go alone. I have unfinished business to handle. I need you to support me through this and let me go." I stopped a minute and rubbed the back of my neck before looking up at him, "because we're friends."

It looked as if a sweat was starting on his forehead, but he conceded. "Don't be gone long." As I walked past him, he reached out and grabbed my arm. "Don't tell your father I let you go alone today, *please*. I'm his slave first, his Commander second. I trust that you know what you're about to do."

"Our secret is safe with me." I reassured and gave him a light smile to cement it, patting his hand until he finally let go. We could be friends, I guess.

I didn't bother with sneaking through the garden or with hiding myself as I strolled into the market. The booths were thin and there were far more jewels and clothing than there were food stalls. The food stalls that were open had wilting crops from the sun and fewer bags of grain than I'd seen before. The price of bread was far too high, but the people were cramming in to get what was left.

I waited there in the center of the market, watching the people pass by me on either side as they bustled around from booth to booth. They recognized the armor of the King's army and made sure to give me plenty of space as they passed. Children played on the edges and beggars sat in the shade holding clay jars over their heads to collect coins.

Yurdell would know I was here. He would smell me or feel it from the venom. I felt it pulse in my wrist. I refocused and the pain ebbed away. It wasn't Yurdell that came up behind me though. I whirled when I felt the presence there.

"Coming to finish the fight he started?" Aluxious asked with a soft worried smile.

"Yes, but it seems he's not comfortable with me setting the time and place. I haven't seen him yet."

"You haven't been waiting very long either."

"I shouldn't have to. He wants my life and I'm serving it to him."

"You're a brave woman. There's something different about you this time. Kyier was right. You're ready now." His compliment made me want to cling to him for support. I could feel the fear and anxiety eating at my mind as I tried my best to ignore it. I was choosing this. His hand rested on my shoulder for comfort. I placed my hand over his, trying to siphon confidence off of those words. He was the first person to believe in my strength before questioning it, even when I wasn't ready to fight. Aluxious didn't have the intuition or judgment of Kyier, but he meant well.

The crowd parted, withdrawing from the path as the predator stalked into the market. The people avoided him like a sickness, turning their noses away and covering the eyes of their children. He looked grotesque and heavy. As he moved closer the venom pulsed harder through my veins, begging me to return to him. It took every ounce of focus I had to draw the venom back and make it quiet. Yurdell appeared engorged, his stomach bloated, and his skin shone an odd shade of near pink through the yellowish pale.

Normally I would swoon over him, have little to no control, but I could tell at this moment he was ugly. He'd been feeding, gorging himself. Yurdell was engorged on the blood of his victims. He'd be stronger, faster, and more lethal with his hunger so thoroughly saited.

As Soilts feed they become increasingly more like the monsters they were created to be. There were rumors that the more they fed the closer to their death they would become. Legends were told that a Soilt could be fed to death. Eventually it would be too much, and they would drown in it. They became cocky and reckless. No matter the speed and agility they were granted with their full bellies, they would best themselves. Being engorged made them lose their hair, changed the color of their skin, made their eyesight hazy, and loosened their good judgment.

Yurdell bared his fangs, making the searing pain race through my body stronger, harder to ignore than before. My knees buckled beneath me as I fought back, focusing my energy in my core and targeting the venom as it moved. I got my bearings and withdrew my axes from my harness. This is what I came here for and by the look on his face he was surprised to see I returned. If he wanted me to fight for my honor, I would.

"Are you challenging me?!" Yurdell threw his arms out and laughed wickedly. He paced closer to me, an arrogant smile on his face. Blood was dried to his lips and his eyes were rimmed in a dark black. "I'm presented with the opportunity to take your life. Are you sure this is what you want?"

Aluxious backed away, no intent to interfere. I lowered myself and brought my axes into the ready position. With the pain in my limbs and throughout my body it was more difficult to hold my axes steady. My arms shook slightly, but after a moment I was able to steady and tighten my grip.

"The princess has made her choice. Are you afraid, Yurdell?" Aluxious taunted him. "Maybe she'll put your head next to the assassins."

Yurdell unsheathed his blade and took a ready position. He stood with the blade upright, the point glistening in the moonlight. A relaxed position for someone that knew the outcome already, as if he'd peered into the future by drinking the blood of his Aylish victims. His grip was tight and unwavering. He took a power stance, one that was used most often when the wielder used force and power to overwhelm their opponents. He held onto the hilt with both hands, resting it back into his chest as if he were going to charge.

I baited him in with a half step to the left, but I withdrew and stepped back just as he barreled forward. I rolled to the side, avoiding contact as he swung wildly. Every move he made, foreshadowed in his stance and steps. He was an open book, worse than that of Inara. Yurdell was being a lazy fighter. Was it because I was a woman? I waited again. This time I relaxed and flipped the ax in my right hand, catching the handle again and resetting. I was playing with him. I could see his frustration growing. I circled to the right, but he didn't follow in the dance. Instead, he remained fixed and followed me with his eyes. This wasn't something Inara would do. He believed in always keeping his enemy in front of him. Yurdell was attempting a surprise attack, one I couldn't judge by his footing or the movement in his arms.

I took advantage when I was at his back. Swinging an ax across the midline, but Yurdell turned and parried the attack easily, sensing my every movement. He laughed at me, his eyes smiling, glistening with amusement.

"You're an amature!" He teased.

"Don't listen to him. He's trying to frustrate you." Aluxious shouted from behind me. It was nice having someone in my corner that didn't doubt me.

This time as I circled, Yurdell followed. One step at a time I closed the gap between us. He would have to move backwards to get a good swing in. I was catching him off guard. He wasn't expecting me to advance offensively.

I swung my ax, cutting him across the chest as he attempted to dodge backwards. A beaded line of blood formed. Soon his shirt was soaked in his blood, or maybe the blood that filled his belly, but he didn't cringe or quit. He barely showed his pain at all.

"A scratch won't put me down." Yurdell said when he noticed that I was surprised he was playing indifferent to the wound. Soilts were strong, I should have known better. I shouldn't have doubted him, or that one wound would cripple him in my favor.

He swung his sword, but this time not in a powerful way. This time he moved with agility and speed. I knocked one blow away, the next I side stepped, barely missing me. My cape suffered the brunt of the blow, severing it in half.

I groaned as I kicked it out of the way. "I really liked this cape," I said. "Why are my opponents always ruining my favorite clothes?"

As Yurdell watched me kick the scrape of fabric out of the way he laughed. For a moment he lowered his sword and ignored the second roll of combat that Inara had taught me.

"Never doubt your opponent! They are always a threat!" His words rang through my mind when I doubted Yurdell's capabilities just before, and then it dawned on me that from the very beginning Yurdell was doubting me… giving me an unknown advantage over him. He wouldn't see my attack coming, not if it was planned just right.

I backed away. Resting one of my axes on my shoulder, lowering the other altogether. This was it. This was my chance. Yurdell was unaware.

"Are you quitting, Kastell?" Yurdell asked, a glint in his eyes as he lowered his sword entirely, letting the tip dangle just above the ground. He wasn't accustomed to being in a dance for so long. He was tiring as well, giving me more of an advantage. He was tiring with the dance he was using to tease me.

    I dropped the ax in my left hand, it bit into the dirt, the handle upright, waiting for me. As I stepped away, I could feel the Fae magic in it calling me back. I picked up the severed cloth of my cape I had previously kicked away and shook the dirt from it. Aluxious even looked perplexed at my actions. I could tell he thought I was quitting; the disappointment was all over his face.

    I smiled as I examined the cloth. "My mother was strong, unwavering. I remember her constantly challenging the patriarchy. She wore trousers and rode horses. She even learned to read and write, the first woman in her family to do so. It's because of her that I've become the way I am no matter how propper everyone tries to make me."

    "Her legacy was to lead you down a path to your death." Yurdell countered, watching me examine the cloth. "We can quit this, Kastell. I can give you another taste of my venom, sedate the pain. I can help-"

    I cut him off by throwing the fabric in his direction, blocking his view. I stepped to the left, just over my dropped ax, and threw the one on my shoulder in his direction. The ax cut through the center of the fabric and I heard the telling thud of contact. The fabric drifted slowly to the ground, resting into the dirt at Yurdell's feet. He was in shock, the tip of my ax buried deep into his chest. The pink color of his skin faded as the blood drained from the gashing wound down the center of his chest. Split ribs and meat from inside his body were turning outward to embrace the ax where it rested.

Yurdell fell to his knees and gripped the handle of the ax. His grip fumbled and his hands shook feverishly as his own blood coated the handle, eventually pulling it from his chest. "No." He whispered as he tried to cover the profusely bleeding gash just to the right of his heart. The white of bone was strikingly bright through the frayed muscle of his chest.

"I can't die. Not here." He said frantically. He rested back on his legs, one arm bracing the ground as he became weak. "My sister… My father." His whispers became incoherent as his eyes rolled slightly.

"You will die." I said. I knelt on one knee in front of him, my second ax in my hand. I showed it to him as life started to drain from him, the brightness of his eyes pulled to the core of his being to be swallowed into darkness.

"This ax was crafted by dwarves, and etched by fae." I said as I let the moonlight catch the flawless tip of its steel. "They say the Fae are the master's of time itself." I snicker to myself under my breath. "I can only hope that when you saw the blade of my ax hurling towards you that it felt like a thousand years, hanging in emptiness, but unmoving from your course."

"You're unnatural!" He spat, blood dripping from his lips.

I could feel the venom dying inside of me as life left him. "No. You are. You proved that when you preyed on me, putting that vile venom in my veins. It's sickening now, but if you would have given me half the chance without treating me like a victim, I may have actually liked you. It really is a shame."

His eyes met mine then. I remembered their stunning beauty the day we came together for a short kiss in the market. I remembered the way the sun reflected in them and the happiness I saw there in that moment. I remembered the moments I thought he was a good man, despite the way others judged him for his breeding.

"I'll remember the day you kissed me." I said as his jaw became slack. I moved closer, my lips next to his ear. "You could have been a good man."

I looked around us, realizing that our duel was spectated by the crowd. Recognition dawned on their faces and whispers and chatter spread. They knew who I was now. The moment of my opponent's defeat would be remembered by those that stood watch. Some of the bystanders looked shocked, some of them looked scared, and some of them cried for Yurdell. There were times in his life he was a good man. Those moments would be remembered alongside his death.

"Thank you…" His last words barely escaped on his last breath. I felt his life leave him as the venom finally left me. His body fell into a puddle of mud at our feet.

I stood above him and with the final swing of my ax I took his head from his shoulders. I took it by the hair and carried it tangled in my fingers. His scalp was cold and dry to the touch and his hair felt wiry, not like before.

I walked off then, pushing through the crowd that crammed forward to see the body of the dead delegate I left in the dirt. Aluxious followed close behind me. "Princess!" He called, but I didn't stop. "*Kastell!*" He shouted.

I turned to him then, stunned that he used my name for once. "What?"

"It's always a pleasure to watch you in the heat of glory."

I shrugged. "This isn't something to glorify. Yurdell was a good man before he did what he did. I'll remember him that way." I continued towards the gate to the castle, Aluxious walking beside me. He ignored the racing tears he saw on my face, just as I tried to. There was an erratic raising to my chest, the pain I didn't want to give credit to, the one that reminded me I was good. My heart ached for killing him. This time it wasn't a stranger's head I carried, but a man I was sure I loved, even if only through the lies of his venom, it still felt real in my heart. Even as the pain from his venom was gone there was a lingering pain in my chest that was independent, it was the small bit of me that may have really loved him. Did it bloom there in the market, the same place I killed him and severed his head, or the hillside outside his elaborate estate?

"The right thing to do often hurts," Aluxious said after a moment, "but I'm still left in awe of you." He added. I didn't respond. Aluxious went on then. "Will I see you again soon?"

I stopped at the gate, mulling over my answer. I wasn't sure I would be ready to face the outside world so soon. Not after watering the ground of the market with Yurdell's blood. How long would it be before a rain washed the blood out of the ground? I expected that when I returned my security would be doubled, if not only Inara, but other guards as well. Yurdell had a family that would surely come after me later. If they didn't, we would all be surprised.

"I'm not sure I'll be ready." I said shortly.

Aluxious smiled at me. "I'm sure you can find a way. I'll be waiting for you when you are."

"I hope I can." I said with a small fake smile. It took a lot to muster something I wasn't feeling. I directed my attention to the guard above the gate. The gate was already beginning to open. "Get me the Commander!" The guard hurried off to do as I asked. No one second guessed me like they once did. I turned back to see Aluxious walking away, his back turned without even a goodbye. He was already disappearing around a few buildings into the heart of the city.

19 Kastell

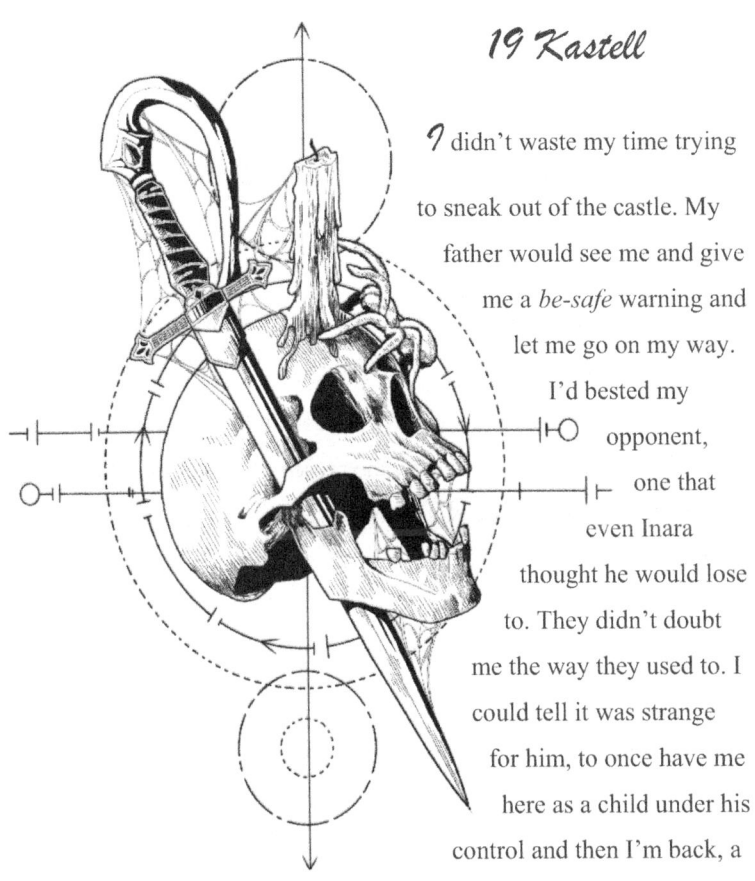

I didn't waste my time trying to sneak out of the castle. My father would see me and give me a *be-safe* warning and let me go on my way. I'd bested my opponent, one that even Inara thought he would lose to. They didn't doubt me the way they used to. I could tell it was strange for him, to once have me here as a child under his control and then I'm back, a woman that he no longer has the right to control. Now, with the strength and means to protect myself. My need for him was less than ever. I didn't mean to push him away, but I enjoyed the freedom I felt now without his looming presence, without the guards, without a leash to control me.

I passed guards coming and going from the stable tucked behind the castle. Some threw me curious glances, but no one stopped. The stables were nearly empty apart from two workers grooming and cleaning horses, tack, and equipment from the guards that had returned. I prepped an empty stall with a saddle and my saddle bags.

When I turned to leave towards the field with a harness and lead, I was surprised to see Safrim opening the barn doors, my mare coming in behind her.

"I saw you come in." She said with a soft smile as she led her into the stall. I watched as she tethered the lead and helped me to lift the saddle onto her back.

"It's been weeks." I mentioned casually as if it didn't matter, but I was excited and comforted by the presence of another woman. My father had stopped allowing Kendra to have visitors and I wasn't so sure why. I didn't care to ask, as long as he made sure she was well fed and cared for while she was here. However, he'd continued to see her twice a week regardless of his restrictions on everyone else.

Safrim shrugged. "I was posted at the farms for security, but my time there is over. They're starting to rotate the security more. They're worried we'll get complacent, they're not wrong. It was dreadfully boring, and the men wouldn't spar with me. I've gotten weak."

I chuckled. "I doubt that." I didn't mean to hesitate, or to drag a silence between us, but it was odd having someone to talk to. I didn't realize how quiet my life had been since the duel with Yurdell. I'd closed myself off to others. *I just need time;* an excuse I repeated to myself repeatedly.

"W-would you like to join me?" I asked, a short stutter through the awkward silence.

Safrim looked up with a bright smile. "I'd love to, but I'd have to admit my intentions are a bit selfish."

I shrugged. "I need the company of another woman. I don't mind. If there's something you want to talk about, then why waste the time on small chats?"

"I like small talk with you." She said and started to saddle a second horse a few stalls away. "It's unbearable to deal with men for weeks at a time. Most of the conversation was less about conversing and more about me being the center of their jokes. I'm just glad to be back."

We led our horses outside in silence and used our legs to heft ourselves into our saddles. The feeling was strange and uncomfortable for a moment. Weeks away from riding made it nearly feel new, but then familiarity took over and I was comfortable, gently tugging the reins and the horse obeyed like we hadn't been apart for so long. The sound of her breathing and the steady rhythm of her hooves on the path eased away my worries. Even my emotional torment seemed dull in the sound.

Safrim talked about her time away at the farm postings for most of the ride. I was relieved to have someone fill the empty silence, and she didn't judge me or send me snide looks the way Inara would when I didn't answer. I listened and that satisfied Safrim.

I led the way through the Market and went to the only place I could think of visiting in the last few weeks. The tree here had leaves that turned a deep red and the grass around the base was thoroughly overgrown. The estate below the hill was dark and untouched. Sure,

Yurdell's sister still occupied the residence, but she didn't do nearly as much as he had to tenderly care for it. Yurdell liked his home here.

    I dismounted and dropped the reins to the ground. My mare wouldn't wander. She was a gentle and lazy beast. I moved to the edge of the hill before its steep decline and sat into the grass, pushing it over for Safrim to fit beside me.

    "What's this?" She sat quickly, folding her legs under here and scanning over the estate.

    "The last good memory I had with Yurdell was here. I think that's when I really started to care for him." I plucked at the grass and dirt, just enjoying the soft breeze and trying not to let any tears out of my eyes. I saw his face frequently. He visited me in my sleep. Sometimes I saw the bloodied man and his wounds, and he blamed me for his death and his choices; sometimes it was his sweet smile and bright eyes full of ambition from times we spent in places like here.

    Safrim's hand hesitated, but then she was soothing me with a hand on my back. Part of me wanted to cry even more, but I bit back the urge and leaned into her touch.

    "Word travels fast, not to mention, a lot of people have been drawing and documenting his death in their journals. Some of the guards found out and that's how I heard. I thought you were courting?"

    I nodded. "We were, but he used his venom on me. He betrayed my trust for greed. The only way to get it to go away is to kill the Soilt."

    "I couldn't believe it was you that did it."

"It had to be me." I sat up straighter. "It was my fight. Yurdell was preparing to die in the arena, but when he faced me, he saw an opportunity to fulfill his destiny. He thought he was supposed to kill me. My father still thinks there's a plot unraveling that we're unaware of. I know there is, but I want time away from the hassle. Sometimes I wish I could go back to the Sanctuary."

Safrim's hand fell away and she chuckled harshly. "Running from your problems won't help, I promise."

"What can make it better?"

Safrim laughed then, excitedly as she pulled out a small pouch from her leather pouch she kept strapped around her waist. "Now, I know you're looking for an escape, but running isn't the right thing, so sometimes when I'm feeling down, I use these."

She passed me small dried thin mushrooms that were an assortment of bright colors with spots on the cap. "They help me to relax and to see things a bit more clearly."

I've heard of them before, but surprisingly during my rebellious phase I never tried them. The trip was soft and delicate. Mostly colorful and hours slipped into one another silently. There were no harsh after tastes and they didn't make you groggy when you woke up. For the most part, they were rumored to be only what she promised, an escape.

I wanted to scold myself the way Kendra would have if she would have seen me shoving a handful of the mushrooms into my mouth. Instead, I giggled. It was a quiet, breathless moment, but it lightened the burdens in my chest. Has it been so long since I felt light and happy over anything? Safrim put three or four into her mouth and raked a hand through her hair. She leaned back, hugging her knees to her chest and rocking slightly as her eyes drifted closed; eyelashes shyly tickling over the pale of her under eyes. Safrim craned her head back, elongating her neck and breathing deeply, letting the escape wash in, silent and beautiful. I turned my own face to the open sky and basked in the light breeze on my face that made me feel like I was flying as my eyes shut. It was the mushrooms, but I swore for a moment I was leaving my body, leaving the heavy stress and distasteful circumstances.

Hours passed slower than the drip of molasses. I was pleased with each slow moment, one more moment away from everything I'd been worried about. What was I worried about anyways? Weren't all my problems gone with Yurdell?

My chest ached at the thought, surfacing his beautiful face and his elegant smile that curved just right at the corners, mischievous and handsome; before he'd gorged on blood, killed others to feed his insatiable appetite all because he knew he'd die. Before then.

I wasn't aware I was crying out loud and ugly until Safrim's firm hand on my shoulder shook me. We had laid side by side in the grass as we enjoyed our escape from reality. My eyes jerked open at the sudden commotion and the sound of my sobs hit my ears. I'd been ugly crying.

Safrim sat up beside me and helped to wipe away my tears. "It's okay to be hurt. No one understands the pain you're going through. I don't care if it was chemical or natural, or a spell!" Safrim shook my shoulders, forcing me to look up at her. "It's okay to feel this way."

"I shouldn't!" I barked back, wiping my tears erratically and choking back another biter sob. "He betrayed me, he hurt me, he put venom in me!"

"Everything he did was wrong. You handled it the way you thought you needed to. Stand by it. Embrace your choice, or no one else will."

"Will you be there for me?" I asked, my voice shaking. "When it gets hard like this, will you be there?"

Safrim wrapped me in a tight hug, squeezing me with everything she had. She even kissed my temple. "I'll always be here."

"Does this make us friends?" I asked after a moment of clearing my throat and stifling my cries.

Safrim didn't just chuckle, she laughed, and I couldn't help but join her. The feeling was freeing. She shoved me lightly and then pulled me into her side. "Yes, we're friends." After a long moment of looking out into the darkening sky, Safrim cleared her throat. "Because we're friends, can you tell me about Inara?"

I snapped my head to the side. She was blushing and trying to hide it with her hand. "You and *Inara?*" I asked coolly, without giving too much away. I didn't know what she knew about our new arrangement, or if she'd known anything at all.

She nodded stiffly. "I heard the two of you are courting now." The statement was blunt, not a question, and not a judgment. I was relieved.

"Yes, but to be fair to him, I haven't been acting like it. I barely talk to him aside from our time training. He's been patient, but I can tell it's irritating him now."

Safrim chuckled then. "He sent me away because he didn't want me to interfere. He said this was the King's choice."

I swallowed a hard lump in my throat. "Actually, I was the first person to nominate him as a suitor. He didn't seem so eager about it then either, but he's trying to make the best of it."

Safrim nodded. She turned to me then, her eyes pleading. "I love him very much; you must be kind to him. Don't make him suffer. If this is the will the Collective will support, I will not interfere, but you must promise to care for him."

I took her in my arms as her own tears started. We were both going through a heartbreak. Mine was chosen. I'd forced her pain upon her. I decided then, with my friend in my arms, that I wouldn't accept this courtship. I wouldn't bend to the vote of the Collective. I'd tell them no. I'd find someone suitable later, but I wouldn't continue to hurt Safrim this way. Nor did I wish to cause Inara any discomfort. We may have been at odds as children, but if he loved someone now, I wouldn't ruin that. We were friends, right?

20 Gideon

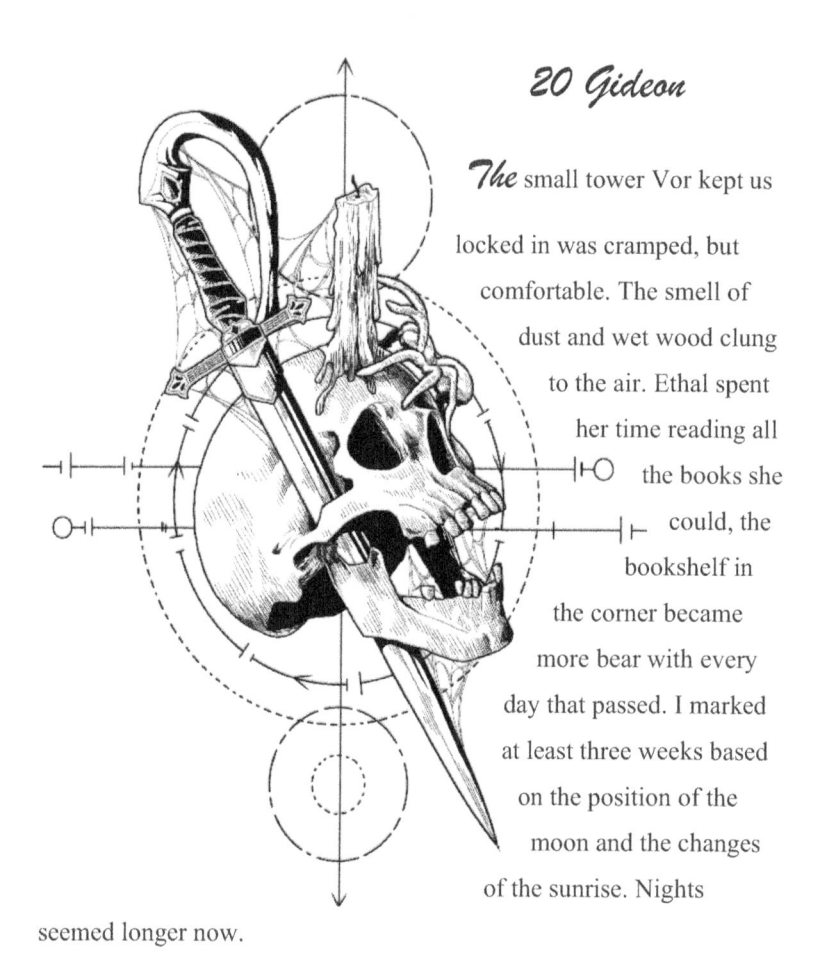

The small tower Vor kept us locked in was cramped, but comfortable. The smell of dust and wet wood clung to the air. Ethal spent her time reading all the books she could, the bookshelf in the corner became more bear with every day that passed. I marked at least three weeks based on the position of the moon and the changes of the sunrise. Nights seemed longer now.

I could watch Ethal all day, sitting by the window with her nose in a book and the sun pouring through the strands of hair that hung loosely around her thin face. The sight of her was calming. Her presence in a room made me feel light weight, the world was more bearable when she was around. I was glad we were able to make the journey here together, no matter the amount of discomfort we had to go through. With her by my side I felt like I could endure anything.

Guards had walked us around the palace every other day and food was brought to us three times a day. We were granted two waste buckets. Ethal and I had to get very comfortable with each other in three days' time, now we didn't mind. We turned our backs on the other and ignored the smells. With every day that passed my impatience grew. Ethal knew I couldn't be kept prisoner, and the King must have too, because he made no move to bind us or lock the doors. He knew I'd come for a reason, and I wouldn't leave until I'd gotten what I wanted.

I flopped back into a chair that was conveniently placed in front of a wood stove. Most of my time was spent pacing and grappling with the minds that passed through the castle, gorging on any information I could use to make Vor agree to a diplomatic solution. Enough blood has been spilt.

"I can't imagine how much longer he'll have us locked away." I huffed out a long breath in irritation. I could sense the tension in the castle. There was a raid on a farm, burning their grain stores. There were arguments between the Commander and his guards about their duties. There were rumors of cheating wives, unfaithful husbands, and the dirty thoughts of the men that rarely saw the comfort of a woman. I could hear their thoughts and worries mingling together in a wave as if they were all one, swarming up to me in the late evenings and throughout the day. There were a few things that gave me footing against the King's resilience.

Ethal ignored my comment. She had stopped reassuring me after the first three times I mentioned he was making me wait. I liked to complain about things just to have something to talk about with her. Yet, she preferred the silent company I provided more. Either the King was scared of my power, or he knew my power and kept me here, spying on everyone's thoughts, a pawn for him against my own will. I wouldn't understand his position until I could see into his mind.

Ethal closed her book and got down off the window seat in a fluid and graceful motion. The dress she wore had a slit up the side, giving me a momentary look at her pale thigh as she reached her foot for the floor and came to sit on my lap. Instinctively I wrapped my arm around her and rested my head on her shoulder.

"Do you know what you're going to say to the King?" She asked. We haven't talked about this yet.

I shrugged, taking her sweet smell in for a second. "I have an idea, but I'm not sure how much the King already knows. I hear them all, all the time." I nestled my head into the crock of her neck, her hand aimlessly drawing on the back of my neck, holding me. With my head on her the thoughts around me became muffled and bearable. "I could only be repeating things he already knows of." I went on, "I'm afraid I'll have nothing to offer to help settle this war. Aluxious is counting on me. The people of this Kingdom are counting on me, and they don't even know it yet." I took in another deep breath, relaxing into her more. "Aluxious is still gathering an Army. If he needs to he will retaliate. He will weaken the King's people as he needs to. They've already burned grain stores close to here. I know the rebels are itching for vengeance. If he gets the diplomatic solution he wants, who's to say they'll accept it?"

"Gideon, stop worrying about everything and everyone else and focus on the king. Focus on what we came here for." Her hand played in my hair at the nape of my neck, sending a chill through me.

I closed my eyes and focused, letting my mind draw away into a quiet place deep inside of me. I tried this before, but I couldn't find him then either. I searched every open mind within the castle, moving like smoke through the air from one open mind to the next. I still couldn't find him, but I could sense his presence. It was taunting me from behind a closed door. I couldn't see it, but I could feel it tugging at me in circles. A void in the center of the castle that I couldn't breach taunted me. He was in his office with the Commander, both silhouettes casted across the gray void. I could feel their minds side by side, one dark and menacing, one clouded with doubt and unease.

I was able to skim through the memories of the Commander, but so many of those memories were clouded and altered. I could sense that he was protected against me from the first moment I was there. As much as I could have gotten into his thoughts before, now it was impossible. The King's mind was rattling at me from beyond the void, tempting me to press onto it. I was hurtled back out and back into my own mind when I tried. A headache pulsed behind my temples. The sudden retreat was harsh and hard.

I opened my eyes slowly, trying to avoid the light pouring in from the window. Ethal was staring down at me expectantly, but I failed again. Why did I have to keep telling her I failed?

"I can't see into his mind. It's right there, it's so close, but I can't get to him! There's something in my way," I said. I gritted my teeth in frustration.

Ethal stood and went back to the bookshelf, scheming over the torn and beaten bindings that waited impatiently to be chosen next. Some of the books poked out from the others, desperately vying for her affection. "You can see the Commander though, and you're sure of what you saw, before it all became clouded?" Her long delicate fingers ran over the binding of a thicker book, but then paused before choosing it next. She clenched her hand into a fist and put it at her side.

I hesitated a second but reached out for her wrist, pulling her back to me and guiding her to stand in front of me. She stood between my knees. I grasped her hand and laid it against my cheek, savoring her warmth. I wanted her to touch me the same way she'd delicately touched the books. I wanted to be chosen for her affection.

"Entirely, without doubt." I said as I leaned into her touch. Her fingers ran down my cheek the way they had on the bindings. She knew what I wanted without question. I wanted her touch. I *needed* her touch. "The King and the Commander are together often. If he already knows then he's biding his time." I kissed the inside of her hand, my lips brushing gently over an old scar left on her from when she was a slave; the only remnants of that life were the marks on her body. I loved them all. This one from a rope she had gripped to steady a stallion as it tried to rip away from her.

I chuckled and with one hand on her waist, brought her closer to me. "My power is the stallion." I whispered against her palm. "I'm sure you won't let me go either."

"Not for a moment." She said, a smile crossing her thin lips. Her eyes sparkled with mischief, enthralling me in their gaze. She lifted her left leg, the slit in her dress parting as she rested her foot on the chair just outside my knee. I instinctively reached for her, an invitation I couldn't reject. I traced the length of her leg with my hand, stopping just under her knee and laying a stream of kisses on the inside of her thigh, each one closing in on her control. I felt it as her breath hitched and the light shiver that passed over her. When I looked up to meet her eyes, I wasn't surprised to see a deep fire raging in them.

I rested my head on her knee, and held her leg there in that spot, watching the fire dancing in her big, beautiful eyes. "I need to be careful not to disturb the fragile peace within the castle."

"Disturb what you must." For a moment I could swear she was talking about her self-control. She wanted me just as much as I wanted her. "As long as we end the war. I want somewhere peaceful to live out my life, don't you?"

I let out a deep breath, stilling my self-control. "Not here." I whispered and lifted my head towards the door. "We're not alone here."

She groaned a light protest, the soft fire in her eyes ebbing away. No, one day I would have her, but it wouldn't be here. I wanted to save those blissful moments for a time where they could be enjoyed and not drowned out by the rest of the world.

Ethal removed her leg, but I caught it there and left another searing line of kisses on her calf, her toes curling as I pushed my thumb into the arch of her foot. "One day soon." I said as I gave her a crooked smile.

Ethal went back to the shelf, her leg disappearing under her dress again. I only gave myself a second to feel disappointed that I wasn't going to have her right here and now. My magic was strongest near her, and I wondered if her own magic would become reckless when we were together. She hardly used it. I wanted to see her wield those flames in her eyes. I wanted to see her in all the glory she was made to be.

Without hesitation she pulled a book from the shelf, the rustling of the covers grinding against each other and the leafing of the pages breaking through my thoughts. "Some of these are accounts of the history of Ayles and the fae. I like this one the most." She turned a few pages and read: *"Fae master time and history. Through them we can see our true origins."* She closed the book and handed it to me. "Do you think there's things we don't know about the origins of our people, or there's?"

I looked over the worn yellow binding and noticed it was written by a Varius. "It's possible, but I'm not interested. I am especially not interested in anything written by Varius, no matter how old. They could all be lies."

"I'm interested." She said dreamily. "I want to know of the heroes of our past."

I went to her and draped my arms around her, my head resting on her shoulder, looking at the dusty book. "I am your hero." I said softly in a pathetic attempt to get her attention.

She turned and met my gaze, a smile coming to her lips. "Of course, you are." Her lips touched mine briefly when the door burst open, and the King stepped in. I chuckled then, realizing that if I had lost my control, he would have been looking at a much more intimate embrace of the two of us.

"Come with me." He demanded.

I began to follow him down the long flight of stairs, he didn't care to wait for a response. Ethal started to follow me, but the King turned on his heel, stopping our descent. "The woman stays."

I shrugged and left a fleeting kiss on her knuckles and continued downward.

Vor led me to his office where he abruptly closed his door and locked it. "Kendra told me you're here to find a diplomatic solution to the war. I told her I wanted you for your power. That's the *only* reason I wanted to meet with you. How can you find a diplomatic solution if *I* can't?"

The King crossed the office and sat in his chair, pulling out a tall bottle and two glasses. I declined his offer, and the second glass was returned to its place in his desk. I meandered through the room, admiring animal mounts and swords hanging on the walls.

"You're a hunter?" I remarked, avoiding the question. A beast hung over his desk. It was a hybrid of sorts, old mutations left by years of the animals living in a post human war. This one was a northern animal. Its hide was thick and white, the face of a bear with horns protruding from its head in every direction and curling at the tips from ramming them into trees and fighting. A crown of its own.

"And a Swordsman." He said with a raise of his brows. He watched me study the mount. "It's a Neborake, aside from the menacing teeth, they're docile creatures. They eat bark and berries, maybe a few fish during the migration. However, they're very territorial. I've never seen more than one within a two-hundred-mile radius unless it's during heat. Aren't they magnificent?" The bear had to have been over six hundred pounds. It loomed over us, its red eyes fixed on the door.

The King sipped his drink, not minding as I looked around at the stacks of maps and papers around the office, covering every exposed surface except for his desk. "Is there anything you see that you like, or would you like to sit down and get to business?" He said, gesturing to the chair available for me.

I sat down in the worn chair across from his desk. "You can't use my powers to win this war," I said. I wanted to be clear from the start. I had something to offer him, but I wouldn't be used as a weapon against anyone. Not against my will.

"What can I use to win the war then? There's nothing you can offer me if it's not your Claret Magic."

I wiggled my finger at him. "You're wrong. Before Claret Magic- I mastered compulsion and mind magic. The Claret Magic only amplified those strengths. I spent only a few moments in the room with the most important people in this castle and I know all their hidden secrets. They were shouting them at me. Apart from yours." I pointed. "You're using something to keep me out." I narrowed my eyes on him. "And now the Commander has something similar guarding his mind, albeit it's weaker than yours."

"That's very keen of you to notice." Vor jingled a gold bracelet on his wrist. "Something a friend made for me. She said you wouldn't leave me alone until you got inside. This means you have to trust me, and I have to trust you. She sent it to me before I sent my envoy." He took a long sip from his cup and placed it on the desk. I could see the circular stain on the desk as if he put the cup down in the same spot every time. "I'm not too fond of the impressions you left in her memories."

I sat back in my chair and stared at him. *Kendra.* "All I want is for this disgusting war to be over. Yet, I find myself more concerned about the internal affairs of your Collective." I said back. What I did to Kendra was wrong, but I wouldn't find myself intimidated by an Ayl that let the Collective control his every waking decision as King.

"The Royal Collective?" Vor asked, confused. "They'll back whichever decision I make, diplomatic or not. You shouldn't let them impede our discussions."

"I don't want anything to do with them, but I've learned a little secret about one of them. He's a traitor, and he's looking to dismantle the peace you've worked so hard at by taking the throne. I know his name and Kastell's life hangs in the balance. The traitor will only use her as long as she's useful and dispose of her soon after."

"Yurdell was killed in one-on-one combat, by Kastell herself. Nothing you've brought to me is new." Vor stood impatiently and ushered me to the door, opening it. The Commander was on the other side waiting. "Escort him back to the tower, he doesn't have anything I want. They'll be leaving soon."

I shrugged and crossed through. "*Yurdell* wasn't the traitor I was referring to. There's another, someone that had their hand in his back pocket the entire time. If you wish to know the name, you will have to come to a negotiation with the Rebel King, myself, and you. Three days! We'll meet at Crystal Falls- *at sunset*. If you fail to show I know which side of this war I will be fighting for."

Vor scoffed in frustration and slammed the door, leaving me face to face with Commander Inara. "You're a big man." I commented dryly as I looked him over. "So much taller than I expected."

"You're scrawnery than I expected for an all-powerful Warlock." He said back snidely.

"I guess all our expectations can't be met. Your mind just seems… *smaller*." I measured the size of his mind with two fingers, only a pinch. I focused my eyes on his and stole a look at his thoughts. Visions of me in chains. A few thoughts of Kastell, but they were guarded. I held my wrists out to him teasingly. "If it would make you feel better, I suppose."

The Commander shoved me in the direction of the tower. "Keep your insults to yourself and stay out of my head." He spat through clenched teeth.

J. L. Cross

Ethal and I were fetched just as the sun was beginning to set. It was the young Princess that came for us. She was as beautiful as everyone made her out to be. Her hair was a vibrant golden white against her light-colored eyes and pink lips. Every curve of her face was highlighted by the way her bangs wisped in front of her face. A soft warm color rested in her cheeks as she noticed I was staring at her.

"There's a passage I can take you to. You don't deserve to go the same way you came. I'm heading out myself and figured you could accompany me. It'll make your presence less questionable."

I laughed, clapping my hands together once. "Sneaking out before dark, what fun!"

"It's not really sneaking when my father told me to take you with me. He's the only one in this house that hasn't tried to put me on a leash recently. The Commander's horrified that I might come back with another head for my rotting collection."

Kastell led us down the stairwell and out the front door of the castle. No one looked twice. She had more freedom here than I thought. The night air was cool and crisp on my skin. I flipped the hood of my cloak over my head to keep the air off my face. Ethal stood beside me and took my hand as we crossed the front courtyard and found ourselves in an overgrown garden.

I ran my hand over a tall rose and pulled at its petals. The deep red petals fell one by one to the ground, engulfed in tall grass. "It's so uncared for. What a shame." I said in a low tone as I picked one of the flowers and handed it off to Ethal.

She smiled and blushed, even her nose turned red when she looked up at me. "Thank you." She whispered.

"A beautiful rose for a beautiful woman." I said back and pushed a strand of her hair out of her face.

"Here." Kastell called, pointing at a low hole in the wall. "The brush is overgrown, so you'll have to fight through it a little."

Kastell pushed the wiry bush and dark green ivy in front of the hole out of our way, allowing Ethal and I through first. Ethal made it look easy, but she was also a remarkably small woman. I laid on my stomach and crawled through.

I straightened myself and dusted my cloak and trousers. The wall was a light tan that illuminated under the setting sun. I waited and helped Kastell to her feet. There were no guard escorts with us, but I knew there should have been.

"Your father sent you alone with us, does he trust me with his most precious daughter so easily?"

Kastell shook her head and smirked. "My Father knows that you wouldn't touch me. He told me that there's someone else trying to use me to get to the throne. He knows you have good intentions and Inara is nowhere to be seen tonight. I figured while he was gone, I'd step out one more time. Kendra reassured me that you could be trusted.

Unfortunately, I don't trust Inara to do the right thing by you. He doesn't seem to like you much, but he doesn't really like anyone."

"Give Kendra and your father my gratitude." I said as the Princess passed by me to make her way through the little homes. It was then I noticed her two shining axes draped across her back in a dark leather harness.

I ran up beside her. "Are those crafted by the *Fae*?" I asked excitedly.

Kastell gave me a warm smile. "What would you know of it?"

"Well, I know that it's been a very long time since someone has lived long enough to tell the tale of living among the Fae. They're elusive beings, hiding in their forest in the North. I've heard a rumor that the forest is dying though. I wonder if the Fae are really there?"

She rolled her eyes at me and continued to walk slowly beside me. "My sister lives with them."

I took in a light sharp gasp. "Have you had contact with her since she left?"

"No. I just know in my heart she's safe." The princess sounded sure of herself.

"Did you know that the Fae are masters of time itself? Some people think they can travel freely through it."

The Princess nodded. "It could all just be a rumor. I guess no one will ever know." She seemed a bit sad. "I don't think I'll ever see her again."

"I'm sure she's happy with them." I added to reassure her, but the truth was that her sister was probably already dead. The Fae didn't appear often to anyone, and if they appeared to her sister, it could be a sign of favor, or a sign of death.

Ethal came to me and touched my arm. "We know him." She said curtly pointing across the market square opening in front of us and across towards the tavern. Sure enough, our Arvor tri-breed friend sat at a table alone, staring down into a beer.

"Aluxious!" I yelled, opening my arms and rushing to him.

"Just kill me please…" The burly man said in irritation as he stood. I threw my arms around him. He shoved me away quickly. "What are you doing here?"

"Summoned by the King!" I said with an excited display of enthusiasm.

Kastell came up and stood beside the three of us, placing three coins on the table and waiting for a barmaid to bring her a foaming beverage. "You all know each other?" She asked as she took a seat at Aluxious' table.

"Well actual-"

"We're acquaintances." Aluxious interrupted me. My brow furrowed. He was hiding his real title from her. *Proxy Rebel King, The Devil.* That was none of my business, but it made sense to conceal himself here. The King wasn't even aware of their leader's name. Aluxious prided himself on concealing his identity and living two separate lives, the one of the beasts, and the one of the man.

"Yes. We met not so long ago. It was a pleasure." My mind raced as I watched the two of them look at eachother. They were waiting for Ethal and I to leave. "It seems like you two have hit it off quite well." I thought that Aluxious was only joking when he said he liked her, but now I had enough evidence to tell me it wasn't a joke. My head filled with that hate again. The fear of mixed children that had every great power of all the races, all except the Fae.

"I think so." Kastell said nonchalantly. "Maybe tonight I won't be killing anyone. That would change it up for us." She giggled and stood. "I'm going to get us drinks." The barmaid never came out to deliver a drink to Kastell. Other patrons stood and moved out of her way as she approached the bar inside. They were *afraid* of her.

I turned my gaze pointedly and accusingly on Aluxious. *She doesn't know.* I didn't have to say the words for him to see them in my eyes.

He shook his head, ashamed. "I don't want her to hate me. She already has resentment for her father after she was left at the Sanctuaries. Then everything with Yurdell. There's no reason she should know."

Ethal slammed her hand down on the table, drawing both of our attention. She was always a shadow in the background. Her presence and anger were strong now, *demanding*. "You best tell her, or she'll never forgive you." She warned. "Kastell deserves better."

I motioned to Ethal, picking up Aluxious' drink and taking a long drink from it. The liquid was warm and tangy. I winced at the grotesque aftertaste it left on my tongue. I set it back in front of him. "She's right. You'll have to tell her."

"I don't see why. Maybe when the war is over." Aluxious said, scratching at the table surface mindlessly.

"Before then." I stressed sharply. "We will be meeting with the King. I made our meeting place Crystal Falls in three days. I know your birthplace has a rather special meaning in this war."

Aluxious rolled his eyes. "I can't wait." He paused for a minute. "Have you decided on what diplomatic solution will work best?"

"*A Union*. There was a lot of *mind-chatter* about ensuring a good marriage for the throne." I said simply as Kastell was making her way back to the table with three pitchers, leaving one in front of Ethal and myself. "Thank you!" I said enthusiastically. "You're so kind."

"I heard something about unions." She pointed to Ethal and me. "You two?"

Ethal giggled. "That's absurd. We don't need such trivial ceremonies. We're bonded on a much deeper level." She took my hand and held it tightly.

"We were talking about our friend, Anxious, or rather someone he *knows*." I turned my eyes on him and saw that he was shocked, his jaw slack and his gaze clouded. His mind was racing with thoughts that I didn't care to know, except that they were screaming at me. "A friend of his is to have a union, *an old man*." I kicked his boot under the table, snapping him out of his trance.

"You never mentioned having any substantial friends." Kastell said as she leaned back into her chair, her half empty beer hanging from her fingers.

"It's not something I expected. It's *arranged* and I'm sure he's not going to be happy about it either. He's not really a friend, more like family, and he's very estranged." He said stiffly, but he couldn't meet her eyes then. I could see the truth heavy on his shoulders.

I stood then to leave. "I think we'll be off now."

"Perfect timing." Aluxious grunted.

21 Kastell

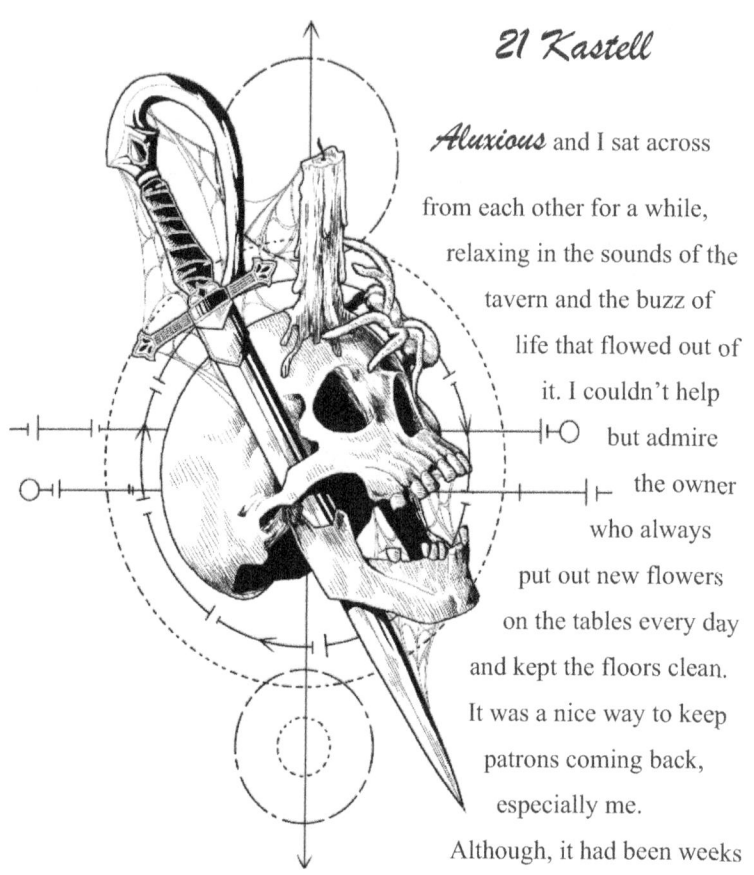

Aluxious and I sat across from each other for a while, relaxing in the sounds of the tavern and the buzz of life that flowed out of it. I couldn't help but admire the owner who always put out new flowers on the tables every day and kept the floors clean. It was a nice way to keep patrons coming back, especially me. Although, it had been weeks since my last visit here. My time with Safrim opened me back up to the world. She was right, I needed to embrace the choice I made, and no one would question me. If I continued to sulk, everyone would notice and bring more attention to it.

My eyes were drawn to the spot in the market square where I had challenged Yurdell and won. I never expected to win that battle, sometimes I thought that maybe I was trying to escape my responsibility to the Kingdom and the pain I endured for it through death that night. Other than my pride, there was no logical reason for me to fight him. I could have walked away again. *I should have walked away.* The thought played repeatedly in my mind. He should have lost his life honorably against Inara in the arena. Not to me, a woman. I'd marked his memory with humiliation.

A small smile crossed my lips thinking of it. A woman defeated such a noble fighter because he was too full of himself during the heat of the battle. He was too cocky. He was far too arrogant, leaving himself wide open for a calculated attack. It still haunted me, the time I enjoyed with him in the Market. I wished he could have stayed that way. He was good to me, respectable even. I made a fool out of myself being seen with him. I knew everything he had done was an act to get closer to me, but I still enjoyed those moments. If only he would have left well enough alone.

Man Killer, Carver, Butcher, Executioner. The names they whispered behind my back made me giddy with pride, and more often than not they made me cringe. I wasn't sure if I wanted to be pleased with myself or regret what I did. I was only now accepting that it had been done.

I remembered my father's reaction when I came in that night, the word of Yurdell's head mounted outside the castle gates already reached him before I could deliver the news on my own. At the time I was covered in his blood. He was furious, but still proud. I stood up for myself, I defended my own honor, but now he had the Royal Collective and Inara to deal with. Inara felt cheated out of an oppertunity to win his freedom from slavery. Yurdell's lands and titles still needed to be dispersed, it was only logical for my father to hand them off to Inara, but I saw in his eyes the way the idea didn't sit easy with him. Something about the Commander wasn't sitting well with my father. Inara was right, I may have cheated him out of a better life. My father had insisted that we court, knowing that the Collective would most likely rule in Inara's favor. He would be a remarkable delegate. Commander would only add to his titles.

"What's on your mind?" Aluxious interrupted my racing thoughts.

"What about you, this sudden marriage that you never talked about before?" I retorted back. "I didn't know you had those sorts of friends. Something about this arrangement seems suspicious. I feel like you would have told me."

He looked away for a moment and then met my eyes. "I asked first. You tell me and I'll tell you."

"Fine." I said as I leaned forward, planting my forearms on the table. I met his eyes and realized he was attempting to flirt with me. I steeled myself against it, not willing to admit just yet that I was technically already promised to someone. "I regret killing Yurdell. It was public, and I stole an opportunity from someone else. I've accepted it though. I made my choice, but I still think about it."

"Are you talking about that arrogant Commander I met the other day?" Aluxious had a chill that passed over him. "He smelled funny. Plus, it wasn't his fight anyways."

I laughed then, unable to hold onto my seriousness. "He could have gained his freedom in his battle against Yurdell. I only had to walk away."

"No!" Aluxious shouted, planting his palm onto the table, jostling our drinks. "You stood up for yourself, put the boot down on the spider taking advantage of you. Don't you ever regret that! Every person in this city has a newfound respect for women, and that started with you."

I blushed. I was bringing a change to the Kingdom. "You're not serious?"

"Women will start fighting their own battles and standing their own ground now. You gave them that courage." He confirmed with his mouth a broad smile.

I shrugged, running my finger over the wet rim of the mug until the glass hummed. "I guess I never saw myself doing that sort of thing, even though it felt good at the moment."

Aluxious stood and motioned for me to walk with him. "Don't let it bother you for too long. You made a decision and it's over with now."

I didn't hesitate to follow him this time like I did prior. I learned that he didn't have poor intentions and he was someone I could trust. He took me out back behind the tavern. I was a step behind him, taking in his broad shoulders and tall stocky frame. Aluxious was a man of pure strength. His arms were lined with muscles that begged to be touched and used.

What am I thinking? I scolded myself and looked away. *You're promised to Inara. Stand up to the Collective and then come back for what you want.*

A few scrawny Ayles lounged around smoking something out of a wooden pipe and passing it along. Two of them were wearing aprons and covered in blood, butchers after a long day.

Aluxious went to a large vertical wooden beam that held up a long and wide overhang attached to the tavern. He patted the beam. "Show me those throwing skills again. I'd love to learn!" He moved out of the way.

"I think I'm going to need another drink for these games. I must admit, I enjoy these kinds of things less than sober." I joked.

Aluxious stepped around me and leaned into the door to the tavern. "Another round!" he yelled.

I withdrew one of my axes and flipped it a few times in my hand. "Would you like to hold one?" I asked and held it out to him. He hesitated, but took it, studying it thoroughly. As he looked it over, I watched him get uncomfortable under my gaze. "Don't think I've forgotten our bargain. Tell me about this marriage." I reminded him.

He huffed and held the ax tighter. "It's arranged. It sprung on me out of the blue."

"To whom?" I pestered. "Does he like her?"

Aluxious scoffed in irritation. "It doesn't matter. He doesn't know. I'm standing in his stead as a proxy. I'm not entirely thrilled to have to deliver the news."

I laughed and teased him. "I think it clearly does matter. Friend of Foe?" I teased again. "I'm sure he'll be pleased as long as her hips curve and her lips part."

His head snapped up and his gaze met mine. "She's very close to an enemy, but she isn't my enemy herself. She hasn't been informed of our engagement yet, nor have all the terms been agreed to. I don't think she'll take it kindly when she finds out. This is *very* arranged."

"Poor girl." I said with a hint of amusement. Arranged marriages were common. The closest we've gotten was him demanding I court Inara. I was still lucky that I knew who I'd be forced to marry. If I had to learn to fall in love again, I wouldn't have chosen him, but I imagined I could. It was also the betrayal of Yurdell that made me turn up my nose to love. I wouldn't be lonesome forever.

Aluxious handed my ax back to me. "I don't want to talk about it anymore. Throw." He demanded and then swiftly changed the subject. "Our army doesn't have the pleasure of such gorgeous weapons, crafted by masters."

I showed him how I balanced the axes for throwing, ignoring the comment. I didn't want to talk about the war now. I showed him how to follow through with the throw properly to hit a target. Repeatedly I struck the same spot in the wood. Each time he was even more impressed. When he tried the same thing, it failed him time after time. Aluxious only became frustrated and decided he had enough.

"I have a game for you." He said as he lifted his mug to his lips. "For every time you hit the beam in the same spot- we drink!"

"You're insane!" I shouted. "We would be drunk within the hour."

He lifted a shoulder in indifference. "I wouldn't complain."

"I would." I retorted. "I have to deal with Inara when I go back. I let his prize prisoners out the other day. He hasn't spoken to me since. He thinks my father made a terrible decision. He's bound to ask if I'm so foolish to think Gideon is not a threat. Or, he'll ask if I don't trust his judgment. All those things I'm not prepared to answer or patient enough to deal with after a few drinks. How did you know Gideon anyhow?"

"The war." Aluxious said while rolling his eyes. "I've made quite a few undesirable acquaintances since I started fighting in the war."

I sat against the wall of the tavern, watching him as he looked uneasy. "Why do I get the distinct feeling that we may not be on the same side of this war?" The realization that Aluzxious was indeed a Arvor tribrid and that most Arvors fought alongside their own kind made my heart sink. I wanted someone on my side, not someone I was going to lose due to a difference in our stance on the war. It made his comment about not having fine weapons make more sense. Our armies were armed well.

He saw the concern in my eyes and kneeled in front of me. "That's something else I think doesn't matter."

I looked away before he could see I was upset. "It doesn't matter until we meet on the battlefield."

Aluxious chuckled and sat beside me. "You're a woman, not that I think it matters, but I doubt your father will allow you into battle."

"My father can't make my decisions for me. Surprisingly, he tries not to make decisions for me. I want to be a good Queen. I don't think a good Queen would hide behind her high walls while her men die for her."

"No," he said shortly. "That's what most Queens would do. You're not like most." He confirmed. He rested a hand on my knee. "I think both sides of this war are hoping for a Queen just like you. Don't lose hope."

I put my hand on his and he clasped it tightly. "Don't let me find you out there," I said.

"Don't throw an ax in my direction if you do." he joked and let go of my hand. He shot to his feet and offered me his hand to help me to my feet. "This is depressing."

"I should be going anyway." I said as I dusted my trousers off.

"What a shame. Let me walk you back to the gate?"

"I don't see the harm."

We walked next to each other in a comfortable silence. The crowds in the tavern and in the streets were dying, children were running home giggling and shouting. How had I missed how happy they were even as war raged, and famine was weighing on their shoulders? A little girl ran between Aluxious and I attempting to outrun a few boys. Her dress was made of a simple heavy weight fabric with cuts in the side for her arms and in the top for her head. She used an old piece of twine to tie it in at her waist to give it a more feminine cut. Did they all have such poorly made things? The two boys bolted around us after her and they were dressed in a similar fashion. All three of them didn't have shoes.

"Could you imagine having so much energy?" Aluxious said and pushed a hand through his thick red hair to push it out of his eyes.

"Could you imagine not having shoes, or decent clothing?" I said back.

"I don't know…" he said. "After sixteen I spent a lot of my time learning to shift. It was easier to wear less clothing, especially ones the sisters didn't mind being destroyed."

My head snapped in his direction. "You lived in a sanctuary? I did too!" I didn't think we would have shared something so unique and intimate in our pasts. "I miss it now." I added.

Aluxious smiled down at me. "I was seven when my father took me there. My mother was dead, and he was going off to war. They hadn't seen a Tribrid in a long time, so they welcomed me, like an experiment. They were still nice though."

"How long were you there for?" I asked.

"Until I was seventeen. My father came back for me. The sisters were afraid of me by then. For a while I couldn't control my shifting, and it happened at random." He shoved his hands into the pockets of his trousers. "I miss it too. It was peaceful. They wouldn't understand me, even now, but I would do anything for that sort of peace again."

We paced forward a few more steps before I asked. "Does shifting hurt?"

He looked down at me, a glint of amusement in his eyes. I was clueless about these things. "The first few times. Now, it's second nature. The beast and I are one being."

"Wait." I said stepping in front of him and placing a hand on his firm chest forcing him to stop. It was hard to admit that feeling his steady heartbeat pickup its pace under my hand made me blush, and I liked it. "Is the beast its own being in the beginning?"

"Well, no, I guess not, but it's like I was inside a different person when I shifted; there were a plethora of personality traits and tendencies that were all my own but suppressed. For a while it felt like a second personality, a new person. It's not like that now. Him and I, there's no difference between us. I am both the beast and the man. When I was young it was like a switch flipped in my mind when I was inside of him. Not anymore." He swatted my hand from his chest in irritation. "Does it really matter to you? You're an Ayl" He continued walking without me. His words stung more than I expected them to. At first it seemed like he welcomed questions about him and then he channeled that feeling into irritation and anger. Was that a part of the beast? Was it a part of him that liked to shove others out?

I was stunned at how defensive he was getting with me. "Yes. It matters to me." I rushed to catch up beside him. He was taking long impatient strides now. He was speeding up to get rid of me faster. "You're one of my only friends. Even if I am an Ayl."

He chuckled in disbelief, slowing to match my pace. "That's impossible."

"You're one of the only ones that doesn't want something from me."

"What do you mean?" He prompted.

I let out a deep sigh. "My father wants me to be a good Princess and a good Queen. Kendra, my mentor, has these standards she expects of me. If I told her I was out drinking with a tribrid she would lose her mind. Inara wants me to marry him so he can have the throne, but my friend is madly in love with him. Neither of them deserves me. Yurdell wanted more power. He wanted to be the next King. No matter who it's been, they've always wanted something, especially the throne." I paused, grasping his arm for a moment. "Not you. You want me to throw my axes like an entertainment act, you want to walk with me, and talk with me."

"It *is* very entertaining to watch you. Even more so with that Soilt hybrid scum on the other end of it." He stopped just outside the gate. It was him that looked up to the guard and called. "Get the Commander."

"What are you doing?" I asked and shoved him. "I don't want to be anywhere near him. He's upset with me, and we're courting. I'm going to try to end it. I told you my friend is madly in love with him." I said in a huff.

"Well," Aluxious watched as the gates opened. "I was curious who the groom to be was."

"Are you jealous?" I asked.

"Not at all, within a few days I'll be happily a proxy for a marriage. I don't have room to be jealous, although he does dote on you; maybe I wished my friend's future wife would think of him that way."

I smiled. "Just be kind to her when you meet. I'm sure she'll come around, and so will he."

"I'm sure she will." He said doubtfully under his breath. I felt bad for him. It was one thing to be forced into a courtship with someone, but for him it was worse. It was someone he didn't know, and he'd be the one standing in proxy for two people that had never met. I could imagine the stress he was facing of having to win her over for someone that couldn't even be there.

The gate swung open, Inara staring out at me with disdain and anger. "Why are you always going out on your own and what in the Devil's name-" his words faltered when he noticed Aluxious standing beside me. Was that anger or jealousy that swam in his cold eyes?

I motioned to the axes resting in my harness. "I think I've proved I can take care of myself." I said back in defiance.

"It was actually remarkable to watch." Aluxious chirped up from behind me, filling me with pride in myself and self-confidence. Why couldn't Inara take that same approach? "She was magnificent." My heart leapt at his words.

"Who do you think you are anyway?" Inara inquired with a bitter curl to his lip and turning his nose up.

I swatted him. "Don't be so rude. This is Aluxious. He's a good friend of mine."

J. L. Cross

"Smells like a dirty Arvor to me."

"Only partly." Aluxious retorted. "But mostly because I don't bathe in... *vanilla*?" He sniffed at the air like a dog, "and the essence of a woman." He harassed Inara, clearly trying to get a rise out of him.

I leaned towards Aluxious and realized he did have the hint of a smell of dog on him, but also the scent of grass, wildflowers, and the sun. Was that the scent of the mountains? He smelled more manly than Inara.

"Your new friend is rude." Inara accused.

"You are too, sometimes." I countered. He sighed irritatingly.

"It was really nice to meet you." Aluxious held his hand out in greeting to Inara. Inara took it after hesitating and quickly released it.

Aluxious met my eyes. "I look forward to running into you again. Be careful out there." He turned and left, again not looking over his shoulder or hesitating. He wasn't one to hang around for a long time. He knew when it was time for him to leave or when he was unwelcomed. Aluxious wasn't bothered by it either.

"Kastell?" Inara held his arm out for me.

"Are you still angry about me stealing your thunder?" I asked as I took his arm and let him walk me to the castle. There was an aching in my chest after Aluxious left, and even more so because this is where I belonged.

He laughed then. "I wasn't angry with you for *stealing my thunder*. Even though I had my eyes on you afterward, I was shaken. I want to be there to protect you and fight for you. As a man that's my purpose, I live to protect you."

"That's sweet, but I don't need you like that, Inara."

"I'm more than aware of that now." He let go of my arm and he turned me to face him. "What do I need to do to make you see me again? We're both in this courtship together." He traced the shape of my cheek with his finger and pushed a floating strand of my hair back behind my ear.

I pushed his hand away from me. My skin tingled where his finger lingered. I felt something for him, and he was trying, but I couldn't do this to Safrim. "Stop treating me like a damsel in distress. I can take care of myself. I don't need a nanny."

"Fine. It's hard not to want to protect you from everything."

"It feels like you're trying to *seclude* me from everything and turn me into a shell to wither away and die. My father is going to have the Collective vote tomorrow about your claim on Yurdell's lands and titles. After that I can only imagine my father will have us married, *promptly*. You need to start treating me like a King, not a Queen. Let me lead us through this."

He chuckled. "You want me to treat you like a man?"

"If it means you'll stop following me around and trying to protect me from my shadow… then yes. Sometimes I wish you were still chasing me in the garden like we were children, even if you were bullying me." I touched his cheek then; it was a matter of time before Inara was the new Prince to the throne and I would have to live out my days with him if I couldn't control the Collective and my father. I didn't want this marriage, or any, yet.

He nodded in agreement. "I'll try."

I let my hand drop and turned away from him to go into the castle. I wanted to see Kendra. We hadn't talked since she woke up and I wasn't going to keep letting my father keep us apart. She suffered a hard hit to the head making her drift in and out of consciousness and she was constantly under observation of the healer for the first week. That time had passed.

For the first time Inara didn't follow me. He let me leave in peace. Finally, I respected him.

22 Kendra

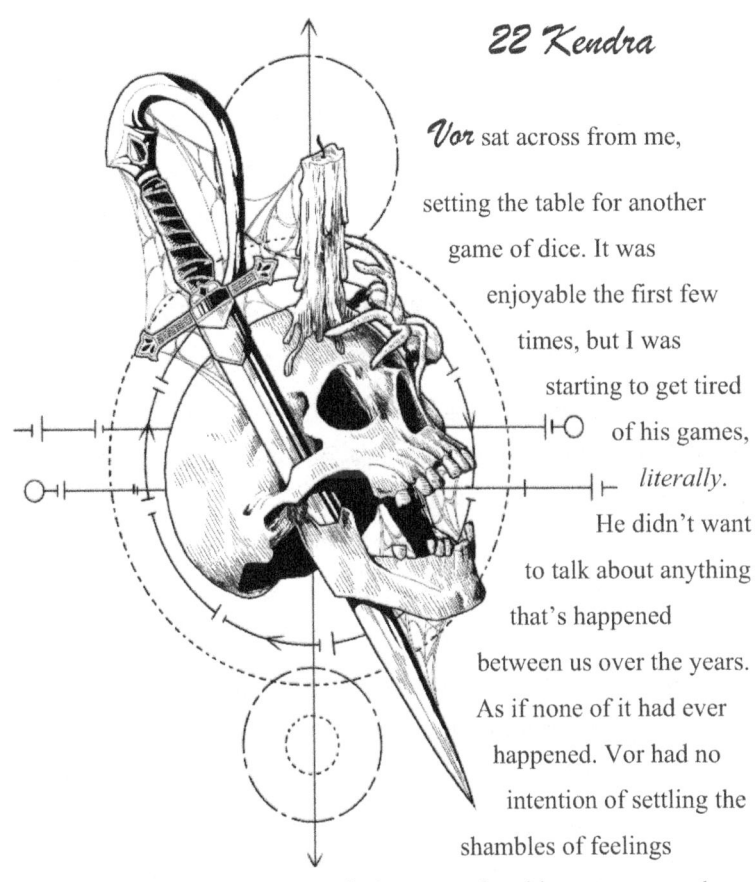

Vor sat across from me, setting the table for another game of dice. It was enjoyable the first few times, but I was starting to get tired of his games, *literally*. He didn't want to talk about anything that's happened between us over the years. As if none of it had ever happened. Vor had no intention of settling the shambles of feelings between us that were left. It made for uncomfortable company, and mostly silence. To make the best of it I was constantly trying to clear my mind of all the angry and hurtful things I wish I could say to him. Instead, I acted as if I didn't know him at all, which wasn't so far from the truth. He was essentially a stranger to me now, but I was the same to him, only grayer. We parted on horrible terms. I suffered years of the self-torment that I experienced after sending someone to kill his wife, *someone that we sent.* Hasn't he felt that same torment knowing that he had planned it alongside me for us to live out our lives together?

Back then was like looking into a fogged window, some of those memories were hazy and difficult to interpret. With old age my mind became weaker. Even my magic was starting to fail me, but I still had a few things in my repertoire no one could imitate. One of those things was still fastened to his wrist. A never-ending spell to protect its wearer from outside influences. With Gideon gone, I imagined he would have parted with it, but there it stayed.

It was brilliant seeing him after so long, almost like a dream after years of nightmares and loneliness. Age was taking my body, but he still seemed young and intact, just as I last knew him. The graying in his long hair and in his eyelashes was all that spoke of his age. I could tell that his joints ached as he set the dice board, another telling sign of his age. His hair was more combed and finer than it was so long ago. It used to be heavy and full of volume. Now it lay flat against his head and thinning. The features in his face were a bit sharper and gaunter than I remembered. Being a King, and alone, did not treat him fairly.

"Why have you been coming down here to see me if you don't want to talk?" the words poured from my lips before I could think twice about them. I twisted those same words a million different ways in my mind, knowing that I needed to ask for my own sanity.

Vor's head snapped up, and we made eye contact for less than a second before he looked away. Kastell and him were more alike than I'm sure they knew. They moved the same, their eyes were reflections of each other.

"There's nothing to be said." *lies.* His twisted brow and his narrowing eyes on the dice told me he had a lot to say, but he was holding it hostage behind his teeth. *Coward.*

My constant supervision by guards would cease when Vor came to visit, as if he needed privacy in these silent stolen moments. It was the only time we could speak freely. I didn't want to rush into the conversations that we needed to have, but I couldn't keep ignoring them either. Vor was always good at hiding his feelings behind a stoic mask of perfection. That mask wasn't nearly as thick as it used to be.

"Did the bracelet work, did it keep Gideon out?" I asked, motioning to the gold band.

He nodded.

"Good, he doesn't know boundaries."

I squared my shoulders and sat up straight, knowing that what I would say next would trigger a reaction. All those years ago all he did was barge in and react, he never gave me the chance to bare my truth to him, and now seemed like a better time than any. "I didn't send that woman to kill your children. You know better than that. We should have known better about bargaining with a witch." I scoffed at myself, the irony. "*I* should have known better. We never set an expiration date. I only assumed she'd died, or maybe you sent her away."

Vor slammed his fist on the table, shaking the legs and rattling the dice. Each dice fell to the floor one after another as his hand continued to shake with rage no matter how much effort he put into trying to make it still. I couldn't blame him. I'd lost him in almost the same manner he had lost his wife, but they would never have such a warm reunion. All the years he spent with her before her father passed, and after he was crowned King, one only grows to love someone more. After he abandoned our friendship, it was as if neither of us existed in the other's life. All I had was letters to his daughter to comfort me.

"Don't you dare bring that up." He unclenched his hand and stretched his fingers out over the surface of the table. I wanted to comfort the pain and anger he was feeling, but there wasn't much I could do for him. I was the reason his wife was dead, and his three young children nearly lost their lives. The witch meant to end his bloodline and the Varius.

I sat with my hands folded in my lap. "We need to talk about it. You told me what to do. You assured me that we could be together, that it was the right thing to do! You did this as much as I did." I didn't see his hand, but I felt that sharp stinging pain in my cheek, a thousand little pricks all at once from the impact. I could feel the red creeping into my skin as I held my hand to that tender spot.

Holding my stinging cheek, I looked up at him in shock. "You're such a petulant child." I spit the words hoping to insult him, but he wasn't one to easily offend.

"You're out of line." He barked back, his voice smooth as ice. "I know my part in what happened. I was a fool. I somehow learned to love my wife, despite her family. I didn't expect to feel so broken- every day I hoped you would send another to put me out of my misery once my children were all taken away from me. Taria fled with the Fae as soon as she was old enough; she refused to suffer the fate of her mother. My son turned into a brutal animal, but even my wife couldn't have stopped that. With Vlad out there, a genuine threat to Kastell, *my only true heir*, I had no other option but to bring her to you. Despite my despair, my anger, and my feelings- I knew she would be safe with you."

"I never meant to cause you such pain." The words were hard to pass, but I knew my rule and he had suffered over the years on his own. My pity for him didn't hinder the fact that I wanted desperately to hit him back, but I was a weak old woman. He brushed my attempt off by swatting my hand away when I finally made the decision to take a swing at him.

He stood, staring down at me. "I'm sorry for my anger. I shouldn't have hit you. I'm burdened every day with my part in her death, but I also suffer every day from when I had to let you go. How could I have taken you in good conscience after her end?" He wasn't looking for an answer.

Vor left then, not sparing me a chance to say anything else. Was it still too late for us? I picked up the dice and folded the board and placed it in the center of the table. My room was small and cramped, more like a renovated closet to accommodate my stay. There were no windows to the outside, so I was always asking what time of the day it was. I started tracking the passing of days with the coming and going of the guards outside my door. I could hear their chatter and sometimes the telling thud of weapons on the stone floor.

I was foolish to believe that I wouldn't be treated like a prisoner here. I'm a witch. Witches don't get a free pass. Vor had to keep up appearances in the castle. If the Collective or guards expected him of catering to witches or warlocks, he would be killed and strung up by the Collective as a traitor to the crown. While the relationship between the Ayles and Witches seemed smoother now than before, that was only outside of the city walls. It was obvious that people within the city walls didn't feel the same way as we did. There was still a raging hate for us here. My skin crawled thinking of having to confront the same people that threw stones at me on the streets. These people were hostile. The realization that our journey into the city gave me was chilling. Vor couldn't do much in the face of hate, the Collective would come against him every time. Maybe the way things are isn't entirely his fault like we would like to think.

I heard a rustling in the hallway and a happier than usual voice. *Kastell.* She only came to visit me once before, but she was being kept away as much as possible by her father, or by the Commander that seemed to follow her everywhere. She told me the last time that they were preparing for the Collective to meet. It would be the first gathering after the initial one of her returns. I heard of her activities since our last visit. She had killed the man that poisoned her heart with Venom. I couldn't believe she stayed away for so long, but it wasn't surprising either, she probably thought I would be disappointed in her. I wasn't. I was proud of her for standing up for herself. I needed her to be strong without me.

The door creaked open, and she stepped through, axes displayed across her back and a lightweight cape that hung off one shoulder. It was deep red and much different from the one she wore before that covered her back. This one looked more ornamental.

"What's with the change in attire?" I said as my finger dragged over the soft fabric when she sat beside me in the same chair that her father was just in. It groaned softly.

A smile spread across her face as she showed me the axes. "Aren't they wonderful? Commander Inara gave them to me."

I nodded. "A gift?" I said as my eyebrows rose suspiciously. "Does he have any other intentions beyond flattery?"

Kastell started to fidget. "That's why I came here. I was meaning to visit, but I didn't feel the urgency of it until last night. He's trying to be different. He's trying to understand my independence, but I'm not sure I want to be understood by him at all, not the way a man does a woman in a union. My friend, Safrim, she's madly in love with him. My father's insisting, we court, but I can't stomach it."

I motioned for her to go on. I could tell her shoulders were heavy now, was it the weight of his gift or the weight of the life she had taken?

"I don't love him." She said suddenly as she picked at her nails. "I thought I was going to fall for him, madly fall for him before the venom. I realized after the Venom wore off that I don't have anything in my heart for him. With Inara I have a history, but he was mean to me when we were children. I don't think he's really changed. It's hard to believe he could. He obviously admires my body as a woman, but I'm still that girl he chased down and picked on. I don't think he'll change, or ever be the man I need. He's not the man I want."

I took her hand in mine and brushed my thumb over her pale skin. "Well, you can't assume anything, but you can be cautious.

Sometimes it's a facade because it's what everyone around him wants. He wants you to be safe, or else he wouldn't have given you weapons of pure destruction. I think you need to make a firm decision. You were falling for him and then you were hurt by someone else. That kind of injury doesn't heal so fast." I waved my hand in the air as if to summon the words from my mouth, "and this friend of yours…. *Safrim*, if she loves him so much, then why would she ever stand for your union? You are left to make the choice. This is a man your father and his Collective would choose for you. Is he someone you would choose for yourself? I think you already know the answer."

Kastell took an ax from her back and held it up to the light. "Do you know what it says?"

I studied the etchings through the head of the ax, only picking up a few of the Fae letters and words until I could piece something together. "*Through time I shall answer.*" I touched the golden letters and leaves in the handle and smiled, feeling the warmth of its desire to hunt and be used. I could feel their magic deep within. "These are meant for great destruction. You should respect them."

"They're very ornamental though." She said back in defense, motioning to the weapons and their beauty.

I laughed, knowing all too well her weakness for shiny gold things. She was always coming home with brooches and hair pins at the Sanctuary, but I was always selling them back to teach her not to covet material items. "Kastell, these are made by the dwarves, the race that is known to build weapons of mass destruction. They fuel the war even now."

She winced a bit, scrunching her nose up at the idea. "They served me well."

"As I've heard."

"He wanted me for the throne."

"Are you so sure?" I fired back, but I knew that she was right. "Venom doesn't mean he was playing an evil game with you. It's in their nature as beasts in the night." I didn't mean to defend him or make her feel bad, but I needed her to learn to work through her own feelings and confusions without me there to validate them.

Kastell huffed. "Don't do that. Don't make me feel like I've made a mistake." *I was right.* She regretted her battle to the death. She regretted taking a life. "He was manipulating me. He was hoping I would challenge him so he could make me feel useless and defenseless. He was arrogant and thought he would win. I wasn't going to let him walk away with my pride. Yurdell was playing a part for the Rebel King, *the Devil.*" The name fell off her small lips like a curse. She validated her own feelings, sorting through them in front of me; While she was also finding someone to blame.

I stroked her hand again. "It's okay to feel regret, even if he was guilty. Always remember first that you chose him as well, and you landed yourself in a bad situation." It would never be easy to take a life, and with everyone she took it wouldn't get easier.

"I'll get over it." She snapped. Quickly she changed the subject. "When the Collective gathers tonight they're going to vote to pass Yurdell's titles and lands to Inara. He'll hold the worth he needs to offer me an official courtship. I'm going to decline. *Politely.*"

I let out a deep breath and touched her hair, moving strands from in front of her face. "Is that what you want?"

She hesitated. "I-" and then there was silence for a moment. I could see the gears turning in her mind through the vacant stare of her eyes. She finally came to a conclusion. "I couldn't pick a man right the first time. I don't trust myself, but I'm not looking for love anymore. My father thinks this is right, but I know it's not. I should trust myself again."

Pssh. I couldn't help letting out the sound of annoyance and I rolled my eyes and dropped her hand. "Your father makes a ton of mistakes. He may seem sure of himself now, but if you aren't ready don't you dare let him push you into a union. Courtship is one thing but handing the Kingdom over to a man you don't approve of is different, and it's the sheer truth about being a woman in your position. The Collective will approve the Commander and that's the only reason your father has selected him."

Her breath caught. "Should I distance myself?"

I shrugged. "If you want to. *What do you want?*"

A sharp laugh passed through her gritted teeth. "I want someone I can't have. It would be so wrong too. My father would be furious if he knew I was associated with this person. I guess he's a friend, but he's complicated. I don't think he's very interested in unions."

I giggled at her. "That's the person you should be distancing yourself from. It seems to me like the Commander is willing to give you gifts and this other man is looking to give you a heartache, maybe even a bastard."

She twisted her hair on a finger. "I'm not sure. He's nice, he's sweet, but he hasn't treated me like a conquest. Inara sometimes does. I'm a means to and end for him, he gets the throne. Hell, my friend doesn't even treat me like I have a throne."

I nodded, understanding. "I think your heart is telling you what you want, but you need to use your head. Your friend is unavailable and even though he isn't trying, he's going to break your heart. He won't be breaking his commitments, that's clear. If he had intended to pursue you, he wouldn't have been so open about his distaste for a union. Men like him can't have women like you."

"We're both being controlled by forces other than our own." Her head dipped as she stared into her lap. She looked up at me determined to be confident and strong. "A Queen has to make hard choices." her voice quivered once, pulling at my heart.

I nodded, smiling at her reassuringly. "Everything will be fine. You don't have to do anything you don't want to."

"But I will, for my Kingdom."

I shook my head. "Not even then. You don't have to be like your father. You don't have to give everyone else what they want."

"I'm not even sure what I want anymore. I thought it was Inara, and then I knew it was Yurdell, and then I was crushed, and now I want someone else, but I can't have him. I'm not even sure how I want him, or if I'm just being selfish and want him because I can't have him. I don't know what I want."

It was hard to see her this way, but I wasn't surprised. I knew she was bound to face challenges like this when she returned. I also knew there would be men preying on her for the throne. I wished now more than ever that Gideon would find a way at ending the war so that Kastell wouldn't be held to making such hard decisions so fast. Her father was aging, and the Collective would demand a suitable successor, and for a woman they would require her to be in a union. If only the war wasn't motivating them to fill those shoes so quickly, she could have more time and explore love the right way.

I stroked her hair until she sat up straight. I moved my chair to sit beside her and wrapped my arm around her, pulling her into me. "Love isn't easy on anyone."

"I think I know what I'm going to do."

I laughed at the smile on her lips. "Well, don't tell me, because I'd rather be surprised."

23 Kastell

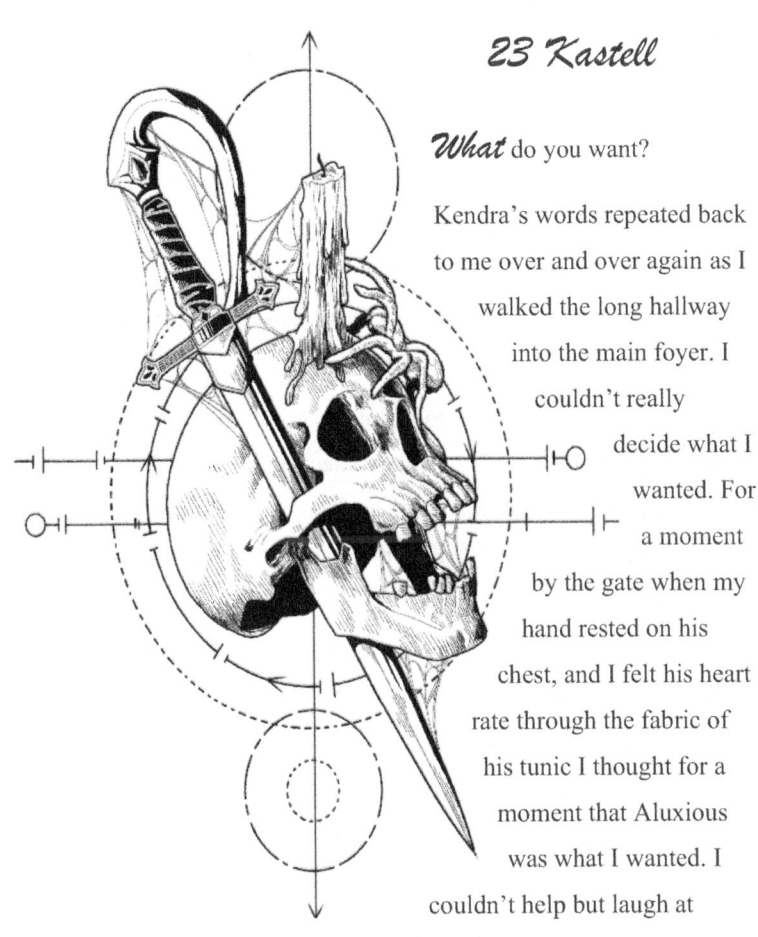

What do you want?

Kendra's words repeated back to me over and over again as I walked the long hallway into the main foyer. I couldn't really decide what I wanted. For a moment by the gate when my hand rested on his chest, and I felt his heart rate through the fabric of his tunic I thought for a moment that Aluxious was what I wanted. I couldn't help but laugh at myself. Aluxious is a hybrid, he wouldn't be taken as the next King, not with the current Collective, and I couldn't stomach giving up the right to the throne.

I used to read books about the Varius reign, not my mother's, but her father and her grandfather before him. They were terrible tyrants. The rifts between the species only grew deeper and deeper with every passing decade they had remained in power. With the succession of my father our people were brought into a new era, but here we were at war with the Rebels for an action my brother took. His heart festered with hate even from a young age. The embodiment of the old Varius values and mannerisms. Horrific. Those same values were still held by many of the elderly Collective members. It was owning the right to the throne that would guarantee the Collective couldn't elect someone like that again, or worse… Calling on my brother to ascend, wherever he may be.

My heart leapt at the sound of a courier being let into the castle. A young boy, no taller than my knees with a broad smile on his face and dirt smudged cheeks ran to me when he spotted me. The servant that had let him in tried to grab his arm to stop him, but he ignored her efforts.

"Princess!" He shouted and skidded to a stop in front of me, clearly out of breath as if he had run the whole way to the castle. "I've word fer ya." He looked around nervously and motioned for me to lean in. "Yer Rebel is waitin," he said. I couldn't help but giggle. I knew without a doubt Aluxious had sent the dirty little boy.

I waved the servant over to us. "What's your name?" I asked the boy as the servant approached, disapproving of the small boy.

"Firmir." he said. His hair was caked with dust and old mud, but I could tell he had jet balck hair buried in the dirt.

I said to the servant. "Get Firmir cleaned up, something clean to wear, and a good hot meal."

The boy looked up at me, his eyes protesting. "I can't! I've got work ta do!"

J. L. Cross

I kneeled in front of him and met his eyes, pulling a sack of coins from my waist band. "This is thirty full pieces, earnings to equate two weeks for a courier."

"I shouldn' take it." He complained. I jingled the small pouch and his eyes lit up, without another protest he snatched the coins and tucked them into his satchel. "Thank ya!"

I nodded to the boy and the servant took him by the hand and led him through the castle to be cared for. I listened to the servant and the boy chatter as they walked away from me. He was glowing with excitement. This was the change I wanted for my people.

The main gates loomed ahead, sealed tightly. I motioned for the guard to open them, but a voice from behind him denied me.

"Wait." I turned to see Inara, sizing me up and down. I didn't say anything. I didn't have to do anything he wanted, and I made myself clear about this. I thought he was trying to turn a new leaf by removing my leash, but by the angry look in his eyes I could tell he wasn't as committed to it as I thought he was.

"Don't go off to meet that *dog*." He snarled, his lip curling with hate.

I laughed at him. I couldn't help but think he was childish in his hate. "Really?" I lifted an eyebrow, tempting him to challenge me further. "We went over this. You need to back off."

He looked away from me then, clenching his fists at his sides. "I don't want to see you get hurt. He's an Arvor, or at least there's a part of him that is, and they're dangerous."

I could tell he meant well. Inara wanted to protect me, but he needed to relinquish whatever leash he thought he had. "I'm not someone you can control." I said softly. "Not all of them are dangerous. It's those thoughts that are going to continue to fuel this war."

"Your people are starting to slowly starve to death as we run out of rations, and yet you want to dine with the same people that are taking those precious resources?"

I froze for a moment. It was never something Aluxious had ever talked about. We always let topics involving the war pass. We weren't interested in them when we spent time together. Maybe I was foolish not to question it.

I walked to Inara and squeezed his hand. I felt the tension leave his body for all but a second. "I'll ask him about it. Maybe someone on the inside is what we need right now. Let me go." I whispered.

He waved for the gates to open but clung onto my hand gently, coaxing me to stay with him. "Just be cautious."

I left him with not much more than a small smile. I was shocked that he had actually decided to let me go. I admired him for putting his best foot forward. I was still irritated with how clingy he had become. Every time I turn my head he's there, lurking in the background. His need to protect me was hard to stifle, especially after the intruder. Or was I only so important because without me he had no chance to be my father's successor? I first noticed how irrational he was becoming after the intruder. He trusted me less after my combat with Yurdell. He told me to not look for trouble, and on the first chance I got I created trouble. I could understand why he wanted to be everywhere with me, but I didn't need his protection.

The walk to the market square was quiet and filled with the song of birds for a change. They were nesting in the crevices of the roofs and overhang beams. The nests grew still and soundless as I passed beneath them. We were racing to the end of the warm season. It wouldn't be long before the chicks were jumping into flight from the nests.

Today was unusually still. There were no children running in the streets and the market was unbearably empty apart from a few stalls. The bins were near empty, hanging off the sides and being cooked in the heat of the sun. Rotten and moldy vegetables were all that remained in some of the baskets. Some of the merchants were packing up their stalls early, their baskets and crates that they loaded empty or spoiled.

I was passing by the mouth of an alley when I was pulled into the shadows of one of the townhomes and a hand pressed over my lips. I tried to scream but every cry was muffled. I kicked furiously and tried to bite at the calloused skin but failed.

"Damn-it, stop!" A growled whisper so close to my ear a shiver went over my skin. *Aluxious.* That growl was more animal than man.

My heart started racing out of pure excitement. I pulled his hand from my mouth. He had me pressed against a townhouse wall, our bodies held together by his sheer strength. I swatted at him, but he didn't back away. I could barely catch my breath under him. I wouldn't ever be excited this way by Inara.

A hood covered his face, keeping it in the dark. "*Stop.*" He said more sternly. The demand and power in his voice made me go entirely still. "You're being followed." His voice was deep and raspy.

He gestured with a slight tilt of his head to the mouth of the alley. Aluxious was massive enough that with me pressed under him no one could tell who either of us were.

I turned my head enough to see past Aluxious's dangling hood. Children were playing in the open market and the traders were packing all of their empty crates. Only a few moments passed before Inara walked past the alley. He stopped and stood in the center of the market for a moment, kicking at the stones and dirt, his hands in the pockets of his trousers and his blade was slung on his back rather than hanging from his belt as usual. His back was to us, and it was the first time I cared to notice that he stood with an aurora of cocky arrogance.

I scoffed in frustration, my teeth grating together. "I can't believe him. We just talked about this."

Aluxious turned his head to look back at me, searching my face for answers. "He's clingy? For you or the throne? That's what's so annoying to you?"

I nodded. "I can't seem to get away from him." I looked away from him and stared out at Inara, expecting him to turn around and spot us.

Aluxious caught the worry in my face as my muscles tensed. His hand grasped my chin lightly, turning me back to him. His thumb traced the curve of my jaw. "He's not here for you. You don't need to worry." After a moment of staring deep into me, touching my soul with his eyes, he looked back to Inara. "I'll protect you if I need to, but I don't think he's looking for you. He's waiting for someone."

My face was burning with heat when I looked away. I could feel his wide muscled leg between mine, shifting to keep his balance, but never faltering to hold me propped up and hidden under him.

His jaw was wide and sharp and a chiseled, defined chin. His cheekbones were tall and prominent. Aluxious had tan taught skin, kissed by the Mother herself. His checks seemed more flushed than usual. Was it because of how close we were getting?

I reached out and gently placed my hand on his chest and felt his heart racing. "Why?" I asked softly.

He turned to me, studying the hand on his chest and then our eyes locked. "You make me nervous." He said and then turned back to Inara. Honesty rippled off of him. How could I make someone as large and strong as him *nervous?*

When I was able to take my eyes from him, I could swear his throat bobbed, relieved that my gaze was shifting from him.

Inara was talking to someone, a maiden from the tavern. I could see the frustration rolling off of him as he straightened his shoulder, laying a purse of heavy coins into her hand. He turned back towards the road that led to the castle gates. At least he wasn't following me for a change.

I knew in my gut that trusting him was far more complicated than everyone made it seem. Here he was, right in front of me passing money to a barmaid, and what for? What purpose did he have to be here? In all the time I was home I never saw Inara freely make his way to the market for a chit-chat with a barmaid, and he'd never gone drinking. He did that in the privacy of his chambers.

Aluxious eased away from me, setting my feet back on the ground and helping to straighten my cloak. "I didn't mean to take you by surprise." His voice was even now, not so much a whisper as it was a moment ago.

"It's alright," I said. My attention focused on the market. "Why is it so empty and quiet? The market was buzzing with life before."

Aluxious heaved out a deep breath. "Rations have been going missing for weeks, because the Rebels and Ayles have been fighting over them. My people need to eat too, so they're doing all they know how to do. But suddenly within the last few days silos and barns are being emptied and burned every night, there's no possible way the losses can be recovered."

"How is that even possible?" I said, fueled with anger. These were my people that were slowly starving.

Aluxious met my eyes. "We don't know. Rebel sentries are trying to protect what's left of our own sources, but time and again they're being slaughtered in the night. We don't have enough men to post more."

I gasped. "Both of our people are starving. Someone is pitting us against one another, making us think the other is taking the food."

Aluxious bit down on his lip. He knew this was happening. "I think I know who, but I don't want to jump to conclusions. I'll dig around about it and maybe take a posting myself. That would be the sure way to know who's behind it."

The air got thick and caught inside my lungs for the span of a heartbeat. "You can't do that. If the sentries are dying, why would you think it would be different for you?"

Aluxious turned back to me, closing the distance between us until my back was pressed against the wall again without anywhere to run. His hands braced on the wall beside either side of my head. He dipped his head down, his breath mingling with my own.

"Are you worried about me?"

"Always…" The truth ripped off my tongue without a second thought. "You're a man, you're more likely than me to end up at a posting that will get you killed."

A sly smile spread over his full lips. "That's sweet. I worry about you, too."

"I'm super safe up there." I said sarcastically, waving in the direction of the castle. "I won't be seeing battle until my father assembles the troops to run down rebel pods." I traced the edge of his jaw with my thumb, desperate to touch him, to absorb the warmth coming from his skin. "It's a shame, really, the Rebels stopped moving in large pods after the first battle we won."

He laughed and his smile grew. "You trust so easily, everyone up there. Not everyone is good, Kastell." he paused. I could see the debate in his eyes on what he would say next. "And I prefer it this way. If they moved in pods they would be slaughtered. Thankfully, you'll never see a posting and we won't be seeing his army move in force, leaving you safely tucked away from battle."

"Are you a good man?" I ignored his smug comment about me never seeing battle. He would eat his words one day. I wanted to be out there fighting for my people.

His smile faltered then; a million thoughts were running through his mind. I could see the wheels turning as he stared at me. "I'd like to think I am."

I touched my hand to his chest, and suddenly the panic in his eyes seemed to vanish. "Promise me something." He said then, putting his hand over mine and pressing my hand into his warm chest.

"Anything."

"If you ever see the other side of me, the beast, don't be afraid of him."

I laughed and pushed him away from me, taking my back off the wall. I remembered the fear I had when I was surrounded by his kind. Could I really make such a promise? "You don't scare me. I doubt you could." I lied. What else was I supposed to do? I couldn't admit to him that there was an untamed fear inside of me because of what had happened.

J. L. Cross

He smiled then, hope gleaming in his eyes. I wasn't afraid of much, but something about Aluxious was primal and angry, strong and fierce. Something inside of me screamed that I *should* fear him, but I couldn't.

"I have somewhere to be, but I wanted to say goodbye before I went." He brushed his knuckles against my cheek, pushing strands of my pale white hair out of my eyes.

My heart gave a small painful lurch. He was probably going to be married. His arranged marriage slipped my mind so easily when I was close to him. I didn't want him to go. I was getting used to our meetings in the evenings at the tavern. Who knows how long he would be gone, and I didn't want to ask. He would send Firmir again if he was back.

"Don't be gone long." I whispered, my voice caught in my throat, even though I knew deep down I wouldn't be seeing him again soon.

"I can't make any promises to you." The pain in my heart grew. We lived two very different lives. It was only by chance that we had been in the market on the same day at the same time when he first approached me. Lucky chance didn't mean that this was a fate the Mother intended for us. Our lives tangled beautifully that day, but she was inevitably going to force us apart.

Aluxious bent and brushed his lips against my forehead and turned away from me and walked towards the city gates. I wanted to run after him, but I held myself still. I watched him as he disappeared through the gates. He never turned back to look at me. Was it hard for him to keep walking, ignoring me like we hadn't been so close? Was it hard for him not to come back and steal the kiss that had lingered so patiently between us?

I straightened my cape and turned to the tavern. I crossed the empty market and slammed myself down into an empty chair. The maiden that had talked to Inara came out and gave me a small glass.

"We don't have much left." She commented dryly and held out her hand for coins. I put them in her palm, she grasped them tightly. "Only one per customer." She turned on her heel and went back into the tavern. I almost considered asking her what they talked about, but that was a question better posed for Inara. Would he pay someone to keep tabs on me?

I sighed in frustration and leaned back into my seat. I stared down into my drink and ran my finger over the lip of the glass until it hummed an awkward pitch. Another piece of my heart was undoubtedly going to break, and I was doing my best to ignore it.

"Can I sit here?"

I looked up to see Inara pulling out a chair.

"Sure- fine." I said in irritation. "I thought we were past this."

"I wasn't here for you." He said bluntly and quickly stood again before he even touched the base of the seat. "I was just meeting someone and saw you here as I left. I can tell you're in a... *mood*. I'll see you back at the castle."

"I'm sor-" My words trailed off into silence. He didn't acknowledge my attempt to apologize. I let him storm off in anger. It served him right. I wanted space more than anything from him, from my duties. Yet, they followed me everywhere I went.

I drank down the bit of hard cider the maiden had given me, letting it burn the back of my throat as it slowly trickled down. It was disappointing that even the cider was running thin, although my father still had his special stock below his desk. I considered stealing one tall bottle for myself when I got back. So be it if he caught me in the act. My heart ached, I wanted to drown it.

Aluxious and I both knew that we lived different lives on two different sides of the war. I would be foolish to believe he would be back for me again. Our encounters would start to run dry and become less common. He was just attempting to make his parting less painful for us both. We grew closer than I thought we had. It would have never worked, no matter how we tried. I'd be expected to make the best decision for my people, but it was the one decision I wouldn't like. I knew what I was going to do.

My room was cold, the fire died while I had been out and as the sun sank it filled it with a horrible chill that reached my bones. My teeth clattered as I started the fire in the hearth and sat there for a moment drawing from the blissful heat. Everything green outside was starting to die. The cold months weren't far off now. I'd be spending a lot more of my time bent in front of my fire.

The door to my room flung open and Della stepped in carrying a large box with a massive cream bow on the top. She huffed in irritation and dropped it on the bed. "I'm sorry, I didn't think a fire would've gone out so quickly."

I shrugged.

"Up with ya." Della came beside me and attempted to hoist me to my feet. She wasn't a strong woman, but she pulled until I gave in and stood up. "What's wrong with ya?"

"I don't want to make hard choices."

Della scoffed. "This is about a boy."

"A man." I scolded.

"Fine then- a man." She laughed. "The heart is fragile an' fickle. You'll move on."

I nodded, straightening myself. I couldn't sit back and feel sad forever. Aluxious and I were never more than friends. We never had a chance to cross that void into something more. As much as I wanted to believe we could have made things work. It didn't matter- our feelings- I was to be Queen and the Collective would never allow someone of his bloodline to be on the throne. I was the only one standing between the progress my father has made for the Kingdom and their desire to tear it down and make it what it once was.

I went to the box on the bed and pulled at the bow. "What is this?"

"The Commander sent it." She said, filling a hot bath and setting the vanity with pins and hairbrushes for after. "He would like ya to wear it for him." She wiggled her eyebrows as mine furrowed. Our eyes locked from across the room.

"He was upset with me the last time I spoke with him." I bit the inside of my cheek nervously. "I was rude."

Della's eyes shot up to mine. "Why? That man is good to ya."

"I need space. After Yurdell my heart hasn't been the same. Everything about him doesn't seem right anymore. This is what everyone else wants, but no one has asked me."

Della came to me and helped me out of my clothing and ushered me into the bath water. "If ya heart is going to hurt, child, at least hurt over a man that will benefit this Kingdom."

I dropped my head, looking into the water. She was right. I should have wanted Inara the entire time, instead I was seeking out Aluxious. My heart needed a friend at the time, and that friendship blossomed somewhere deep inside of me into something more, surprising me at the last moment. Inara deserved that much from me.

"You know," I said flatly. "The Commander is someone worthy."

Della tisked and snapped her finger in front of my face. "Wake up, child!" She hissed. "A good man will never think he's worthy of someone like ya. When he needed ya to be persistent ya decided ta turn ya back. *Foolish.*" She rolled her eyes at me and went back to the vanity. "None of the men here are worthy of you."

Was that really what I did? My heart tightened and squeezed every drop of sorrow out inside of me. I was so blind. In the end I moved on and left him in my wake. If Della was right, Inara had felt what I wanted to feel for much longer. The moment I walked out the castle with Yurdell was the moment I snapped something inside of Inara. Worthy or not, he committed, and he's tried to right the wrong ever since, throwing himself in my path at every opportunity as if his chances were quickly running out. They had been all along.

While I was getting annoyed with him trailing behind me, protecting me, and treating me like a delicate flower, he was just trying to make himself an undeniable part of my life. The Kingdom deserved someone like him. He'd given up someone he loved to be the man the Collective and my father wanted him to be. They needed someone to commit, to do what was best for the people. I could love him, but it wasn't fair. Safrim wouldn't hold it against me, but I would. My heart stuttered at the thought of facing her if I decided that following my father's lead was best.

I'd pushed Inara away, and now I knew I had to stop. He deserved better, and the Kingdom deserved him.

Della laid a towel over the side of the tub for me. I stood and dried myself, making my way to the vanity to have my hair finished. I stared at myself in the mirror, remembering the first days I was infected with the Venom. I could see him carved from a memory lounging on my bed as I sat in this same chair. I had tried to seduce him then. It was after his finger touched the skin of my breast that the Venom penetrated every piece of me, stifling those desires with disgust. Were my feelings for him so easily doused? Was there anything left or was I right to want to leave it behind and move on without him. Safrim would be good for him. Didn't she deserve to be happy, too?

I faced the vanity mirror and took in the elaborate dress. It cascaded over me and clung to my curves, making me look sensuous and womanlier. My trousers and tunic hung loosely on a hook in my dresser. I wanted more than anything to be comfortable, but with the Collective gathering I had to make a proper appearance. Inara picked this just for me. He had a good eye for style.

Parts of the dress were sheer and light weight with only enough thick fabric to cover my chest and just below the waist. The light blue fabric made my eyes glow. The ice blue met with the green near the pupils. After debating it for a moment I took one of the teal scarves that Aluxious had bought for me and wrapped it over my shoulder. The silk was soft and cool against my bare shoulders.

Della came up beside me and fluffed the tulle skirt of the dress. "Very beautiful. The Commander won't be able to look away from ya."

I gave her a weak smile. I chose this. I could have run after Aluxious this morning. I could have gone after him. *I chose this. I would have been miles away from my responsibilities by now.* My mind whispered to me. Della spent hours pinning my hair into an intricate crown design over the front but flowing luxuriously down over my shoulder. She used a hot steel rod that she heated moderately over the flames to put curls into my thick white hair.

She stood in front of me now, making her masterpiece perfect. "Very good." She said more to herself than to me. "When ya done at the gathering call for me, I'll help ya put this away. Please, *do not* get this one covered in blood." Her eyes darted up to mine, silently scolding me for the last dress I had ruined, although that one had belonged to my mother.

I wasn't entirely surprised that most of the fabric was sheer and see through. Inara was illuminating all the womanlier features I possessed. The dress would make a statement to the Collective that I wasn't a child, and I was prepared to assume my duty as the heir. They continued to doubt my capabilities on the mere fact that I'm a woman, but my father and Inara both stood in my corner when I needed them to, a weapon ready to be harnessed against the Collective.

I was beside myself about wearing it in the first place, it would certainly send a statement to everyone else in attendance as well. First, I'm supporting Inara's claim to the lands and titles. I believed he deserved them after so many years in service to my father. I really believed that much. Two, accepting a gift from him was a sign that I would be accepting his offer of a courtship, but when I publicly denied it then maybe everyone would acknowledge that I wasn't going to play by the rules of the society they created.

The dress was in the color of Inara's banner, a sky blue, light and airy, just like the dress. My father's banner was darker blue. With gatherings like this one, it was expected for guests to dress according to their banners, but tonight I would undoubtedly support his claim. Such intimate gifts aren't to be taken lightly: clothes and jewelry for the most part. I never thought to consider the gift of my axes to be intimate, but instead only one from a teacher to the student. I should have thought it through before accepting them in the first place. Third, I would be solidifying the choice I made not to go after Aluxious. This was the end of that path. I would be staying here to defend my right to the throne, with or without a man beside me.

Della herded me to the door, making sure my dress was moving right and not getting caught. She swung the door open, and Inara stood on the other side, hand raised to knock on the wooden frame.

"I'm sorry." He said quickly, his eyes locked on mine first before scanning over me. His brown eyes sparkled with life and happiness at the sight of me in the dress he had sent. "I d-don't…" He cleared his throat. "I don't mean to intrude." He finished slowly, stumbling over his words before getting his bearings.

"She's ready now." Della said as she moved away from me, stepping to the side, waiting. During events like this one she stayed close to me, fetching me anything I may want or need. She would know when I was ready to depart and come back to the room to fill the bath and heat the sheets.

Inara stepped back from the door to give me the room to move through the door, maneuvering the tulle skirt with me. His eyes were glued to me with every step I took, worshiping my grace silently. He offered me his arm, his hand steady against his chest. I hesitated a moment, I wanted to turn and run away. Change into my trouser and tunic and run for the wood line, screaming for Aluxious to find me. I knew he didn't live in the city. My best bet would be that his Arvor-senses would sniff me out or that he would be waiting for me to come to him.

You're crazy. Stop it. I scolded myself and pushed those nonsense thoughts away. How naive could I possibly be? Aluxious wasn't waiting for me. He didn't feel the same way for me, and if he did, I didn't know for sure. It's possible he only needed a friend, and I was an easy target. How would I ever know what his true intentions were? I would never know if we shared the same feelings, or if it were just me. I hoped, even as I slid my hand into the loop of Inara's arm, that he had felt the same for me, even as that future died with every step I took forward.

"You look stunning." Inara said, ceasing my racing mind. His lips were a breath away from my ear, the warmth of it making my skin tingle. His voice was even and soft, soothing. He calmed me without even knowing it.

I blushed. I couldn't help it; flattery was one of my true weaknesses. He was always good at that.

Stunning; absolutely magnificent. I remembered the first time he had whispered that complement in my ear.

I smiled as I looked up at him. He was smiling down at me, entranced by me. The look in his eyes failed to stir something that had been waiting dormant since the day I removed Yurdell's head from his shoulders. I had to make the best of this.

Inara walked me down the stairs and as we came to the doors of the ballroom, we found my father standing there. Inara bowed, "Your Highness."

"Commander." He said curtly. Then his gaze shifted to me. "Gorgeous. As always." His compliment was guarded, his eyes shadowed. He wasn't the happy man he usually was. I hadn't seen him in days, something was happening, and I was being held at arm's length. His face seemed more stern and less cheerful to see me than usual.

I put my hand on his arm, drawing his attention back to me. "Is everything okay?"

"I'm just thinking through some things." He said curtly, brushing my worry away. "It's nothing serious."

24 Ethal

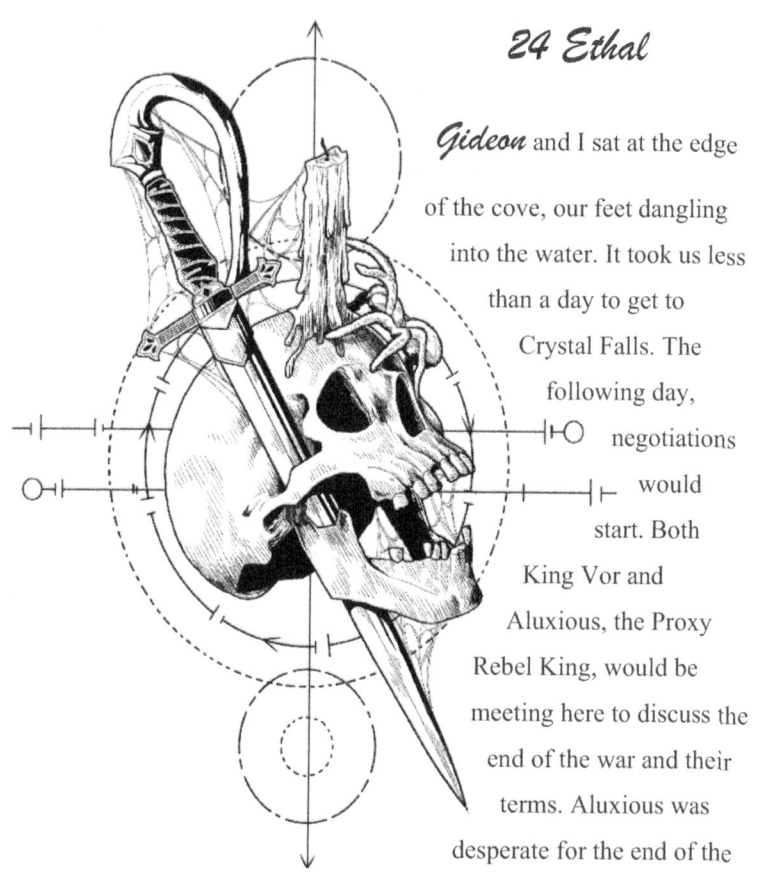

Gideon and I sat at the edge of the cove, our feet dangling into the water. It took us less than a day to get to Crystal Falls. The following day, negotiations would start. Both King Vor and Aluxious, the Proxy Rebel King, would be meeting here to discuss the end of the war and their terms. Aluxious was desperate for the end of the war. The King, however, was not. Both sides of the war wanted to see an end, but the Ayles made that end look distant. Gideon would demand the King sacrifice the heir to the throne, his favorite child, straight to the Arvors- *Literally*.

Gideon lounged against a rock, staring off into the cover, the water rushing in from the channel over a short waterfall. The water was so clear it looked like shards of glass flowing over the sharp edges of the fall. It was mesmerizingly beautiful.

The small village behind us laid in ruin, unbuilt from the attack that started the war. Vlad, the King's son, long forgotten by the Rebels. They could care less *whose* actions started the war, only that the Ayles paid for all the things they did over the years: the first war with the witches and the segregation and hatred that followed. After the first war the Ayles treated everyone like lesser people. The Rebels wanted them to recede into the shadows of the world and take their hate with them.

Rebel forces were gathering in the west coast and moving East slowly. Gideon reached out to contacts he established long before his first death and before Claret Magic. Many of the warlocks grew old and gray, while Gideon remained unchanged by time. These warlocks were paired with the rebels. It wasn't just the Arvors versus the Ayles. It was different now. It was all the people versus the Ayles.

Gideon twirled a piece of grass in his fingers. "How do you think the rations are doing? There can't be much left."

I shrugged. This was the part of Gideon that scarred me. If I weren't on his side… What would become of me?

"Claret Magic is strange." I said, shifting my eyes away from him. "How did you do it?"

Gideon sat up straight, excited to part what he knew. "When we first walked through the city, it was waist deep with people, but when we left… *empty.*" He said with a sly smile on his lips. "I heard them all. Every mind as we walked those streets. I couldn't help but get into their minds, toy with them. I needed a catalyst after all."

"Why- why did you need to destroy their food? People will die."

"With war comes sacrifice." He said sternly. "I will gladly let another few thousand Ayles die to see the end of war."

"Gideon…" I plead, my voice begging him to see the consequences of his actions. He didn't tell me what he had done until we were traveling here. I noticed the emotionless venders, the rotten foods, the depression and bitter hungry stares of those Ayles. "Tell me why." I finally demanded.

His cocky smile dropped from his face when he took in my real anger, my distaste for him. "How else would the King be convinced to come here? He wouldn't. His people are starving at an unprecedented rate, soon enough, that will overflow into the castle. The Rebels were only stealing the Rations they needed, but now it looks like they're destroying it all, making the Ayles suffer."

"They *are* suffering." I said adimitally. "Even the children."

"And because of their suffering he will come. I planted the seed into their minds and within only two days the rations were targeted, and their sentries died as well." He paused. "Don't worry. My footprint has been erased. The Ayles that did my bidding killed themselves not long after. Now the Arvors think the Ayles are starving them and vice versa."

"It was wrong." I snapped.

"No." he corrected, "it's ending the war."

"And if he doesn't show?" I spat back at him. "You'll have to live with those deaths. I'll have to live with them as long as I possess your life force."

Gideon crawled to me and laid his head in my lap. I felt Claret Magic before I saw it. The air vibrated and hummed. The magic wrapping around me in a soothing red blanket of comfort. My anger and my thoughts of those emaciated and dying Ayles and Arvors leaving my mind.

"He will show. Have faith in me."

Faith bloomed where only doubt was before.

The village of Crystal Falls was nothing, but half burned buildings and ash. We stood in front of the town hall building in the center, the least burned of the village. Gideon took it in and cocked his head to the side, observing and processing.

"This will do." He held his hands out in front of him, his eyes rolling back into his head as the Claret Magic pulsed from his hands in waves, humming and vibrating us. The sound of wood against wood and the cracking and creaking of it pierced the quiet as the Claret Magic engulfed the building, obscuring it from our view. The haze of red mist gathered stronger and thicker.

The air pulsed and vibrated so quickly I couldn't hear anything, it felt as if time halted for a brief second. Gideon snapped his fingers and the magic rushed back into him, pouring in through his eyes, ears, nose, and hands. Anyway, it could get into him, it moved to get there. He took in a sharp breath as the mist disappeared into him. He heaved an uncomfortable sigh of relief when it was finished.

Gideon's body hunched over as he moved forward. His body was sapped bare. The power he had gathered in his core and away from his access so it could recover. I could see the pain on his face and went to slip his arm over my shoulder to hold him up. *I'll have faith.* I said to myself as I held his weak body.

He motioned to the newly restored building. It was long and two stores tall. The exterior was a dark brown and the roof shone jet black against the orange and red trees in the forest beyond. Those woods belonged to the Arvors.

I helped Gideon in through the wooden doors and set him down in a rickety chair at the long table in the center of the gathering hall. Bookshelves lined every wall, most of them bare. Some burned books scattered through the shelves. Even the drapes were rehung and in pristine condition.

"If you could do all of this, why couldn't you add some books?" I asked playfully.

Gideon chuckled. "I can't create things that don't already exist in the space I'm reconstructing."

"What a shame."

I moved around the room, lifting open some chests to find blankets and clothing. There was a small kitchen and a few private rooms. The upstairs was only a balcony that went the length of every wall, lined with more bookshelves. I could see the door to one bedroom up there.

"Why here?" I asked as I sat across from him at the table. It was too wide to reach across for him, but I was still angry about what he had done to the food supplies. I wanted him to know I hadn't forgiven him yet.

"This is the village where the war started. Vlad came to collect taxes, but instead he killed everyone he could find." Gideon stood and went to the mouth of the kitchen and stopped just before the doorway. He bent and picked up the corner of the rug and peeled it away, showing me the locked entrance to a cellar. "Aluxious spent days in this cellar waiting out the sounds of the Ayles ransacking this place for all it was and all it had. His father led this community. It wasn't a pack, mostly loners and exiled Arvors. They had their own little democracy here, like the witches do in most of their villages. He allowed anyone that was willing to pull their weight and obey the laws to build their homes here."

I leaned forward on the table, listening. "What was his name?" I asked.

"Alcux." No one knows what happened to him. When Aluxious turned seventeen Alcux went to the sanctuary to claim him and then after a year of introducing him to the Rebels as the new proxy King, the heir to the Rebel throne, Alcux left. He abandoned them all.

No one knows where he went. I know someone that could tell us though." He met my eyes, a wicked smile playing on his lips. "A Fae."

"Impossible," I said.

The door to the building burst open. Aluxious strode through stark naked. A scowl was plastered across his face. "I can't do this. Not to her." He said, his lip curling with pure rage.

"What a marvelous appearance." Gideon said, slowly clapping. He strolled around Aluxious, taking in the man's sun kissed skin, broad chest, shoulders, and the sheer power and strength those muscles screamed to have as they flexed when he moved.

"The Mother has made a stunning piece of art out of you." I commented as I picked at my nails, heat rising in my cheeks. I tried not to stare at him.

"This is wrong, Gideon. I can't force her into this." Aluxious ignored us. "And I know what you've done to the food, don't think I'm fool enough to blame the Ayles for this. I know better."

"You will, or you won't have peace. I told you what the consequences would be if you refused." Gideon warned.

"Change your mind. There has to be another way to find peace." Aluxious pleaded. "I don't want her to know me like this, she doesn't know who I really am, *as a beast or as a man."*

Gideon braced himself on the table. "There is no other way, Aluxious. I wish there were. I've already dug myself too deep into this plan. The people of Civith both fear and cherish their Princess. The people will not go to war against her. This gives me enough time to figure out what to do with her brother. That's a whole season of peace and trading. Isn't that enough for you? The King will not bend to anything else. If you want him to bend to peace, this is it."

"I do." Aluxious said, his head dipping in shame. "I'm not worthy of her, not the way I am. I've killed too many of them. When she finds out who I am she'll never accept me. Nor will she accept the man she's really going to be forced with."

Gideon chuckled. "We told you to tell her."

I leaned forward, cocking my head to the side. "I told you to tell her, didn't I?"

"It doesn't just roll off the tongue: *just to clear the air, I'm the Proxy Rebel King. I shift into a mangy animal that killed hundreds- no, thousands of Ayles to fight back against the Patriarchy that's made everyone else suffer. I hope you can still love me.*" He mocked.

"That sounded pretty good. I mean, you could work on the presentation a bit." I said, trying to hide my amusement. "Though, no one is promising love."

"Tonight should be fun then." Gideon said with a clap of his hands.

25 Kastell

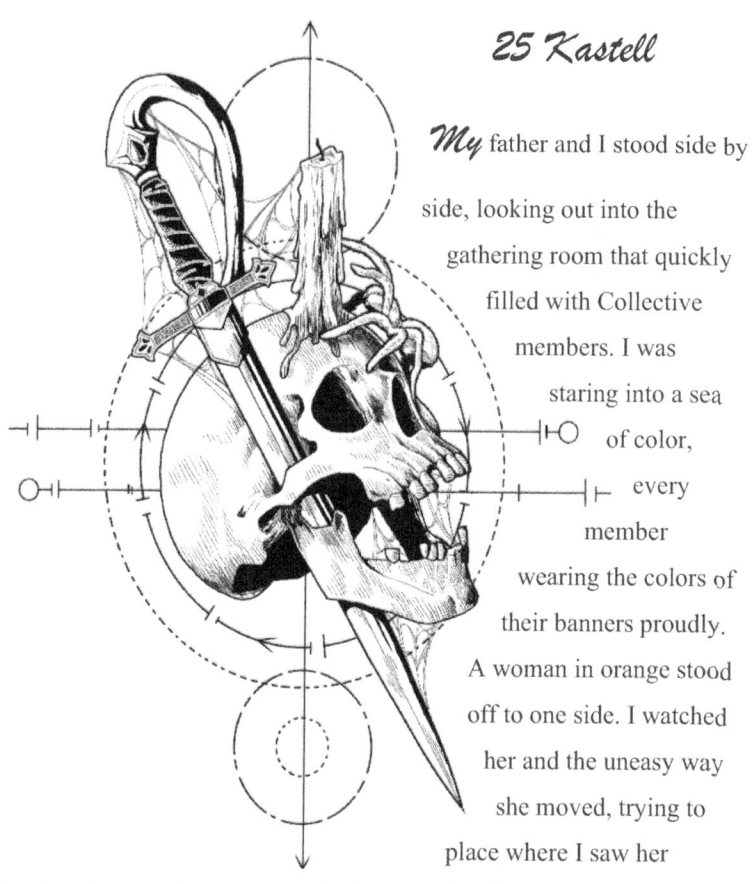

My father and I stood side by side, looking out into the gathering room that quickly filled with Collective members. I was staring into a sea of color, every member wearing the colors of their banners proudly. A woman in orange stood off to one side. I watched her and the uneasy way she moved, trying to place where I saw her before. She was in trousers and a fancy tunic with an overcoat. Upon the first glance she almost looked like a man, except the swell of her breasts that told you otherwise. She was gripping a small glass of cider and looking into the crowd, analyzing them. She looked at them the way a predator would. Her hair was short and black, smoothed over one side of her head, cascading in front of her dark black eyes. They looked soulless.

With a tilt of my head, I looked to my father, posing the question with my eyes. She was new here. He looked then and ground his teeth. "Yurdell's sister, Yimra. They're twins."

She was like looking into the past, the first time I saw Yurdell standing in this very room. "Why is she here, wearing his banner colors as well?" I pointed out. "Women can't hold positions and titles in the Collective. Isn't that the very reason the Collective wants to force me into a union?"

"No, they can't." He said dryly. "She's been running the farms, estates, and market district since his death. I tried to rush this gathering to push her out of it, but with the time that's elapsed, she's going to wish to retain lands and a sum of his fortunes to tide her over." He saw my curious gaze and smacked his lips. "She's not a good woman, Kastell. She won't be welcome on our land after tonight. The money she wishes for would get her home, or to a new land." He warned. "Yurdel and Yirma are opposites. If he would have been anything like his greedy sister, we would have killed him in his sleep, but the Northern King of Vortich has a claim on her life. I didn't wish to spark a second war with other peoples, so she's slid by in the darkness until now."

"You would risk dishonor by carelessly murdering a delegate without the Collectives' agreement?" My mind spun in circles, his eyes confirmed what I didn't want to believe, and they didn't linger to absorb my anger. Why would my father not make that same rash decision the night he had Yurdell's life in his hands? Was it only to give me the opportunity to fight for myself, or was the threat Yurdell posed to me not equivalent to the threat his sister posed to others? How did I fit into the equation? Something in my chest tightened and caught in the back of my throat. Were those tears? Here? Now? *No! Pull yourself together!* I snapped up, straightening my back and swallowing my furry. He'd given me the chance to act, but it could have been over sooner. He could have done something, and he wasn't nearly as concerned with the way the Collective would view him for doing so. He wallowed in the weeks it took me to come to terms with what I would do, when he had clearly made up his mind in the moments, he'd found out about Yurdell's betrayal. He could have ended it. He would have ended it regardless of Inara's interference, but he'd left the life of the delegate in my hands.

My father met my eyes and gave a curt nod. The confirmation that made me want to weep. Did he hurt in the weeks like I had, allowing me to make the decision? "She keeps a house of slaves and treats them poorly. She sells their blood to the Soilts that seal themselves in the north. Yirma steals from the people, and she hasn't done anything about the rations that have gone missing in the regions since Yurdell's passing. She's letting control slip out of her fingers and doesn't realize it. She's here for the money. I wouldn't be surprised if she used it to build a manor south of the city and bought more slaves to butcher. Anywhere, but not on my land. Not anymore."

I gasped. "She's awful."

"Very." Inara said from behind us. "She used to come to the Collective meetings before." He shivered. "She wanted me to pursue her. I couldn't stomach it. She smells like blood and copper all the time. *Revolting.*"

I covered my mouth when a giggle erupted from me. Not much made Inara flinch in disgust, but he clearly was disgusted by this woman. "Looks like you may still need to fight for your right to get your lands and titles," I said.

Inara smirked and said teasingly, "Except, more diplomatically. I don't think I'd like to fight a woman. Both you and Safrim have bested me, I expect that I'm not nearly as skilled as I once thought. Not against the beauty of a woman."

I couldn't help but smile. I missed this bantering. When he saw me in the dress it was as if his worries and fears melted away, leaving him more relaxed and easier going. He was so high-strung. He followed my father's lead without question. He'd abandoned his lover for the will of the King. I could only imagine that most of his time was spent overthinking the situation we were in together. How could he possibly make me want him, the man that my father would finally choose? In a desperate attempt he followed me around to make sure I was safe. Everything to him was a challenge. Leaving someone he loved would have been difficult. I underestimated what he would do to protect the throne.

I turned to my father. "What are we waiting for? An invitation?"

Della came running down the hall behind us then, dragging a chest behind her. She stopped and unbuckled the latches, taking out my father's crown and placing it on his head when he bent forward for her.

I didn't get the chance to see him in his crown until then. My father wasn't one to wear it around for no good reason, but in front of the Collective it would be a symbol of his power and position as King. I forgot the grotesque look of it. Crafted out of the blackened hand bones of Arvors, the claws extended into the air over his head and the thumbs lined his cheeks, the claws coming to a point just at the base of his jaw.

She pulled a second smaller and delicate crown from the chest, a polished white bone crown. It was crafted from the bones of a bird, the skull mounted at the front, the beak would touch the spot between my brows. A crow. The bones of the wings tilted back and into the air in a permanent predatory dive. This was my mother's crown, one for a Queen, not the crown of a Princess.

My father saw my worry as I studied the crown. "I figured the more they see you in the seat of power as Queen, the less they'll challenge it later, but I don't think now is the right time."

Della placed the delicate crown in the chest again.

Inara strolled past me, his shoulder grazing mine gently as he passed. He stopped in the mouth of the door and a drummer boy off to the side of the room started to beat on his drum, a steady and heavy beat matching the steady pulse of my heart. "Vor Kest, first of his blood, prevailing ruler and *Vanquisher*. Kastell Kest, sole heir to the throne and undeniable Queen, *Carver of Men*."

My father grasped my hand tightly in his and put it in the curve of his elbow and led me into the room at his side. Everyone dropped to a knee, head bent. I looked to my left and saw Inara there, staring up at me on his knee. This was a man that would let me lead him in our rule together.

"Rise." My father's deep voice bellowed through the room, the drums ceasing. "Is the Collective ready to convene?"

A farming district governor that I remembered vaguely meeting on my homecoming stepped forward. He was an older frail man with long thin hair that was wiry and dry from the hours he spent in the sun. His skin was golden from the long summer. His eyes were a dull shade of brown, the life in them wearing thin and weary. He was a thin man, his dress tunic swaying two sizes too large around his emaciated frame.

"The Collective is ready," he said. The man's voice sounded dry and raspy, dehydrated and starved.

My father led me to the head of the long table in the middle of the room. He let me sit to his left and took his own seat. After we were both seated at the head of the table the other men of the Collective, and Yirma, made their way to their chairs. The chair at the other end of the table was now occupied by the old frail man, where Yurdell once sat tall and proud.

The chairs scraped against the marble polished floor as they took their seats. Yirma made a show out of being the last to sit, claiming the seat to the left of the Primary Collective Dignitary. My father made no motion to even look at her or acknowledge her behavior. The other men caved and stared at her as she moved elegantly through the room and into her chair. Her steps were smooth and fluid, the way Yurdell's were before he'd gorged and turned into something unrecognizable.

"Now that we're all gathered there's a few matters that should be discussed." My father began. "Yurdell Ravine was relieved of his titles and lands, passing to his sister Yirma Ravine after his death in combat as a steward of the name. The Collective will make recommendations to the successor, and we will have a vote. I will part with my vote last." My father paused, glancing at me, considering what he was going to say next. "On another note, regarding the war and more pressing matters, I was offered a negotiation. The Proxy Rebel King, myself, and select guards. We will be negotiating terms to end the war. The attacks on our food supply have forced my hand. I will need to negotiate peace, or we will not have enough rations to go around for the winter. Our people are already dying; many more will follow if we let our hate for these creatures stand in our way of finding peace."

Gasps echoed through the chamber. The frail man at the other head of the table shot to his feet, shaking as he did so, his hands clenched at his sides. My father cooked his head to one side in interest.

"Yes." My father said giving him the acknowledgement to speak.

"Absolutely not. We will not negotiate with the rebels that are burning our food stores to the ground and letting our people starve. We should act while we are still strong, attack them on the coast where they hold their ground, drive them back across the sea where they came from!" There were whoops of encouragement and furry passes between the men.

"I'm hearing a reason *to* negotiate." My father said calmly. "The famine is growing; people will die if we don't cease this war. I've already lost a lot of my men in my army due to the famine. They're deserting our cause to make way for their families. Many of them are desperately trying to provide. Children and women are dying quickly, especially the ones carrying a child. Our numbers will be greatly affected from now to another generation if we continue to fight. They're winning this war. Normally I would hold my deserters to the stake and roast them in front of their men, but wouldn't I also put my children first before losing a war? I beg you to listen to yourselves, you will bring your own end. If we go on, we will have no one to trade with and the winter will kill us all. We still have the last harvest approaching. We can still salvage this coming cold season."

"We should attack! Kill their children and their sentries! Make them pay with their lives for the ones we've lost!" He spat.

"Please, sit." My father coaxed, his voice deep and soothing.

"You're a coward!" The man hollard, his voice cracking.

My father shot to his feet, slamming his fists into the table. "*Sit down.*" His voice reverberated through the room. The elderly man fell back into his seat, my father's voice hitting him like a wave of pure presence and power.

My father returned to his seat, straightening his jacket and clearing his voice. "I will be attending. If the Rebels are doing this, then we need it to stop."

J. L. Cross

"I want to go." I said from beside him.

He shot me a glare, but after a thought he nodded. "Yes."

Inara tensed in his position behind my father. I could see he was almost trembling with rage. I hated to see him so angry with me. I wished I could let him know I would be fine, or that he could come with us, but I didn't dare speak when my father commanded the room.

"We'll discuss rationing first. What do we still have? A negotiation does not guarantee any success on our end. We may very well still be at war by the morning." My father demanded.

The farmer at the end of the table gestured to a younger man to his right. "My son, Zerun, will lead with his inventories." Young men in many families were brought to these gatherings to learn to lead in their titles before the untimely passing of their fathers.

The young man, just cresting his teens, straightened, his voice trembling with nervous quakes before evening and becoming still. "We have the stores that are held within the city at the beginning of the year, in the case of a famine or drought. We'll be opening these warehouses within the next few days. We have wheat, flour, corn, and barely. Just enough to make it to the fall harvest if we limit who receives rations. The tavern and all trades outside of the city walls will cease. Our people here are more important. All the other storehouses have been burned, one or two were salvaged and the repairs were begun, but unfortunately there wasn't much food left. What we did have was given to the families that tilled those lands to tide them over. We have an abundance of fall harvest: apples, pumpkins, and an array of other late season vegetables, but we will need to arrange an immediate inventory after the harvest in the coming weeks and plan the winter accordingly. Those outside the city walls will receive rations. If our resources begin to fail us, we will need to lock the city down, abandoning those on the outside. We can rebuild the farms in Spring. I would like advice that we do not tax those that have lost their men or their fathers due to the famine in the early part of the year. We will need to support whoever is left to rebuild."

My father looked back at the frail man. "Your suggestion."

"Cease trades, close the tavern, and reach out to your home villages. The Silver Sage village is more than capable of offering us wheat and barley for the cold season. The Arvors may have left them untouched. It is the only village that stands independent from the crown, a growing and healthy democracy, but if the famine touches them as well, then they will need to surrender to the crown. We've been wanting to add them to our territory for generations. This gives us cause to approach them on the subject."

My father nodded and gestured for the man on his right to make a note. A scribe. "Write a letter to Silver Sage, bring it to me within the hour. I want it in the hands of a courier before I depart for my negotiations. We will not be asking them to concede to the crown. Not yet. We only breach the topic of the famine." The scribe only nodded. My father addressed the others again. "Officer." He motioned to a man in a leather military uniform.

The young officer wasn't accustomed to sitting at the Collective. It would have been Inara's seat. While he did not have a formal title or lands, he still advised my father, giving him a seat at the table. With a pending vote in his name, he couldn't take his seat at the table.

The officer didn't make much of a fuss of himself, but he wrung his hands and loosened his gauntlet on his right arm as if he were uncomfortable. "I've taken the liberty of searching every attack from the Arvors since the storehouses were targeted. We're finding one or two sentries from the Rebels and usually one Ayl. All of them are dead when discovered. It's known that the Arvors are allowing the Ayl time to call out for help before slitting their throats. The Arvors look to be slaughtered, beaten to death. We still don't know who it is that's killing the rebels. It's perplexing. We thought someone would step forward and take the credit, but nothing yet."

My father rubbed his jaw. "Rebels have made a point to be discreet for so long. Why are they suddenly seeking attention before they kill their victims?"

Inara shifted behind me and cleared his throat. "Could I suggest that their forces are becoming restless after going so long without a battle?"

The officer nodded in agreement. "This is my theory as well."

My father chuckled. "Great, so it looks like careless, restless dogs are attacking our food stores out of *boredom.*" He took a second, thinking and then moved on.

"Yirma." He said pointedly. "You do not have a vote at this table. You wouldn't have come if you didn't have something you would like to add. This is your chance to say what you wish." My father motioned for her to begin.

The tall slender woman cleared her throat and stood. "My brother, Yurdell, commanded respect at this table for years. I wish to maintain his fortune, in payment for his service to the Collective."

My father laughed and wagged a finger at her, leaning forward he braced a hand on the old wooden table. "I just told my daughter you would be asking for such things. You're rather predictable."

Yirma brushed her hand through her hair and let out a nervous rasp. "I have the right to be cared for after his sacrifice."

"You have no right!" My father clenched and slammed a fist down again. His face distorted in rage again. "You have none." He repeated more calmly. "Yurdell was being bought in the market district. He allowed rebels into my streets, receiving payment for their passage. He was trafficking child slaves in the walls of the city so that you could pay your debt to your father, which he refuses to accept as payment. Yurdell delivered venom to my daughter in a failed attempt to lay claim to *my* throne!" My father stood and straightened his back, walking around the table smoothly, a powerful man on the prowl, his footsteps heavy with every step. "You've lost control of the district in a mere few weeks. When we are done here tonight, you will not have any claim to lands, titles, or coins in my territory. You will be nothing. Run back to your father in the North or cower away from him on someone else's land, but you will not be welcome here."

"I've been thinking, the Collective is in need of reform." I said, as my father stopped behind one man that began to quake at my father's presence, his hands gripping the arms of his chair tightly. My father didn't challenge me when I interjected.

"My daughter took the first step, luring out and destroying a corrupt piece of waste." He flashed a proud smile in my direction. "Yet, so much remains. I think she's right; we are in need of reform."

He stopped by Yirma's side, studying her. Only a few inches from her. I could see the sweat breaking out on her forehead. My father drew a knife from his waistband, sharpened to a fine point. "Would anyone like to do the honors?" He stared around at the Collective, a vile smile playing at his lips. The sight of it made my stomach turn. My father was truly the character he needed to be when he put the crown atop his head.

"No one?" He asked, lifting an eyebrow to suggest that I do it. I shook my head, begging him to leave me out of this, but I knew he was calling on me to do what a Queen would do to protect her people. Kill the corrupt. Weed out the weak. I'd volunteered the idea, now he would make me follow through. *Show them your strength and let them tremble, Carver of Men.*

My stomach clenched, but I stood and came to him, taking the knife. "Who would you like first?"

He shrugged nonchalantly as if we weren't debating on taking a life. "What do you want, Kastell?" My head spun with a million things I wanted for our people. Every person in this room could be a conduit to making it happen for them. "Should we weed out the pathetic, the tax collectors that speak in our name and give fear to our people? Maybe the accountants that look after those funds and refuse to spend it on their own people who suffer, on the homes that are weathered and collapsing within our city. Yet, their own pockets are lined and heavy. How about the constructors who failed to build us homes that will last and stand for centuries, despite the resources we've given them?" All were viable options, all had their faults, and even more- my father was calling them out one by one, acknowledging that he knew they were crooked and deceitful.

"What do you want, Kastell?" He prompted me again. The same question Kendra had asked me. The same question I had been silently asking myself over the last few weeks as they passed, leading up to this moment.

I hesitated but grabbed the knife tightly that he now offered to me. Yirma bought slaves and drained them for blood to trade in the North, in Votich. The home of the most powerful Soilts. She had the power to do something about the dwindling rations in the market district by sending food from the farms she controlled, but instead she was letting them starve. She abused her slaves and stole from the people. Who knew what else she had done over the years.

I took one step at a time, finding the power in my legs to move. I wouldn't regret this act as much as the one I'd taken against her brother. This would satisfy me. It would cleanse our city of their unholy bloodline. I stood behind her, watching the sweat glisten on her, smelling her fear. I grabbed her by the hair and ripped her from her chair, she tried to fight but I was quick. I pressed the blade to her throat and split the skin and cut into her throat. Deep red blood spilled out across the table and the sounds of her choking on it pierced the air. The members of the Collective gasped and pushed away from the table and away from me.

J. L. Cross

The same look of terror that they had for my father was on all their faces, but they were looking at *me*. I held the knife out for my father, but he motioned for me to keep it. A prize for my efforts. The feeling of regret didn't fill me as I looked down at her vacant eyes. *Why break tradition?* I asked myself and used the knife to severe Yirma's head from her body. I tossed it to a soldier standing next to the door.

"Keep it safe for me until we're done here." I said.

My father stared into my eyes; his eyes glowed with pure pride. *"What else do you want, Kastell?"*

I locked my eyes on him after studying my bloody hands and ruined gowen. *Again.* "I want all his wealth to be distributed to seamstresses to make clothing for the children in the cities, and shoes for them as well. I want what's left of her home and land to be remastered into another farm. Yurdell's lands and titles will be passed to Commander Inara. In the light of his titles, it is expected that our courtship be made public, but I decline to accept. I will rule, with or *without* a man."

My father coaxed the scribe with his hand to write everything down. "The Queen has spoken." My father said and offered me his arm. I didn't hesitate to take it. He led us from the room and into the hallway away from prying eyes and ears.

Della stood there; her mouth dropped when she took in my dress. "How dare ya!" She yelled. She smacked her lips in irritation and threw up her hands. "I'll run ya a bath." Della was muttering under her breath as she walked away from us.

J. L. Cross

My father turned me to look at him and grasped my shoulders with his large hands. His eyes were filled with sorrow. "Inara has been listening to the rumors in the wind, the Warlock will demand a union to end the war. You must prepare for what will follow. You will be taken from here. If a union is held the Collective will strike your name from my tree. They will call on Vlad, my control and power here will weaken. You will have to make difficult choices, and they will come quickly."

My heart stopped- and sputtered, skipping a beat. "No." I said softly. "Not me." I said admittedly, but he nodded. "*Without a man.*" I repeated sternly. "I am not the means to the end of this war. There must be another way!"

"Yes." He said, the sorrow deepening and hanging in his voice. "They see you as their Queen, as long as I am King, they will not act against you. I needed to see what you would do for your people. You'll do anything, Kastell. You'll give away the purity of your soul and slaughter our enemies to protect these people." He took my chin in his hand and made me look at him as my eyes filled with tears. "What will you do to protect your people, Kastell?" He asked. "I will give my own daughter to the enemy for them."

My father fell to his knees in front of me, grasping my hands and holding them to his face. Tears moistened my hands. When I looked down at him, he was sobbing into my dress and wrapping his arms around me, holding onto me for dear life.

I had come to terms with being bound to Inara, this is why he had shaken with rage, he knew I would agree to whatever I needed to to protect our people. We were the same in that way. I stroked his hair as I cried with him. I didn't let myself weep loudly. I didn't let that pain settle in. I would be leaving this home, *my father, Kendra, Inara*... I would be leaving them forever. I was going to give myself without question to the Proxy Rebel King to end the war. Would I not be giving myself wholly to a man I'd never met, *the King of the Rebels?* My breathing became shallow. He was horrifying, or so the tales said. He left his throne in the hands of a proxy and ruled from a distance, staying in the shadows.

Aluxious would do the same. I said to myself. "I'll do whatever I need to do." I said softly. I knelt and took my father's grief stricken and sobbing face in my hands and kissed his cheek. "I'll do whatever I need to do." As I looked at his sobbing face and he pulled me into his arms for a tight hug I couldn't help the cries that tore through me, though I promised myself that I wouldn't. I was going to make the choice to leave for our people.

I held onto my father as the future I thought I would have vanished. There would be no sole Queen over our land. It would be me bound to a man that ruled from the shadow of his proxy, the enemy, and my own kind waiting to strike, waiting for the King to fail.

26 Kastell

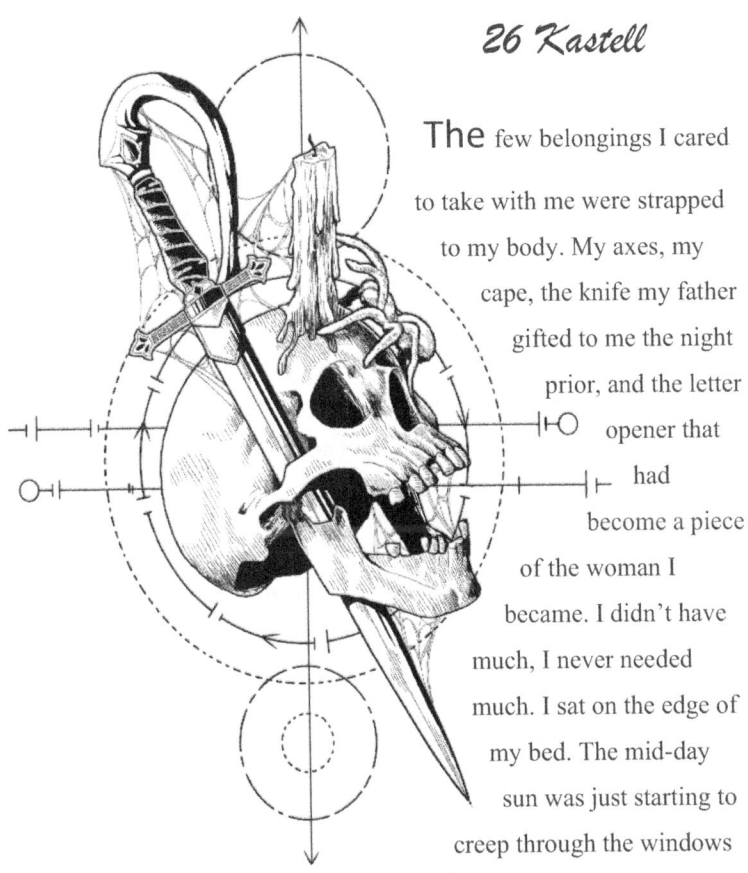

The few belongings I cared to take with me were strapped to my body. My axes, my cape, the knife my father gifted to me the night prior, and the letter opener that had become a piece of the woman I became. I didn't have much, I never needed much. I sat on the edge of my bed. The mid-day sun was just starting to creep through the windows and drapes. The day was long, and each second passed like feathers floating to the ground, slow and heavy on my mind. I thought about seeing Kendra, but I'd had my goodbye with her once before and I wasn't sure I could handle another. Soon she would know the truth and wasn't that hard enough?

I didn't have it in me to seek out Inara after my father had told me about the conditions of our negotiation. I decided *I* would do this. Even though I publicly denied our courtship, I knew it would hurt him for me to leave. I couldn't stand to see that same pain in his face that I saw in my father's. Inara had given himself entirely to the duty of protecting me and now I was abandoning him and his efforts. My father's pain was enough for me.

Who knew what the Proxy Rebel King would do with me after the terms were reached. They called him *The Devil* for a reason. I wouldn't really be his. Would he lock me in a cell to rot away until the true King returned? The Proxy King was covered in the blood of Ayles and his fur coat was as red as the rays of the evening sun. No one knew who or what he was in his human form, he never allowed anyone to see him that way, living a double life.

I wondered then if I would ever see who was really under that fur coat or if I would be killed before I ever had the chance to find out. Would he dispose of me before his own King found what he'd done to end their war?

There was a soft knock at the door. I stood and crossed the room. Della had been checking on me periodically. She tried to bring me lunch after the meeting with the Collective and I refused. My appetite hadn't returned. I was prepared to send a second meal back to the kitchen.

Inara stood there, his eyes dark and tired. His jaw slacked as if he were going to say something, but then didn't. I waited, but he only took me in, studying every piece of me to commit it to his memory for a lifetime.

"Come in." I said dryly and stepped to the side for him.

He sat in a chair at the hearth heavily and stared into the low flames. "I'm sorry." He whispered. "You shouldn't have to do this."

"You knew, before the meeting." I accused him.

A curt nod.

"Why didn't you tell me?" It was more a demand to know than a question. He wouldn't leave alive if he didn't answer honestly.

"You've been so guarded with me. I wasn't sure you'd listen. Plus, admit to me now that if you would have known you would have run off to look for the Hybrid. I know you care for him." He turned his gaze up to me, his eyes wet with tears that he wouldn't let fall. "I couldn't let you make a rash decision that would prevent us from ending this war and saving our people from famine." He looked down then. "I wanted to give you the chance to make your own choices without my voice echoing in your head, but I forced you out of a choice by keeping it a secret. I'm truly sorry for that, yet I'm not. I wanted to give you the freedom you were begging me for, but I have a duty to these people. Yurdell poisoned love for you and you still chose to give me freedom today. Safrim will be pleased. I can't say I've been the same kind of friend to you."

A silent tear fell from his eye. "I'm sorry I didn't tell you, you deserved to have a choice and I stole that away. When you killed Yirma, everyone shuddered in the room. I couldn't keep my eyes off you. I knew in my heart that you would be strong enough for this. You would do anything for your people. I wish I realized sooner and told you about everything. I should have told you about Safrim, but I didn't.

I should have told you about the conditions of the negotiations that the barmaid overheard. I could have been more honest with you."

Tears stung my eyes. Betrayal didn't end with Yurdell. I wanted to run away from it all; from him, my father, the union, but now I understood why fate led me to keep us distanced. My heart couldn't handle all the pain it would have been if I would have been so enthralled with him. If I really loved him.

"Thank you." I said and placed a hand on his shoulder. "You saved me from making the choices I don't think I was ready for. I won't have you to help me with that anymore."

He grasped my hand and pressed his lips to my skin. I wanted to be held, by him, by anyone to ease the unraveling happening within me. At that moment I was glad we'd become friends.

"Yurdell met with someone in the market the day he took me there. Was it you?" I remembered watching Yurdell talk to someone in the alley way, hidden deep in the shadows. I had brushed the incident off as just another shady person, like Aluxious, trying to pay their way for passage in the city. I had caught them out of the corner of my eye that day. The question always nagged at me. What if it had been Inara? Could he have known about everything from the beginning?

Inara's head snapped up. He didn't answer.

"*Was. It. You.*" I demanded.

He shook his head. "No, I was on patrol outside the walls. Everyone was occupied, even your father."

A cold chill ran down my spine. "No, that can't be. I swore it was you. You threatened him. You were there to get me back because you didn't approve." I said, my brow furrowing with anger. "You hated him."

He stood and held out his hand to calm me down. I hadn't realized I reached for the knife on my belt. "Who was it?!" I screamed.

Inara came to me and held out his hand for the knife. "It wasn't me. I would never lie to you so directly. I may have kept secrets, but I wouldn't blatantly lie about anything. I hated him, I didn't approve, those things are both true, but I wouldn't interfere with your choices no matter how angry they made me."

"Then *who* was it?" I asked again, confused. I knew the figure in the shadows was important. I could see the jewels and embroidery on his cape. I saw the way his presence was strong and powerful, looming over Yurdell. Whoever it was played a different game from the sidelines, one we didn't even know was happening.

Inara brought me to sit on the edge of my bed. "It might be best for us that you're leaving. Especially if there's someone behind Yurdell's disastrous plan to take the throne."

I shook my head. "Don't say that."

"I've ignored the rumors passing through the soldiers, my closests officers were reporting that a particularly powerful Ayl returned to the city recently. I thought they were only stirring the pot, mainly because you returned, but now I'm not so sure."

"*Who?*" I begged.

"Vlad. I thought that they were just trying to rile me up. I could never find him. I looked everywhere, but the rumors didn't stop."

"Yirma and Yurdell," I said. "He had to be there with them, hiding on the outside of the city with the two most vile people we know. He would fit right in with them."

"My thoughts exactly. Your brother must have sent that Arvor into the castle. He paid for them to come here and kill you, but the Proxy Rebel King sent a poor half-starved bastard to do that work he should have done himself. If your brother is here this feud will only pause over the cold season. Your brother will do all he can to possess the throne. Your father had me send a letter to the Fae. We're calling on Taria to return. I doubt anyone will hear from her, but he insists that she lives. Your brother will work on persuading the Collective to his side through the cold season. When Spring comes none of us will be safe anymore."

"She won't ever return, even if she lives. She swore off this life."

Inara nodded. "Do what you can there. Gather the Rebel armies, use the power of being his Queen, even if you're forced upon him. Use that power and gather his armies in mass. When Vlad makes his presence known we'll need you to attack him with everything you have."

The whole room seemed to be shrinking around me, the air thick and tight, my vision blurred, my head throbbed. "I can't do this," I said.

"You can, and you will."

"I'll do anything for my people."

Inara nodded and knelt in front of me. "I'll be here, your spy on the inside. I'll come to you, wherever you are. We'll take him down together and we'll purge the court. Safrim will help us. We won't let this Kingdom fall from the inside." He clasped my hands and pressed delicate feather light kisses to them. "Promise me something."

I nodded. "*Anything...*" That word spilled off my tongue the way it did with Aluxious, my heart tugged at me.

"If I'm fighting on this side, you need to keep fighting on that side," he said. I nodded; my voice silent by the pressure sinking in on my shoulders.

I was doing this for my people, and I would raise a new army if I could fight my brother, or I would return and challenge him to single combat for my people. I would die for them. I would die for all of them.

Inara shifted behind me; his back pressed against my own. We sat like that until the time for us to leave approached. His presence was comforting, and his hand lingered on mine, reminding me that he was there still. The weight of him against me calming my racing heart and keeping my worries at bay. The sun was starting to set.

A heavy knock came. And then again, impatient. "Kastell. We only have a few hours to make the ride. The horses are ready." My father's voice shouted through the door.

"No, not yet." Inara whispered. "I'm not ready yet."

I pushed away from him and stood, donning my cape and axes and my waistband with my knife. He propped himself on an elbow, studying my stoic face. "You're just like him," he said. "You have that face, the one that people fear, and love, and that mask that hides everything that's going on inside your mind."

"I won't let anyone know that I'm afraid." I said simply. "I don't need a weakness."

Inara stood and came in front of me, brushing the hair out of my face, "say goodbye to me. I didn't get a chance when your father sent you away last time."

"I shouldn't," I said. "I don't want this to hurt any more than it already does."

"Say it now, before we leave." He said again. "We leave the pain here, in this room. We're warriors out there."

I straightened my cape. "Until we're saying it again later."

"We won't say it. I'll let you go with him, quietly." He paused. "And you'll be strong. You'll go on your own. The pain will stay here." It was a lie. The pain would follow, leaving everything that was comfortable in my life behind. The second time I would be uprooted from this life.

"Fine." I said, a small smile came to me then. "One goodbye."

"I'll savor it for a lifetime. Or until we fight side by side."

I cleared my throat and said it. "Goodbye then." I looked at my feet, ignoring the hurt in his eyes from barely being able to look at him. "Just that one."

"I can do this." He said to himself. "I can say it," but he didn't, and I wasn't bothered. I could be strong for the both of us.

I looked up, meeting his deep eyes that were swimming with emotion again. "You could do it, but you don't have to." I touched his cheek gently. "My father is going to need you when I'm gone."

Pounding echoed through the room from the door. "*Kastell*." My father demanded.

"Coming." At least they would both be with me when I left.

27 Kastell

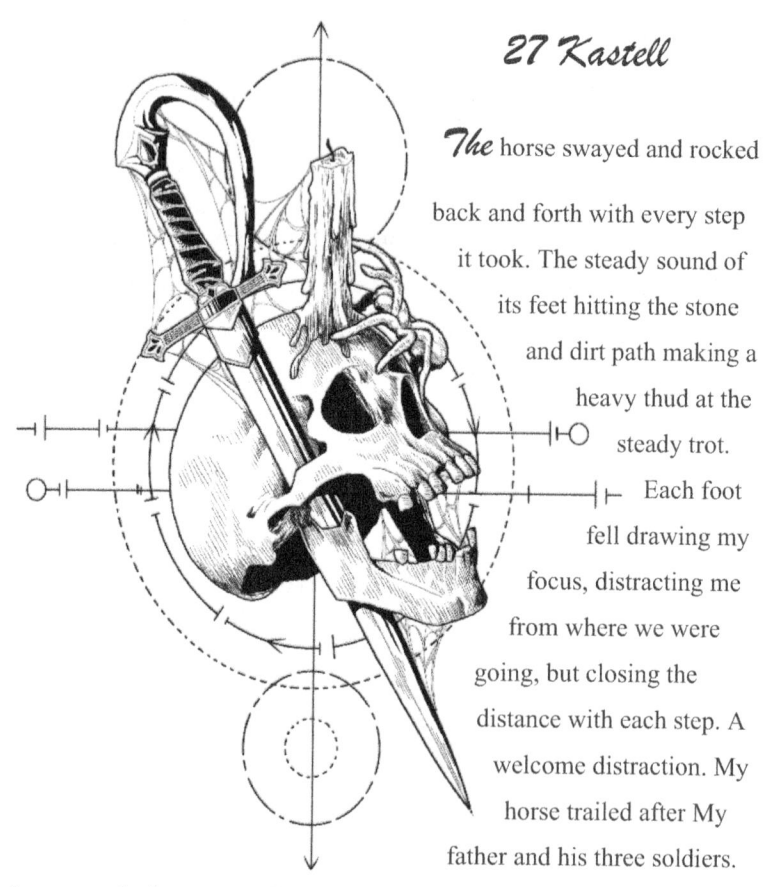

The horse swayed and rocked back and forth with every step it took. The steady sound of its feet hitting the stone and dirt path making a heavy thud at the steady trot. Each foot fell drawing my focus, distracting me from where we were going, but closing the distance with each step. A welcome distraction. My horse trailed after My father and his three soldiers. Inara matched my pace. We were making good progress. The sun was touching the horizon leaving the threat of running out of time balancing on our shoulders. Yet, none of us had the intention to rush.

"Crystal Falls is just over the creek." Inara said, pointing to the large wooden bridge we were coming to. "The beginning of Rebel territory."

"We've been promised safe passage through the village." My father said over his shoulder. "I expect to see sentries posted or gathering nearby. Don't pay them any attention."

My father's crown was black and vivid against the browning grass and orange trees. I would have suggested he leave his crown at home, being that it was made out of the hands of the Rebels, the ones we were going to be making peace with, but my father would have only ignored my suggestion. He wouldn't want to make them think we were afraid to offend them. His crown was a symbol of his title and his throne. The Rebel King had neither a crown, nor a throne. Not in the eyes of my father.

My mare's feet thudded as we started over the bridge. The creek was low but running quickly to get back to the river. The water was murky and dirty. Occasionally, I could see the telling signs of small fish lurking beneath the surface; a splash here and air bubbles surfacing there. The wooden bridge creaked and moaned under the weight as we all crossed.

When I neared the center of the bridge I looked up, gazing into the cluster of burned down buildings in front of us. Each one was caved in, missing entire sides, or nothing more than four corners. The remnants of the life that once lived there clinging to it. A burned doll stomped into the mud just on the other side of the bridge, torn and ripped banners, flower gardens ran out of control and completely consumed old porches and patches. The flowers reminded me that the Mother would always reclaim her land, making it beautiful again.

We were passing through the first rows of burned homes, the smell of pine and sap sticking to me. As the sun set a fog rose from the wet blades of grass into the air. The last rays of the sun were threatening to disappear, flashing through the gnarled near-naked arms of the pines that moaned when a light breeze caught their tops, pulling them back in the direction of home. *Home.*

I wanted to go home. I wanted to turn my mare and run all the way, or as far as she would go before quitting. The weight of where I was going and what I was going to do pressed down on me the closer we got. It threatened to pin my heart and soul to the ground. Inara only sparingly glanced at me, checking to make sure I was still determined to follow this path. I would be used, I would be targeted, and I would be preyed upon because of my grasp on the throne. No man could be trusted. Not after I had trusted so easily before. Whatever I was walking into would be more complicated and dirtier than a simple union under my father. I had to be prepared to do all I could to bring control to the situation.

Inara had taken the brunt of my hate after I killed Yurdell. My guilt haunted me. Sometimes when I closed my eyes, I was able to see him the way he was in the market square, how happy he appeared to be. That's how I wanted to remember him, but my dreams were different. That taunting looks on his face as he talked down to me. All because I'm a woman. *Aluxious would never talk to me that way. He admired me.* Sure, I was right about that, but Aluxious was unique. He wasn't like most men. Aluxious wasn't interested in a woman that needed to be protected or wanted to be protected. He treated me like an equal. I couldn't have him though. Nor would he have me. That future was washed away now when I refused to go after him. Although he is a rebel, I could be seeing him again, especially if the Proxy Rebel King hauled me around everywhere with him like some fairly won prize, a living symbol of the peace being forged between our people.

I *could* see him again, but I doubt it would make a difference. He wouldn't want anything to do with me once he sees me with the Proxy Rebel King. He wouldn't risk such a delicately designed peace for his own pleasure. No, instead he would be a constant reminder of my decision and all the things I was walking away from now.

"Kastell," I was staring down at the horn of my saddle when my father called to me. "I'm sorry." The apology was sincere, but it would be the last I heard about it. My father was a man that committed to his decisions well before he acted.

"You're only doing what you think is right."

Inara gripped the reins of his horse tighter until his knuckles paled. I wished I could say something to ease the tension, but it would be futile. Inara would be facing my brother again soon, a childhood friend of his.

A large community building stood untouched in the center of the town. It was entirely out of place. The only thing that resembled living civilization, but it was so out of place it made my nerves scream that it wasn't right. Ivy was climbing up one of the walls, the shutters open to catch the last of the sun for the day. Old drapes wafted in towards the center of the building, waving at me through the window.

The wooden sides of the building were deep rotting brown with patches of moss growing from the crevices between the logs. The dying grass around the edges made the last late season flowers look just as out of place. A sunflower was standing tall and proud at the corner of the building, tilting slightly towards the horizon where the sun was vanishing. The wooden shingles had the remains of black soot and burn marks on them, the only cue that there were once fires that tried to claim this place.

A candle lit inside the building, a welcoming flicker beckoning to us. Inara dismounted and tied his horse off to a nearby post. I followed suit, leaving the reins tied loosely in case I changed my mind and bolted at the last minute. I gripped the hilt of my knife tightly in part to stop my hand from uncontrollably shaking.

Inara put his hand on my arm, a simple attempt at calming my nerves, but the sensation to hurl the few contents of my stomach up clenched onto me. I swallowed hard, holding the urge down even while the flavor of bile took my mouth.

I walked to the open door of the community building and stepped through. My father and Inara followed me, allowing me to make the first move, the deciding steps. Gideon and Ethal stood on the other side of the table clothed in robes of red and black. The black velvet cloaks touched the floor, dusting over the splintering floorboards. The inside of their cloaks were blood red. Deep Red rope tied the cloaks closed at their fronts.

A massive thick tapestry covered the floor, leaving only a few feet of space from the walls exposing the hardwood flooring. There were only enough chairs at the table for five. A carefully selected amount. Only the immediate parties of the negotiation would be present.

My father's soldiers stepped to the edges of the room, taking a still position like statues.

Gideon waved his hand in dismissal. "Soldiers are not permitted." He narrowed his eyes on Inara. "Especially you, Commander."

Rage flared in his eyes as he gripped the hilt of his sword. I put a hand over his and that anger seeped away. He knew to trust me.

"We knew what this was going to be. Wait for my letters." I said and motioned him towards the door. We didn't need another heartfelt goodbye. My heart would feel every second of this moment over and over again for the rest of my life. This was the day my father would let me go, for the second time. They weren't going to fight for me, not now when all our people were starving. I wanted them to fight for me. Deep down I didn't want to be turned over like a mere bag of coins, but I understood why they were.

The guards stepped out with Inara, leaving my father and I to sit at the table. Gideon sat across from us, then Ethal. He held out his hand for her as she glided into her seat.

"I don't believe the King has been formally introduced." Gideon gestured to Ethal. "King Vor, this is my... *handler.*"

My Father's eyebrows twisted. "Handler?"

"Claret Magic needs a connection to life; therefore, Ethal is that divine connection. Our magical bond is very delicate. I'm inclined to do just about anything she wants me to. Aren't you lucky that she's a very passive and caring woman?" Was it only me that noticed how he divulged his weakness to us all? I knew better. He wanted us to have someone or something to focus on that wasn't him. If we destroyed Ethal it wouldn't end. He had to have other weaknesses that were more heavily guarded. He wouldn't tell us those.

"How does it work?" I said before allowing my father to press his own questions. I was intrigued with them the first time I saw them in the castle. They looked as if they feared being separated more than death itself.

"I'm not entirely sure. Claret Magic has never been harnessed this way before. With every passing day there's something new. As our emotional and physical connection grows I've found that there's more for this bond to offer. I can hear her wants and needs whispered to me, but unlike everyone else…" he paused, his eyes finding hers. "I can't hear her thoughts. With her the world is quiet again."

"Endearing." My head snapped up and turned towards the door. *Aluxious.* He strode into the room with a level of demand I never saw him harness before. Even my father's eyes were wild with rage and wide. Both of us had been conned. *Liar.* I wanted to snarl at him. My heart lurched into my gut and twisted my insides like a knife in an open wound. I wanted to scream and hurl my axes with all the force I had.

I stood to my feet, half of me wanted to run to him, the other half wanted to bury an ax in his chest. *Betrayal.* My mind hissed. I knew this feeling swelling inside of me, the same feeling that blossomed when I discovered the truth about Yurdell. Aluxious was here because he needed to be. *The Proxy Rebel King, The Devil.* He was the man that had the lives and blood of thousands of Ayles on his hands. I spent evenings bantering with him, drinking with him, laying under the stars- all to find out he was in fact the Proxy Rebel King himself.

Just that morning I had been presse under him in the market, ready to enjoy my last glass of cider within the city walls. I admired him in those moments, his strength and his beauty. Now, I saw the monster he was. Did he lie about the Arvors dying to protect our food sources? Was he trying to pry at my heart because he knew for days now that *I* was the woman he would be marrying to his King? Is that why he had gotten so close and personal with me so quickly? Was he just trying to stir some part inside himself that could accept me as his new Queen, or had they plotted this from the day he'd given me that first coin for food?

"You're a monster." I said behind gritted teeth.

Aluxious met my eyes. "No, your father is, but your eyes are clouded by the luxury of your castle, the sisters of the sanctuary kept you hidden away from the real world for too long." He scoffed. "You call me a monster, yet your brother slaughtered my family, *in this very home.*" His eyes flickered a daring amber, threatening to ignite the beast under his skin. "Your father protected him. We want vengeance. *I want revenge.*"

I rolled my eyes. "This is absurd, this war you're fighting is because you want to see my brother dead?"

"Personally, yes. Among other things. The city is closed off to my people: witches, warlocks, and Arvors. The Ayles over tax and take our food, they used to leave us with only enough to get by in the winter. My father constantly went without dinner to feed his family. The Ayles once took our people for slaves and beat them and traded them for fun." His voice grew loud and angry. *"What's so special about the Ayles, Kastell?!"*

Gideon stood up, a wicked smile on his face. He placed a hand on Aluxious's chest, easing him back into a seat. I sat down heavily, my eyes never straying from his.

"Just for the record." Gideon snapped his fingers. A quill, ink, and parchment appeared on the table. The quill moved itself, a blood red mist guiding it. "I did tell Aluxious to tell you."

"The time wasn't right." He grumbled.

"The time would have never been right, thank the Mother for circumstance." I said back bitterly. He only rolled his eyes.

My father still hadn't found his voice. I looked to him to make sure he was at least still breathing. That's when he broke his silence. "We've met before."

Aluxious smiled, a cunning smile on his lips. "A year or two ago."

"Yurdell introduced you to the Collective as a visiting diplomat. You were interested in our crop trading."

Aluxious nodded. "How did you think we knew where to hit when we needed the food? The Ayles started starving the Rebels long before now. We only took what we were due."

Gideon held up his hands to silence them. "We need to start. I have a few things that will be worked into this treaty. These are non-negotiable."

Ethal smiled, excited. "The city will have five full moons to prepare for a public opening."

"No." My father said sternly. "I will not open my city to wicked creatures to come in and destroy what we've built."

Gideon tisked. A red mist appeared from his finger, snaking around the table. A bind of it shot around my father's face and Aluxious's. Their mouths sealed tightly. They both grumbled and mumbled their displeasure but quit complaining when they realized there was nothing they could do. "No more interruptions."

"Secondly," Ethal continued. "There will no longer be a tax on food, or travel. The Kingdom will tax for land and per head in a household and no more. Gideon and I have done the figures, this would be enough to fund the army and repairs within the city while sparing the people from being overtaxed. Third, the Rebels will owe the taxes for the last two years, the date of Aluxious's ascension as Proxy, only the years he's responsible for, back to the Kingdom. We decided it wouldn't be fair to ask the now Proxy King to pay for the deeds of his father. There is one condition to these back taxes. The Kingdom will use them exclusively to rebuild Rebel villages. The Kingdom must hire both Rebels and Ayles to do the rebuilding. This will strengthen the alliance if they're forced to work together. Fourth, defectors to the alliance will be punished accordingly. Vlad was banished for slaughtering a whole village, and that will never happen again. Death will be met with Death. Anyone unwilling to live within the Alliance will be asked to relocate across the Kingdom's southern border or north of the river. There will be no exceptions."

No one knew what was beyond the Southern border. I only saw it once as a child. It was like looking into a deep void of sand. The green lush life of the Kingdom just *ended*. Explorers that went in were never seen again.

Gideon clapped his hands. "Now to the fun part. This alliance will be sealed by the union of the Princess to the Rebel King, via his Proxy, Auxious. I've decided that a traditional union will not work for this. I will perform a binding ceremony. A binding ceremony will link Kastell's life force to the Rebel King's and vice versa. If one of them is threatened- so is the other. This ensures that neither of them can work to undermine the Alliance. I hope this will also sway King Vor from making a rash decision in the coming weeks."

A binding Ceremony? They were sacred and blessed unions traditionally done by the Sister Witches, calling on the Mother to bind two souls until their death. Rumor was that these unions went beyond the grave. Bindings are a painful tradition that died as we modernized, but every so often one would be announced. The Mother splits a piece of your soul and gives it to your partner. In return you receive a piece of them. It changes people, and not always for the better. These unions were phased out because they were dangerous and uncalled for.

"There hasn't been a binding in over a century." I remarked, hoping that the Sister Witches wouldn't be able to recall how to perform one, but intense magic wasn't easily forgotten.

Ethal lifted a shoulder. "I think you're wrong. The Mother bound me to Gideon, and him to me. We didn't ask for this union, but we were blessed by it. I doubt the Mother will oppose a union of your caliber. I'd like to think she wants peace for her children as much as we do."

I glanced at my father then at Aluxious. I could see the clouding dark in his eyes. He didn't want to be part of a binding; he was horrified at the idea. This wasn't going to affect him, but someone that wasn't here to decide on his own. Making Aluxious uncomfortable made me smile with pleasure. "I'll do it." I said then. That pain in his eyes swelling.

Gideon cocked his fingers, the quill and parchment drifted to me. "Very well."

"How long does this treaty last?" I asked as I grasped the quill tightly.

"Great question, a smart question. I was hoping you wouldn't ask." His lips twitched at the corners. "At first the treaty will have ten years to be fulfilled. If an heir is born to the Rebel King the treaty cannot be broken, sealed by the combining of both peoples."

"I have ten years?" I bit the inside of my lip. "I can wait ten years."

"*Mmmm.*" Gideon grumbled. "Don't be mistaken, this is not an escape clause. This is a death sentence. If you do not bear a child in ten years- you will die, the sacrifice the Aylish King *should* have made after his son slaughtered those villagers. *His heir will die.*"

My heart was racing, the quill hovering over the parchment. Gideon was giving me full control. This treaty was my decision. No one else. I couldn't help but imagine a baby boy with Aylish ears running around at my feet. I never thought of children so thoroughly before. At the thought of Aluxious my stomach turned. He was the monster everyone made the Devil out to be. Politically and violently. He was cunning, he was a liar, and he was betrayal. Knots twisted in my gut. Ten years. The treaty wouldn't be indefinite until my death sealed it.

"Take your time." Gideon coaxed. "Remember, my threat to either side was that the party that withdrew from the negotiations would be guaranteed that I would be fighting against them."

I swallowed hard. Without the witches on our side, we couldn't afford to have an enemy as powerful as Gideon to fight against. He would ensure the Ayles were wiped from the face of the Earth.

Gideon's magic pricked at Aluxious drawing blood. "The Arvor will not have a choice in this matter." Aluxious's blood curved and signed the document. I could hear him groaning in protest across the table. "He has taken the choice from his King, and so his choice to withdraw is revoked."

Ethal sat forward in her seat to see the blood dry on the parchment. "He gave up his chance at a choice when he gave up telling you the truth." *Consequences really are a bitch.*

J. L. Cross

I knew what I needed to do for my people. I couldn't allow anyone to continue to starve. I couldn't allow there to continue to be a war. My death would ensure peace for generations to come, I would still have ten good years to live. I could do that. I could sacrifice that for my people.

I scrawled my signature at the bottom, the fine red mist tightened around my wrist, drawing a definite red line there, a scar to tell the tale of what I had done. The blood from it dripped onto the parchment.

Everything was quiet as the men were released. Neither of them looked at me. I had the power in this room, and both sat by useless. I stood then, making my way outside. Inara waited by my horse, helping me mount.

"Don't be alarmed, but Vlad has come." Every muscle in Inara was taut as if he would be ready to fight or defend.

I looked around until my eyes landed on the disproportionate man. His walk was teetering, and his leg was an odd, mangled shape. His hair was grimy and matted, but his clothes were pristine and clean. The undersides of his eyes are dark and gray. This was the man from the ally.

My father stepped out of the house behind me and groaned. "Hasn't there been enough in one day?" He asked as my brother hobbled closer.

Vlad chuckled a dark and bent sound. "You killed my lover this morning, *sister*." His eyes found me, boring into me, challenging me to say something, but I refused. I wouldn't fall for his games.

"What do you want?" My father asked.

"I deliver a message from the King of the North. You've stolen his children and he has sent me to steal your throne and your lives. First it was only the throne, your lives were for my own liking, but now he wants it all the same."

My father laughed, uncharacteristically amused. "He sent a banished cripple to do his work."

Vlad huffed in irritation and moved his hands, casting some spell with magic no one knew he possessed. My father's face twisted, recognizing the power Vlad was using as if it was something he'd had once himself. Was it a gift from the Northern King? An invisible hand gripped at my father's sword and yanked it from its sheath. No one could move quick enough before it was buried into his chest and blood sprayed out of the wound.

Aluxious ran out from the building to me and hoisted himself onto the back of my horse. He saddled up behind me, my body frozen in place. My eyes fixed on my father's now vacant eyes as he slowly collapsed to the ground.

A hard yank on the reins and we were taking off towards the coast where the Arvors called home. I tried to throw myself from the horse to go back to where my father laid, but we were deep into the woods by now, flanked on all sides by running Arvors, their claws digging into the ground as they hurled themselves forward to their home, keeping up with us easily.

His arm was wrapped securely around me, holding me firmly in place. There was no going back. Things were in motion now that no one could right. Vlad would be coming for us.

Screams I couldn't hear myself were tearing out of me. Every part of me shook with anger, fear, and anguish. My father was taken from me. Everything meant nothing now, all that I was trying to become was fading into a basin of darkness. Vlad came to claim the throne and he would have it.

My screams echoed and reached my own ears.

I wasn't screaming for my father. I wasn't screaming for my friends. I screamed for *him*. I screamed for my protector, my weapon. I thought the name only rang in my mind, and then I was hearing it in the air, bouncing off the trees around me.

"KYIER."

"KYIER."

"KYIER."

Every syllable of his name lengthened by the rasping scream of my voice that was starting to die.

When I couldn't scream anymore, I only wept. My face was buried in my hands. It was then that I heard it and the magic of the Relic confirmed for me.

"I hear you, my Queen. I hear you." A whisper only my soul could hear.

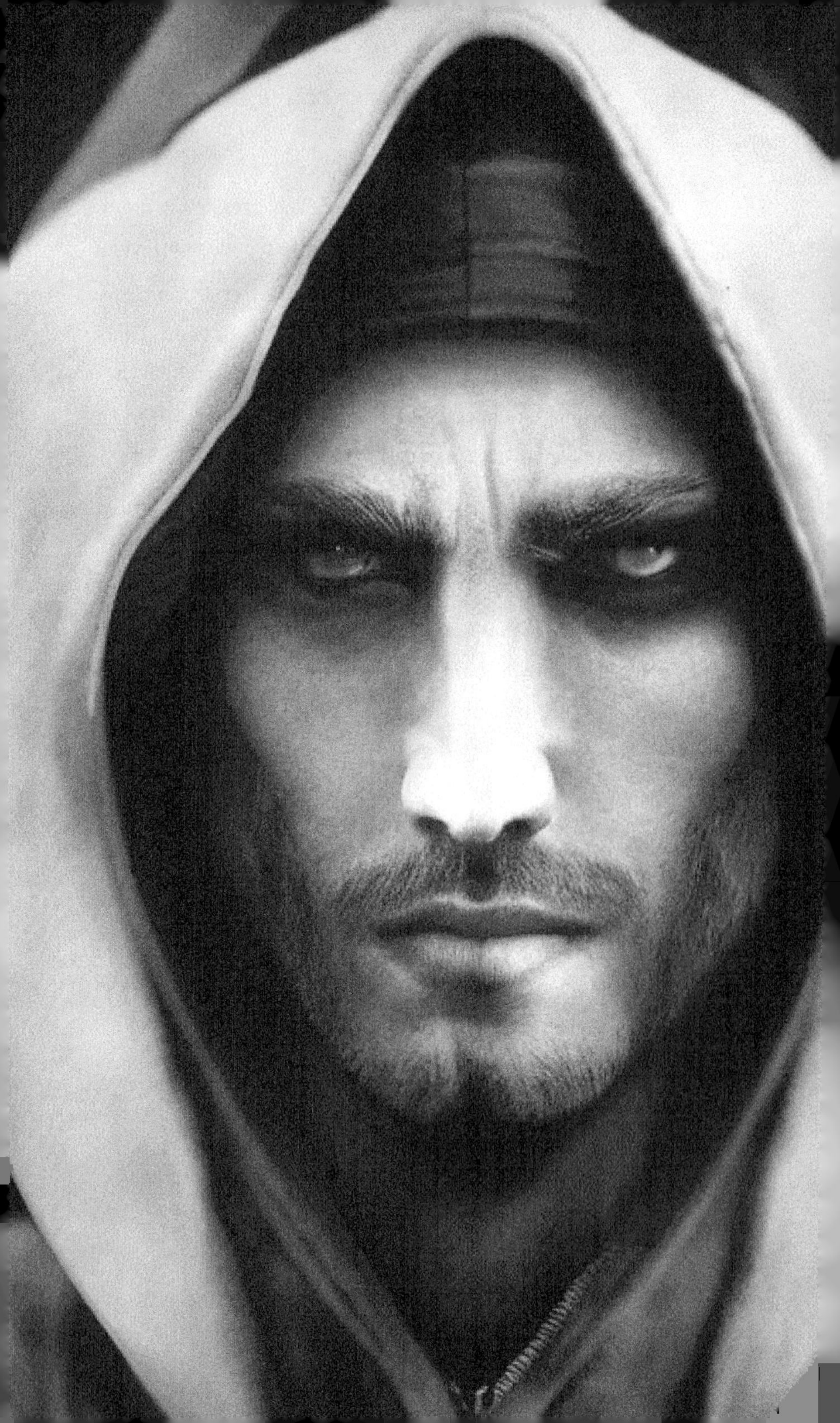

About The Author

J. L. Cross has built a quiet life in Iowa with her husband and their children. She served six years in the United State Air Force and left the service to be home with her family. The birth of her daughter was the motivator behind wanting to become a full-time Author. However, J. L. Cross is still far from that luxurious lifestyle. Becoming an officially published author has ticked a few items off the dream sheet for her, to include cementing something as fact for her daughter to grow up knowing- that dreams, regardless of their prestige or their importance to others, are worth chasing. As an Author, J. L. Cross has accomplished her dreams and continues to build on them, living as an example for her children to follow.

While she enjoys writing, J. L. Cross also revels in a good book, following various genres to include fantasy, dark fantasy, and rom coms. There's always something for her to learn in the words and worlds crafted by other great Authors.

J. L. Cross

586

Made in the USA
Monee, IL
11 October 2022